DOW/T

a
BERLIN
LOVE
SONG

SARAH
MATTHIAS

a
BERLIN
LOVE
SONG

troika books

Published by TROIKA BOOKS

First published 2017

Troika Books, Well House, Green Lane, Ardleigh CO7 7PD, UK

www.troikabooks.com

Text copyright © Sarah Matthias 2017

A CIP catalogue record for this book

is available from the British Library

ISBN 978-1-909991-40-8

1 2 3 4 5 6 7 8 9 10

Printed in Poland

*For my husband for his unfailing
support and encouragement,*

*and in memory of my father (1924–2016)
who loved my writing but was sadly never
able to see this book in print.*

Sultry wind in the tree at night, dark gypsy woman,
World full of foolish yearning and the poet's breath,
Glorious world I always come back to,
Where your heat lightning beckons me,
where your voice calls!

'Glorious World'
Hermann Hesse

Pallid face
dead eyes
cold lips
Silence
a broken heart
without breath
without words
no tears.

'Auschwitz'
Santino Spinelli

'Strange friend,' I said, 'here is no cause to mourn.'
'None,' said the other, 'save the undone years . . .'

'Strange Meeting'
Wilfred Owen

PART ONE

RUMOURS OF WAR

A Garden in Berlin
Spring 2013

MY NAME IS LILI PETALO. And this is my grave. Well, not my grave exactly, because I'm not in it. Not my bones anyway, in this small sun-filled garden in Berlin, under the pear trees foaming with pink and white blossom. When you've finished my story you'll understand why. Look. Can you see the design carved into the smooth, cream granite? Put your hand out and feel it. It's the *chakra*, the wagon wheel that's on our flag. We never had a flag when I was alive, but now we do. Our flag is blue on the top and green on the bottom. Blue for the heavens and green for the earth. And there's a wagon wheel in the middle like the one on this stone. It stands for our wandering life, but on the flag it's red, for the burst of fire at creation.

You see, when I was alive I was a *Zigeuner*, as the Nazis sneeringly called members of my tribe when I was a girl growing up in Germany. A gypsy. I was beautiful though, whatever the Nazis thought, or so Max used to tell me. My hair was like a horse's mane, black and poker straight. *'May kali i muri may gugli avela,'* I used to whisper in Romani as he lay sleeping. *The darker the berry, the sweeter the fruit* . . .

Max Hartmann. With eyes bluer than thrush eggs and a floppy light brown fringe. He wasn't a Romani like me. Just a Berlin boy of seventeen who loved me in that long autumn of 1942, when war was raging all over Europe and my people weren't allowed to travel any more. And I loved him back desperately, since our love was forbidden. For he was the son of a rich professor of medicine at the Charité Hospital in Berlin. And I was *Zigeunergeschmeiss*. Gypsy scum.

Pandora's Box
Berlin – October 2012

MAX HAD FOUND THE OLD leather suitcase one chilly afternoon in October. He hadn't exactly forgotten about it. It had always been there, lurking in the shadows of his memory, and he'd been meaning to brave the steep steps down to his cellar for a while now, just to check it was still there. But his feet were so clumsy these days, and besides, he wasn't even sure he wanted to rake over his past again. Surely he had enough to be disgruntled about at his advanced age, without picking at old scabs. But as he'd switched on the radio that autumn morning he'd heard the voice of the German chancellor opening the long-awaited memorial in Berlin's Tiergarten park.

'I hope that the inauguration of this new memorial, to the

hundreds of thousands of Roma killed by the Nazis, will ensure that what has been called the forgotten holocaust will now receive the attention it deserves . . .'

A flurry of clapping and then the weather forecast – windy with scattered showers. Suddenly Max knew he must finish the business. He had to go down there, even if it did mean awakening the spirits of the dead.

Wheezing heavily at the foot of the cellar steps, Max flicked the light switch. A dim yellow glimmer struggled into life, revealing the shadowy form of a dressmaker's dummy, a rusty tin bath, an old piano. The power had always been feeble down there. It brought back memories of air raids and smoking oil lamps and his little brother Rudi's ridiculous terror of spiders as they huddled in the darkness, listening to the hollow howling of air-raid sirens, and the cacophony of whines and crashes from outside, as the whole cellar convulsed and boxes crashed down on their heads.

The battered suitcase sat on a stone shelf next to an empty gas mask canister and a tin of ancient sardines. It was small and square with two silver clasps and a hard metal handle – a gift from Tante Ida for his First Communion. He'd chosen it himself from Wertheim's, one of the most magnificent department stores in Berlin, and it had travelled with him on every family holiday, school trip and visit to his grandmother in the Bavarian mountains until the shiny brown leather was scuffed and the silk lining shabby. If you could call a piece of luggage a friend, then that suitcase was an old and intimate one. A trusty hideaway for his most precious things.

Max carried it carefully, almost reverently, over to a threadbare armchair and lowered himself down, stiffly at first and then heavily as he let his body slump those last few tricky centimetres, sending a huge sigh of dust glittering upwards in the dim light. He hesitated, feeling rather like Pandora in his favourite Greek myth. The story had been on his mind a great deal whilst planning this visit to the cellar. Of how Pandora must have felt as the contents of her mysterious box whispered to her to release them. The difference was, of course, that Pandora had no way of knowing what slimy, snarling things her box contained, whereas Max knew only too well what he was about to let loose.

He closed his eyes and tried to breathe slowly, just as Doktor Seligmann had told him to do when his heart beat out of time, but the trick wasn't working today. He felt like a schoolboy about to turn over an exam paper, not knowing if he was equal to the task. He thought again of Pandora, and how she'd lived to regret what she did, but the contents of his suitcase were shifting impatiently now, jostling one another. Calling insistently from the past. *Let us out. It's easy. Just lift the lid.*

Max pressed upwards with his thumbs. Even before he opened the lid he could hear the music of his memories rising to a crescendo: the shrill tinkle of circus bells, the dying notes of a gypsy fiddle, the gurgling of a steaming samovar in a bow-topped caravan, the crack of a horse whip and the tantalizing cry: '*Roll up! Roll up! Welcome to Circus Petalo, the greatest show on Earth.*' And underneath it all, Lili's deep, silky voice, murmuring in his ear, soft and full of promise: *'May kali i muri may gugli avela.' The darker the berry, the sweeter the fruit.*

Max groped under the cloth of paisley silk that covered his secrets. Somehow he could bear it more to feel before he looked. Yes, here they all were: the rusty horseshoe with the nails still in, the silver bells from her stallion's harness, the tarot cards in their bag of embroidered silk, his Hitler Youth knife that he'd used to carve their names on the tree in the Grunewald, the lock of twisted hair. The portrait. He let his fingers explore, tracing the swastika pattern on the front of his old diary, caressing his soft-backed Hitler Youth songbook, snagging against the jagged edge of the broken scroll from a gypsy fiddle. He stretched his fingers. Where was it? That last thing?

You don't have to do this, Max. Close the suitcase. Put it back on the shelf.

But in truth his mind was made up. He closed his eyes as he pulled his clenched fist from under the cloth, slowly turning it palm upwards and opening his fingers in the feeble light. Tears began to well in his eyes, trembling on the lower lids as a faded black triangle of rough fabric stamped with a Z gently uncurled in the hollow of his hand. The bulb in the low ceiling flickered suddenly more brightly, made a sizzling sound, flared and went out. Velvet darkness reclaimed the gloom, dense and crackling with life. He couldn't see her, but he could feel her very near and he could smell her familiar scent, like roses – deep and slightly spicy.

'Write our story down, Max,' came a soft voice from the

darkness. '*Write it down for Rollo.*' Her voice shivered down his spine.

'Lili?' he whispered. Memories surged about him, crowding in the spidery corners, thronging the shadows cast by the broken remnants of forgotten lives. He pressed his hand to his chest, trying to calm his galloping heart. 'But you were always the storyteller . . . not me.'

Her voice hung in the air, insubstantial, like the shadow of a breeze. '*But I'm not here to tell stories any more, Max. Not in your world. So you must write the memories for us. Now, before it's too late.*'

A Garden in Berlin
April 2013

MAX SAID GOODBYE to his sister Gretchen as she was waiting for her taxi to Margot Kruger's house in Dahlem for a day of Bridge. 'I've left soup and a roll for your lunch,' she said. 'Take things easy and I'll be home by seven.'

Max tapped his stick impatiently. He wished she wouldn't worry so, although to be fair he could hardly blame her. Perhaps she feared he might slip off whilst she was out and *join his ancestors*, as Lili would have put it in her inimitable way. After all, Doktor Seligmann had warned her he might, given the perilous condition of his heart.

'And mind you don't catch cold!' she called, banging vigorously out of the front door like a woman half her age.

Max breathed a sigh of relief. Bridge parties were a rare

opportunity for some peace these days. A welcome chance for some time alone.

It wasn't that he wanted to exclude Gretchen exactly, although for years he could hardly bear the sight of her, striding along with her friends from the Hitler Youth group, carrying the flag of the *Bund Deutscher Mädel*, the *League of German Girls*. But they'd buried their differences long ago, and these days Max was more grateful than he'd ever thought possible for her care in his declining years. Nonetheless, for this task, this closure, as it were, of a chapter, he needed to be alone with Lili.

For a few days now Max had sensed time running out. The pains in his heart were sharper and just lately when he climbed the stairs, his chest made a sort of musical whistling, like a model train. So when he'd woken this morning to a perfect April day, he couldn't help wondering if something . . . someone . . . was telling him that now was the time to bury the past. That if he waited until the days grew longer and the sun less pale in the sky, he'd find he had left it too late.

The last six months had been painful. Listening to Lili's voice in his head as he wrote. Reliving their memories. But on this bright April day in Berlin, Max knew he had done his best. The sun felt warm on his back as he sat at the green garden table at the foot of the old stone steps, gazing at his precious things for the last time. He nodded contentedly. The memorial stone looked just as he'd hoped it would – the sixteen-spoked wheel beautifully carved, and the sandy hole the gardener had dug beneath the headstone the perfect size for a small suitcase.

Max stretched out his hand, hovering uncertainly over the contents of his memory box as they lay on the table. 'Best begin at the beginning,' he muttered to himself as he selected the rusty horseshoe and the pack of tarot cards and placed them on his knee.

A gentle breeze rustled the pages of his manuscript.

'*Is that our story, Max?*'

Max felt a sudden jolt of happiness, like a shock of electricity. He looked up, peering into the stippled patches of lemon-coloured light between the trees. Was she just a shadow in the dappled shade, an echo on the wind? 'Is that you, Lili?' he whispered, narrowing his eyes against the glare. And then he smiled, his face alight with pleasure. 'I've done my best to capture your voice,' he said. 'But as I told you in the cellar, you were always the storyteller, not me.'

Max cupped his hand around his ear and leaned towards the sunlight. Was that a smile in the voice on the breeze?

'*I trust you, Max,*' said Lili.

Circus Petalo

I WAS BORN in a wagon in the middle of a show, amid the smell of canvas and sawdust, greasepaint and cheap perfume, my birth cry drowned out by applause from the big top. Ma told me the first thing I ever saw was a clown with tri-coloured hair. No wonder the circus was in my bones.

My people were showmen, part of a group of families travelling with horses and a menagerie of animals in brightly painted bow-topped vardos – caravans with narrow, diamond windows and high wooden wheels. Romani families are big and boisterous. *But chave but baxt*, as we say in our language – *many children much luck*. Yet I was the firstborn of only two, and I'd been a long time coming. By the time I turned up, Nano Florian, Pa's younger brother, had three girls already and a baby boy with Ma's sister Bernadine.

So there was a rumpus when I came howling into the wagon in the interval between the trick cyclist and the fire-eater. Friends rushed straight from the ring between acts: acrobats in ostrich plumes, trapeze artists in shimmering leotards with chalk still white on their hands. Even Nano Florian left the big top to welcome me – and he was ringmaster.

Then a year later my sister Frieda arrived and that was it. Pa always wanted a boy, but no more babies came their way. Pa didn't let it bother him. 'If you can't have what you like,' he said, 'then like what you've got!'

Circus Petalo was our family business, begun by my grandad, Guno Petulengro, before the First World War. Circuses were all the rage back then, especially in Germany – the home of Hagenbecks, the famous lion tamers, and Sarrasani, one of the world's biggest travelling shows. Some even had buildings, like Circus Busch on the banks of Berlin's River Spree, with bandsmen dressed in white tuxedos, and chandeliers in the stables.

Grandpa Guno started small, with a couple of monkeys, a dancing dog and a star-spangled tent for fortunetelling, but the crowds just kept coming, and before long he had a score of scarlet wagons with copper lamps and gold-leaf trim and *Circus Petalo* in curly letters on the sides. It was a traditional show. No swanky wild cats for Guno, even though he knew cage stunts pulled the crowds. 'A lion will lick your head today and bite it off tomorrow,' he always said, but that wasn't the real reason. Truth is, he hated seeing big cats in cages. 'Like Romanis forced to live in brick.'

Don't get me wrong. Circus Petalo was no fleabag

show. Guno just kept it simple, that's all: clowns, jugglers, trapeze artists and horses in the ring. He had some of the finest ring horses in Europe: white Lipizzaners for the fancy stuff, graceful Arabians for his liberty acts, where horses do tricks on their own. And broad-backed Belgian Vanners for his *rosinback* stunts – that's *bareback* in circus lingo, after the rosin we spread on their rumps to give the riders grip.

I never knew Grandpa Guno. He went to join our ancestors when I was a baby. But I've heard so many stories from Baba Sara, as we called my grandmother, that it feels like I did. Romanies don't write things down. Stories around the campfire – that's how we keep memories alive. Like how our circus got its name.

Now, Petulengro means blacksmith, a common Romani name, but Guno wanted something more romantic. One day, as Baba Sara was scrubbing clothes in the river, she saw a silver fish leap three times from the water. As she tried to catch it, it slithered clean out of her fingers, but as it did her hand snagged on something sharp. A rusty horseshoe with the nails still in. Well, my grandmother ran barefoot, her feet grey with dust by the time she reached the camp. 'Guno! Guno! Look what I've found!'

You see, iron has magic power. That's why our men wear horseshoe nails round their necks to hold off Beng, the devil, but to find a shoe with the nails still in . . . that's the best luck of all. Guno appeared at the vardo door, the sunlight shining on his golden earrings. 'It's a good omen,' he laughed. '*Kushti bok*. Fortune is smiling!'

Petalo means horseshoe in Romani. Baba Sara used to say that she chose the name for our circus, but I reckon the name chose her. Guno hammered the horseshoe above their vardo door, with the prongs pointing *up like a cup, not down like a frown*, to hold the good luck in. And Guno never looked back. Our vardo was stuffed with photos of him, standing by his skewbald horse in leather riding boots and wide corduroy trousers, a dozen watch chains dripping coins stretched across his waistcoat, and Baba Sara standing all chuffed by his side with gold round her neck and silver in her ears. They wore their luck, you see, and what they couldn't wear, they hid behind secret panels in the wagons. Banks were for the *gadje*, as they called outsiders. Not for the likes of them.

Life wasn't always *kushti*, though. Times were hard during the First War when they lost their horses to war work. It broke Baba Sara's heart to think of her gentle bob-tailed Percherons dragging gun carriages through the mud. After the war, Circus Petalo joined Blumenfeld's, the famous Jewish circus, but soon they'd built up their own horses again, and Guno and Sara were going it alone with Romani performers, just like the old days. Except, that is, for Pali and Tamas, a couple of Jewish tumbling clowns, twin dwarfs from Blumenfeld's. They rode stocky Shetlands bareback and could sing in four languages, accompanying themselves on child-sized fiddles, with their painted-on faces – one happy, one sad. They'd grown that fond of Baba Sara that they stowed away in the kettle-box under her wagon the day she left Blumenfeld's, and only came out when they'd travelled too far to go back. In fact, Baba Sara was glad. Circus Petalo didn't have any little people and what circus is complete without them?

They'd made a canny choice, as it turned out. In fact, their love of my grandmother probably saved their lives.

Gems on a Necklace

M Y FIRST THIRTEEN YEARS were sweet as honey cakes. I loved the roving life and Circus Petalo was a true roaming band, a *kumpania* we called ourselves, rolling along between showgrounds with our canvas big top.

One of my earliest memories is bouncing along a rough German road, fields of poppies either side, waving to passers-by with my sister Frieda and our cousins, to the heavy rumble of the wagons and the clucking of the bantams in the kettle-box that swung beneath our vardo. Our dogs are barking and the fancy birds are squawking in the hooped cages roped to our *taliga* – the open cart we've hitched to the back of our home.

The birds are Baba Sara's, her Feathered Fantasy, as she calls her act: rose-breasted cockatoos and peach-faced lovebirds and a rainbow of noisy macaws that can bark, whistle and even squawk popular tunes. She's squatting on the back porch of our wagon, puffing her pipe, ribbons of lavender-grey smoke weaving patterns round her black straw hat, with Maestro, her magpie, cackling on her shoulder. He's the star of her show, tapping tunes on his bird-sized piano with his beak. He's cocking his head as if to say, 'Look at me! She loves me best!'

Memories fizz and sparkle, like bubbles in a glass. I can see it all so clearly – the long trail of wagons snaking into the setting sun, slowly rocking towards the rim of the sky, like bright-coloured gems on a necklace.

My pa, Josef Petalo, was a bareback rider, and my ma and her sister Bernadine were stars of the high wire and flying trapeze, so me and my sister had our pick of circus skills. Ma started training us on the wire when I was only four, and by my sixth birthday I'd crossed the ring standing on Ma's shoulders, twenty metres up in the air. We rode ponies before we could walk, so we could have been *rosinback* riders, no problem. But for us, there'd never been a heartbeat's doubt. We were born for the flying trapeze.

We'd been training with Rollo, our friend, since we could sit on a stool without tumbling. First two metres above the ground, then higher every day, until we had to use a ladder to reach the perch. We practised sailing through the air, shoulders screaming with pain, until we made the trapeze look like a baby could fly it. 'You can't peel an onion without crying,' Ma used to say, as she rubbed our red-raw hands with hazel balm. She was hard on us, was Ma. She said the Angel of Death sat in the front row at every show, waiting for the tiniest slip.

When we stayed anywhere for more than a few days, Pa would send all us *chavvies* to school. Pa was our *Rom Baro*, our *Big Man*. He made all the rules, and he was fixed on us getting book learning. We were a brainy family. Pa spoke loads of lingos and could solve any riddle you asked him. He read big books with small writing and wrote a dandy hand with curly bits on the letters, and he could spell right too.

So wherever we happened to stop, we'd join the local school. We were never exactly welcome. Mothers would huddle in the playground, whispering about locking doors. 'Watch your washing lines,' they'd mutter darkly, as if we'd want their drab old clothes. And the teachers never gave us any books. They said it was because we weren't stopping long enough but we knew they thought they'd never get them back.

One memory has always stuck. We'd arrived at Oberbiel, a small German town, and turned up at the local school. It was too rainy for tennis so the other kids were inside picking teams for gym. Their apparatus was rubbish. Just a few ropes and a leather horse. All the same, we knew what would happen. Frieda and me would be left till last, like outcasts. But we hadn't reckoned on a mean teacher too. 'You haven't been trained on the vaulting horse,' she said, smirking at her girls in their tidy gym skirts and skinny white legs. 'You can't learn in an afternoon and you'll be gone next week.'

Frieda winked at me and I winked at Frieda, and as the girls queued up in a smug line we lounged by the wall like we didn't care a button. Then as soon as the first girl set off I was away, wheeling down the gym in perfect cartwheels faster than the girl could run. I heard the other girls gasp as

I made a nifty handspring up onto the horse. Then I grasped the pommels and went into a sequence of swings and scissors and then flip-jumped to the ground without a shake.

'And that's on a stuffed horse,' I told them. 'Try that at a canter!'

The girls were so startled they hadn't noticed Frieda shinning the ropes, so when a high-pitched giggle came from the ceiling, they nearly jerked their heads off in surprise to see my sister dangling upside down.

Our ticket wagon was busier than ever that evening and I couldn't help grinning when I saw the teacher queuing up. We brought the house down that night. And for that stay at least we were the most popular girls in school. But nothing lasts, and the next week we were back at the starting post, in a new school and begging to borrow a book. And it was hard to keep smiling when the kids danced round us in the playground, chanting:

Dirty gypsies, put them in a tub,
Their skin will be white
When we've given them a scrub!

The cheek of it! We despised the *gadje* and their baths. Fancy washing your face in the same *chikly* water as your you-know-what! Anyway, we didn't need *gadje* friends. Our troupe was one big family, and Ma made us proud of our skin. This is a story she told us when the going got rough.

In the beginning when God made the world, he shaped
little people out of clay. Then he built an oven to bake his
first batch. But the elephants were playing leapfrog and
pulling each other's trunks, and God got distracted and

the people got burned. That's why some skins are black. He tried another batch, but this time he was so worried they'd burn he pulled them out too soon. They came out pasty white like dough and that's how white people came to be. Then God tried one last time. He didn't leave the oven. He timed it not too long and not too short. When he pulled the people out they were baked just right, toasty brown. And that's how the Romanies got their skin.

Ma meant to make us feel special. But circus folk feel special anyway. And it was only a bit of taunting in those days. We weren't called 'the gypsy menace' back then. At least not officially.

When the weather turned wet it was back to Berlin. We always parked in the same field owned by Herr Scholl, a friendly grocer. He'd give us his damaged vegetables at closing time and we'd fix his baskets for him – tit for tat. I remember how the rain drummed on the thin walls of our wagons and the wind keened through the short stovepipe that stuck up from our roof. We'd put stones under our wheels to stop them bogging down and make stable tents for the horses, then spend long, dark days in the light of the flames that leaped beyond the rim of the old blackened stove, seeing to the winter mending. And at night we'd cuddle together inside feather quilts, planning new stunts for next season until we fell asleep among the chickens that always hogged the warmest spots next to the pot-bellied stove.

'The hens are warmer than us,' we'd moan.

'Happen they are,' Ma would say. 'But we'd never put you in the pot!'

Happy days! My early years were full of joy and laughter. We didn't see the storm clouds gathering. We were busy just living our lives.

The Gathering Storm

I DON'T SAY we hadn't heard rumours. We often met wandering bands on the road and shared a fire. Like the Lalleri Roma, coppersmiths we met near the Polish border, who told us about German soldiers going round the villages killing Sinti, the brick-dwelling Roma, and whole camps of wagons torched and the people hauled off to special prisons. But truth is, we couldn't credit it. Everybody loved Circus Petalo. Our big top was always packed, so why should these Nazis hurt us? Romanies live from day to day. Not like the *gadje*, always fretting about the future.

I still remember the night Pa came home from a meeting of the Association of Circus Performers in the summer of 1938. He used to go every year to catch up with old friends and he always came back fizzing. But this time he was on the quiet side. Ma knew something was up and she winkled it out.

A Jewish elephant trainer Pa knew from Blumenfeld's was emigrating to America. 'We had to queue all night at the embassy for visas,' he'd told Pa, 'but we're all set now. Who wants to stick around here and get sent to a labour camp? You should come too.'

Pa told his friend he couldn't afford the passage. 'I've a wife and children and a troupe of acrobats. And, anyway, we don't speak American.'

'It's English over there,' laughed the man, 'but who needs lingo? Acrobats don't need talk and elephants speak elephant. Circus folks are better placed than most to get out. It's not just Jews they're after now, you know . . .'

'Well, nobody's given us any grief so far,' said Pa. 'Our big top's stuffed with Nazi uniforms.'

The elephant trainer had shrugged his shoulders. 'I'm only saying. We've been friends a long time, Josef. I wouldn't want . . .'

Pa told us he'd felt sorry for the man. He'd heard about the Jews and their troubles. It was hard not to, even if you didn't read newspapers like us. So Pa just shook him warmly by the hand and wished him *Latcho drom*, which means *Good journey*, and said we'd wait and see which way the cat jumped.

Ma went very quiet.

Pa guessed she was thinking about Pali and Tamas, our Jewish clowns, so he did his best to set her mind at ease.

'Don't worry, Ma. That pair speak Romani just like the rest of us. And besides, who cares who's working in a circus, as long as the punters get their thrills? And if a clown's gotta hide there ain't no better place for it. You could be anyone under all that greasepaint.' He laughed in his easy way. By convincing Ma, he'd put his own frogs back in their box. Pa never fretted for long. It wasn't his way. He truly believed we were safe. We were Circus Petalo. We came from a different world . . . beyond the Nazi's reach. Or so we thought.

Opposing Currents

I HAVE TO SAY right from the start that I wasn't a founder member of the Hitler Youth. I know everyone pretended they'd been forced into it – after the war was over and we were ashamed even to admit we were German. But in my case it was true. We were a devout Catholic family, and in the autumn of 1939 I was almost fourteen. A schoolboy at Canisius College near the Tiergarten, the famous park in the middle of Berlin.

My father, Julius Hartmann, was Professor of Medicine at the Friedrich Wilhelm University and director of the Kinderklinik at the Charité, the oldest teaching hospital in the city. He was a jovial man by nature, so it seems unfair that I remember him as often angry. That's what the Nazis did to people back then. They got under their skin, chafing away like crumbs in a bed. My father never stopped ranting about how impossible it was to run his clinic ever since the Nazis had dismissed his Jewish colleagues and filled their posts with 'inferior minds'.

Whenever I think of him now, I see him in the old leather chair in his study, poring over one of his medical texts in the glow of his brass desk lamp, wire-rimmed spectacles reflecting the firelight. We said his glasses made him look like Himmler, Chief of the SS. That drove him wild, which was out of character too. A sign of the constant tension everyone felt in those days, like an electric current crackling through the air.

Vati, as we called my father, thought Hitler was completely mad. He hated the whole idea of the Nazi youth organization, with its banners and parades and swearing oaths of allegiance to Adolf Hitler. And in some ways I was proud of him for daring to say what he thought, but mostly I just wished he'd keep his mouth shut, or better still, join the Nazi Party like most of my friends' dads. My best friend Hans Rust had been to torchlight demonstrations with his father, marching behind the swastika banner singing the Horst Wessel song: *Raise high the flag! Stand rank on rank together!* I couldn't help envying him, but Vati wouldn't dream of letting *me* join Hitler Youth. At least, not until he absolutely had to.

My mother didn't believe in National Socialism either. But she wasn't strong like Vati. Mutti, as we called her, met my father in France in 1917, in a casualty clearing station near Amiens. He was a barely qualified doctor of twenty-three. Mutti was a trained nurse, but even she hadn't seen such injuries – wounds so hideous that death was a mercy. Day and night they operated together in a cramped mobile hospital amidst the roar of heavy guns. Vati didn't talk about it much when we were children, but he did tell us how he'd fallen in love with that young nurse, Maria Junger, who became his wife after the war, and later on our Mutti. 'She was strong and beautiful in those days,' he used to say with a wistful smile, as if talking about someone he'd once known and somehow lost.

My mother tried to be loyal to my father, but the Mutti we knew was different from the one he'd fallen in love with. The war had shattered her nerves. She'd had a breakdown soon after she'd married my father, and so Vati's widowed sister, Tante Ida, had moved in with them whilst Vati finished his training. And then we children began to arrive and Mutti never nursed again . . . and Tante Ida never left. The fact is, we'd never known life without my aunt's fierce nose – pure beak from bridge to tip – poking into everybody's business in a scented whirlwind of lavender cologne and peppermint drops.

Vati had always found his sister difficult, even before she joined the Nazi Party and began to influence Mutti in ways he didn't condone. She'd lost her husband, Onkel Manfred, in the First World War. He'd died after a botched amputation, but not before he'd received the Iron Cross First Class for his trouble. 'Just like our esteemed Führer,' Tante Ida would say, smiling proudly as she arranged the twin photographs of Onkel Manfred and Adolf Hitler, both sporting identical medals, on top of the baby grand on which she taught piano to terrified children.

Vati would sigh behind his copy of the *Deutsche Allgemeine Zeitung*, one of the better papers of the day. 'Except Hitler didn't die of his wounds, Ida. More's the pity!'

As a schoolboy I was utterly confused. How on earth could I choose between my father, who I loved and respected, and my friends in Hitler Youth who badgered me to join them every day? 'We were born to die for Germany!' they'd tell me, smart as Sunday in their regulation brown shirts, their voices breathless with longing and their hair so short their ears stuck out like lollipops.

'Your friends have been brainwashed,' said Vati. 'Hitler's a crazy maniac!'

Herr Meissen

'WHAT ARE THEY TEACHING you in school these days?' railed my father one evening as I dumped my empty satchel in the kitchen yet again. It was a Wednesday. Hitler Youth *Heimabende*. The club night Hitler had declared homework-free. 'You do nothing but sport at school nowadays. What use is it to our medical schools that students can run sixty metres in twelve seconds if they know nothing about chemistry?'

I was just about to point out that I wasn't personally responsible for the new curriculum when my sister Gretchen sprang in through the kitchen door. '*Vati!* I could hear your voice in the street! *Anybody* could be outside! *Mien Gott!* This family!'

'Don't blaspheme, Gretchen,' snapped Vati.

'*Gretchen! Gretchen! Heil Hitler!*' squawked Otto. The African Grey belonged to Tante Ida, a second-hand purchase with a second-hand vocabulary that could mimic the doorbell as well as greet our Führer.

'Do keep your voice down, Julius,' pleaded Mutti, glancing gratefully at the parrot's cage.

You never knew when our block warden, Frau Schneck, the Party representative in our street, might be lurking outside with the excuse of delivering an official circular if anyone caught her with her ear to the keyhole. She used to be a Communist, but overnight she'd become a Nazi spy, snooping on neighbours and carrying tales to Gestapo headquarters that could bring the police knocking on your door in the small hours of the morning.

Vati lowered his voice, but only slightly. 'Just look at little Gretchen here. She has a first class mind but her head's stuffed full of baby care. At eleven years old! Do you know what she told me last night? "My body belongs to the nation!" Where does she hear this rubbish?'

Gretchen was the keenest of all of us to join Hitler Youth. My aunt had bought her an album last Christmas, *Achievements of the Third Reich*, and it was already full of cigarette-cards of girls in the gymslips of the *Bund Deutscher Mädel*, performing synchronized gymnastics like healthy waving corn. I could hear her in her bedroom at night declaiming slogans she'd already learned by heart. 'Motherhood is a woman's supreme function! I will provide the Reich with racially healthy children!'

I put Siegfried on the lead and slammed out of the front door, kicking angrily through the leaves on Tiergartenstrasse as I towed our fat, old dachshund down the pavement. It wasn't his fault he was spoilt and smelly, but I couldn't help taking my frustrations out on him. Deep down I knew Vati was right. School was a complete waste of time. I was clever. I hoped to study the violin at the Berlin Conservatoire after I'd passed my Abitur exams, so I was definitely fed up that we didn't learn anything useful any more. But I wasn't a swot either. I was crazy about sport, and Hitler Youth sounded tremendous fun to me: games every Wednesday afternoon, swimming and athletics all day long on Saturdays, camping in the forests around Berlin. How I longed to eat stew out of a tin bowl at the *Heimabende* on Wednesday nights, huddled around the clubhouse wireless listening to *The Hour of the Young Nation*. Or ride around on my bike like my friend Hans Rust with a handwritten notice, *Hinein ins Hitlerjugend – Join Hitler Youth*, attached to the handlebars with string.

My mind was in complete turmoil. I felt literally ripped in two.

It was around this time that school finally became unbearable. There was hardly a teacher left who wasn't in the National Socialist Teachers' League. All non-members had been dismissed, including my violin teacher, and now I had lessons with a fool who hardly knew a bow from a broomstick. Our class teacher, Herr Meissen, was a powerful little man with one fierce blue eye and a patch over the other – a fanatical Nazi and a commander of storm troopers in his spare time.

He told us he'd lost an eye in the World War, but rumour had it he'd lost it in a beer cellar brawl. When we weren't doing drills with flags, he taught us to hate those conspiring Jews who were busy taking over German businesses and stealing babies from the hearthsides of good German families. 'Jews walk differently from Germans,' Herr Meissen informed us one day. 'Their feet are flat and their arms are much longer than ours.' And then he'd pin up savage illustrations of the differences between Jews and Germans. Grotesque drawings of fleshy hooked noses, thick sensual lips and evil goggle eyes. We committed endless details about our blessed Führer's life to memory like a religious creed.

'When was Adolf Hitler born?'

'Twentieth of April 1889,' we'd chorus without a moment's hesitation, lest the sharp edge of Herr Meissen's ruler came down on our knuckles.

'What medal did our blessed Führer win in 1918? What is our leader's favourite composer? What is the name of his dog?' Our teacher spat questions like bullets from a gun and woe betide anyone who got caught in the crossfire.

I remember one day in particular, just before the final tightening of the rules on joining Hitler Youth. I still wasn't a member although Herr Meissen had been on my case for weeks, giving me low marks for good work and sending me on long errands when I was supposed to be having a violin lesson. I knew I was in for it that afternoon, because of the way he'd been glaring at me as we lined up in the playground.

Unfortunately my desk was the old-fashioned kind with the seat attached, so there was no escape as he bore down on me, fists like Christmas hams. He grabbed me by my left arm and hauled me to my feet so that I smacked my shins against the sharp wood of the lid, twisting my arm behind my back so violently everyone heard the bones crack.

'I looked around our playground with pride this afternoon,' he roared, the veins pulsing within his stand-up collar. 'I saw a brave sea of children all clad in the uniform of the Hitler Youth. And then I saw how one worthless brat destroyed the blissful scene. The only boy in my class who prefers his bow to his banner!' He dropped me back like a broken puppet and I fought down tears of agony for the remainder of the afternoon, praying for the bell to ring.

As it happened, Herr Meissen had chosen a convenient day to break my arm, since Frau Schneck had called round that very afternoon to bully Mutti yet again. My mother had been home alone, she told us later, holding her breath behind the spyhole and praying for Frau Schneck to go away. 'Your children will be sent to a state orphanage, Frau Hartmann, unless they join up right away,' she'd shouted shrilly from the other side of the door. 'It's now compulsory, you know!'

Mutti had finally given way and opened the door, pretending she'd been having a nap and hadn't heard the bell. After all, she couldn't have Frau Schneck screaming in the street. 'I . . . I expect you want something for the Winter Relief . . .'

'I most certainly do! And I suggest you review your contribution. This household has a larger than average income.'

I could imagine the size of Frau Schneck's eyes behind her pebble glasses as Mutti gave her an extra large donation to the *Winterhilfswerk*, the Nazi fund to provide the poor with coal and blankets, and a couple of Vati's cigars for her husband. But even this bribe hadn't gained Mutti the extra points she'd hoped for.

'And by the way, Frau Doktor,' she'd said, stuffing the cigars greedily into her tombstone handbag, 'someone in this house has been playing that *Niggermusik* again. You should know that Reichsführer Himmler has decreed that youngsters who listen to American jazz should be put to hard labour. You'd better have a word with your Erika! *Heil Hitler!*'

'*Heil Hitler!*' squawked Otto, removing Mutti's need to reply.

So when I staggered in that afternoon, face grey with pain, and collapsed on the green and white tiles of the kitchen floor, poor Mutti's nerves finally gave way and she begged Vati, almost on her knees, to let us join the Hitler Youth.

There'd been times in my life when I'd found Mutti's anxiety stifling. A parent's worry can be a suffocating thing. But just this once, I could have kissed her.

In Uniform

'**P**INCH ME, AUNT,' said Gretchen, gazing joyfully at herself in the hall mirror in her long blue skirt, black neckerchief and white blouse of the *Jungmädelbund*, the junior wing of the BDM. She turned full circle. 'Oh, Aunt! I'll be the best *Jungmädel* ever.'

Tante Ida had made a cake to celebrate, and Gretchen had decorated it with black, white and red berries in a swastika design. And before we could blink, she was head over heels in love with her Den Leader, Helga Eckart, and busy learning how to make a tourniquet out of a pair of suspenders, and other such vital skills.

My older sister, Erika, had a lucky reprieve from a uniform that would definitely have cramped her style. At eighteen, she was just about to begin her *Landjahr*, her compulsory year working on a country farm. I certainly couldn't imagine her in the braids and white ankle socks of the BDM. Not Erika, with her hourglass figure and scarlet nail lacquer. She modelled herself on film stars like Greta Garbo and went to bed with a dab of *Midnight in Paris* behind each ear and her hair in complicated rollers to impress her boyfriend Georg, an officer from the tank training school in Krampnitz. She was lively and fun, with a terrific collection of jazz and swing records that she played with the volume turned up, dancing on the parquet in her high-heeled shoes.

My little brother Rudi, on the other hand, was desperate to join up. You had to be at least six, even for the *Pimpf* – the little fellows – as the junior section was called, so at only five and three quarters, he had to be satisfied with helping me polish my belt buckle until his round face shone in it. I didn't feel too sorry for him. Tante Ida bought him a red bicycle to make up for it, and he seemed happy enough riding it up and down the street outside with his gas mask on.

Gretchen had always been a prig, but once in uniform she became insufferable. At eleven years old it was clear she would never be a beauty. I used to think Erika had taken all the best genes and left the ones she didn't want behind for Gretchen. They fought like cat and dog. 'Did you know that if a woman smokes, her breast milk will contain nicotine?' announced Gretchen one morning, adjusting her beret in the drawing-room mirror. 'The Führer hates smoking.'

Erika blew a cool smoke ring at the ceiling. She smoothed her dress over her flat stomach, fixing her eyes just below

Gretchen's waistband. 'I've heard he also says women shouldn't be too thin. It makes them infertile. But that needn't worry you, Gretchen. Your hips are broad enough.'

A mottled flush spread up Gretchen's plump neck, bright against the starched white expanse of her *Jungmädel* blouse with its white buttons embossed with the letters JM. 'Well, at least I don't drink. You stank of wine last night. The Führer says German women should shun alcohol . . . *and* lipstick. And every girl needs nine hours' sleep.'

Erika appeared in the mirror behind Gretchen, nudged her aside, and applied a perfect bow of lipstick to her mouth. 'Oh, that explains it,' she exclaimed in mock relief. 'I wondered why you were in your nightie so early these days. I feared you might be ill. And by the way, Gretchen, I've taken your tin of Nivea from the bathroom. The Führer says you're not to use Jewish face creams, darling, so I'm only helping you out.'

Erika bent over her gramophone, with its huge horn like a giant brass lily. She cranked the handle and soon the strains of Benny Goodman were resounding through the house at full volume. She flung herself down on the sofa, inhaled deeply and blew twin streams of smoke through her nose. 'Oh, Gretchen,' she sighed, kicking off her shoes. 'Don't you just *adore* American jazz?'

I stifled a giggle. I loved being 'in' with Erika. It made me feel grown-up, although in truth I was just as pleased as Gretchen with my uniform. I was thrilled with the triangular badge on my sleeve embroidered with *Mitte Berlin*, our local branch, and from the first moment I pulled on my black shorts and fixed my neckerchief in its leather toggle, the organization dominated every aspect of my life. There was so much choice: the *Flieger-HJ* for daredevils who wanted to fly gliders. The *Marine HJ* if you wanted to sail. The *Motor HJ* where you could learn to ride a motorbike. There really was a niche for everyone and my boyish heart raced with pride as we marched through the streets, police stopping the traffic to give us right of way as Berliners saluted our flag.

Vati was bitterly disappointed, so I pretended I didn't enjoy the military part of it – the drums and the fluttering banners. I avoided his gaze as I raced to my post as altar boy at St Hedwig's, hastily pulling my cassock down over my new uniform. I put Vati's face firmly from my mind as, amidst the glow of torchlight, I raised my right hand at shoulder height. '*In the presence of this blood banner, I swear to devote all my strength to the Saviour of our Country, Adolf Hitler.*' I couldn't help it. My spine tingled. Before long, I stopped going to the cathedral altogether.

Parsley Tea

FRIEDA COULDN'T WAIT for me to start bleeding like her. You see, she was in love with Rollo, the catcher from our act, and couldn't wait to be wed. 'Fly to your catcher like a lovebird to her mate,' Ma always said when we were training, and Frieda had done just that. Frieda was taller than me even though she was a year younger, so I'd been used to being taken for the baby. But the eldest must be betrothed first in our tribe and that can't happen until you're a woman. Truth is, I didn't mind one bit, because I knew what it would mean. My betrothal to Rollo's big brother Marko would be on me as fast as a sparrow could fly through the big top.

Frieda was impatient, though, and she'd been nagging Baba Sara about herbs to bring me on.

'Don't rush her, Frieda,' Baba Sara had said, pouring scalding black tea from her silver samovar. 'A lifetime of good things awaits you both.' She smiled a deep brown smile, like wrinkled autumn leaves. Baba is a name of respect in our tribe, and everyone listened to my grandmother. She spat a stream of tobacco juice through the gap in her front teeth as if the subject was settled. But Frieda wasn't having it.

'Can't you give Lili some parsley tea? That's supposed to work.'

Baba Sara fixed Frieda with one of her looks. 'I didn't know you were our new *shuv'hani*.' That means *wise woman*, and my grandmother was ours. 'Anyway, what does Lili want? It's her body.'

Frieda clattered down the vardo steps with a face as long as a fiddle, but she needn't have fretted. At nearly fourteen I was definitely changing shape. I'd looked at myself in the mirror screwed to the back of our door that morning and I'd noticed my breasts were swelling. I was on the brink of womanhood. All the same, I would avoid parsley tea.

I had a problem, you see. I just couldn't love Marko. At least, not like a girl should love the boy her pa's chosen for her. I did love him, but only like a brother, which is what the Camlo boys were to me – ever since their ma died in a *rosinback* accident, one night in a village outside Hamburg. Lala was Pa's partner in the ring. It wasn't his fault she fell and broke her neck, but he took it hard, especially as her man Otto was his best friend. Our ma did her best to make amends. She was as good as a real mother to those Camlo boys, and our two families were as close as hairs on a horse's tail.

I tried hard to feel the way I should. Marko was sweet and gentle and a natural with the horses. He was always bringing home wrecks with running sores he'd haggled for at horse fairs, and nursing them back to health. My own horse, White Lightning, was once a skin-and-bones all covered in sores that Marko had rescued. I was grateful to him, but that's not the same as love. I used to lie awake on summer nights gazing at the stars and imagining how real love should feel. It should feel thrilling, I told myself. Like when I'm poised on the perch of the flying trapeze, about to swoop down the black chasm of the swing, my belly full of butterflies.

Now as I just said, Baba Sara was our *shuv'hani*, and she'd been teaching me to read the tarot since I could shuffle the cards without dropping them. And just lately, since this business with Marko, I'd been more fixed on the cards than ever. Most Romani families own a set but I'd never seen a deck like hers before. The hand-painted scenes were based on the circus. Even Death himself sat on a canvas big top, with his hood up over his sightless face and his bow-top vardo in the background, just bursting into flames. Whenever we got the chance, Baba Sara would light the ruby lamps in her vardo and I'd sit cross-legged at her low card table, studying the pictures – *The Hanged Man, The Fool, The Lovers* – trying to learn their meanings. Every card has its own special charm, but my favourites were definitely the face cards. I'd turn them up one by one, wondering which queen was me. Cups, Swords, Pentacles or Wands? And just lately, I'd been fixed on the knights. *Which knight was he? Which knight for me?*

'The Knight of Cups is loyal and dependable,' Baba Sara

said with a wink. 'He moves slowly but surely towards his goal.'

I knew what she was thinking. I turned him over – face down. 'The Knight of Swords is a thinker,' she told me.

I picked him up to look closer. I liked the birds on his waistcoat but nothing moved inside me. I didn't like the Knight of Pentacles, I told her. His horse was ugly.

Baba Sara shot me one of her looks. 'He's a gentle wagon-pulling horse. Steady baggage stock, but none the worse for that.'

I turned him tail side up. Time and time again I thumbed the cards and always came back to the same one.

Wands is the suit of fire, and something about this knight on his chestnut charger, flames springing from his emerald bandana, made me return to the card again and again.

'A confident, energetic knight,' Baba Sara told me. 'Impulsive and passionate.'

I thought of Marko and how nothing moved inside me. And at night in my narrow bunk, I dreamed of my Knight of Wands.

It was August and we were camping in the Grunewald, the lovely forest on the edge of Berlin, taking a rest before our last run of summer in the Tiergarten. A few of us were out scroggling for mushrooms with shallow willow baskets. There was Florica and Fonso – our Spanish flamenco dancers, and their little Fifi, who'd just made her first public performance, juggling saucers on a unicycle. There was me and Frieda, Rollo and Marko, Pali and Tamas the dwarfs and their little dog

Spitzi, and a straggle of barefoot *chavvies* from the troupe.

I'd forgotten my troubles for a while as I filled my basket with curly chanterelles and the kind we called hedgehog mushrooms because their gills are spiky and brown. I knew better than to eat chanterelles raw but we'd eaten our fill of bilberries as we rambled so I'd managed to persuade myself that I'd eaten too much fruit . . . until the cramps bent me double.

Frieda was at my side in a twinkling. 'What's the matter, Lili?' Her sharp eyes missed nothing and nor did mine. I'd seen her hanging back with Rollo, crouching too long behind the bushes and coming out with her hair in a tangle.

'It's nothing. Go on without me. I . . . need to water the horses.' Which is what we say when we need to you-know-what. Then I waited until they'd gone before I curled up in a ball on the forest floor, groaning and clutching my belly. Truth was, it had nothing to do with bilberries. I lay like a hedgehog curled up for winter, my nostrils full of the smell of moss and fungus, and cried and cried for my lost childhood, as if my heart would break.

It's like trying to hide an elephant in a hen house, keeping secrets in a vardo, and Pa wasted no time in arranging my betrothal. It was the Romani way, and that was that. 'My father chose your pa for me,' said Ma. 'And we're as happy as fleas on a dog.' So my bride price was fixed, and a week later, Pa held my *pliashka* – my engagement feast.

Pliashka

M Y BLACK HAIR was braided with scarlet ribbons and Marko's was shining with oil. He beamed at me so wide his teeth gleamed in the firelight. I looked down coldly, fighting back tears of despair. I watched numbly as Otto Camlo presented Pa with the traditional bottle of *tatti-pani*, brandy wrapped in a bright silk handkerchief, a chain of gold coins round its neck. They embraced warmly, slapping each other's embroidered waistcoats, and then Marko's pa unwound the coins from the bottle and placed them round my neck as a sign to the other boys that I was now betrothed. Marko's eyes shone with pride. Then both our pas drank a toast from the bottle to seal the promise. '*Baksheesh!*' they laughed.

Marko's arm slipped shyly round my waist. I shrank inside myself. Why were they toasting my good fortune? Surely they knew I didn't feel how I should. They must have seen Frieda and Rollo. How they giggled and touched when they thought no one was watching. Surely they knew it would never be like that between me and Marko. 'Poor soil never grew fat marrows,' Baba Sara used to say. And yet now I must wear his *diklo* – his neckerchief – as a scarf around my hair.

Then everyone clapped Marko on the back and he was grinning from ear to ear. Then Florica danced for us in her polka-dot dress, with Fonso in his matching waistcoat and flat-topped *sombrero cordobés*. Those two were so much in love, and they'd designed a special betrothal dance in our honour, whirling and spinning as Florica's brother, Manuel, tapped a rhythm on his guitar, fingers flashing.

Before long the men were drinking deeply – dark homemade liquor from an earthenware crock. There were chickens and stuffed mackerel. Plump brown trout, juicy moorhens with fennel and wild thyme, and our favourite delicacy: *hotchi-witchi* – fat hedgehogs speared through the back legs and roasted with wild garlic.

I slipped away to find White Lightning. He was tethered to the back of our wagon on a long rope, so I followed the tether under the trees until I found him, chomping the grass in the stippled moonlight. He pushed his muzzle into my palm and I kissed his soft nose. 'Lucky boy,' I whispered. 'Your life is so simple.' Then I climbed up on his back and lay full length with my arms round his neck, telling him my dreams until I fell asleep.

In the morning Marko was angry. He said I'd shamed him in front of the *kumpania* by going missing. He'd looked everywhere for me. Which just goes to show how little he understood me. If he'd known me at all, he'd have guessed where I'd be.

The Royal Path
Wednesday 30 August 1939

W E WOKE EARLY, harnessing the horses and breaking camp in the Grunewald where we'd spent a couple of lazy weeks. Pa broke a brandy bottle over the ground to thank the forest spirits and then we were off in a jangle of trace chains. The night before we'd been frantic with the dandy brushes, rubbing down the horses until their coats gleamed like copper kettles, varnishing their hooves and braiding their manes and tails with ribbons. We took more money in Berlin's Tiergarten than anywhere else all year, so we had to look our best.

It was midday when we reached the showground. There was a tense kind of feeling in the air that day. And there were even more of those ugly banners than ever, dangling from each lamppost like a line of red and black washing. And the traffic! We'd heard rumours of war but we hadn't reckoned on this. Soldiers were streaming down the road in army vehicles, grocery trucks, school buses – anything with wheels. When we came to the traffic circle in the middle of the park, we thought we'd taken a wrong turn: there was now a massive new column three times as high as the big top with a golden angel with outspread wings. As we trotted round the column we were nearly mown down by an army lorry, hooting so loud it panicked the horses.

We were glad to turn off the road into the clearing we always rented for our showground. It was quite a business, getting twenty wagons through the gap in the railings without scratching our paint. We were still struggling with the baggage stock when a couple of red-faced policemen came puffing up on bicycles to check our documents. We weren't to light any fires tonight, they said. There was going to be a blackout in the city and a pretend air raid.

Pa pushed a couple of free tickets into their hands. It was typical of Pa to make sure his bread was buttered on both sides. 'Will there really be a war?'

The policeman shook his head. 'I don't think so. Hitler's pulled back from the brink. This is just a precaution – to make sure the sirens are working and everybody knows where the shelters are. You'll hear planes overhead tonight, but don't worry. It'll only be our own *Luftwaffe*.'

'Well, I'm glad it's not tomorrow. A big top without lights is like a hedgehog without spikes.' Pa slipped them a bottle of sloe schnapps to go with the tickets and off they peddled, pleased as pickles.

The police weren't the only ones hot and bothered. We had to finish the set-up before nightfall. Soon the Tiergarten would be ringing with the sound of the rig-team, the thump of sledgehammers and the clanking as they raised the king poles of the big top. And we had to open up the sideshows so we could get earning straight away. We had a carousel with pretty horses, a steam calliope with a brass keyboard, and a shooting gallery where you could shoot paper flowers for ten pfennigs. And Baba Sara's fortunetelling booth. I was feeling pretty chuffed that day, as she'd said I could mind it while she paid a visit to her sister in Friedrichshain. She'd never asked me to help her before, but now I was a woman she'd begun to treat me different.

Now, telling fortunes for the *gadje* is as easy as shelling peas. You just tell them what they want to hear and they go away happy. The star of her show was a green parakeet. For twenty pfennigs it would pick out a scrap of paper from a pile with its beak. There wasn't a bad prediction in the heap and the punters loved it. So I knew what I had to do that afternoon. Read a few palms, the crystal ball. Maybe give the parakeet a bit of an airing. Make as much money on the side as I could. And if I hadn't meddled with the tarot that day, everything would have been just *kushti*. Truth is, I had no one to blame but myself for what happened.

Baba Sara had a motto: *let your life dance lightly*, and she always was the first to make merry. But there was something about the tarot that brought out her solemn side. 'Never mess with the tarot, Lili,' she used to say. 'Remember, "tarot" means "the royal path". Our destiny lies in our own hands, but the tarot shows us the way.' I didn't properly understand her. Not then. But I came to understand only too well. Things might have turned out different if I'd heeded her warning. By the time I understood what my grandmother meant . . . it was already far too late.

Glove Puppets
30 August 1939

THERE WAS A CURIOUS ATMOSPHERE in Berlin that last week
of August – the week before war broke out. Day after
day, the sun burned down from a cloudless sky whilst we
prayed for peace and prepared for war. We'd thought of
nothing but blackouts for days – Tante Ida striding in and
out of rooms, carrying rolls of black paper, Gretchen trotting
obediently behind with the scissors, and now anti-blast strips
crisscrossed the windows. We'd expected war a year before
over the Sudetenland and yet Hitler had negotiated peace.
There'd been practice blackouts back then until Britain and
France had backed down and left Czechoslovakia to its fate.
So maybe it would be the same with Poland . . .

Vati wasn't so hopeful, but then he'd read *Mein Kampf*.

'Why are the statesmen of Europe so blind?' he asked, knocking the ash out of his pipe so hard he chipped the ashtray. 'Hasn't anybody else read Hitler's book? That gangster's after only one thing, and that's another war!'

For weeks now, the papers had been full of so-called Polish outrages, the headlines two inches high:

THREE GERMAN PASSENGER PLANES
SHOT AT BY POLES!

GERMAN FAMILIES FLEE FROM
POLISH SOLDIERS!

All day long, Hitler's voice screamed from loudspeakers on street corners: 'Germany will never again capitulate to Britain!'

And now the Rally of Peace, as they were calling this year's Nuremberg meeting, had been suddenly cancelled. We could feel the danger getting closer and closer.

We duly prepared our cellar. We had room for thirty and Tante Ida had filled shelves with home comforts: kerosene lamps, a first-aid kit, some board games for the local children complete with folding card table – even a dressmaker's dummy. Vati said it took up the place of a whole person, but my aunt was adamant. 'We might be interred for days if the house collapses. I, for one, will keep busy whilst I wait for the fire brigade!'

It was a Wednesday before school and we were unusually quarrelsome. Our gardener and maid, Herr Müller and his wife Heidi, had just handed in their notice, so we'd had to make our own breakfast and the coffee was lukewarm. It was a great blow. The Müllers had been with us for years and Rudi especially adored them, so it was ironic that the final straw had come because of him.

Rudi used to spend hours pottering in the garden with Herr Müller and his wonky old wheelbarrow, or sitting on a high stool as Heidi made pastry, shaping little men from the spare cuttings. They hadn't minded one bit when Rudi named his two pet rabbits after them, even though both were male. But there'd been a problem with the Müllers for a while now.

Vati had ignored Walther's dwindling moustache as it shrank from a large caterpillar to a small toothbrush. And he'd got used to the sight of his brown uniform and pillbox hat and the fact that he used our garden shed to store Nazi Party pamphlets. '*Heil Hitler*, Herr Doktor!' Herr Müller would say with a challenge as he gave my father the stiff-armed salute in the middle of the garden path.

Vati would clear his throat uncomfortably, raising his Homburg hat. 'Yes, well, Herr Müller, and a good morning to you too.'

But this time Herr Müller had gone too far. The previous week he'd given Rudi a tin of cigarette cards of Hitler and his henchmen. Vati had confiscated the tin, making a mental note to limit Rudi's time in the garden. But the evening before that quarrelsome Wednesday morning was the final insult. Coming out of his study Vati had found Rudi scurrying by with two glove puppets. On one hand sat Adolf Hitler in his black SS uniform, brandishing a club, and on the other a caricature of a hook-nosed Jew in a long black caftan and curling sidelocks. 'They're a birthday present,' wailed Rudi as Vati wrenched them from his grasp. 'From Herr Müller and Heidi . . .'

There was nothing else for it. The Müllers would have to go. He'd tell them first thing in the morning. As it happened, Vati was spared the embarrassment of giving them the sack. They got in first. They didn't feel they could continue working for an employer who refused to join the Party, especially with the situation in Europe so grave. So it was burnt toast for breakfast . . . and frayed tempers all round.

We'd been discussing how to celebrate Rudi's birthday, and as usual Tante Ida was informing Mutti of plans she'd already made without reference to her. 'The zoo on Saturday followed by a cherry slice at Café Kranzler. And there's a circus opening in the Tiergarten tomorrow night.' She stroked Mutti's arm as if petting a lapdog. 'According to my diary, Maria, you and Julius have tickets to hear Wagner's *Meistersinger* at the Volksoper tomorrow night. So it will be just Rudolf and myself unless anyone else cares to come?'

I was definitely on for it. I loved the travelling circus. I always went to watch them raise their big top, enthralled by the dark-skinned strangers who would arrive mysteriously from nowhere with their blazing campfires, weave their magic, then disappear as suddenly as they'd come. Everyone else was too busy. Erika had tickets to see Zara Leander in *The Desert Song* at the UFA Palast, and Gretchen announced that she was playing her clarinet in a *Jungmädel* concert in aid of the Winter Relief Organization.

'Good for you, Gretchen,' smirked Erika, reaching for

the lukewarm coffee. 'At least *somebody*'s doing good works in this family. Are you folk dancing too? You look like a Bavarian milkmaid in that blouse . . .'

Herr Müller averted the impending fireworks just in time with a sharp ring on the doorbell. Newly kitted-out in the green overalls of an air defence volunteer, he'd come to deliver a pile of empty sandbags and some stern orders. Always on the short side, Herr Müller appeared to have grown ten centimetres with his newfound responsibility. Clipboard in hand, he lectured us as if we were complete strangers rather than his employers until only the day before, informing us that school was cancelled because of an air-raid protection exercise. Had we prepared our shelter? he asked, much to our surprise, since it was he who had done most of the work, reinforcing the ceiling with planks and wooden props. There'd be total blackout at nine o'clock sharp, he told us, with German bombers flying over the city to add realism. Selected buildings would be 'bombed' and our house had been chosen for a direct hit. Then he handed us two cardboard signs, one labelled *Serious Head Injury* and the other *Trapped in the Rubble*. There would be stretcher-bearers to administer pretend first-aid and we'd to choose two people as 'casualties'. Then, with a self-important *Heil Hitler*, he was gone, leaving us to squabble over the starring roles.

No one fancied *Trapped in the Rubble*, but Gretchen was eager for *Serious Head Injury*. Erika announced that she was washing her hair this evening, and if anybody thought she was going to an air-raid shelter with her hair in curl papers for a false alarm, then they could think again.

Twenty Pfennigs

I'D IMAGINED that this glorious day off from school would be my own to use as I pleased, until the evening's air-raid drill. My aunt, it seemed, had other plans.

'You'll look after Rudi this afternoon, won't you, Max?'

It wasn't a question. Mutti had disappeared to her bedroom with a headache and my aunt was driving Gretchen to Broadcasting House where her recorder group was performing for the wireless. 'You can buy him some sweeties from Frau Günther's, then take him to the Tiergarten to feed the squirrels. And whilst you're there, you can buy circus tickets for tomorrow.'

Rudi was ecstatic. There was nothing he liked more than going out with me in my Hitler Youth uniform, except perhaps tea at Kranzler's. So all was settled.

Frau Günther's confectionary shop on the corner of Potsdamerstrasse was a schoolboy's paradise, with its red and yellow awning and polished mahogany counter. Behind the old-fashioned till, row upon row of glass jars glittered with jewel-coloured sweets. I still think of her, even now, every time I smell that seductive aroma of liquorice and mint humbugs that always brought saliva flooding into my mouth. Frau Günther's was possibly the most popular sweetshop in Berlin and she had the reputation of having tried every sweet in the shop, which was probably true as she was as wide as she was tall. She would always add an extra ounce to the paper bag when children came in, and two ounces if your name was Rudi Hartmann. Her face split into a delighted grin when my brother sprang excitedly through the glass door, although she couldn't resist a disapproving glance at my swastika armband.

Our family knew Frau Günther from St Hedwig's, where we all went to Mass on Sundays, and I knew she was no lover of Hitler. So I was surprised to see that some jars had been newly shifted to make way for a framed photograph of our Führer himself. 'I've cleared a nice space for the required picture, as you see, Max.' She smiled, following my gaze. 'Squeezed him in between the bitter lemons and the sour cherries!'

We all jumped as the bell clanged to admit an SS officer in high boots and black uniform with silver facings. '*Heil Hitler!*' he barked, before imperiously demanding cigarettes. 'And be quick about it, Frau Günther!'

'There you are Rudi, *Liebling*.' She beamed at my brother, ignoring the impatient drumming of the officer's fingers on the counter. 'A little bird told me it's your birthday soon, so I've slipped in some marzipan sticks too.' She glanced towards the SS officer. Frau Günther had a subtle way of winking that you could mistake for a tic of the eyelid. 'Goodbye, Max,' she said cheerily, handing me a bar of Ritter's Sport chocolate. 'Slip this in your pocket. Share it with your friends from Hitler Youth!'

By the time we turned into the Tiergarten opposite the grand stone arches of the Brandenburg Gate, the shadows were lengthening on the yellowing grass. There were uniforms everywhere: grey-blues and greens of the armed forces, Party uniforms in tan and black, brown shirts and black shorts of the Hitler Youth, and girls from the BDM looking hot in their long blue skirts, taking cooling drinks at the outdoor cafés. Everyone seemed to be out enjoying our famous Berlin air, and there was a definite holiday atmosphere, despite the silhouettes of anti-aircraft guns on the tops of buildings and the new notice on all the billboards: *POLAND ORDERS GENERAL MOBILIZATION*. People seemed oddly hectic, as if they were trying too hard to enjoy themselves and determined to ignore the gangs of Hitler Youths busily daubing kerbstones with fluorescent paint ready for the blackout, and the ominous drone of bombers flying overhead in an easterly direction.

I bought some nuts for the red squirrels from a kiosk and then we strolled through the garden until we came to the large clearing by the Goethe memorial where the circus always raised its big top. A cluster of wagons, brightly painted in red and gold, stood under the trees, each with a different design on the side: a laughing clown with his dog in a matching ruff, a horse rearing up before a lady in yellow, a girl on a trapeze, her black hair spread out behind as she flew across the paintwork. And on every carriage the same slogan in swirling gold letters: *Circus Petalo. The Greatest Show On Earth!*

The big top still lay in a crumpled heap and yet the magic had already begun. An exotic fellow in a striped turban sat cross-legged, charming snakes with a fat-bellied flute, and we stopped to take a flyer from a chimp in school uniform, complete with satchel. Rudi was still hungry, so we found a stall where he chose some salt-studded pretzels, washing them down with a glass of lemonade. 'That's definitely your last treat,' I said firmly, 'or we won't have any ticket money.'

The queue at the shiny red booth was already long, as if people were buying tickets as a kind of talisman, and Rudi clapped in delight as a tiny black-faced monkey in a fez danced along the counter, delivering our tickets with his curly tail. It was hard to drag Rudi away but I was starting to get bored of child-minding, so it was with some relief that I finally pocketed the thirty pfennigs change and announced it was time to leave.

It was as I turned from the ticket booth and began to edge through the crowd that I first saw the strange wagon. It was parked on the edge of the showground under the linden trees, between the shooting gallery and the merry-go-round. Maybe it was the unusual colour that caught my eye, or perhaps the golden steps peppered with silver stars. Or was it something else? Whatever it was, some magnetic compulsion was drawing me towards it, driving all thoughts of home from my mind, and as I began to drag a startled Rudi across the showground, I heard him squeal that I was crushing his fingers.

The wagon was a deep royal purple decorated with silver moons and astrological symbols, with a picture of a dark gypsy woman and a glowing crystal ball within a circle of stars. And above her head, in curling silver writing: *Sara Petalo. Fortunes read. Futures foretold. 20 pfennigs.*

Just twenty pfennigs. The price of a newspaper. Or a bar of my favourite Ritter's chocolate. I glanced over at the merry-go-round with its horses with wide grinning mouths. *10 pfennigs a ride . . .*

My throat felt so tight I could hardly breathe as I pushed a puzzled Rudi towards one of the golden-tailed ponies and hurriedly helped him up, pressing a ten-pfennig piece into his hand. 'Give it to the man with the colourful neckerchief.'

Rudi grinned happily, not quite believing his luck, as I turned and walked quickly towards the wagon. At the top of the stairs I put my hand in my pocket where the two remaining small brown coins were silently burning a hole. I took a deep breath.

Futures foretold. Twenty pfennigs.

Crystal stars hung on beaded threads at the doorway. Pushing them aside, I stepped into the velvet darkness. There was a scent like roses, deep and slightly spicy, mingled with a faint odour of sweat. The wagon was lined with candles that cast a flickering light on an ornate silver samovar, and as my eyes grew used to the light, I saw the arched roof was dotted with silver stars.

'I can read palms . . . tea leaves . . . the crystal ball . . .' said a voice in German but with a gentle foreign burr.

The girl had startled me. I hadn't seen her at first, gazing at me from the shadows. She wore a headscarf, but I could see that her hair fell down her back to her waist, thick and straight. Her long neck glowed like burnished copper and her earrings glittered in the flames. I noticed everything about her, so that when I lay on my bed that night, I could recall every detail: her high cheekbones, strong, straight nose, even the bronze-coloured hairs on her arms as they caught the light.

'S-Sara?'

The candlelight danced in her eyes as she smiled. She shook her head. 'Sara is my grandmother. My name is Lili.'

Knight of Wands

L ILI GESTURED towards a small table spread with a velvet cloth. Two silver chairs stood opposite each other, like props from a circus ring. 'Sara isn't here . . . but I can read your palm for you if you like. Please. Sit down,' she said, pulling the scarf from her hair and dropping it onto the floor.

I fumbled clumsily with the chair and half sat down and then stood up again to scrabble in my pocket for the two coins. Her hands were cool as she took the twenty pfennigs and I noticed her nails were lacquered. Not scarlet, like Erika's, but purple. She took the opposite chair, smoothing her skirt beneath her. I was trying not to stare, but it was hard to look away. Her lips were reddish brown, like oaked wine, her teeth strong and white, and as my eyes slid down her neck to the soft hollow at the base of her throat, I saw that her blouse was cut low, showing the golden curve of her breasts. I was spellbound. I waited, tongue-tied, willing her to speak first.

'What brought you here today?'

I shook my head. 'I . . . I don't know. I can't explain . . .'

'Not everyone knows,' she said quickly. 'It really doesn't matter.' She held out her hands. 'May I see your palms?'

Her hands were large and muscular and I noticed the sinews, like narrow ropes stretched taut under her skin. 'Do you work in the circus?'

'I'm a trapeze artist,' she said, as casually as if she worked in a post office. 'My hands always give me away.'

A trapeze artist! The image sent thrills down my spine. 'We . . . we have tickets for tomorrow night. It's my brother's birthday.'

'Then you'll see me,' she smiled, tracing the lines on my palm with her finger. My hands were shaking. What was it she'd asked? *What brought me here today?* I really had no idea.

'I . . . I suppose everyone wants to know the same thing . . . Will there be war?'

She raised an eyebrow, as if the question on everyone's lips in Berlin was a surprise to her. And to be honest, just at that moment I hardly cared either. She sat very still, a frown like an arrow between her brows, and then, dropping my hand, she pushed back her chair and disappeared behind a velvet curtain that hung at the back of the wagon. I felt suddenly bereft. Had I said something wrong? Was it the mention of war?

I don't know what made me reach down and take the headscarf. But before I knew it I'd snatched it up from under the table and stuffed it into my pocket. I could hardly believe what I'd done, but here she was already, slipping back through the velvet drapery, the brass rings jangling. I felt my guilt glowing like a brand on my forehead, but she seemed oblivious, intent instead on a small bag of embroidered silk that she'd placed on the table between us. I watched as she pulled the drawstring, aware of a sudden spicy aroma of tobacco. She wrinkled her nose. 'My grandmother smokes a pipe,' she said, as if a woman smoking a pipe was quite the usual thing. She removed a pack of cards from the bag, then slowly began to shuffle the deck, passing the cards effortlessly from one palm to the other in a cascade of deep purple backs and silver shooting stars.

'I thought you were going to read my palm . . .'

She smiled and closed her eyes. I took the chance to stare at her again. I noticed the darker pigmentation under her lower lashes, like the faintest bruise. She was very beautiful.

The cards looked hand painted, and they were worn too, as if they'd been shuffled hundreds of times. And yet the colours glowed bright in the candlelight. 'My grandmother's tarot,' she said in a low voice. 'The Petalo deck.' She glanced anxiously towards the beaded curtain that hung over the entrance, as if she thought someone might be listening outside. 'This is her wagon. She's teaching me to read . . .'

'Futures foretold,' I said, remembering the painted sign.

'Are you going to tell mine?'

She hesitated. 'It's not that simple. Tarot means "the royal path". It shows us possibilities. What's likely to happen. Not always what will.'

I smiled inwardly. *Hedging your bets*, I thought. 'But that's not fortunetelling!' It came out before I could stop it.

She shook her head. 'You misunderstand. The tarot isn't about telling the future. The future is never cast in stone.'

I was about to ask what the point of a reading was if the cards didn't tell the future but she seemed to see into my mind.

'The cards show us what will happen if things stay as they are. We're free to choose our own lives. The tarot just shows us the way. Shall we lay a spread? It's up to you.'

The air hummed between us, static with energy. The samovar gurgled and hissed. Outside, a barrel organ played a mechanical tune, wavering and slightly off pitch. I felt half scared, half excited, like on a Hitler Youth courage exercise, where you jump over a parapet not knowing how far the drop is on the other side.

She fanned the deck. 'You have to choose a Significator to represent the Querant. That's the person asking the questions. Take your time. Choose the card you're most drawn to.'

One card stood slightly proud of the arc – just a fraction out of line. I slid it out with my finger and handed it to her face down. 'Is this one all right?'

'How can it be wrong? The card chooses you, not you the card.'

I put my hand to my heart. It was struggling to find a rhythm. 'Are you going to show me?'

She held my gaze. 'I know who you are even without looking,' she said softly, closing her eyes. 'You are the Knight of Wands.'

Slowly she flipped the card. I felt a jolt of surprise. The picture wasn't what I'd call a knight at all, but a young man in an embroidered waistcoat astride a chestnut horse, flames leaping from a green bandana tied, circus style, around his head. In one hand he held a flaming torch and behind him a fiery sun was setting over an autumn field. I felt my cheeks flush. I liked the look of the figure on horseback. He might not be a knight on a charger, but I liked his sturdy horse and rippling muscles. It made me feel strong and glamorous. I stretched out my hand to touch my knight and as I did our fingers met.

'Wands is the suit of fire. This knight is energetic. Quick tempered but loyal. He must beware his passions. Once he has made his mind up, nothing can change it.'

For a few moments we sat silently, our fingers touching, and then Lili gathered the rest of the cards together and tapped them expertly into a neat pile.

She handed me the deck. 'The Querant shuffles, but don't worry. The cards shuffle themselves. Just concentrate on one question and then draw seven cards. There are many tarot spreads – the Star, the Fan, the Celtic Cross – but time is short. So I'll read the Romani Seven.'

A Moth to a Flame

Baba Sara always visited her sister Ana when we came to Berlin, which is how I found myself alone telling fortunes in her vardo that afternoon. Ana had caused us great sorrow by leaving the roaming life for a Sinto man, the settled kind of gypsy who lived in Germany at that time. She'd gone to live in brick in a place called Friedrichshain, with a roof that didn't leak and a flushing toilet. Baba Sara said it could have been worse. At least she hadn't disgraced herself by marrying a *gadjo*. But Sinti ways are nothing like ours, and Ana's husband kept a vegetable stall in Alexanderplatz, so she may as well have married a *gadjo* as far as Pa was concerned.

Frieda was helping Rollo and Marko at our shooting

gallery nearby, handing out gingerbread hearts to the winners and exchanging moony glances with Rollo, and to be honest I was glad of an excuse to get away from them. I didn't mind a bit of my own company. Marko had been acting like we were married already since our *pliashka*. 'Where have you been, Lili? Why aren't you wearing my *diklo*?'

Even Pa had been on at me, like he was trying too hard to make things right. 'He'll make a fine husband. Life's not like fairy tales. Love at first sight and all that. Real love grows, you'll see.'

It was quiet in the vardo. Everyone wanted to be outside in the sunshine and I'd only read one palm for a soldier and the crystal ball for a widow whose only son was going to the army. I pitied her, so I told her he'd come back safe and sound, and she'd given me all the coins from her purse and covered my hand in kisses. There'd been no more customers for ages and I was wondering whether to get the cards out and do a sneaky reading, when I heard a footfall on the stairs. And there he was, standing in front of the beaded curtain, in that ugly uniform all *gadje* boys wore in those days, with short brown hair and a fringe that flopped half over his eyes. I didn't notice how blue they were until he sat down opposite me, but I did feel how my belly went suddenly wobbly, like it does in the ring. Lying alone in my bunk that night, I couldn't remember when exactly I fell in love. Was it when he shook his fringe out of his eyes or when he did that silly stand-up-sit-down thing to get his money out of his shorts? All I know is that I recognized him the moment I first saw him. My Knight of Wands.

I only meant to read his palm. Honestly I did. But I felt like a moth caught in the candlelight. I knew I'd burn my wings but I couldn't help it. I don't remember fetching the cards. But before I knew it I was sitting at the table, shuffling the deck, with my heart leaping so high I thought it might jump on the table. I knew it was wrong. Baba Sara could be back any minute and I didn't want to be caught. Which is why I chose a quick reading. The Romani Seven.

The Devil Reversed

THE FIRST OF MY SEVEN was another knight – a bareback rider in a crimson vest on a white circus horse with flowers on its bridle. The rider held a water pail high above his head.

'The Knight of Cups,' she said. 'The suit of water. It's a positive card. It sits well with the Knight of Wands.'

'Sits well?'

'The first of the seven represents the present – your inner self. This knight stands for someone carefree and unattached. Loyal and faithful. You're artistic . . . a musician, maybe?'

I put my hand to my lapel. It was all nonsense, of course. She must have seen my orchestra badge. I knew fortunetelling was about guesswork – picking up clues and pretending you had second sight. *Don't be gullible, Max,* I told myself. *She'll be far away by the time you discover she's given you an earful of rubbish.*

I fingered my badge. 'I . . . I play the violin . . .'

There was a challenge in her eyes, as if she'd read my thoughts. She shrugged. 'Draw again, and place the card to the right of the Knight of Cups.'

All fingers and thumbs, I fanned the deck and slipped one out from the middle, laying it face up beside the bareback rider on the white horse. A man with a crown sat on a throne with something that looked like a circus ball between his hands, although it might have been a coin. Both feet rested on two similar objects, as if guarding them.

She gave a short laugh. 'The four of Pentacles. A typical *gadjo* card.' She touched it lightly with her finger, moving it into line with the others.

'A *gadjo* card?'

She glanced at me shyly. 'That's our name for outsiders. This man is making sure no one touches his coins, and he can't go anywhere because his feet are holding them down. The *gadje* spend their lives trapped by possessions. Building houses and filling them with things . . .'

I frowned. I'd never thought of myself like that. We gave to charity and supported good causes. We were better off than many of my friends but we didn't live grandly. I felt annoyed at being judged by a stranger. 'A bad card, then?'

There was a silence. 'Not necessarily. It shows the things that you want from your life now. You can always change those things. The cards only show us possibilities.' She shook her head. 'And anyway, no card alone is ever bad or good. The cards must be read together.'

She gestured towards the deck, meaning I should draw the next card. The five of Swords, she told me, meant family and friends. 'It shows conflict. Not fighting, exactly, but not peaceful.'

I nodded.

'Arguments at home?'

I nodded again. 'It's a worrying time for everyone,' I said, 'wondering about war and everything.' I thought of Gretchen and Erika at each other's throats and the Müllers leaving. *It's just clever guesswork*, I told myself. But I didn't care. She could tell me whatever nonsense she liked so long as I could keep looking at her. I was captivated.

'Your next choice indicates past influences. The things that led up to today and made you what you are.'

I drew again. The two of Cups was a positive card, she told me. I felt absurdly relieved – like a schoolboy with a good report after a bad one. 'You have talent but you've also practised hard to get where you are.'

I thought of rifle practice instead of school orchestra, and my violin lessons taken over by playground drills. 'It's hard to practise these days,' I said, following her gaze towards the curtain that hid the inside of the wagon from the world outside. She seemed anxious, as if someone might interrupt us, and suddenly I remembered Rudi on the merry-go-round. The music had stopped. I really ought to be going.

'Choose again,' she said quickly, as if she too was in a hurry. 'The next card is important. It indicates your hopes and dreams.'

That sounded better. Thinking about school had altered my mood. I needed something hopeful but somehow I felt nervous. The atmosphere had subtly shifted and I was dimly aware of an ominous feeling, as if the next phase of the reading might not be so good.

I placed my fifth card beside the others underneath the Knight of Wands. Swords is the suit of air, she told me, and the mind. And the ace indicated an emotional relationship – one that might cause trouble. She touched each card lightly with her finger, a small arrow of concern between her eyes.

'Something wrong?'

'It's confusing,' she said at last, 'as if there's joy and pain all mingled together. There's trouble brewing . . .' She met my gaze. 'You're on the edge of something . . . but there's still time to pull back. It all depends on you.'

She gestured again. That hurried flutter of her fingers. 'The next card shows the near future – the direction of events if things carry on the way they are.' She nodded. 'Go ahead. The next two cards are the most important in the whole reading.'

There was a new urgency in her tone. I felt a shiver, like an icicle sliding down my spine. I held my breath as I drew the next card, turning it over slowly. Half afraid, half longing to see. I heard a sharp intake of breath. 'The Tower! Our first *Boro Lil.*'

A crumbling turret stood on a rocky crag under a stormy

sky. Flames sprang from its narrow windows, and from the castellated top a falling figure, its cloak billowing behind like a flag. Forked lightning sliced the image in two. A cold hand closed round my throat. '*Boro Lil?*'

Lili was staring hard at the cards, as if willing them to rearrange themselves. 'The tarot is divided into two sets. The *Boro Lil* and the *Tarno Lil*. The *Big Book* and the *Little Book*. The ones you've already drawn are either pip cards, or court cards from the *Tarno Lil*. They just cover the day-to-day business of life. But when a *Boro Lil* turns up . . .' She looked troubled. 'They stand for the decisive events in our lives.'

'Another bad card, then?'

There was a catch in her voice but still she kept her eyes on mine. 'The Tower is a dark card, I can't deny it. It usually means turmoil . . . dramatic change . . .'

'What . . . what sort of change?' Why did I feel uneasy? Wasn't this just a bit of fun? An innocent flirtation. And yet I felt a definite shiver, raising those tiny hairs on my spine.

Her voice was unsteady. 'Illness. An accident, perhaps . . .'

I took a deep breath, telling myself again that this was all nonsense, but the look on her face told me that she, at least, was deadly serious. She put her hand to her chest. 'I'm sorry. I shouldn't have done this. But it's too late now.' She swallowed, nodding anxiously towards the cards. 'You must draw your final card. I can't leave a reading unfinished. The last card shows the final outcome. A positive card now might change the whole reading.'

The cards with their purple backs and shooting silver

stars lay on the table, jealously guarding their secrets. Which one concealed my destiny? What was it she'd said to me? *Concentrate on a question you want answered and choose the card that draws you.* I held my breath and fanned the cards, my right hand hovering uncertainly over the deck. Then I focused on the question uppermost in my mind, and this time it had nothing to do with the war. I slid the last card on the right slowly from the fan and flipped it over, placing it face up in seventh position.

Lili let out a cry. 'Beng reversed!'

I can only describe the feeling as falling. I felt a sharp pain in my chest and I swear I heard a noise in my head like a scream. I stared at the card. The inverted image of a goat, winged and horned, sat crouched above two naked demons, each tethered to his seat. 'Beng?'

Her voice was a whisper. 'Beng is the Devil. Another *Boro Lil.* Cards have different meanings depending on which way up they appear . . .'

Her words hung trembling in the air between us. 'And the Devil *reversed?*'

'The Devil is not always the bad card people think . . . but reversed it means total evil . . . upending of the natural order.' She took a deep breath, then stared at me, forcing me to meet her gaze. 'I need to ask . . . What question did you hold in your mind as you drew the final card?'

The atmosphere was icy cold, as if a Baltic wind had sliced down unseasonably early, cutting a knife through the warmth inside.

'Whatever happens, I'm glad I came,' I heard myself

saying. 'You're different from anybody I've ever met . . . and you're beautiful too.' I almost looked over my shoulder to see who had spoken. I'd never said anything like that to a girl before. I'd had a crush on blond Sophie Fischer from the cathedral last year, but I was definitely more interested in football than girls. What on earth had come over me? I reached out and placed my hand on hers. I could feel its knotty sinews. I imagined her flying through the air, high above the circus ring, hands clutched tight to the flying trapeze. Suddenly she pulled her hand away, as if my fingers were rods of white-hot iron. She looked at me with a strange intensity.

'What tempted you here today? Why did you come?'

I opened my mouth but no words came.

'With one behind, you can't sit on two horses,' she said, as if to herself.

'I don't understand . . .'

'It's a Romani saying. It means you can only live in one world. You have to choose.'

We held each other's eyes for what seemed like eternity. The Petalo deck lay on the table between us, full of signs and warnings. Of different paths to choose. How long we'd have stayed there locked in each other I'll never know, for suddenly, in a clatter of beads, a tall, scowling woman burst through the curtain, her hair escaping wildly from its pins. An olive-skinned boy of about my age hovered behind the old woman's shoulder, glaring at Lili, eyes full of reproach.

The woman's eyes glittered in the candlelight. 'What's going on, Lili?' Silence filled the narrow wagon as she glanced towards the table where the Romani Seven lay in a neat row. 'What are you doing?'

Her shadow loomed huge on the curved walls as she took one pace across the small space towards the table. I'll never forget her look of horror as she stared down at the cards.

'The Tower and the Devil *reversed*!' she gasped. And then she looked at me for the first time. Nobody had ever stared at me with such hatred before, as if at some kind of poisonous insect. '*Gadje Gadjensa, Rom Romensa,*' she muttered under her breath. 'Get out, *gadjo*! Out with you!'

And then she turned on Lili, her eyes on fire. 'May our ancestors forgive you, Lili! You've betrayed my trust, and now look what you've done!'

Sprechen Verboten!

THERE WAS THE MOST DREADFUL ROW when I got home. I'd known there would be just as soon as I ran back to the merry-go-round and found Rudi gone. The gilded horses were rigid and still on their golden poles, the steam organ's wobbly voice was silent and the ticket-man with the gaudy cravat had disappeared. Everyone was drifting home to get ready for the air-raid drill and nobody had seen a small fair-haired boy in brown shorts wandering around looking for his brother.

I had no idea how long I'd been in the wagon with Lili. Time had stood still, and when I first emerged, blinking into the sun-drenched afternoon, I didn't remember Rudi. All I knew was that I wanted to get away from the fierce old woman and the boy with the accusing stare. I'd almost reached the Goethe memorial when I suddenly remembered him . . . too late. When he'd finished his ride he'd looked all over for me, burst into tears and then been rescued by a neighbour from the apartments at the end of our street who'd spotted him being sick by the gate.

Tante Ida was furious but I was pretty cross with Rudi, to be honest. After all, he shouldn't have wandered off. And I wasn't to blame if the greedy little pig had made himself sick with sweets. I did feel guilty, though. I'd deserted him for a reason I didn't even understand myself and couldn't possibly explain to anyone. I was excited, confused, angry with Rudi – all rolled into one. I didn't want to talk about it. I just wanted to be alone. Just like any teenage schoolboy, I suppose, who finds himself suddenly, unexpectedly, hopelessly in love.

The air-raid drill was scheduled for nine o'clock. We had a hurried supper made by Tante Ida, and Vati was bad tempered because it was *Eintopf – one-pot* – a disgusting pork and sauerkraut stew that Hitler had decreed we must eat on the first Sunday of every month, so we could give the money saved to Winter Relief.

'It's not even Sunday,' moaned Vati, but Tante Ida was unashamed.

'We'll have to get used to going without, now our ration cards have been activated!'

I decided I shouldn't eat anything at all, like people do in novels when they fall in love, but suddenly I found I was ravenous. I'd eat just this once, I decided, and then I'd starve myself. 'I thought you weren't hungry, Max,' said my aunt. I made a kind of grunting sound.

'Don't talk with your mouth full,' said Gretchen.

All in all, it was a tense evening. After we'd helped with the washing up I escaped to my room – alone at last. As I lay fully clothed on my bed, waiting for the air-raid siren, I tried to make sense of the afternoon – the old woman who had yelled at me, the hostile boy, and the strange tarot reading. I must admit I felt a bit foolish about the tarot cards now I was back at home, but Lili had definitely had me worried for a while. Up in my bedroom, surrounded by piles of *Der Kicker* football magazines and my posters of flying aces from the World War, I managed to find some perspective. The guttering candles and the strange smells had drawn me in. And the mysterious wagon all painted with symbols. Anyone might have fallen for her confidence trick. It was a sham, and not a very nice one either – making money out of people's anxieties. But I had to admit she was quite a performer. For a few minutes I'd almost begun to believe in it myself.

I stretched luxuriously on my bed. I could put the foolish tarot business behind me, no problem, but I couldn't get the girl out of my head. I pulled the guilty headscarf from my shorts pocket and breathed into its folds, drinking in the spicy scent of roses. Then I wound it twice around my neck. There was a pleasant haze in my mind, like on the day I'd had too much wine after my First Communion. I ached all over with a delicious weakness. I thought of the silly fumblings behind the clubhouse when I'd kissed Sophie Fischer. How could I have thought she was pretty? So blond and pale. I'd even written a poem about her once, after I'd seen her in her games kit! Well, I'd definitely gone off her now. I hugged my gas mask and imagined I was holding Lili to my chest. I was just kissing her softly when . . .

I leaped off the bed nearly halfway across the room. The unfamiliar, long drawn howl of the sirens – bang on time, in true German fashion. Up down! Down up! Up down! Three wailing tones announcing the presence of Allied bombers within Berlin's ring of defences. And then I heard the drone of aircraft flying right over our roof. We'd been warned there'd be real planes but I found myself shaking even so. And when we heard the *tak tak* of anti-aircraft fire from the Tiergarten and the yells from outside: '*Lichter aus! Sprechen verboten!*' Rudi started to scream.

'God in heaven,' cried Mutti. 'Where's Rudi's gas mask?'

Gretchen sprang from her room, swathed in bandages in her role as *Serious Head Injury* only to run smack into Erika emerging from hers in her blue silk dressing gown, hair in curlers.

'*Erika!*' hissed Gretchen. 'It's the air-raid drill! We've got to go down to the cellar.'

'Oh fiddlesticks! If you think I'm spending the night in the cellar for a false alarm you've got another think . . .'

'Shhh! *Sprechen verboten!*'

'Don't be daft, Gretchen. What are you whispering for? Do you think the *pretend* enemy can hear us up in their planes?' Erika flounced back into her bedroom and a moment later we heard her gramophone crackle into life.

By this time Mutti had manhandled Rudi into his gas mask and was dragging him, bug eyed and pig snouted, towards the cellar stairs.

'It's only a *practice*, Maria,' snapped Vati. 'He'll break his neck on the stairs with that thing on. And then he won't need a gas mask!'

Overall it was a restless evening, what with the *Luftwaffe*'s antics overhead, the clanging of fire engines and the tremendous lightshow as the feathery sprays of searchlights swept the skies. Gretchen was thrilled. Clearly being bumped over rough ground and dumped onto a heap of other groaning casualties was the best thing that had ever happened to her. 'Just think of it,' she declared, placing her cardboard label in the centre of the mantelpiece. 'Me, Gretchen Hartmann, carried up Tiergartenstrasse on a stretcher in my nightie!'

After the long All Clear had sounded and we'd managed to persuade Rudi that it wouldn't be fun to sleep in the cellar, Vati turned on the wireless in case of important news. I retired to my bedroom to think some more about Lili. I tweaked the blackout curtain. The streetlights were still out and the stars were beautiful. I'd always noticed them at my grandmother's in the mountains but never until now in Berlin.

Tante Ida had given me a brown leather diary when I'd joined Hitler Youth with a swastika embossed on the front. It had days in it but not dates – the kind meant for writing your memoirs. I'd thought it was a funny present at the time. Surely only girls filled diaries with secrets. But that evening I slid the neat brown volume from my desk drawer, smoothing it open at the first page. I sat back in my chair, sucking the end of my fountain pen, and then I began to write . . .

Stars over Berlin

Diamonds sparkling in a crow-black sky
Raven hair sprinkled with autumn rain . . .

I'd already written half a page of crossings outs and blots when I heard Vati's low, worried tones on the landing. I tiptoed across in my slippers and opened my door just a crack.

'Hitler has formed a war cabinet. Göring to preside. Mark my words, Ida. The sands are running out . . .'

I closed my door softly and picked up my pen. *My life is changing,* I wrote dramatically, *in so many ways . . .*

The news on the wireless next morning, however, was complacent with success, if you didn't count the man who'd fallen off the Anhalter railway platform in the blackout and been hit by a train.

'*The air-raid practice went off last night with exemplary calm, and Berliners are back on the streets this morning going about their usual business.*'

Vati snorted over yet another slice of burnt toast. '*With exemplary calm!* Clearly that fellow was nowhere in the vicinity of the Hartmann household last night!'

Warnings

I FOUND OUT LATER why Baba Sara was mad as a frog in a sock, and it wasn't only because of the tarot, or the fact that Marko told her I'd been a long time alone with a *gadjo*, although she was certainly snarky about that. '*Gadjo Gadjensa, Rom Romensa – Gadjo with Gadjo,*' she kept saying, '*Rom with Rom.* It's the Romani way.' But there was another reason for her to be cranky too, and that probably made her madder with me than ever.

You see, Nani Ana had told her a terrible story, and that night Baba Sara told the troupe. The night before a show we'd usually be putting the final touches to our costumes or going over a routine or two, but it was hard to do much in the blackout. So we squatted Rom fashion around the clearing where the fire should have been and listened to her story instead. It wasn't the best time for a story like that, what with the air-raid practice going on all round us. But I don't suppose there'd ever be a good time for what she had to tell.

Last autumn, just after we'd left Berlin, there'd been a bucketful of trouble for Ana's husband Maritz. It started with a bit of name-calling and some jostling in the street. Then one day some kids toppled his cart all over Alexanderplatz, squashing his fruit and playing catch with his marrows. You'd have thought the police would have helped out, but they didn't. They just stood there laughing. And it got worse, till it was happening every day. Then one night the Gestapo came for him, hammering on the door long after they'd gone to bed, and arrested him. Just like that. Ana didn't know where he was for weeks.

And then one day in April he just turned up. He'd been in prison in a work camp called Sachsenhausen, in Oranienburg, north of Berlin. Ana didn't recognize him when he knocked on the door. She thought the skeleton with the shaved head was a filthy beggar. He'd been building a prison camp for almost half a year – a concentration camp he called it, although really it was just a pigsty. And he had a letter burned on the skin of his arm – Z for *Zigeuner* – and a number after it, just like you'd brand an animal.

I'd never seen Baba Sara so jittered before. You see, prison wasn't the worst thing that had happened to Maritz. One day, a big Nazi came to the camp, high ranking, so Ana said. He called all the gypsies together and told them they were thieves and parasites and that's why they'd been locked up. And then he made them an offer. The Nazis didn't want them breeding in Germany, but if they agreed to be sterilized, he'd let them go. He'd brought two doctors with him to do the cutting. The doctors made out they were doing them a favour. They'd only chosen gypsies who'd fought in the World War, so they said. The others wouldn't be so lucky. Well, Maritz had been in the trenches in 1917, so they said they'd let him go if he agreed to the operation.

What else could he do? He didn't think he could face another winter in that place. His chest was already bad from the gas in the trenches, and he'd almost coughed himself to death in the camp. They'd been bullied, starved and punished like animals. And this was a chance to get out . . . so he'd agreed. But now he was home he couldn't hardly speak without stuttering. They hadn't done the numbing properly and he'd felt the whole thing, start to finish. Ana said he dreamed every night the Gestapo had come back for him and he'd wake up screaming and covered in sweat.

We couldn't believe it. 'Why pick on Maritz?' said Ma. She'd never had much time for the Sinti, but Maritz was Ana's husband after all. 'He's lived in Berlin all his life. He has a good trade. They don't break the law.'

Baba Sara shook her head. 'It's not just Ana and Maritz,' she said. 'That's the trouble.'

A new office had recently opened in Gestapo headquarters in Prinz Albrecht Strasse, she told us. They'd sent Maritz a letter. All Sinti had to report for registration. Well, Ana went along to the office with Maritz and they were treated like criminals. The police took their fingerprints and then gave them a brown registration card to show they were true bloods. Brown for full-blood gypsies and blue for half-bloods – *poshrats*, we called them. And now there were new rules coming out every week. Gypsies weren't allowed to marry non-gypsies. Gypsies couldn't collect letters from the post office or go to school. And now they weren't even allowed to keep dogs and cats!

Well, Baba Sara couldn't bite her tongue. 'I won't say I told you so, Ana,' she'd said, 'but you should never have gone to live in brick with a Sinto. There's safety in the wandering life. I'd like to see them try to take our fingerprints.'

But Ana wouldn't have it. 'You've got wax in your ears, Sara. How can you know what's going on if you never stop in one place? Don't you talk to other Roma on the road? Well, if you don't, you should, and then you'd see which way the cat's jumping. It's not just Sinti they're after. I'm telling you, your travelling days are over.'

We were as shocked as Baba Sara. We tossed Ana's story back and fore in usual Rom fashion, the men speaking first and then the women, while the little ones wandered off to watch the light show from the anti-aircraft guns. Was it really as bad in Berlin as Ana said? She'd always been a funny one. But what if it was true? Should we harness the horses and leave tonight whilst the Nazis were busy with the practice? Or should we go on with the circus? Everyone said their bit, then all of a sudden Pa called for silence. As *Rom Baro*, he always had the last word.

'*Hush kacker!*' he said suddenly, thumping the silver-headed cane he always held when we were having a *kris*. 'I said, shut up and listen!' We all waited as he sucked on his pipe. 'It's rubbish,' he said at last, looking straight at Baba Sara who'd been chewing baccy to calm herself. 'Think about it, Mother. I'm sorry for Maritz . . . if it's true. But you heard what Ana said. Those work camps ain't for people like us. They're for lazybones. Maybe the authorities have got to do something about people who won't work . . .'

Baba Sara spat out her baccy in a way that told Pa what she thought of that. 'Maritz kept a vegetable stall. Got up at the crack to go to market. Hardly a lazybones!'

Everyone started talking at once, so Pa had to bang down his cane for silence. 'It's always the same. Three Romanies, four opinions! But I'm *Rom Baro*, so listen to me.' Ana had always been a worrier, insisted Pa. That's why she'd left the wandering life and gone to live in brick. 'Look at the facts. We talked to the policemen today. They didn't say nothing about registering, or fingerprints, or brown cards. They even took tickets for the show. We work hard. We're almost sold out for tomorrow already . . . and you mark my words, half the punters will be in Nazi uniform.'

Baba Sara tried again. 'Just because Ana married a Sinto doesn't make her a fool, Josef. We should be grateful for the warning. At harvest time it's too late to sow. Let's make sure *we* don't leave it too late.'

'And as you taught me yourself, Mother, a rabbit with only one burrow is soon caught. The Rom know how to survive. We've got plenty of holes we can hide in . . . if ever the time comes. But that time ain't come yet. The *kris* is over, Mother. I've decided. Circus Petalo will stay.'

And so we talked and smoked and passed round the brandy bottle, on into the night as the air-raid practice went on over our heads, the droning planes like tiny silver crosses caught in the searchlights, until suddenly the All Clear sounded.

'Let's light the fire,' said Pa, 'and have some dancing.' He caught my eye, sitting hunched like an owl on the edge of the circle. 'Cheer up, Lili. You look like you've swallowed a frog. Go fetch my fiddle, that's my girl.'

I scrambled to my feet to do as I was told, but I didn't have the heart for dancing. Not tonight. As the siren faded into the night air and lights began to spring on again in the Tiergarten, I had a sudden sick sort of feeling that somehow today marked the start of a bellyful of trouble. I'd been scared by Baba Sara's story, coming right on top of the ill-starred tarot reading. For a few minutes her news had driven the handsome *gadjo* from my mind. But now he floated back into my thoughts, and as I tramped to fetch Pa's fiddle, I heard Baba Sara's voice in my head: *Gadjo Gadjensa. Rom Romensa. Gadjo with Gadjo. Rom with Rom.* And then I thought of the way his long eyelashes cast a shadow on his cheeks in the candlelight, and the way he flicked his fringe out of his deep blue eyes. I'd never seen him before today, so what was it about this strange boy that set my heart aflutter? After all, he was just a schoolboy in a silly uniform, who'd tipped me right off balance, crept in without warning and completely stolen my heart.

The Greatest Show on Earth
31 August 1939

THE AIR-RAID PRACTICE had shocked everyone. Somehow war seemed more possible, now we'd actually heard the sirens and seen the searchlights. Everybody was talking about war and almost everybody was against it. People felt angry about being kept in the dark. 'We know nothing! Why don't they tell us what's going on?'

Most people had spent all day awaiting developments, glued to their Peoples' Receivers that by Nazi design could only pick up local wireless stations. But you can only remain at fever pitch for so long, and by evening most people had given up waiting and gone out. My parents, resplendent in evening dress, had departed for the opera house, and Erika to the UFA cinema with her friend, Klara. And Gretchen to her charity concert in her Bavarian milkmaid's outfit.

'Thank goodness they've all gone,' sighed Tante Ida, waving Gretchen off down the garden path. 'Now, when you've tied Rudi's shoelaces, Max, we'd better be going too.'

As Rudi skipped excitedly along the pavement, Berlin seemed blissfully normal again, with people crowding into restaurants and bars as if nothing were amiss. We stopped briefly at the entrance to the Tiergarten to admire a poster of a girl in a sequined bolero perched on a dazzling white horse beneath a curly red banner: *Circus Petalo, The Greatest Show on Earth!* I couldn't help thinking it looked rather odd, squeezed in between a poster of Adolf Hitler announcing the sale of four million copies of *Mein Kampf* and an advert for the Nuremburg Rally of Peace, with the ominous word *CANCELLED* scrawled across in diagonal black letters.

We could feel the throb of the generators even before we reached the showground, so that when we finally saw the big top, the rumblings seemed like the heartbeat of an enormous beast. Circus Petalo lay sprawled across the Tiergarten, a glittering confusion of candy-striped tents. In stark contrast to yesterday's blackout, bright bulbs from sizzling food tents spilled their light over the milling crowds, and hundreds of coloured bulbs lined the seams of the big top. My mouth began to water as the aroma of onions tickled my nostrils, carried on a warm breeze that stirred the magic lanterns into a swinging dance. A pair of miniature clowns in cone-shaped hats waddled along in oversized shoes offering candyfloss to excited children.

Rudi's eyes were gobstopper round. 'Why is that clown sad?' he asked, pointing at the one with the painted-on frown. 'And the other one happy?'

I tried to think of something clever to say, but he was onto the next question before I had the chance.

'Will there be lions?'

I said I didn't think so but there were sure to be lots of horses. I'd glimpsed a fair number, corralled behind a canvas wall, gorgeously plumed, their gleaming coats reflecting dancing patches of green and yellow light. My eyes raked the showground, searching for Lili, and my heart almost stopped at the sight of a girl in a feathered costume selling programmes. I broke into a run. 'Do you want one, Rudi?'

The girl smiled as she took my coins, but it wasn't Lili. We gave our tickets to a clown in striped trousers and hurried to our ringside seats under the glare of the arc lamps, breathing in the heady odour of tan-bark and sawdust. The band was playing the stirring *Entrance of the Gladiators* by Julius Fučík. I recognized it from school orchestra. The piece always made my spine tingle, even in the school hall. I hugged myself in anticipation as I settled back in my seat to read the programme.

The show was divided into two halves. I ran my eye hurriedly down part one. *Bareback Dog Spitzi with clowns Tamas and Pali* began the programme, followed by *Fifi, the Amazing Child Juggler*. Then *Liberty Horses* followed by *Trick Ponies* and *Otto and Marko Camlo, the Amazing Bareback Riders*, finishing before the interval with *Franco and Bernadette, Celestial High-wire Thrills – Guaranteed*, said the commentary, *to bring the audience to the edge of their seats.*

No sign of Lili so far.

I hastily scanned part two. More clowns, then *Pierrot, the Mind-reading Horse* followed by *Florica and Fonso Botello and the Amazing Grace and Power of Flamenco.* There were sword swallowers, dancing dogs and then – there it was at last, squeezed in between *Chimpanzees' Playday* and *The Grande Finale: Rollo and the Sensational Flying Petalos – Birds Without Wings!* I sank back in my red plush seat. I'd have to wait until almost the end of the show . . . but I was actually going to see Lili again.

At first I didn't know how I'd make it through the first half, but the clowns were wonderfully funny in their absurd hooped trousers. Cracking heads, skidding on banana skins and bouncing off each other, they clung together, howling stage tears whilst the audience roared their sympathy. Then, with the aid of collapsing ladders, exploding bouquets and leaking buckets, we were soon reduced to hysterical laughter, especially when their shaggy little dog rode a pony round the ring facing the tail.

The bareback riders were thrilling too, somersaulting from one horse to the other as they cantered gracefully around the ring, tails flowing like silk. I had a feeling I recognized one of the riders – the boy from the vardo the previous afternoon – but I couldn't be sure, and before I knew it the ringmaster in white jodhpurs was announcing the interval, and Rudi was begging Tante Ida for a *bratwurst* with onions.

I stayed in my seat. I claimed I wanted to listen to the orchestra but the truth was I couldn't bear to leave the ringside. Just to be there made me feel closer to Lili. It had been a sensational first half, but not much had happened in the dome except for the tightrope artist who'd thrilled us by cooking an omelette on a stove balanced on a gleaming silver wire. But now I was aware of a lot more activity up on high. Men in black were climbing the rigging, right into the dome towards the narrow platform that was fixed to the central pole, checking everything, testing the trapeze bars and ropes and scattering chalk on the wooden boards.

As I gazed up at them I felt an unpleasant churning in the pit of my stomach, like something cold and slimy in my guts. I'd suddenly remembered the tarot card with the burning tower and the falling figure, its cloak billowing out like a flag. I watched as the men slid deftly down the ropes and left the ring through a crimson silk curtain, clapping chalk from their hands. Feeling slightly sick, I fished the crumpled programme from my pocket and scanned the running order again. *The Flying Petalos – Birds Without Wings!* The words swam in front of my eyes and I found I was clutching the programme so tightly I'd pierced the cheap paper with the nail of my thumb. I closed my eyes and breathed in deeply. *Let it start soon*, I prayed silently. *The sooner it starts again, the sooner it will all be over.*

White Heather

I'D BEEN OBSESSED with Alfredo Codona ever since Ma took me to see him perform his famous triple somersault at Berlin's Wintergarten Theatre when I was only seven. In fact, it was that very night that I made up my mind to follow Ma on the flying trapeze rather than bareback riding like Pa. By that time The Three Codonas were world famous, especially Alfredo, who'd performed this stunt for the first time a year before. Every fancy circus in the world wanted to hire them: Ringling Brothers, Barnum and Bailey's, Hagenbecks. They were sensational, and Alfredo was the best of them all. From the moment I saw this amazing feat and heard the great gasp of admiration from the spectators, Alfredo became my hero.

We'd been able to do the Double Double for years, and,

to be honest, I was a bit bored of our act, so all that summer of 1939 I'd been practising a two and a half with the life belt – Rollo as catcher. The danger's in the speed. Your brain loses track at sixty miles an hour, so it's hard to know when to reach for your catcher, and if you miss and drop badly into the net, you risk a broken neck. I wasn't too worried. Ma had taught us how to fall properly, and by the end of August I was making a good nine out of ten and I'd been pestering Ma to let me give it a go in public. She wasn't sure. She still didn't think I was ready.

I remember every last detail of that summer evening. I can see the dressing room near the entrance to the big top, its table cluttered with pots of rouge and powder. Pali and Tamas are already whited-up, finishing each other's smiles and frowns with sticks of greasepaint. Frieda is taking off her earrings and reminding me about mine. We never fly with jewellery or anything that can flap or tangle. Then she helps me into my fleshings and my silver leotard with the turquoise spangles. Then we paint the cork-black round our eyes followed by thick scarlet lipstick so we won't look drained under the lights. And last of all we chalk our forearms, to stop them slipping in the catcher's grip.

When we're done, Ma braids our hair. Mine first, then Frieda's. It has to be in that order, like a kind of superstition. There are plenty of those in the circus – like always putting your right foot in the ring first and sewing garlic into your costume. Or putting white heather in our braids. We'd brush out our hair after every performance and there it would be – a tiny piece snagged in our combs.

Frieda and Rollo had been cold with me all afternoon. In fact, they hadn't really spoken to me since I'd been discovered reading the tarot for that *gadjo* boy, and spending too long with him in the vardo. So I was relieved when Frieda helped me into my costume. You've got to be in tune with your partners when you fly the trapeze. And before he climbed the Spanish web, Rollo squeezed my arm – just to show we were still friends.

I still don't know what went wrong. Ma hadn't wanted me to try the two and a half – that's for sure. 'You're not ready, Lili,' she'd said. But had I really not told Rollo that I planned to give it a try? Afterwards my head felt so confused, like when you've done too many cartwheels and you've gone all giddy. Maybe I *thought* I'd told him. Or maybe . . . just maybe . . . I knew in my heart that I hadn't. Perhaps I'd got carried away, showing off. And worst of all, showing off for someone I hardly knew. Someone I wasn't even sure was watching me at all.

Birds Without Wings

' A ND NOW, LAAADIES AND GENTLEMENNN . . . *children of all ages! I have great pleasure in presenting the act you've all been waiting for! Please welcome the undisputed stars of Circus Petalo . . . our very own Birds Without Wings! THE EXTRAORDINARY! THE DAZZLING! THE SPECTACULAR! THE FEARLESS!'* A roll of drums and a clash of cymbals. *'THE BREATHTAKING FLYING PETALOS!'*

I stared in the direction of the ringmaster's gloved fingers, heart hammering, eyes on stalks as invisible hands drew back the curtain, and before I knew it there they were, three slight figures in silver and turquoise running into the sawdust arena, silver capes flying as the orchestra burst into frenzied life. With a flourish, they handed their capes to the beaming ringmaster and bent their heads to thunderous applause.

The two girls looked very alike, one slightly taller than the other. I wondered if they were sisters. With their braided hair and identical spangled figures it was hard to tell them apart. They rose up from their bow, acknowledging the cascades of applause with dazzling smiles, and then I recognized the shorter one as Lili. You might say the other one was prettier, with a round, soft face and wide-set eyes. Lili had a strong jaw with a long, straight nose, and yet she was the one that sparkled like a firecracker.

The Three Petalos held their arms in the air to show that the act was about to begin and then threw themselves into a succession of handsprings like whirling silver Catherine wheels until they reached the rope ladder at the side of the ring that snaked up into the shadowy darkness of the dome. And then, in a spine-tingling roll of drums, the two girls ran lightly up the ladder with as much ease as if it were a flight of shallow stairs, reaching the top in a clash of cymbals, whilst the boy shinned a rope, hand over hand, muscles rippling as he climbed.

There was absolute silence from the band. I knew it was deliberate, to increase the dramatic effect, and yet still it made my flesh shiver. For a moment they stood motionless on the platform and then slowly, dramatically, the boy took the trapeze in his hands. In an instant he was flashing through the air, swinging elegantly backwards and forwards as if to gain momentum before executing a number of moves, until he was hanging upside down by his knees, spangles twinkling.

The crowd roared its approval. I was relieved to see a safety net at least, although it seemed a long way down. And now the other girl swung out in a graceful curving flight, turned a somersault and landed in the boy's strong grip, the pair of them swinging together until, on the return sweep, the girl sprang lightly into the air, nimbly catching her own trapeze, and in a second she was safely back on her perch to gasps of admiration from below.

I was clenching my teeth so hard my jaw ached. Then Lili was off, but instead of turning one somersault, she turned one and a half, landing neatly in the boy's outstretched arms. I had to close my eyes, only opening them again when a burst of clapping told me she was back up in the dome. I felt sick to my stomach. I wished I hadn't come but I couldn't leave now – not until I knew she was safely down in the ring.

Two and a Half

PICTURE ME THERE on the springboard, the chalk white on my arms and my leotard glittering in the arc lights high up in the dome. We've nearly finished our act. Me and Frieda have just performed a passing leap, returning to the bar with a double pirouette. It's one of those fancy stunts an audience goes wild for – all top show but not much risk. So far I've managed to keep my head. I know I mustn't look down. You can't see anyway in the dazzle of the lights but that's not why I don't. We're superstitious in the circus, and trapeze artists never tempt fate. Yet right now I want to know if he's there. It's all I can think about. He said he had tickets for tonight. So is he down there in the crowd? Is he looking at me? My heart misses a beat, fluttering out of its usual rhythm, a little out of time because that boy might – just might – be watching me.

Steady yourself, Lili, I tell myself. *You can't afford for anything to be different – everything must be accurate. Not a split second out.* And then I hear Baba Sara's voice in my head. *Gadjo with Gadjo. Rom with Rom. It's how it must always be.*

I look towards Rollo, hanging by his hocks from the catch bar. He gives me the sign that he's ready for the double somersault. *'Allez!'* His face wears its usual calm expression, our catcher who I trust with my life. My hands are steady on the trapeze bar as I measure the distance with my eyes. I wait for the roll of drums – the signal to the audience that they're about to see something grand – and then the clash of the cymbals and I'm off. I get in a couple of wide swings first and then at the shout from Rollo I launch myself . . . *'Hup!'* . . . into the two and a half.

Tears of a Clown

I HEARD THE LONG, terrified scream as if I'd been waiting for it all evening, echoed by a scream that went up from the crowd as the spangled figures plummeted through the air. I can still hear the resounding smack as they hit the net, first Lili and then the boy. The crowd held its breath, praying that this was a stunt . . . waiting for the artists to bound up from the net, turn a somersault down into the ring and bow smiling to an audience that's suddenly applauding more wildly than ever, through sheer relief . . .

The two bodies lay limp, unmoving in the swaying net, and then a collective groan of horror mingled with screaming filled the dome.

Suddenly there was wild confusion. People surged

forward towards the ring as circus attendants ran to and fro, shouting, urging everyone to keep back as the net was lowered gently to the ground. Before I could reach her, the mêlée of people parted, and Lili and the boy were borne from the ring, out through the curtain behind the orchestra. And then, incredibly, like a scene from a Hollywood movie, the bandmaster raised his baton and the band began to play as spectators started rushing for the exits. I heard the voice of the ringmaster, shouting above the hubbub. 'Laadies and gentlemen! Remain seated, if you please. People will get hurt!'

'Come on, Max,' said my aunt in a grim voice. 'We need to get Rudi out of here. He's had a terrible shock.'

'Get out of my way!' Elbows out, I thrust a path through the spectators, shoving people aside, ploughing towards the exit. I scanned the fairground, and then I began to run, wildly from tent to tent, around the perimeter of the big top, around the sprawling showground, until I noticed a huddle of clowns and acrobats in their costumes at the entrance to a plain canvas tent. No one noticed me hovering at the back.

The boy lay on a low ottoman, his head resting on a folded blanket. A dribble of blood ran from his nose and mouth, pooling into a dark spreading patch on his chest. His kohl-rimmed eyes stared blindly.

Lili's partner knelt by the bed. 'Don't die, Rollo,' she sobbed. 'Rollo, please don't die.'

A man with a drooping moustache sat holding his head in his hands, slowly shaking it from side to side, his shoulders heaving. A miniature clown with a painted-on smile and tears coursing down his face placed his hand on the girl's arm. 'Frieda, please. He's already dead.'

'No. Not dead,' said the girl softly. 'He's still warm. Can't you feel it, Pali?' And then the girl let out a great cry. I'll never forget it. It was the most hollow, desolate sound I'd ever heard.

I turned quickly on my heel. I could still hear the thrum of the generators from the big top. The shocked crowd was dispersing noisily. The boy was dead. I was sure of that. But what of Lili?

The War is On!

Back home that night, I couldn't speak to anyone. I flung myself down on my bed in my clothes, and tossed and turned all night until dawn in an agony of despair, running over and over the events of the evening. I'd only just dropped off into a fretful sort of doze when I became aware of someone roughly shaking me awake. I sat up in bed, dazzled by the sunlight streaming through the shutters, wondering why I was still wearing my shoes, then suddenly the feeling of loss and grief rose up again and swamped me.

Vati didn't seem to notice. He'd switched on the wireless at seven-thirty in the morning only to learn that last night, as he and Mutti were listening to the overture to *Die Meistersinger*, and Rudi and I were sitting in our ringside seats, a million and a half German troops had been pressing on towards their final positions on the Polish border. Whilst Gretchen was playing her clarinet in the BDM band, German tanks and infantry had poured across the Polish frontier and were now on the advance. Vati's voice was quaking with fury. '*Mein Gott!* Isn't one war enough in a lifetime for that Austrian snake in the grass?'

It would be two more days before Britain and France declared war on Germany. But there was no doubt in my father's mind that this was it. The thing he had dreaded most of all had finally come to pass.

The war was on!

I dressed without washing and went out, avoiding the martial music on the kitchen wireless. There was an eerie silence on the deserted pavements. I walked quickly down my street, skirting the Tiergarten, turning left into Hermann Göring Strasse. I was going to find out what had happened to Lili, even if I had to knock on every caravan door in the circus. Even if I had to ask that crazy old woman. I'd been in shock last night. This morning I was going to find out.

It was a gloriously sunny day. The red squirrels were already out, scurrying hopefully along the paths on the lookout for food. The Goethe memorial gleamed white in the sunshine. I stopped dead, staring at the flat yellow marks in the grass where the tents had been, blinking in disbelief at the wide, deserted space. Circus Petalo had gone, leaving only a trail of churned earth and deep scars in the sandy soil. I crouched down with a groan of defeat. Taking a handful of earth, I held my clenched fist to my mouth, then, standing up, I let it trickle through my fingers.

As I was leaving the Tiergarten, I noticed a shiny black Mercedes passing slowly through the Brandenburg Gate, official pennants flying. It turned sharp right, skirting the burnt-out ruins of the Reichstag, then proceeded in the direction of the Kroll Opera House, the German parliament's new home. I looked at my watch. It was quarter to ten. I couldn't face going home but there was no getting away from the public listening stations, so I heard Hitler's ten o'clock broadcast from the Opera House, just like every other German citizen glued to their kitchen wireless.

'I am from now on merely the first soldier of the German Reich. I have once more put on the field-grey coat that was most sacred and dear to me. I will not take it off again until victory is secured, or I will not survive the outcome.'

My aunt washed all our windows that afternoon, scrubbing our front steps with a vigour exhausting to watch. Looking back, I think it was a kind of brave defiance. *Don't come for us, Death. We're very much alive.*

Alone once again in my bedroom, I pulled my diary from my desk. *Deep scars on the ground,* I wrote. *Deep scars on my heart.* Then, with my ruler and fountain pen, I drew a thick black line.

Dead Man's Lament

WE PLUGGED ROLLO'S NOSTRILS with wax and covered our mirrors so his spirit wouldn't get trapped on earth. Our menfolk ripped the buttons from their coats in sorrow and Pa played a haunting *mulengi djili*, a lament for the dead, on his fiddle. Then we washed Rollo and dressed him in his finest clothes, placed money in his pockets for his journey, and buried him in the manner of my people.

'I open his way into the new life,' pronounced Pa, tears streaming down his face, 'and release him from the fetter of our sorrow.'

Then we burned Rollo's things: his pillows and sleeping rugs, his leotards and fleshings, and we smashed his plates, for we don't keep anything belonging to the dead.

I say *we* buried Rollo. By that I mean my people. My memory of that time is cloudy. Gentle voices, kind hands, but little else. I lay for days in Ma's vardo, slipping in and out of nightmares, and it would be many weeks before I would be strong enough to take my place in the troupe again. And by that time war was raging all over Europe and we were many miles from Berlin.

Pa blamed himself for not heeding Ana's warning that night of the air-raid practice. If we'd packed up and left Berlin then, Rollo would still be alive. It was *prikasa* – a *bad omen*. He left the chimps tied up outside Berlin Zoo with notes round their necks: *Please look after us. We're friendly.* Pa thought they'd fare better there in these uncertain times. And he left our cobras in their baskets too: *Safe. No fangs.*

Pa reckoned we should travel southeast. 'We ain't going to be trapped here like crabs in a bucket,' he said. He'd heard about German children leaving Berlin for somewhere called Glatz in the mountains, away from the expected bombing. If the Nazis were sending their *chavvies* there, it would surely be safe for us too.

My body slowly healed but my mind took longer. I couldn't understand how Rollo was dead and I was still breathing. Sometimes when I caught Frieda's eyes on me I felt so guilty I wanted to die. And yet my belly still grumbled with hunger. My heart still beat in my chest.

I often used to run the memory of the accident backwards in my head. It was always the same – grainy black and white. I think it's because of something that happened once at the UFA cinema in Berlin, years before the night I fractured my skull and Rollo died. I'd gone to see *Vaudeville* with Frieda and Rollo and Nani Bernadine's girls. Ma said we should see the film because our heroes, The Three Codonas, were doubles for the trapeze stunts.

The silent film was a love triangle about a trapeze act, starring Emil Jannings with Lya de Putti as his cheating wife. We'd giggled all the way through at the idea of Emil Jannings, at eighteen stone, up on the flying trapeze. Stupid *gadjo* director! Anyway, we watched carefully when it really was The Codonas on screen. Suddenly, just as Alfredo had performed his famous triple somersault, the film projector jammed . . . and then started playing backwards. How we laughed when Alfredo started somersaulting backwards, back onto his trapeze bar, then up onto the springboard. At first I felt bad about laughing at my hero but you had to admit it was very funny, especially the shots of the audience spitting *bratwurst* and onions back into their rolls.

And now I run my own stunt backwards like the film . . . from the moment I thumped into Rollo at the wrong angle, sending us both hurtling into the net fifteen metres below. I imagine us rising up from the net, and as we do Rollo's broken neck is mended and the faces of the spectators change from horror to anticipation. Back, back my memory rewinds as I somersault two and a half times upwards. Up, up towards the safety of the narrow board. I look round at Frieda and she's looking towards Rollo, her eyes alight with love. And in my strange reverse film there's still a chance of a different ending. A chance to heed the warning of the tarot.

The cards show us what might be, not what will. We

choose our own paths. I chose mine and my will was free. I was showing off. I know in my heart that I killed Rollo. If I could spin my life backwards, then I would.

A Garden in Berlin
April 2013

MAX DUG IN HIS POCKET for a handkerchief, wiped his eyes and blew his nose. Then, placing the rusty horseshoe and the tarot deck in the bottom of the suitcase, he stared into the pool of deeper shade behind the memorial. A hazy form eluded him for a second and then slipped back into view.

'It was a coincidence, Lili. Nothing to do with the tarot. You made a mistake because you weren't concentrating. You were showing off for me.'

A sudden cool breeze shivered the pear blossom, casting dancing patterns on the orchard floor. Max cupped his hand to his ear as if listening, smiled sadly and shook his head. 'We'll never agree and I don't want to argue.'

His stomach gurgled and, as if on cue, he heard the

shrill ring of the house telephone. That would be Gretchen, ringing to check he'd remembered the soup she'd left for his lunch. She'd been touchingly anxious about leaving him. He turned over a page of his manuscript, skim-reading the first few lines. This would be a good place to take a break. And Gretchen would probably ring again soon. He hoped so, and then he shouldn't be disturbed for the rest of the afternoon.

Max groped behind his chair for his walking stick, braced himself, then pushed down on the garden table with his free hand. Straightening his back with a sigh of pain, he shuffled towards the stone steps, tapping his stick on the mossy pathway as the telephone shrilled a second time.

'Are you all right, Max? You sound out of breath.' Anxiety always made Gretchen sound cross.

'I'm warming the soup. How's the Bridge?'

'Oh, hopeless! Irma Shroeder's a useless partner! You'd have thought Margot might have warned me she was coming . . .'

'I hope she's not listening . . .'

Gretchen didn't moderate her voice. 'Honestly, she's bid *three no trumps* twice now, when it really should have been *four spades*! Anyway, we're having a spot of lunch, then I'm partnering Margot, and Gretel Schmidt will have the pleasure of Irma, so we might win a few games before it's time for *Kaffee und Kuchen*. Now, you get some rest. I might ring again after tea.'

'There's really no need . . .' said Max lamely as the burr of the dialling tone announced that his sister had hung up.

Max lifted the pan lid, sniffed, and decided he'd just eat the roll. He needed to get on if he was to finish before

Gretchen got home. He pulled a picnic rug from the back of a chair on his way to the door. The sun was warm but there was a chill on the breeze.

Back down in the garden, Max shrugged the rug round his shoulders, then picking up a small buff-coloured book, he peered at the faded title: *The Sun Will Never Set on Us – Songs of the Hitler Youth*. It was a clever design, soft backed and the perfect size for the regulation Hitler Youth pocket. It crackled as he smoothed it open. The black and white illustrations were finely drawn. Boys in shorts waving flags and beating drums. Boys sitting cross-legged around campfires, tents pitched in the distance. He flicked the pages of words and music, and in spite of everything, he still felt a prickle of excitement as he read the titles of the songs he used to know by heart: *'Unsere Fahne flattert uns voran!' 'Our Flag Leads Us Forward!'* Max closed his eyes. He could almost hear the bugles. *Forward! Forward! The fanfares sound!* He shut the book guiltily and picked up the sheath knife, feeling the six-inch blade inscribed with the words *blood and honour* with his thumb. How proud he'd been of it, with its enamelled swastika embedded in the handle. Proud for a while, anyway . . . back in those heady days. He placed the knife next to the songbook, his hand hovering over the twisted lock of hair. Then, with an effort, he picked it up, tracing the plaited strands of black and brown with the tip of his finger, before holding it to his lips.

'Memories of happier times,' he murmured. 'The calm before the storm.'

PART TWO

RUMOURS OF VICTORY

Rabbit *Eintopf*

A T FIRST THE GERMAN ARMY seemed unstoppable. Poland, Holland, Belgium, Norway. 'The British warmongers are utterly impotent,' sneered our Führer. 'The German Reich will last a thousand years!' And certainly for the people of Berlin there were far more casualties caused by the blackout than by enemy action. More car accidents, rapes and murders than ever before . . . but no bombs.

Baths were an early casualty, rationed to weekends only – a state of affairs that would have caused huge rows in our house had Erika been home. Fortunately she'd left for a farm in Potsdam for her compulsory *Landjahr*. Gretchen read out her letters, secretly pleased that Erika was mucking out pigs. She smirked over the photograph of our sister wielding a pitchfork. Mutti felt sorry for Erika, and sent a blue velvet hat with a feather, like Zarah Leander's from her latest film.

'Don't be ridiculous, Maria,' reproved my aunt. 'She's bringing in the harvest, not attending a film premiere.'

To be honest, rationing had hardly affected us – except for the early shortage of toilet paper. 'Use the RAF propaganda leaflets instead,' we were told. 'It's all they're fit for!' And there were certainly plenty of those, falling from the sky like autumn leaves. Vati said we'd be better off wiping our bottoms with the the *Völkischer Beobachter*, the Nazi daily. Otherwise we had plenty of provisions at first. At over two kilos of bread each per week we had more than we could possibly eat. Too scared to put it in the rubbish lest Frau Schneck should come snooping, I was sent with Siegfried to feed the Tiergarten ducks.

At first I didn't mind. I was glad of an excuse to linger alone by the Goethe memorial, gazing over the clearing where the circus had been. For days afterwards I'd scanned every paper for news of the accident . . . and discovered nothing. Hardly surprising in the circumstances, I supposed. And given the circumstances, there was little time for introspection either. Wartime Hitler Youth was claiming me body and soul, and after a week or two spent haunting the Tiergarten, I flung myself into my platoon with added vigour. If I couldn't find out what had happened that night, I thought, then I'd better try my best to forget.

Clothes rationing started in mid-November – a particular problem for Rudi. At six years old, his feet were growing like summer marrows. Tante Ida took him to the new shoe exchange and swapped his old ones for a pair of winter boots ready for his evacuation to our *Oma*, our grandmother in the Bavarian mountains. He'd be out of harm's way there, she hoped, along with scores of other Berlin children. And just in time, it turned out, for the coldest winter in a hundred years.

Even our bones ached that winter. Coal barges stuck fast in the icy canals like insects trapped in amber, and we foraged in the woods for firewood. People joked that the Russians had thrown in bad weather free, along with the non-aggression pact with Hitler. Christmas came and went and still no bombs fell. 'You're more likely to be killed by a falling icicle,' said Tante Ida, gazing out of the window to where they hung from the roofs, at a metre long.

Mutti missed Rudi terribly. With hindsight, he should have taken his rabbits with him. With Herr Müller gone, nobody remembered Heidi and Walther, and they died in their hutches on the night the temperature plummeted to minus twenty-three. Snug in the mountains, Rudi escaped the sad sight of their rigid little bodies laid out on our kitchen table. I begged for a burial but Gretchen produced a recipe from her Young Maiden's Cookbook for a rabbit *eintopf* involving dried eggs and a revolting bunch of vegetables we called *suppengrün*. We ate Heidi first and then Walther. And very tasty they were too.

Play Quietly

THE MOUNTAIN TOWN OF GLATZ was beautiful, with a fortress and an old stone bridge and lots of posh houses – just the kind of place to make pots of money. We'd found our *atchen'tan* – our *good stopping-place* – and Pa and Nano Florian had ridden into town to check the post office for news. The weather was turning and hoar frost clung to the branches like white lichen. That morning Baba Sara was brewing tea in her samovar on the bottom step of her vardo, sending clouds of steam billowing up as I sat sorting hawberries in the doorway, my head bandaged up like a Turk. She'd gathered enough for her famous hawberry brandy, guaranteed to mend broken hearts as well as broken heads. She'd give some to Frieda, she told me, and she'd winked in her old way for the first time since the accident. I was glad the ice was starting to melt. You see, I had a feeling she was suspicious about what happened that night. She never mentioned it straight out. Not the tarot or the *gadjo* boy. But it hovered in the air and she never asked me to read the cards with her again. She poured a stream of dark liquid into Pa's favourite cup as he came trotting back, waving a letter. She grinned at him, gold teeth flashing. 'Black as evil, hot as hell, and sweet as a young bride,' she laughed. But Pa's news soon wiped the smile off her face.

There'd been the usual signs in the town, daubed on shop windows, such as: *GERMANS! DON'T BUY FROM JEWS!* But the banner in huge capitals draped across the town hall was a great blow: *GYPSIES ARE NOT WELCOME IN GLATZ.*

The town was swarming with soldiers, Pa said, like rats on a dung heap. And there was a letter too . . . more news from Nani Ana in Berlin.

We couldn't believe our ears. Ana's neighbour, a decorated Sinto from the World War, had been called up to the *Wehrmacht*, the German army, but he'd been thrown out, almost before he'd got his army gear on, because his name was on a list of Sinti sent by the Berlin police. And there was worse to come.

A truck arrived next morning, and all the Sinti men from their block were herded to the police station and packed onto cattle trucks. 'You can't take our husbands,' the wives had cried. 'They won medals in the war.'

But policemen with pistols struck them to the ground.

'We'll take whoever we like, you gypsy whores!'

She was lucky, wrote Ana. Nano Maritz was away visiting his brother so hadn't been took.

Pa called the men together and held a *kris*. Then the men spoke solemnly to us all, Pa and Nano Florian in their long green poachers' coats, and Otto Camlo dressed head to heels in black. He'd taken Rollo's death very hard. His moustache was long and *chikly*, and there were streaks of silver in his hair. We were safer here than Berlin, Pa told us, standing on his vardo steps, but there was no question of us working any more. 'When the wind is high, move your tent to the other side of the hedge,' he told us. We must go into hiding.

'How will we get by without working?' said Ma. 'There ain't no Herr Scholl here!'

Baba Sara drew herself up to her full height. She spent so much time squatting, it was easy to forget just how tall she really was. 'What's this nonsense you're talking, Rosa? Let the Romani who thinks he needs a *gadjo* greengrocer to survive step forward. And he who does can be buried in a ditch like a dog!'

Nobody came forward. No one fancied that option much.

And so as autumn gave way to winter, we disappeared into the forests. We gathered elderberries while they still hung heavy over the hedgerows and late autumn medlars at their best. *Bletted*, we called them, soft and almost rotten. We dried meat and made jars of preserves. We painted our vardos brown and forest green and removed our brass ornaments and good-luck charms. Our women swapped bright skirts for dark dresses and our men cut their hair. Pa was firm. 'Speak German. Strictly no fortunetelling. And no poaching unless we have to.'

'Play quietly!' warned Baba Sara, although she knew that telling a Romani child to keep quiet was like telling a bird not to sing.

We made changes to the pattern of our lives. We'd met a band of coppersmiths who told us more news, and this time Pa listened. 'They've rounded up whole camps of our people from all over. Bavaria, Austria, Bohemia . . . and sent them to prisons in Poland.' Some of their clan had been arrested for lighting fires – the soldiers said they were signalling to the enemy. So instead of blazing campfires we had glowing embers with buckets of water in case of unwelcome visitors. We disappeared into the forest, slipping in and out of shadows like the witch-bird, until the weather turned too cold for outdoor life and the snows came. The coldest winter for a hundred years.

Honorary Romanis

JANUARY 1940. Birds froze solid on the trees. Snowdrifts piled high against our vardo doors, and no sooner had we dug our way out to rub goose grease into the horses' hooves than another blizzard trapped us in again, even tighter than before. Icicles hung from the ceiling like vicious teeth. And then around the end of the month Pa had a stroke of *baksheesh – good fortune.*

Pa made friends wherever he went and through a bit of secret horse dealing he'd met a farmer, Hans Vogel. Well, one snowy day Pa arrived at the Vogels' farm and caught Hans and his wife listening to a foreign wireless station. They'd thought they were safe as rabbits in a burrow in the freezing weather so they were shocked when Pa banged on the window. Pa couldn't believe the fuss. He'd no idea the Nazis could hang you for listening to the wireless! Poor Hans was gibbering like a monkey – something about trying to find a German wavelength and tripping over a foreign one.

'I don't give a fig who you're listening to,' said Pa. 'I just wanted to swap Ma's jam for some hay.'

Hans really thought Pa might report them to the Gestapo and he'd offered Pa his tithe barn for keeping his mouth shut. Pa was in high spirits. It was the answer to his prayers.

Ma wasn't happy. 'Only a fool swims in unknown waters,' she warned.

But Pa said he had a good feeling about the Vogels. 'I'm sure they ain't Nazis. Else why would they be listening to foreign news? And there's enough room in the barn to drive our wagons and horses inside.'

We lit great fires in the barn every night, stuffing the windows with pillows, and we filled cloth bags with hot chestnuts to keep our feet from freezing. And as the farmer began to trust us more, Pa and Nano Florian would slip into the huge kitchen with its roaring fire and hams hanging from the blackened beams and join them at the wireless. Our men didn't know any English but Myfanwy Vogel turned out to be Welsh, with *grandchavvies* living in Cardiff. She translated for everyone and so we learned the progress of the war.

We got very pally with the Vogels as the weeks crawled by. Ma showed Myfanwy how to skin rooks for a pie, and was pleased as anything when she copied the recipe down in her special book. We even put on a show for them one night. Myfanwy almost split her sides watching Pali's dog pushing a baby carriage on his hind legs. And then Florica danced flamenco, whirling her shawl so the silk birds looked like they were flying. Then Pa played Myfanwy's favourite tune on his fiddle, *Hungarian Dance* by Rachmaninoff that he'd learned by heart from her gramophone, and Myfanwy and Hans sang a duet in Welsh about a gypsy who ran away with a soldier. We made them honorary Romanies for ever that night, for we'd never met *gadje* like them – generous-hearted and willing to share all they had. Pa swore they'd saved our lives that winter and they said we'd put joy back into theirs. They were kindly times. Times to store up in memory's larder against the crueller days to come.

Hans and Myfanwy Vogel were the kindest friends but Romanies can't hide away forever. We'd soon be as white as curd cheese like the *gadje*. We were tense and snarky, and as the snows began to melt in March and the alpine gentians poked their trumpet heads through the soil, Pa made up his mind.

I was helping him shave one day. He was stripped to the waist, a broken shard of mirror propped in the angle between the trunk of a tree and an upright branch. I handed him a towel and he rubbed himself down, shaking drops of water from his hair like a wet dog. Then he stretched and slapped his belly. 'Just look at me! Plump as a partridge. What use is a circus troupe without muscles?' Pa was right. I was bursting from my skirt. 'The leaf is rising. You can see it in the hedgerows. We should be moving on.'

I crossed my arms over my chest, rubbing my hands up and down my muscles. They'd definitely lost tone. 'But I thought it wasn't safe to travel . . .'

He shook his head. 'The kettle that lies face down can't get sunlight. I was born for the wandering life.'

I watched him stomp off into the trees and soon I heard loud chopping, like he blamed the trees for the pickle we were in.

It was at about this time that Pa and Nano Florian began to disappear . . .

They'd be gone for days. Ma was close as a clam. Then one day I found her alone in our vardo kneeling in front of the tin-framed picture of *Sara la Kali* – *Black Sara*, our Romani saint. Ma got up so hasty she knocked over her candle. She pretended she'd been looking for her thimble but her eyes were all puffy so I knew it wasn't true. Then next day Pa and the others turned up and Ma was smiling again. And it kept on happening. They'd be back one day and gone again the next. And Ma would be back on her knees, bothering Black Sara.

We asked Marko if he knew why his pa kept slipping off, or Frieda asked him, I should say, as Marko never talked to me any more. No one had mentioned our betrothal since Rollo died, and these days he walked the other way when he saw me. Anyway, Marko had no more idea than we had, only that two of the open *taliga*s we used for carrying circus props had gone.

I discovered their secret by accident. Pa, Nano Florian and Otto Camlo arrived home one night when I was in bed and everyone else was cooking supper in the barn. It was my time of the month and I'd had a bellyache, so I'd sat for a while on the locker seat opposite the fire, with my feet on the guardrail, nice and snug. I'd felt dozy after a bit, so I'd gone to lie down on my bunk. I was that relieved when I heard Pa's voice I almost burst through the curtain, but we never interrupted our men, not when they were talking, so I lay there quiet as an owl. Nano Florian was there and Otto Camlo, and a few minutes later Fonso joined them. I shouldn't have earwigged, but sometimes it's the only way to find things out.

It turned out Hans Vogel was in a group called the Polish Resistance, and he'd put Pa in touch with a faker – a man who'd make false papers . . . for a price. And our men had been risking their lives running to and fro across the border, taking explosives to their fighters in the forests so they could blow up bridges and trains and make a muddle for the Germans. And in exchange for every delivery they'd get forged passports for our troupe. And now our documents were complete. Pa pulled the last two passports out of his pocket and opened one, reading the Spanish name aloud with a low chuckle. 'Pedro Orosco,' he laughed, as Pali's face stared out at him. 'And his brother Juan. Their new names suit them well.'

It had been Fonso's idea, sparked off one day when Pa had the fidgets. 'Why not travel as a Spanish troupe? Lots of Spaniards are dark skinned and there's Moorish blood mixed with Spanish too.' Him and Florica spoke it fluent and their little Fifi knew the lingo too. They could do all the front of house stuff, he said, and the rest of us could do our acts with a Spanish twist. After all, most of our horses were Andalusians and Lipizzaners. They could do the high Spanish trot, no trouble.

It had all started as make-believe, over a tot of brandy around the fire in the barn, dreaming up Spanish acts and new names: *Julio and Rosario, the Flying Espanas. Pascal and Ervero, Spanish foot jugglers.* We already had *Florica and Fonso, the Amazing Spanish Dancers.* What would we call ourselves? *Circus Escudero,* thought Fonso – the name of a famous flamenco guitarist. And so they talked about it, passing round the brandy bottle, but in Pa's mind at least it was just make-believe to help him pass the time . . . until the night he mentioned it to Hans Vogel.

And a few weeks later, after many dangerous adventures across the German-Polish border, *El Gran Circo Escudero di Andalucía* was born. We all had Spanish passports and forged IDs. And me and Frieda, who'd already decided that horses were safer than the flying trapeze, became *Francisca and Antonia* overnight. *The Amazing Spanish Equestriennes.*

It was a sad parting from Hans and Myfanwy, although I sensed a feeling of relief as they waved us goodbye. The week before, a young partisan had been hanged from a lamppost in the town's main street. The local police chief wouldn't let anyone cut him down. And so the horrible thing hung there for days as a warning to anyone who might feel tempted to join the resistance.

There was no doubt in Pa's mind, he told us, as *El Gran Circo Escudero* bowled down the lanes in our newly painted vardos. The Vogels had literally risked their lives for us.

There's a Romani saying: he who willingly gives you one finger will also give you the whole hand. Well, we didn't want to ask Herr Vogel for his whole hand, however freely he'd have given it. And, anyway, Pa longed for the stars above his head. *'Romano Drom!'* he laughed as our high-wheeled wagons trundled through the early summer hedgerows. 'The Romani road!'

Impregnable City

BY SUMMER 1940, Rudi was back in Berlin. The British couldn't easily reach us, unlike the cities in the north and west. Göring, commander-in-chief of our Air Force, the *Luftwaffe*, had promised no English bomber would penetrate our double ring of defences, and for the moment it seemed he was right. We rejoiced in the streets at the fall of Paris, and Hitler was driven to the Reich Chancellery on a carpet of flowers. You couldn't get away from his voice these days, screaming from loudspeakers in restaurants, banks, taverns – anywhere, in fact, that bore the red and black signs: *Hier! Hören Sie die Führer-Rede. Listen to the Führer's speech here!* We hugged each other in the playground. '*Sieg Heil! Sieg Heil!*' we chanted. *Hail victory!*

Our sense of security, however, proved false, for as 1940 drew to a close we discovered that Berlin's air defences weren't so solid after all. In August the bombers came at last, sending us scuttling to our cellars – forty-three times in four months. The Reichstag was hit, the Propaganda Ministry, Berlin Zoo, the Protestant cathedral. From August to March we went to bed in fear, lying rigid in the dark and waiting to see if the *night pirates*, as Hitler called them, would come for us. Then after the spring of 1941, the bombing more or less stopped and Berliners heaved a sigh of relief, especially as rationing had really begun to bite. Gradually our bread became greyer and the queue at the tobacconist was thirty metres long. *Berlin raucht Juno!* screamed the adverts on our buses. *Berlin smokes Juno cigarettes!* The truth was, Berlin was hardly smoking at all. And with little fruit, we were suffering from skin rashes and a sudden eruption of farting that Vati blamed on the yellow colouring in our *ersatz* butter. Everything was second rate. There was a joke going the rounds about a Jew who'd tried to hang himself, only he failed because the rope was made of synthetic fibre. And talking of yellow, there was a sudden starburst in Berlin; the Judenstern became compulsory for Jews in September, and everywhere we saw yellow Stars of David stitched to their left breasts.

Of course the sight of wounded soldiers was now much more common on our streets. I'd seen the trains myself one day, down at the Potsdamer Bahnhof. The three easternmost lines were filled with trains carrying the wounded Germans from the *Ostfront* to hospitals in Berlin. At first the sight was oddly stirring as the walking wounded emerged to be greeted with *Malzkaffee* from huge metal urns, served by smiling girls from the BDM . . . until they began to unload the stretcher cases. I stared in shock, wondering what horrors lay beneath the bloody dressings that concealed the stumps of limbs. *Wheels must turn for victory!* screamed the white chalk letters on the carriages. There was an old drunk there, leaning over the railway bridge, shaking his fist at the trains. 'From France we got silk stockings! From Russia we get this. Damned Russians! Mustn't have had any silk stockings!'

I made a mental note not to mention the casualty trains to Erika, whose boyfriend Georg was serving with his tank regiment on the eastern front.

Nonetheless, despite what was happening far away, for our family at least, life went on pretty much as usual. Victory had followed victory for three years, and as my seventeenth birthday approached in August 1942, we were once again feeling more secure in Berlin. There'd been little bombing since the previous spring. The theatres and bars were still open and even the restriction on public dancing had been lifted. And for a few glorious months, as the RAF turned their attention to other targets, life in Berlin went back to something approaching normal . . . for the last time.

La Vida es Buena!

CIRCO ESCUDERO was as popular as Circus Petalo had ever been. Fonso swapped places with Nano Florian as ringmaster so Fonso could do the talking – especially booking fairground space and making friends with the local police, although soon Pa could join in almost as well. We'd hardly crossed a border than Pa was speaking the lingo like a native – just like he could fiddle a tune when he'd only heard it once. At first we only went to villages, but as the war dragged on and punters still flocked in, we got braver. We were a welcome tonic, Pa said, from the horrible things folks were doing to each other in the war.

It hadn't all been *kushti* though. We'd had some bad scares. Like the time the Gestapo came searching the showground with their snarling dogs. 'We are searching for Jews,' they told us. 'It is unbelievable, but there are still traitors who are willing to hide them.'

Fonso kept the officers talking, sloshing brandy into tin mugs while Pali and Tamas slid into the kettle-box under their wagon and Pa put up the sign we'd made just in case: *Poisonous snakes! Keep out!* Then Fonso showed them round the tents and handed out free tickets for their kids. '*No te preocupes!*' said Fonso. 'We wouldn't dream of hiding the filthy rats!'

The men went off laughing. He'd got them quite lushy, but we needed some brandies ourselves after that, just to settle our nerves. And that night Pa made the dwarfs bury their prayer book in the woods, the one in German and Hebrew. 'If your God blames you for that,' said Pa, 'he ain't as good as you reckon!'

But that was our only real fright. Our disguise fitted like a glove. There's a Romani saying: you can't hide a cat in a sack. Its claws will show through. Well, we'd proved that one wrong for three years, and as the late summer days grew shorter, Pa turned his mind to winter, thinking longingly of our old rented lot in the Grunewald. It was a lovely place in autumn and near enough to the train station for us to work in Berlin. 'The theatres and bars are still open,' said Pa, who'd taken to paper reading. 'There ain't been no bombs there for over a year.'

And so as we turned our horses' heads towards Berlin we were feeling pretty cheerful. We drank each other's health in Spanish. '*La vida es buena!*'

Test of Courage

THAT SUMMER OF 1942 had been glorious weather, and now even in autumn the evenings were warm, pungent with the scent of honeysuckle. So a three-week Defence-strengthening Camp in the Grunewald for sixteen to eighteen-year-olds should have been a paradise for a loyal member of the Hitler Youth – cooking sausages over our campfire, singing as night drew in and the stars came out, sharp as daggers. But three years on and my love affair with Hitler Youth was well and truly over. Everything seemed to conspire together at once: the punishing new training, the wagonloads of horribly wounded soldiers puffing into Berlin, my doubts about our leaders' motives, and my first startling glimpse of Lili again after more than three years . . .

To be honest, I'd never liked the rigid pecking order of Hitler Youth, where the most vulnerable boys were victimized whilst the most brutal rose to the top. Boys like Martin Gorman, for example, who I had the misfortune to know from my school. He'd been the sort of boy who enjoyed pulling legs off insects and watching their bodies writhe helplessly on the ground, or grinding younger children's faces into the nettle patch behind the bike sheds. The kind of pupil Herr Meissen used to love. So you can imagine my horror when I learned that he was to be my platoon leader for this three-week training camp.

Gorman would make us crawl for hours through prickly gorse, followed by knee-bends until our legs burned in agony. We'd run for miles until our chests were bursting and then run some more because we hadn't run fast enough. We feared leaders like Martin with their petty brutalities, but even more we feared the watchful SS, with their death's head caps and double bolts of lightning on their black uniforms, and their smiles like the twist of a knife.

One of Martin's favourite exercises was the *Mutprobe* – the *courage test*. Each boy who passed received a special knife in a polished wooden box. The test required us to leap over the parapet of a two-storey farmhouse, trusting that the older boys would be ready to catch us in a tarpaulin. We were all terrified, but one boy, Erwin Cornelius, was so scared he was sick on his shoes. Then when he did jump he wet his trousers from sheer panic. So Martin made him walk round the camp for a week with *Bed-wetter* scrawled on a sign round his neck.

And then there was the *Schwimmtest*. I'd seen Martin watching us splashing in the Havel as we relaxed from our daily routines, looking out for boys who couldn't swim. And next day he'd single them out for the ten-metre drop.

His victims, wearing helmets and knapsacks, had to jump from a tower into very deep water. I still don't know whether Martin would have left Cornelius to drown if I hadn't jumped in and hauled him out. It wasn't easy to save a boy weighed down by waterlogged boots. I struggled to the water's edge and flung Cornelius down on the riverbank. His face was horribly mottled and his eyes bulged from their sockets. I was about to start some chest compressions, when to my great relief he gave a sudden shudder and spewed up half the river over my boots. I looked round, expecting a riding crop on the back of my shoulders but Gorman wasn't there. Our brave leader had gone.

Erwin Cornelius was missing at roll call the next morning. Some boys out practising map reading found his body in the forest later that day. He'd stabbed himself with a Hitler Youth Dagger of Honour. Not his own, of course. Martin Gorman had made sure he'd never had the privilege of owning one himself.

It was the middle of the third week of our training and by now we were glowing with health. We'd been pale and scurvyish when we'd parked our green bicycles at Grunewald station and marched to the camp, faces as grey as the streets of Berlin. But for over two weeks now we'd had meat and vegetables in abundance and I'd definitely put on weight. Two weeks grazing on forest fruits had improved our complexions and hiking in the blazing sun had turned our skin a golden brown, like beech leaves in autumn.

We'd been preparing for our war game for two and a half weeks. Of course, we'd played Battle of the Flags before, spending a day creeping through the forest, hunting down our 'enemies'. Such games would often end in fistfights between platoons as weaker boys got thrashed while their leaders stood by encouraging it. But the exercise planned for today was serious reconnaissance training, designed to sharpen our appetite for real-life combat, with actual weapons, under the critical eyes of experienced military personnel. Gone were the days of air rifles and wooden hand grenades. Now we were handling high-powered weapons – Mauser 98K carbines and light machine guns – and my head was full of field exercises and how to dig foxholes under fire. We were given a slogan at the start of each week. Week one – *We Fight!* Week two – *We Sacrifice!* And for the third week of our training: *We Triumph!*

Our black banner with the angular white lightning bolts of victory hung slackly in the still air as we crawled from our tents on the morning of the exercise. We'd been given our 'ribbons of life' the previous evening, so after a quick breakfast of ham, hardboiled eggs and *schwarzbrot*, the 'blues' rushed on ahead to set up their headquarters in some hidden part of the forest. We gave them half an hour and then, at the sound of the Fähnleinführer's whistle, the 'reds' set out to try to capture our opponents' flag. If you found your enemy in the forest you'd to rip off his ribbon and then he was dead. Once 'killed in action' you had to evacuate the battlefield and await whatever ghastly punishment your platoon leader had dreamed up for you, for failing to stay alive.

The sun was warm and I was soon sweating in my thin brown shirt. Cautiously I worked my way from thorny blackberry to prickly gorse, creeping along at a crouch. Sometimes the bushes thinned out, and then I had to pull myself along on my stomach, terrified of feeling the jerking on my left arm announcing that my enemy had found me before I'd found him. After a while, I arrived at a clearing in the pine trees and stopped to listen. I rose from a squat, alert for telltale sounds – a sudden flurry of birds or the snap of a twig – but all I could hear was the familiar drowsy hum of hornets and the rasping caw of a jay.

And then I heard a sound that made my heart leap. The merry ripple of laughter followed by a sudden splash. I peered in the direction of the sound, and as I did, I noticed some deep scars on the ground like the marks made by metal-rimmed wheels, and a line of dead hedgehogs hanging by their hind legs on a piece of twine slung between two willows. And in the distance I heard the plaintive sound of a violin. I frowned at my map, disorientated. I hadn't realized I'd strayed so close to the river.

The Sneeze

THE DROPPINGS OF A FLYING BIRD never fall twice on the same spot, as Pa used to say. So I didn't expect the *gadjo* boy to ever walk my road again, although to say I'd never thought of him would be a lie. Just lately I'd been dreaming of Max, especially now we were camping so close to Berlin, and I longed for him every time I saw Marko and Frieda together.

I don't think Frieda knew she was falling in love with Marko at first. For a year, at least, her spirit had been too fragile to think of anyone but Rollo. But as months grew into years, I began to notice the way her eyes searched out Marko when we sat around the fire and how she seemed more peaceful with him than anyone else. Don't get me wrong. I was happy that Frieda was growing close with

Marko and that nobody mentioned our betrothal any more. But I couldn't help feeling sad that love had passed me by.

The morning Max stumbled back into my life, me and Frieda had been working hard. First we'd emptied the eel traps that we'd set in the river the day before. It had taken all our strength to haul the baskets out of the river and we were pleased with our catch. *Panni Sappor* fried with wild garlic was Pa's favourite. We'd carried the pail downstream between us, checking the fowl traps on our way to the shallow place where Pa said we could wash our hair. It was one of his jobs when we struck camp to divide up the riverbank – water for drinking and cooking upstream, then for washing ourselves further down, then water for washing our clothes.

I was feeling closer to Frieda than I had for months. I'd done my best to let her know I wasn't green-eyed about Marko, and today we were singing and talking, just like the old days before Rollo died. It was a sheltered spot and we'd stripped to the waist and hung our shifts on a forked branch, then waded out to a flat rock. We dipped our heads in the river, working the bright green soapwort into a foamy lather and chattering away like two magpies. I squeezed the water from my hair and stretched my arms up to the sun, enjoying the feel of my lengthening muscles after squatting so long on the rock. Then I began to wash myself under my arms, spreading the lather over my neck and breasts.

Frieda was laughing and pointing. 'Look at you, Lili. You've made a bodice of bubbles!'

And it was then that I felt it. The strange shivery tingle down my spine. Something or someone was watching me . . . and then I heard a sneeze.

Dead! Dead!

TWO GIRLS STRIPPED NAKED to the waist, their bright skirts hitched high so their long, wet legs gleamed in the sunlight. The shock of recognition winded me, like the kick of a rifle, a sudden fierce blush flooding my face. I'd never seen a naked woman before. I knew I should look away but I couldn't drag my eyes from her firm breasts and purple-black nipples protruding through the foamy soap. She looked older than the girl of my memory, taller and more striking than ever, wet hair falling down below her waist. Her cheekbones had lost that childish roundness and her body was curvier, though still hard and toned, like an athlete. The other girl was laughing too as the water trickled down her face and neck, meandering down the valley between her breasts.

I held my breath as I parted the fronds of a hairy willowherb, sending clouds of feathery seeds into the air. Two curious wide-mouthed baskets lay next to an enamel pail containing a knot of grey and silver eels, slithering and glinting like gunmetal. And next to the bucket, an assortment of dead birds: partridge, pheasant, woodcock. No wonder the girls looked so healthy, their strong limbs brown as owls. I blinked in disbelief. Was it really Lili, half naked, laughing and stretching her muscular arms high above her head?

What should I do? Part of me wanted to shout her name but she'd think me a Peeping Tom, spying on naked girls! She wouldn't remember me. She'd probably never even spared me a thought. I was breathless with shock. I didn't dare move, and then I felt a tickling in my nostrils. The air was thick with floating seeds. Horrified, I pressed my hand to my nose but the sneeze just kept on rising . . .

Her body gave a sudden jolt at the sound, and as she turned the sun glinted on her golden earrings, and I swear I felt a dagger of light pierce my heart. Her black eyes widened in surprise. She gave a cry like a startled bird. And then I was off, racing through the undergrowth like a fox with the hounds on its tail. Suddenly the forest came alive, as if my panic had sent the woodland creatures fleeing in sympathy. A rabbit sped across my path and a chorus of rooks rose up from the trees, cawing loudly. Was it my imagination, or was there something behind me, crashing through the gorse, gaining on me inch by inch? My chest was bursting, my throat burning, and then all of a sudden, a monstrous thump. The crunch of another body smashing into mine, knocking me clean off my feet. For a crazy moment I thought it might be Lili, and then I felt the dreaded tug on my left arm as my ribbon of life was wrenched off and my enemy was upon me, sitting astride my body as I lay face down on the forest floor, my mouth full of earth.

'Dead, dead, dead!' screamed the jubilant voice on my back.

I twisted round to see the sweaty face of Baldur Gernot looming over me, brandishing my ribbon of life. He coughed and spat into the bushes, wiping his mouth on his sleeve. 'Hard luck, old fellow. I wouldn't like to be in your shoes. Thank God I'm not on Martin Gorman's team!'

Wild Boar

Frieda hadn't noticed the sneeze but she heard me cry out. 'It must be my time of the month,' I groaned suddenly, doubling over as I glanced slyly back towards the riverbank. The boy had gone, but I could hear the sound of crashing in the undergrowth and a sudden racket of rooks. 'Sounds like wild boar on the riot,' I said. Frieda looked puzzled but I made such a show of clutching my belly that she said I could go on ahead as long as I sent Marko to help her lug the eel pail. I snatched my shift from the branch, hitched down my wet skirt and ran like a witch from white garlic. I just needed to be alone.

We had a book in our vardo about nature. Frieda liked the pictures of baby animals best. But I'd always liked the volcanoes. I loved the way they seemed harmless on top, but deep inside the earth boiling lava was bubbling away, all the gases building up and up until they burst out like a boil, flames soaring high into the air. Well, that's how I felt that day I saw Max again. Like all my feelings had been pressed down for years, so that the outside of me looked just like a peaceful mountain. But underneath it all they'd never stopped churning away and the sudden shock that day made them all erupt. I was fizzing up inside like a pop bottle, about to explode with joy.

As I crouched on my narrow bunk, alone in the small space I shared with Frieda, I told myself over and over that it was all moonshine. We'd been fooling the Nazis for nearly three years as *Circo Escudero*. So shouldn't I be running to warn Pa there were soldiers in the forest, instead of quivering on my bed with my stomach in knots? 'With one behind, you can't sit on two horses,' Pa always said. And look what had happened before when I'd let myself dream. So why did I suddenly find myself standing in front of the mirror on the back of our door, turning this way and that and tossing my hair, wondering if he'd still think I was different from any other girl he'd met? Suddenly I felt my face burning up. What was wrong with me? I should be ashamed that a *gadjo* had seen me mother-naked, instead of slipping off my blouse to see how my breasts looked in the mirror.

Later that afternoon, Frieda sidled up to me as I was chopping the greens. I could tell she was narked with me. 'What are you doing, Lili? I thought it was your time of the moon!'

I felt the blood stain my cheeks for the second time that day. Our time of the moon was *marhime – unclean –* and here I was chopping greens for Pa. Liars need good memories, so Ma always said. 'I . . . I made a mistake. I must have eaten too many bilberries . . .'

She frowned. 'But we weren't eating bilberries, Lili.'

I'd have to be careful with Frieda, I told myself. She knew me far too well.

Double Guard Duty

I'D EXPECTED FIFTY KNEE BENDS straight off for losing my ribbon of life so early on. But Martin Gorman was preoccupied when I got back to camp, grinning and sucking up to the SS like a dog begging for dinner, so I got off lightly. Just double night-sentry duty. Four hours instead of the usual two. It could have been a good deal worse. Such as standing up to my waist in the freezing Havel for several hours, or running through a field of nettles in shorts with no shoes. Martin Gorman could be very inventive when he felt like it.

Today was the end of our three-week training course and it was back to Berlin tomorrow. We were all exhausted, so after a few rousing choruses from our songbook we hauled down the flag. I watched jealously as my comrades crawled into their tents, longing to join them, roll myself into my army blanket, close my eyes and dream about Lili. But a swift reminder of how nettles felt on bare legs kept self-pity at bay.

I'd changed my shorts for the long trousers, warm jacket and black ski cap of our winter uniform. We were in for a cold night, which was probably just as well, I thought, as I slung my rifle over my shoulder and prepared for my night's watch. Sleeping on duty was one of the worst crimes in the long list of punishable offences in Hitler Youth, so it didn't do to be too comfortable.

The camp was noisy for a while, full of the sounds of boys bedding down, laughing and thumping boisterously against the canvas sides of the rows of peaked tents. But soon all I could hear was low snoring, although someone somewhere was playing a mouth organ. I breathed in deeply, savouring the rich, loamy smell of the woods. I can still remember the sky that night, clear and starry, with Venus bright as a splinter of glass above a sharp new moon. *Moon on its back like a smile . . . is it smiling for me?* I made a mental note to find my old diary when I got home, the one where I used to write my poems. I hugged myself, pretending my body was Lili. I hadn't written poetry for years.

The fire had died down to a deep coral glow and my feet were starting to freeze, so I decided to make my first circuit of the camp to check for wild boar lurking in the undergrowth. They'd been known to rampage through the camp, snouting rations from supply tents and running amok amongst the guy ropes. So round and round I trudged with my muffled flashlight, past the rows of trestles where we lay for rifle practice, picking my way between tents, just like any other loyal Hitler Youth on sentry duty. But in my dreams I was back on the riverbank, creeping stealthily in the direction of that deep, throaty laugh. Parting the fronds of hairy willowherb that screened Lili's private place from prying eyes, holding my breath and peeping in . . .

I pretended to myself later that I'd heard suspicious noises in the forest and accidentally lost my way. But the truth is I couldn't really remember what happened that night. I'd somehow found myself amongst the trees like a sleepwalker, wondering how I'd got there. I flicked on my flashlight, checking the bearing on my compass that had somehow found its way into my pocket. To get to the river, I needed to walk due east.

I heard the soft babble of flowing water before I saw the glimmer of the river through the trees. I stopped, inhaling deeply, drinking in its earthy, mineral smell. Someone not far away was playing an accordion and a dog barked sharply, though it could have been a fox. I shone my flashlight along the line of willows that fringed the bank. The row of dead hedgehogs was gone, but I could still see the remains of the twine dangling limply from the willow's trunk. I crept forward, pushing through the undergrowth, until I was staring out across the mysterious black water. The fragile moon swam in its dancing dark shadows amongst a sea of stars. I didn't like rivers at night. I imagined all kinds of slippery things beneath the surface, snaking in and out of the tangled weed. But tonight this shadowy stretch was flooded with the sunlight of memory, of the surprise of Lili's naked body, and the water sparkling as it trickled between her breasts . . .

I switched off my flashlight, preferring the velvet blackness that rushed in like a soft cloak. This was the place. I shivered, surprised to feel tears welling up in my eyes. Suddenly, all the pent up emotion of the last three weeks seemed to come together at once: my hatred of our platoon leaders, the suicide of Erwin Cornelius, the joy of seeing Lili again . . .

I heard a splash. A fish probably, leaping in the river. To begin with, I thought it was the surging of my tears, the way the air seemed to stir and shift. The darkness in front of me swayed. Alarmed, I flicked on my flashlight as a shape rose up from the flat stone at the water's edge. There stood Lili, staring at me, blinking in the golden beam.

'What took you so long?' she said, in her soft, lilting accent.

I didn't trust myself to speak. I didn't want to break the spell. And, anyway, what do you say to a stranger who you feel that you've known all your life? *We were born to be together*, I wanted to say, but it sounded naive. Like the lines from a Hollywood movie. Her hair was almost purple in the pale moonlight, her eyes so dark I saw only the glimmer of their whites as she stepped towards me through the shallow water.

'I knew you would come. I've been waiting for you.'

Words would come later, when we'd sit under the stars and Lili would tell me her wonderful stories: *The Tale of Shon and Chakano* and *How the Gypsies Found Their Fiddle*. The time would come when she'd show me how to fry duck eggs on a shovel and how to skin rooks and cook them in a hay-pit. But for the moment . . .

She placed her long fingers lightly on my chest. I stretched out my hands, letting them rest on her shoulders. I'd imagined Lili in my dreams, soft and pliant, so the hardness of her muscles shocked me. Of course they were. How else could you soar through the air on a flying trapeze? I'd kissed girls before. In fact, I'd kissed Sophie Fischer from the cathedral quite a lot, and I'd liked it at the time. But afterwards I forgot all about her. But here, tonight . . . my heart was drumming in my throat, so hard I could scarcely breathe.

I expected her to pull back like girls always did, but Lili just stood there silently, eyes half closed, her face turned up towards mine. The skin on her throat was warm. I could taste her sweat. And then I had a sudden urge to hug her close like a long lost friend, burying my face in her hair. She made a sound like a sob and then I was kissing her mouth, and she was kissing me back, covering my face with her lips, hot breath on my neck, sending shivers snaking down my spine.

'I've never forgotten you,' I said.

She stared at me, tracing the line of my jaw with her fingertip, and then drew back suddenly, pulling me deeper into the trees. She put her hand to my lips, staring hard across the starlit river. 'It's my pa and Nano Florian,' she whispered. 'They'll kill me if they find me with you.'

Two tall men in long coats were picking their way stealthily along the opposite bank. I could feel her heart pounding against mine.

'It's a poacher's moon. I should have known they'd be out checking the long nets.' She suddenly grasped my lapels, staring into my face. 'You won't tell, will you?' Her eyes glittered in the moonlight. 'There'll be trouble if you tell.'

I pulled her back into my arms. 'Tell what?' I murmured, my lips on her hair. I wasn't really listening. I was drunk on the smell of her.

She shook her head, twisting away. 'I have to go. Ma will be wondering . . . I said I was just going to . . . water the horses . . .' She broke off shyly. 'That means . . . you know . . .'

I didn't know. All I knew was that I couldn't let her go. What if she slipped away into the darkness and I never saw her again? 'Where can I find you?'

She hesitated. 'How do I know I can trust you?' The men had disappeared but I could tell she was eager to be gone. 'Things have changed. I can't explain now. But you mustn't say you've seen me. You mustn't tell anyone you remember us from before. Do you understand? Things are different now.'

I didn't understand but I kissed her softly on her forehead. I was her slave. I'd do anything she asked. 'I promise.'

Lili smiled uncertainly, and I was lost again, heart and soul. 'We're camped over the river. By the side of the Hundekehle Lake. There's a field with a green gate. I have to go . . .'

Unwillingly I let go of her shoulders but I didn't move away. She glanced up at the new moon, now trailing fragments of cloud like smoke. '*T'e avel bachtelo a son nevo,*' she whispered. Then she held my hand to her lips, kissing the tips of my fingers as she stepped away from me. '*Let the new moon bring us happiness.*' And then she was gone, dissolving into the forest, like a dream that slips from your grasp on waking, leaving you cold and alone.

'I'll never hurt you,' I murmured into the darkness. 'You can trust me with your life.'

Tarantella

I HADN'T TOUCHED THE TAROT since Rollo died. I hadn't dared. But that night, when everyone was drinking round the campfire, I crept into Baba Sara's vardo. Softly I unlatched the little wooden cupboard beside her bed and pulled out the bag of green embroidered silk, then struck a match. The candlelight gleamed on the cards' bright colours – emerald, scarlet and gold. I shuffled and cut, fanned and cut again. The pictures were as dazzling as I remembered, and the shivery feeling when I touched them just the same. I crossed back to the door and parted the beaded curtain. Baba Sara was asleep in her blanket under the clear, cold sky and I could hear Pa and Nano Florian tuning fiddles to an accordion.

It felt so good to have the cards in my hands again. I

held my breath and laid a spread for me . . . then just as I was about to turn over the first card, I changed my mind. I heard the fiddles around the campfire strike up a lively jig and I had a sudden urge to dance. To stamp my feet to something wild and romantic, like a Tarantella. The tarot means *the way*. *The royal path to life*, so Baba Sara used to say. I gathered up the cards and slipped them back into their bag. If dark clouds were gathering, I didn't want to know. Tonight I wanted to dance. To forget the future and live for now. I'd seen my Knight of Wands again and I wasn't going to worry about anything. Not tonight. Maybe never. For I knew in my heart that whatever dark shadows the tarot might show me, I'd never swap safety for love.

Strange Cargo

THERE'S A SPRING in my step next morning as we march
through the station tunnel to collect the bicycles we'd
stacked at the front three weeks ago. Grunewald station is
a striking building, its arched entrance like a castle gate.
There's an autumn chill in the air and my breath is milky
fog. I don't mind the cold. I'm warm inside. Every time
I think of Lili, a shock like a silver knife slides up under
my ribcage. I'm flooded with love for everything. I smile
happily at the ladies from the Red Cross standing under
the huge clock, handing out hot drinks to a group of SS
in high black boots. I wonder why they're here and then
I notice a crowd has gathered, mainly women with small
children. They're laughing and shaking their fists.

'Just look at those cheeky Jews!' cries a small boy in a striped hat. He's holding tight to his mother's hand, darting back behind her sturdy woollen stockings as we approach. 'Just a bunch of useless eaters!'

We stop at a command from our leader and turn to stare in the direction of the children's pointing fingers. A train with seven cattle trucks has drawn up at the freight yard to the right of the station, and groups of men, women and children are being loaded roughly in. They're wearing yellow stars and numbered tags. Some men are carrying heating stoves and women clutch sewing machines and pillows. They look pale, scared, tired. Eyes rimmed with red. The men huddle like crows, tattered wings of coats flapping. The children are crying. The train ticks and hisses impatiently, exhaling clouds of steam into the frosty air.

An SS strides forward. He wrenches a pillow from an old woman and slits it open with his knife, feathers flying like flurries of early snow. A necklace falls out. A silver-backed hairbrush. A gilt-framed photograph. The officer raises his whip and strikes her to the ground. Placing his boot on her neck, he scrabbles on the ground for her treasures. He examines the hairbrush with exaggerated care. 'I like it,' he says. Then, laughing, he removes his boot from her chin and stamps on the photograph. I hear the glass crunch. 'Get up, you thieving whore!'

My fingers clench around my knife. Why does no one help her? And then I see the soldier. His machine gun is trained on the carriages. His cigarette glows bright orange and then fades. He isn't laughing. His hand is on the gun and his eyes are on the Jews.

I'm shaking. The sun comes out from behind a cloud, flooding the station with pale autumn light. I shiver. There's light but no warmth.

Lili Marlene

HOW COULD I EVER fit back into my old life? My horizon had tilted. I lost track of those first few weeks after I met Lili again. They spiralled away in a haze of joyful secret meetings in the Grunewald. It was easy to get away. Most men were in the Wehrmacht by now, so Hitler Youth had to take over their jobs as tram conductors, railwaymen, postmen. Soon we hardly went to school at all. I'd never felt so free.

Everything revolved around seeing Lili and I quickly organized my life around her. I volunteered as a part-time postal auxiliary as I guessed it would give me more freedom than working as a tram conductor. I neglected my friends. I'd hurtle round the district on my bike, delivering the post as fast as I could, and as soon as I'd delivered my last letter I'd peddle vigorously out to Grunewald station in the western suburb.

The ride was exhilarating, freewheeling down the Kurfürstendamm, or Ku'Damm as Berliners fondly called our once fashionable shopping street, then out west through the suburbs, past vegetable patches that had once been parks, and lampposts camouflaged to resemble trees. I was intoxicated with the thrill of it all. Dizzy with love and with a grin so wide I began to worry Tante Ida was getting suspicious, especially since the news of the war grew chillier with every passing day.

'I don't know what you're looking so happy about, Max,' she'd say with a weary sigh, lowering her copy of *Frauen-Warte* magazine. 'General Rommel wants us to donate our bridal veils to the Afrika Korps now!'

Mutti looked shocked. 'Whatever for, Ida?'

'They've run out of mosquito nets, apparently.'

I snorted with delight at the idea of General Rommel's men bedding down under wedding veils. My aunt looked at me oddly over the half-moons of her spectacles. She sniffed. 'There's definitely something wrong with that boy.'

It's true, I thought, happiness flooding through me. *I'm ill. I'm sick with love!* I felt sorry for Mutti and Tante Ida – too old for passion. And then I mentally crossed out my aunt, as I couldn't imagine her in love . . . ever.

I'd never met anyone like Lili before. No one had ever made me feel so alive. Everything smelled stronger, tasted better, shone in brighter colours. I saw all nature through

Lili's eyes. Looking back, I have more memories from our days in the Grunewald than from any other time in my life. Of catching river trout and frying them on a shovel. Of carving our names on trees and looping them round with a heart. Of cutting off locks of our hair and twisting them into braids of sandy brown and black.

We'd been seeing each other for over four weeks before I ate *hotchi-witchi* for the first time. It was November, the best month for eating it, so Lili told me, when they'd grown fat for hibernation. After three years of rationing I'd grown pretty used to eating dubious cuts of meat. Mutti claimed she'd even seen a dead donkey in our butcher's backyard. So when Lili suggested stuffing a hedgehog with thyme and wild garlic and roasting it in river clay, I was more than happy to try it.

I was feeling especially happy that afternoon as I wheeled my bike past the big clock over the entrance to Grunewald station. I'd heard the distinctive tones of our Führer on the wireless as I was fastening my bicycle clips under our kitchen window.

'Despite heavy German losses on the *Ostfront*, Stalingrad is on the point of surrender!'

Thank God, I thought. Göring had told us the worst was over. There'd be 'fine food for Christmas,' so he said. Morale in Berlin had been up and down lately, but if everything was going so well on the eastern front, I might not be called up after all. I breathed a hearty sigh of relief. Gone were the days when I longed to be part of it. After all, who in their right mind would prefer the army to an afternoon spent cooking *hotchi-witchi* over an open fire?

I wheeled my bike around to the side of the station and propped it against the wall under a holly bush. The bike racks had vanished long ago. Essential metal for the war effort, I supposed, along with the park railings that had started to disappear. I took off my bicycle clips and peered over the wall into the freight station next door. *Gleis 17.* The platform where I'd seen the Jews.

I'd mentioned what I'd seen that day to Tante Ida. There'd been terrible rumours in Berlin about where all the yellow stars had gone. They'd been everywhere only recently but now you hardly ever saw them. Tante Ida dismissed the stories out of hand. She was tired of the tittle-tattle, she said, invented by people who didn't understand what Hitler was doing for the Fatherland. They were probably off to resettlement camps where they could all live together and not bother the rest of us. Hadn't I said I'd seen women carrying sewing machines? She laughed scornfully. 'You don't encourage people to take sewing machines and then shoot them. Heavens above! This is the twentieth century. You'll end up in a detention camp yourself if you don't stop parroting atrocity propaganda.'

I wished I could believe her. But just recently there'd been a flurry of leaflets too, mysteriously appearing on our tram seats or pushed by unseen hands through letterboxes. *Woe betide our nation if it does not take part in the destruction of the Hitler Beast*, followed by descriptions of the deportation of the Jews.

The freight yard was eerily quiet. I dragged my eyes away.

My aunt was probably right . . . but then what about those leaflets? I pulled off my uniform cap and stuffed it in my pocket, then hurried through the tunnel to the back of the station, whistling my new favourite song under my breath:

'*Vor der Kaserne vor dem grossen Tor,*
Stand eine Laterne, und steht sie noch davor . . .
La la lala lala . . . la la lala laaaa . . .
Mit dir, Lili Marlene . . .'
With you, Lili Marlene . . .

I made a mental note to commit the words to memory. How absolutely perfect! That this German love song had suddenly become so popular, just when I'd met my own Lili again.

The Spider and the Fly

LILI TOLD ME she'd found a special place for our secret meetings, deep in the Grunewald. I'd been learning the *patrin*, the coded signposts Romanies leave for stragglers to show the way: bent flower stalks, notched bones, scraps of rag tied to a fence post. I'd never need my compass again now that I knew how to use the Great Bear to find the Pole Star. She'd leave me a trail, she said, starting at the stump we called the lightning tree at the edge of the Hundekehle Lake.

As soon as I saw the twist of flowery rag hanging in the silver birch I knew I was on her trail. I glanced uneasily at the sky. It was an ominous dirty yellow, the colour of old parchment. A sure sign of rain. I scanned the muddy ground for my next clue, smiling as I saw a small arrow of pebbles pointing into the trees.

The forest smelled of pine resin and the thick carpet of needles squelched under my boots as heavy drops of water seeped down through the canopy, snaking a freezing trail down my neck. The next sign was a line of smooth white stones that bent to the left. By now the pines had given way to beech, their massive silver trunks rearing up from their roots. I knew I was on the right track now. Here was the smooth trunk where I'd carved our names with my dagger. I'd said the beech trunks were like pillars in a cathedral, and Lili had laughed and called me a brick dweller. Didn't I know that the roots were the gnarled hands of old giants and the huge straight trunks their arms? She'd never set foot in a church, she told me, but she still believed in the Virgin Mary, and *Sara la Kali* – Black Sara, the Romani saint – and the tree spirits and the ghosts of her ancestors and the devil, that the Romanies called Beng. It seemed quite a lot to believe in all at once, but I didn't say.

I scanned the bushes for my next clue. A brilliant green bird flashed across my path with a mocking cackle as a fat drop of rain hit the earth with a splatter, and I heard a distant grumble of thunder. At first I thought I'd found a line of baby hedgehogs marching across the clearing. I touched one gently with my foot. It was a cluster of sweet chestnut pods, followed by another and another, arranged at regular intervals, marking my route across the scrubby grass. I took a deep breath as the familiar sick feeling of anticipation rose in my stomach. The rain gusted slantwise as I raced across the clearing, kicking the spiny pods aside as I ran.

I could smell the meaty aroma before I saw the red barn, nestling in a hollow and surrounded by hawthorn bushes, on fire with crimson berries. Perhaps memory tints every good thing with a rosier hue, but the wood of my recollection is glowing with colour, despite the gathering storm. *This must be it*, I thought, bursting with happiness. *Lili's secret place.* Violet lightning flashed as I lifted the rusty latch. I paused, counting the seconds, until I heard the roll of thunder. The storm was nearer now, and as I pulled the door some fallen leaves spiralled upwards in the wind.

It was dark inside the barn, except for the light from a small fire flickering against the opposite wall beneath an empty hay feeder. I jammed the door back against the wind, then peered, mole-blind, as objects slowly emerged from the shadows: bales of hay, broken farm implements, shovels, scythes. I sniffed. Something altogether more mouth watering was competing with the scent of wet straw and cow dung. 'Lili, where are you?'

A soft laugh floated down from somewhere above my head. White lightning exploded, flickering like a movie screen, once, twice, three times against the barn walls. And then I saw her, kneeling in the hayloft looking down at me, the firelight in her eyes.

'How did you get up there?'

'I climbed the wall. I was getting worried. I saw the rain fowl just now.'

'The rain fowl?'

'The green woodpecker. Pa says it always means rain.'

I suddenly felt absurdly pleased. 'I think I saw it too! Bright green with a sort of cackling call.'

Lili imitated the sound. 'Pa calls it the chuckling jester because it's red and green and sounds like it's laughing. It has a cosy hole where the rain can't find it. Like me up here.' She held out her hand. 'I'm in my nest too. Come on up. There are plenty of footholds. The hedgehog isn't ready yet.'

I stared at the blank wall, wondering if the rusty nails and iron hooks were what she meant by footholds. 'I'm not a spider, you know!'

She laughed seductively. 'I'm the spider and you're the fly. I've spun a web and now I want my dinner.' She knelt up against the wooden rail and pointed down. 'There's a ladder on the floor if you need one . . .'

I bent down and hauled the ladder upright in a shower of loose straw, propping it firmly against the floor of the hayloft. Lightning flared and died. The thunder beat its drum. I held her gaze as I placed my foot on the first springy rung. I thought my heart was going to burst. 'Here comes the fly.'

Another lightning flash. She shut her eyes, counting the seconds. 'One *hotchi-witchi* . . . two *hotchi-witchi* . . . three *hotchi-witchi* . . .' The storm was almost overhead.

Dark Berry

I WANTED MAX to track me down. And now I was tempting him. *What's happened to me?* I asked myself. I knew the strict rules of my tribe and this was not allowed . . . with anybody . . . let alone a *gadjo*! I must have been mad, but love is a kind of madness, so Baba Sara once said. And I couldn't help myself. I could hardly breathe for wanting him. I was trembling as he climbed the ladder. I told myself this had to stop. I couldn't let this happen . . . but I couldn't stop. I could have stopped before I started . . . but now . . . I'd waited so long for this feeling. I knew it was wrong . . . but there was no turning back. In the end it was the blackberries that tipped us over the edge, or maybe the blackberries and the thunderstorm together . . .

It was Max wanting to learn the *patrin* that first gave me the idea. And then I found the old red cowshed. The minute I pushed open the door I knew it would be our secret place. I'd planned this day with care: the trail, the blazing fire, the *hotchi-witchi*, the ripe blackberries. Looking back I can't believe I was so crafty. As I said, love is a kind of madness, and unless you've felt it for yourself, you'll never know what lovers will do.

I tempted him on purpose, holding the gleaming blackberry between my fingers as he climbed. I remember every detail. I'm kneeling on the floor of the hayloft. He climbs the ladder and squats down next to me, picking some straw from my hair, and then he bites down on the berry between my fingers, scoring my flesh with his teeth. The juice squirts onto my neck in a streak, like blood. He leans towards me. Licks it off. His tongue feels warm and slippery and slightly rough. I think my heart will stop. 'That's the sweetest blackberry I've ever tasted.'

I stare at him. His hair is shining with raindrops like stars. I put a blackberry in my mouth, then I press it from mine into his with my tongue. '*May kali i muri may gugli avela,*' I whisper, my mouth still touching his. He closes his eyes, swallows, then licks the juice from my lips. His breath is warm and smells of fruit. His voice sends shivers down my spine.

'What does that mean?'

'The darker the berry, the sweeter the fruit,' I say.

Another bright flash. Another pulse of light. He takes my head in his hands like it's the most precious thing he's ever held and threads his cold fingers through my hair. My world stops turning. I gaze into his eyes, blue as cornflowers. 'I can't stop thinking of you, Lili. I can't stop dreaming of you . . .' He slides his hands down my face, following the neck of my blouse, pulling the ribbon undone, sliding his hands inside. I want to tell him how much I love him. The way he makes me feel. How I think it can't get any stronger and then it does. But now he's kissing my mouth . . .

I'm at a crossroads, caught between then and now. My eyes are blinded by a stab of lightning. One *hotchi-witchi* . . . I am taking off his shirt, pulling it over his head without unfastening the buttons. A split second later the walls tremble. I can hear the wind outside rocking the trees. The old Lili is about to shed her skin. I'm on the trapeze platform, quivering on the edge, waiting to swoop down into the dark chasm of the swing. I'm on the brink. It's elation. It's terror. I catch my breath and then I leap from my place of safety, out into the velvet blackness of the big top. But this time I know that I've judged it right. Max will be there, waiting to catch me. I know he won't fail me. I trust him with my life. And when I swoop back up, up to the safety of my perch again, I know I will be changed.

Shon and Chakano

M AX STROKES MY HAIR GENTLY. 'You look different.'
I push his long fringe from his forehead, tracing the shape of his face with my finger. 'I am different. We're like Shon and Chakano. Born to be together.'

'Shon and Chakano?'

'Moon and star. Close your eyes and I'll tell you a story. And when I've finished, the *hotchi-witchi* will be ready.' He sighs and nestles his head in my lap. 'Don't go to sleep,' I say.

Once, long ago, a prince was born and his parents named him Shon because he had a moon upon his head.

That same night a baby girl was born to a Romani blacksmith. 'We will call her Chakano,' said the blacksmith's wife, for on her head there shone a star.

Now Shon was rich and Chakano poor and yet they looked as alike as ripples on the water, only Shon's skin was creamy white and Chakano's dreamy dark.

That very day, Chirikli, the magic bird, visited the king, telling him, 'Your prince will marry the blacksmith's daughter, for if it wasn't for the moon and the star they are as alike as two stalks in a cornfield.'

'Never!' cried the king. 'A chikly gypsy's daughter marry my son? Never!'

That night the wicked king summoned his most trusty servant. 'Take the gypsy's daughter into the woods. Kill her and leave her body for the wolves!'

Now the servant was loyal to the king but he also feared God. So he lined a basket with sheep's wool for the baby and set it upon the river, then taking his hunting knife, he cut open his vein and spread his blood upon his shirt to trick the king.

Next day, an old fisherman's wife was gathering reeds by the river and spied a little basket in the stream and heard a baby's cry. Snatching it up she ran to her husband. 'Husband!' she cried. 'Milk our goat and light the fire! I have found a child as cold as death with a star upon her head.'

Years passed and Chakano grew in beauty and goodness. One day the king brought his horse to the river to drink and there he saw Chakano washing clothes with her mother.

'O fisherman's wife,' said the king. 'Is this beauty

with the star upon her head your daughter?'

'I have raised her as my own, O King,' she replied, 'for I found her in my childlessness, floating in the river.'

And then the king knew he had been tricked.

'Girl,' he said to Chakano. 'I need to send a message to my queen so she will not worry if I am late from hunting. If you get to my castle before sundown I will give you two gold pieces.' Then the king took out his quill and wrote a note.

Dear Queen,
Put this messenger to death for she is really a wicked witch in disguise and means to kill our son.

And Chakano went singing on her way. When she reached the castle gates there was a sudden flurry of wings and the Chirikli bird swooped down and snatched up the note. It flew to the top of a tree and by magic changed the message:

Dear Queen,
Marry this beauty to our son before nightfall, for she is the daughter of a rich king and I want to join our kingdoms.

Then fluttering down, the bird dropped the note back into the girl's hand. As soon as the queen read the message she called the priest and hurried to the chapel.

And as the king was riding home he saw a light shining from the stained-glass windows. Quickly he *dismounted and ran to the chapel doors and flung them wide. There at the high altar stood the prince and the gypsy's daughter, the candlelight gleaming on the moon and stars on their heads.*

'I now pronounce you man and wife,' proclaimed the priest.

And at these words the king gave a mighty shriek, loud enough to shatter the glass in the rose window above the altar. Loud enough to burst the chambers of his wicked heart. And as the echo of his dying scream faded away, the Chirikli bird sang from the rafters, and all the bells of the valley rang for joy.

My story is finished. The hedgehog is ready. Roast *hotchi-witchi* is sweet and juicy. Max watches as I split open its clay jacket. I show him how the bristles and skin come away with the pot. He takes a mouthful. I can tell he likes it. 'May you always have a hedgehog in your pot,' I say.

We hardly speak as we eat. We don't want to break the spell, but every few moments our eyes meet. After we've eaten I nestle against him. His skin is warm from the fire and I want him to melt into me, so that when we have to part I can take him with me, deep inside my skin.

When we leave the red barn the rain has stopped. The clouds have cleared and the sinking sun gilds the dying leaves with gold. Everything is rinsed clean of the dust of summer. I am clean and new, shining like the sun. The sky is on fire. My heart is on fire. I have never lived until now. I will remember this day for the rest of my life.

Cabbage Purée

MY BIKE HAD WINGS as I sped down the eerie tunnel of the Ku'Damm. It was hard to believe it was once ablaze with neon lights as I followed the whitewashed kerbstones snaking away into the distance. It was well after six and completely dark, except for the occasional flashes of light from the S-Bahn. You had to keep your wits about you these days. Apart from their electric blue sparks, the trams were near invisible.

I chained my bike to our drainpipe, since our railings seemed to have disappeared. Then I leaped up the stairs two at a time. The handrail had gone too, but just at that moment, I felt I could fly. One of my aunt's piano pupils was murdering *Für Elise* in the drawing room as I dragged off my boots in the hall. *Best avoided*, I thought with a grin, as I tiptoed towards the kitchen.

I opened the door to the usual greeting of *'Heil Hitler!'* from the parrot to find our two Slavic maids, Mirka and Ludmilla, picking leaves off a sad-looking cabbage at the sink. There was no fire in the grate and I felt sorry for the sullen maids in their thin jerseys. My aunt had found them down at the local employment office. By this time Berlin was littered with rows of flimsy wooden barracks for the thousands of prisoners of war. At least these girls had a proper roof over their heads now winter was on its way.

Gretchen and her best friend Margot were in the kitchen too, looking warmer than our maids, snug in the 'monkeyskin' jackets they wore over their winter uniforms. They were drinking mock orange juice they'd made from soaking swede slices in their sugar ration. Margot, I noticed, was still wearing her regulation beret, pulled steeply down over one ear like Marlene Dietrich. I guessed it was for my benefit. Margot always made me feel uncomfortable, ever since I'd caught her kissing the photo of my passing out parade on top of the piano.

I did my best to ignore Gretchen these days, but I couldn't help noticing she'd changed her hairstyle, swapping her bell ropes for a kind of braided bun, so that she now resembled one of those plump plaited loaves we used to order from the baker's. And she was wearing the full uniform of the BDM. I'd been so preoccupied lately I hadn't realized Gretchen had graduated from the junior branch.

The girls were busy scribbling letters to soldiers at the

front, so I decided to beat a hasty retreat. I wanted to finish my poem – the one about the moon smiling for me.

'Oh, don't go yet, Max,' called Gretchen eagerly. 'Margot's written a letter to the Führer. I'm sure she'd like you to hear it!'

Margot leaped to her feet, her cheeks the colour of mock orange, as she tried in vain to snatch the paper from Gretchen. 'Don't, Gretchen, *please!*'

Gretchen cleared her throat. '*Dear Herr Hitler. I have nothing to give you except my love. I know this is perhaps a strange suggestion but I would like to have your baby. It really bothers me that a man like you is childless . . .*'

My snort exploded like a cork from a bottle, although I wasn't exactly surprised. I'd seen crowds of girls like Margot, flooding the streets to see the Führer, literally swooning and strewing flowers in his path. It was well known that love letters arrived at the Reich Chancellery every day by the sack load, along with hand-knitted socks and jerseys.

'Well, he's such a nice man!' wailed Margot. 'It's a pity he's not married. He needs a wife. He's so sincere . . . and he loves children . . . and dogs. But who looks after him? Who warms his slippers by the fire?'

'Who warms whose slippers?' It was Tante Ida, fresh from Beethoven's deathbed.

'The Führer's,' simpered Gretchen. 'Margot's written him a lovely letter about having his baby.' She beamed at Tante Ida. 'We should all bear children for the Reich, shouldn't we, Aunt?'

I heard the front door slam. 'What's happened to our

railings?' Erika slid into the kitchen, blue and sophisticated in her new Signals Auxiliary uniform, complete with boat-shaped hat, pencil skirt and seamed stockings. Her job operating a teleprinter definitely suited her better than bringing in the harvest. She swept the kitchen with an accusing stare. 'Well? Where've they gone? I nearly fell down the front steps!'

I stared at her legs with a brotherly eye. Were those real silk stockings or just gravy browning and a line of pencil? She looked ravishing in a trench coat, like Greta Garbo.

'The Führer needs our railings for the war effort,' said Gretchen piously. 'It's a small enough sacrifice, Erika.'

'What on earth does he need railings for?'

Gretchen rolled her eyes. 'We were talking about having babies for the Reich, Erika. Have *you* ever thought about it?'

'Not specially,' she said, grinning at me in the mirror as she unpinned her hat. 'But if *you* have, I've got some tips. I read an article in the paper about the *Lebensborn* project. An unmarried girl can go to a special Party home to become pregnant by a member of the SS! As long as she's got the right credentials, of course. Girls are flooding in, apparently.' She patted her hair. 'Personally, I'm not interested in a random SS officer . . . but Gretchen and Margot might be persuaded . . .' She stopped suddenly mid-sentence, her eyes widening in horror. 'Oh, Gretchen! Goodness me. You've changed your hairdo!'

I caught Erika's eye. 'Yes, Gretchen,' I said casually. 'I'd noticed too . . .'

It was no use. My voice had begun to tremble. I took a deep breath but it didn't help. My shoulders were shaking and I felt that dreadful bubble rising in my stomach. *The uncontrollable urge*, Erika used to call it. 'It's funny, but you *do* remind me of something with your hair like that. What is it, Erika?'

Erika's eyes had started to water in her effort to gain control. And then the storm broke. Erika and I were doubled up, gasping, catching each other's glance and starting the other one off again. 'S-sorry, Gretchen,' she stammered. 'It's only that . . . it makes you look so . . . so . . . so very like . . .'

' . . . a plaited loaf!' I exploded, holding my stomach.

Even Margot was giggling by now, no doubt relieved to get her own back on Gretchen for the letter. 'Gretchen thinks it makes her look like Helga Eckart – our BDM Führerin!'

'Really?' I squeaked. And off we all went again, drowning in gales of laughter.

Tante Ida waded to the rescue. 'Max! Erika! That's extremely rude! Just ignore them, dear. It suits your face, in my opinion.' She placed a comforting hand on Gretchen's shoulder. 'You're much too old for pigtails now you've graduated. This new style makes you look very . . . mature.'

Erika wiped her eyes on her handkerchief. She swallowed hard, but I had a feeling she had another arrow for her bow. 'Well, you'd better not look too *mature* Gretchen, or Tante Ida might march you off to the *Lebensborn* project. Oh, don't look so horrified! I'm only teasing. But you must have heard what they're calling the BDM these days . . .'

Gretchen scowled. 'No. I haven't, as a matter of fact. But if it's something horrible I'm sure you're going to tell me . . .'

'Oh, not *horrible*. Just rather amusing. The *Bund Deutscher*

Matratzen . . .'

I stifled a laugh. *The German Mattresses League!*

Erika shrugged. 'Well, it's hardly surprising. The girls of the BDM have been putting themselves about so much . . .'

My aunt banged the table so hard that mock orange sloshed from the glasses. 'That's enough, Erika! I can't imagine where you heard that filth, but all I can say is it's a case of the pot calling the kettle black. Your skirt's far too short. And you'd better start knitting some stockings pretty quickly. We've run out of gravy browning.' She flashed her tombstones at Margot. 'That's a very thoughtful letter, Margot, dear. I'm sure the Führer will appreciate the sentiment, if not the deed. Now, I think supper is in order. Mirka. Ludmilla. If those sausages are ready, I'll start serving the cabbage.'

Jingo Jango

IT WAS A TENSE SUPPER, the atmosphere crackling with animosity. Rudi had brought his latest collection of *Abzeichen* to the table – the collectable badges that showed you'd donated to the week's Winter Relief appeal. There was a new set every week. No one dared walk in the street without the latest badge pinned conspicuously to his lapel. Rudi had every set ever issued: embroidered crests of the German lands, resin portraits of German musicians, animals of the Reich. This week's were a collection of tiny booklets with intriguing titles such as *The Führer and the German Army* and *The Führer's Battle in the East*.

Tante Ida swept them off his plate impatiently to make space for the cabbage purée that came plopping from the ladle in an unattractive heap. I was still enjoying being 'in' with Erika, so I began to pick them up one by one, reading out the titles for her amusement.

'*The Führer and the Hitler Youth*. I think I know enough about that,' I sighed. '*Hitler and the Jews*.'

I sneaked a glance at Vati but his gaze was fixed on his plate. I picked up another little book. The odour of cabbage was nauseating but it wasn't the smell that had suddenly made me feel sick, but the book's title: *Hitler and the Gypsies*.

Erika was flicking through *Hitler and the Jews* with her lacquered nails, squinting at the tiny pictures. 'Well, I've never seen a Jew with a nose like a curly sausage . . . or feet this big. Have you, Rudi?'

My father cleared his throat and laid down his knife and fork. 'Of course he hasn't. It's called propaganda, my dear. It's not only untrue, it's downright wicked.'

I heard Gretchen draw breath, about to launch into one of her usual tirades, but Vati had her trapped in his steely glare. 'And you, Gretchen, my dear, will keep your opinions to yourself whilst I'm eating my supper. I can't control what you say in your BDM clubhouse but I can dictate the conversation at my own dinner table. People seem to have forgotten that our Lord was a Jew.'

Tante Ida laughed unpleasantly. 'And who betrayed Jesus? Answer me that? Aha! I seem to have you there.'

She smiled triumphantly to herself and began to attack her sausage. I thought no one had noticed me palming one of the tiny books and dropping it into my lap. I'd underestimated Gretchen. 'Why have you taken one of Rudi's books, Max?

Rudi! He's pinched one of your books . . .'

Rudi made a lunge across the table, cabbage purée flying from his fork. 'Give it back! It's mine.'

My face was burning up. 'You can have it back, you little beast. I was only looking . . .'

'Well, you can't look at it on your knee,' persisted Gretchen. 'Which one are you so interested in, anyway?'

I'd often felt an overwhelming urge to slap Gretchen. For once I envied Mutti, eating supper alone in her bedroom. I scraped back my chair on the parquet, casually flicking the tiny booklet back onto the pile.

'Excuse me, Vati. May I leave the table? I assume there's no dessert?' It wasn't really a question. Tante Ida hadn't mastered puddings without sugar. But I might have guessed that Gretchen hadn't quite finished. She carefully selected the offending booklet from the pile in the middle of the table.

'Is this the one you were looking at, Max? *Hitler and the Gypsies?* Yeuch! They're almost as dirty as the Jews. Look at their wild, greasy hair.'

My aunt's smile could have curdled vinegar. 'They're a social nuisance, Gretchen. Deceitful and work shy! Even *worse* than the Jews, if that were possible. The blessing is that there aren't so many of them.'

'Django Reinhardt's a gypsy,' said Erika. 'And he doesn't have greasy hair.'

My aunt emitted a powerful snort. 'Who's *Jingo Jango*? Another of your lovesick American crooners?'

'Actually, he's a famous jazz guitarist.' Erika began to

hum a catchy tune, tapping her fingers on the edge of her plate. 'You must know *Minor Swing*. I've got a record of him playing with Stéphane Grappelli in Paris. He's amazing! He lost two fingers in a fire in his caravan and the doctors said he'd never play again. I can put him on the gramophone if you like . . .'

'You'll do no such thing, Erika,' said Tante Ida, rolling her napkin. Even she seemed to have given up on the cabbage. 'I've had my fill of complaints about your nigger music from Frau Schneck. American records are now officially banned, as you well know. It's downright unpatriotic to play enemy music when fellow Germans are fighting so bravely.'

'Himmler says young people who listen to American jazz should be put to hard labour,' said Gretchen.

Erika blew out her cheeks in mock relief. 'Just as well he's French, then. You had me worried for a minute. And he's a gypsy not a nigger, so that's all right too!'

Poor Foxy!

I WAS THANKFUL to leave the battlefield of the dining room,
yet as I tiptoed along the landing past Mutti's door I felt a
worm of worry uncoil in my stomach. *That horrible little book!*
How I wish Gretchen hadn't seen me slip it onto my knee.
As I passed her bedroom, I couldn't resist the temptation of
the new poster she'd pinned to the door – a smiling family
under the wings of a Nazi eagle: *The Nazi Party Safeguards
the People of the Nation.* I dug in my pocket for a pencil stub
and sketched a pair of spectacles on the wholesome baby on
its mother's knee. It made me feel slightly better, but not
much. I'd imagined myself spending the evening in my room
dreaming of Lili, going back over the afternoon and thinking
about her hands on my body, the complicated smell of her

skin. Now I couldn't get the dinner conversation out of my mind.

It was cold in my bedroom so I pulled on one of my aunt's fur coats. I have to admit she'd been generous with them ever since that freezing winter of 1939. There was a large mahogany wardrobe on the landing containing my aunt's passion. She had every kind of fur you could think of – silver fox, chinchilla, muskrat, Persian lamb – in jackets, coats and stoles. She'd let us choose one each that first Christmas, and what with the permanent coal shortages, we'd been allowed to keep them. Rudi had chosen a silver fox wrap with sharp pointed ears and four dangling paws and a thick brush, with a snout that clipped onto the tail, and eyes of shiny jet. 'My poor foxy,' he called it, and took it to bed every night.

Of course Erika had taken full advantage of my aunt's generosity. 'Give that girl a currant,' said my aunt, 'and she'll always take the bun!'

I was just warming up in bed, drifting off into dreams of Lili, when Erika knocked on my door. She looked as if she'd been crying, although she still managed to look like Marlene Dietrich in my aunt's beaver lamb stole – a type of lambskin designed to look like beaver fur. 'Gosh!' she said, gazing at my posters. Long-dead flying aces from the World War competed for precedence with members of the Hertha football team. 'A bit different from my room. Clark Gable kissing Vivien Leigh!'

'I thought you liked Georg better than Clark these days,' I laughed, realizing too late that I'd said the wrong thing. She collapsed on my bed and burst into tears. It turned out she'd only just seen the letter that had arrived that morning. She was usually pretty jolly after a letter from her boyfriend, even if there was little left after the censors had finished with their black ink. This letter had somehow escaped, brought out by a daring pilot in a mailbag. She read me edited highlights.

I'm sorry, my darling, but what they're saying in Berlin about beating the Russians is just lies. If you could see what Stalingrad has done to our army. There are bodies everywhere, left to rot where they fall. When will this slaughter be over? Home by Christmas? What rubbish!

I squeezed Erika's arm. 'He must have had a few bad days, that's all. Stalingrad is as good as taken. I heard it on the wireless this afternoon. England's about to surrender . . .'

Erika blew her nose. 'It's all lies, Max. I showed this letter to Vati. I surprised him in his study, with his head under a pillow, listening to the German language broadcast from London. The news from the east is as bad as it could be and the Allies have landed in North Africa. We're not winning this war – and that's a fact!'

I dug in my pocket for half a Juno I'd saved for later and coaxed it into life with a match. Erika accepted it greedily, inhaled deeply, then handed me the butt end. She laughed bitterly. 'How are the mighty fallen! I used to smoke Passion Brand in an ebony holder, and now it's the scrag end of a Juno on my brother's bed. But thanks all the same.'

A sudden pounding along the landing shattered our

intimate moment. Gretchen hurtled into the room clutching a greenish mess in her hand, water snaking down her arm. 'Ah, there you are, Erika! You've been using my soap again!' The tiny monthly soap ration was a constant source of friction. '*And* forgotten to put it back on the grid. It's nearly melted away. I know it was you . . .'

Erika sucked in her breath. 'Oh, get lost, Gretchen! You really are the limit.'

Gretchen stamped her foot. 'You're so unbelievably selfish. It's baths at weekends only, but Erika takes them every day. American jazz is banned but Erika plays it on the gramophone. Girls are supposed to dress modestly so Erika draws seams up the back of her legs. And on top of everything, someone's drawn spectacles on my poster! If you don't stop this I'll report you to my leader . . .'

Erika sprang from the bed. At first I thought she was going to punch Gretchen but instead she just shook the letter in her face. 'Shut up, you little prig! Soldiers are dying and all you can think about is whether someone's borrowed your soap.' She pushed past her roughly and then turned back. 'Oh, by the way Max, if you want to hear that Django Reinhardt record, come to my room . . .'

'But the Führer says –'

'*Damn* the bloody Führer!' Erika's green eyes were glittering with malice. 'Go on, Gretchen! Report *that* to your precious BDM leader, you stupid German milk cow!' Tears started in Gretchen's eyes. Erika smirked contemptuously as she retreated across the landing. 'Oh, haven't you heard that one yet? It's another name for your precious BDM. The

Bund Deutscher Milchkühe!'

I heard two doors slam. Alone at last I sat at my desk and pulled open the drawer. I'd filled page after page in my diary since meeting Lili again. Poems about her. Things she'd said. The stories she'd told me. Tonight I'd write all about the lovers, Shon and Chakano . . .

My stomach lurched. My diary wasn't there. I heaved the heavy drawer out further until it tilted down towards my lap. And there sat my precious book, right at the back, as if someone had flung it in hurriedly, rather than putting it carefully back in its place. I frowned. I never locked my room. I hadn't thought there was any need . . . until now.

A Garden in Berlin
April 2013

MAX PLACED THE BUFF-COLOURED SONGBOOK in the suitcase along with the Hitler Youth dagger and the twisted lock of hair.

'We could never have been together, Max, even if there hadn't been a war . . .'

Max sat completely still, hands clutching the edge of the garden table, the breeze gently lifting his hair. 'We could have tried. Love can conquer everything, so the poets say. We were Shon and Chakano . . .'

Lili's laugh was a breath of wind. *'Shon and Chakano were just a fairy tale . . .'*

'What's that, Lili?' Max frowned. It was the breeze, he told himself, blowing her words away. 'But you always said . . . I mean . . . we did love each other, didn't we?'

The trees shivered. '*Oh yes, we loved each other, Max. But you're wrong about Chakano. I never really thought I was like her. In my mind I was always Pokhalo.*'

'Pokhalo?'

'*I thought you used to write my stories in your book.*'

'Maybe I found it too sad. Remind me . . .'

'*The one about the Romani girl who fell in love with a magician's son. And when he found out, he imprisoned his son in a tall tower, wound about with poison ivy . . .*'

'Yes, I remember now . . .'

'*She begged the magician to release him and so they made a deal. If she could weave seven golden cloaks in seven days, she could marry his son.*'

'That was a hard task . . .'

'*Not for Pokhalo. She was handy with the loom. She could make a cloak in less than a day, but he cast a spell, so as soon as she'd woven two threads, one came undone. So on she stitched, two threads forward, one thread back, but by the sixth day she'd still made six cloaks. Then while she was weaving the seventh she fell asleep . . .*'

'So they never married?'

'*Worse. The magician hadn't done with her. When he saw her tears he laughed until his sides hurt. "The foolish gypsy is weeping for her unfinished cloak. If she loves weaving so much I'll turn her into a spider. I'll call her Pokhalo – Little Cobweb." And to this day Pokhalo spins and spins, spreading out her threads to dry, and when the sun shines and you see dewdrops on the threads you know that Little Cobweb has been weeping for her lover.*'

'That's the saddest tale you ever told . . .'

'*No sadder than ours,*' said the wind in the trees.

Max wiped his eyes. It was never going to be easy. He'd known it the day he opened his Pandora's Box. He put his hand to his chest, pressing gently, in the middle and slightly to the left. The pain in his heart was sharper today – although a broken heart, as he knew to his cost, hurt most in the stomach. *Slowly*, Max, he told himself, feeling that curious tingling in his left arm again. *Remember what Doktor Seligmann said.*

But his mind was already racing ahead with Lili. Already he could see the lights of the Wintergarten. Hear the music in the auditorium. Feel the cheap paper of the programme in his hands. Perhaps his memory was playing tricks but he was sure he could smell sweat and stables, horseflesh, dung and sweet straw. He hesitated, fingering the circus bells on the table. He wasn't sure he could bear to hear their trembling sweet-tongued sound. The bells shivered as he lifted them to his lips. His memories were as fresh today as ever they were, even after a lifetime spent nursing his wounded heart.

Writhing Snakes

24 NOVEMBER 1942. *Terrible news from the eastern front is trickling in faster now*, I wrote in my diary. *And today . . . the first public admission – a Soviet breakthrough of German positions southwest of Stalingrad.*

Then on Christmas Eve, the chilling news on the wireless: *Twenty divisions of General Paulus's Sixth Army – encircled in an icy wilderness.*

We'd already guessed what the recent shortage of news from Russia really meant, despite the weekly newsreel of jolly soldiers on the eastern front, merrily baking Christmas cakes in improvised fuel containers.

'I bet those soldiers have never been further than the Babelsberg film studios,' sniffed Erika. There'd been no more letters from Georg.

Mass on Christmas Eve and dark by four thirty. We all donned Tante Ida's furs, and with our feet wrapped in newspaper inside our boots, we struggled through the snowdrifts to the cathedral. We were all downcast at the news. Apart from Rudi, that is, who seemed pleased enough with his only Christmas gift – a flimsy cardboard game, *Hunting for the Coal Thief*, designed to promote energy conservation. We waved at Gretchen as we skirted her BDM choir on Gendarmenmarkt solemnly singing *'Stille Nacht'*, with the new National Socialist words:

Adolf Hitler is Germany's star
Showing us greatness and glory afar,
Bringing us Germans the might
Bringing us Germans the might

Whatever the Nazis had tried to do to Christmas, they hadn't succeeded at St Hedwig's. The blackout blinds had made its grand cupola almost invisible from the outside, but within was a blaze of light. Two vast Christmas trees flanked the altar, warmed with a bloom of creamy candles amongst the gilded fir cones, each topped with a five-pointed star. I glanced at Tante Ida, remembering that first year of the war and the ferocious row about the jewelled swastika she'd put on the top of our *People's Christmas Tree*, along with the baubles with the image of the Führer's face that she'd hung amidst the spruce branches.

It was more crowded than usual in St Hedwig's. People

were standing in the aisles, coats studded with the fluorescent good luck symbols everyone had taken to wearing these days in the shape of horseshoes and four leaf clovers. I closed my eyes and breathed in the heady scent of frankincense. If I kept them shut I could almost imagine it was a normal Christmas Eve, especially when the organ struck up with my favourite hymn by Bach: *'From Heaven Above to Earth I Come'* . . . Except for the fact that, try as I might, I couldn't shut out the sound of weeping. Women in black armbands, softly weeping.

I knelt and prayed harder than I'd ever done before that no harm would come to those I loved. *Maria, hilf uns allen aus unserer tiefen Not. Mary, help us all in our deep distress.* I prayed for Erika and her Georg on the eastern front. I prayed for Vati and his hospital work with the wounded. I prayed for Lili and me. But most of all I prayed that no bombs would fall on Berlin. We'd been lucky for the whole of this year, I thought, as the priest laid the host on my tongue at the altar. But how long would it last? As I returned to my pew I felt snakes begin to move, coiling and uncoiling in the pit of my stomach. I had a terrible premonition that my life, so safe for the last three years in spite of war raging all over Europe, was just about to change.

I linked arms with Erika as we left the cathedral and picked our way down the slippery steps, wishing friends a subdued Merry Christmas. Perhaps it was the shock of this evening's wireless announcement that had awoken my writhing snakes. But I knew in my heart that this wasn't the real reason. Vati had told me something before we set out for the cathedral. He'd asked me into his study and spoken to me, man to man. He'd heard some other news, he told me, whilst listening to the BBC. There was a new man at the head of Britain's bomber command: Sir Arthur Harris – a man with new ideas. And a new bomber too. The Avro Lancaster, he informed me, could do the work of three bombers of the 1940 vintage. For three years Berlin had been too far northeast for large-scale bombing raids . . . until now. Would I do Vati a favour after dinner tomorrow whilst the others were playing Christmas games?

'Not a word to Mutti just yet,' he confided. 'But it's probably a good idea to check on the sand buckets and make sure the stirrup pump still works. I caught Tante Ida using it during the summer to wash caterpillars off the cabbages!'

Stolen Horses

WE CELEBRATED CHRISTMAS EVE, *Vilija* as we call it, with sweet *bobalky* sprinkled with poppy seeds with a silver coin inside. Ma used ground up nuts instead of flour to bake the rich milky bun and I was the one who found the coin. *Good fortune for me this year!* I remember Pa going round the table with the usual gifts: a sieve full of grain, a purse of money, and a bunch of basil and wild garlic to ward off evil spirits. 'Good health!' toasted Pa, raising his glass to everyone and beaming broadly at Florica, who sat cradling her new baby in her lap. 'And new beginnings!'

On the eve of the old year, I sat by the glowing stove replacing missing sequins on my costume. I licked my finger and selected another spangle from the wicker basket, hugging myself with happiness. I had two reasons to be happy now. I was in love for the first time and no one else in the history of the world had ever felt this way. And as if that wasn't enough, Pa had just found us jobs in the Wintergarten Theatre with none other than Fredy and Rolf Knie, the famous Swiss circus. I'm not joking. *Fredy Knie*. The most famous horse trainer in Europe! Opening on 18 January.

'We'll make enough money,' said Pa, 'to see us right till we can start travelling again.'

I ignored that bit. Like most people in love, I didn't look beyond the end of my nose.

It had happened like this. I'd been so wrapped up in myself that I hadn't noticed Pa's usual winter fidgets. So I was pretty surprised when he returned to camp the day before Christmas Eve like a dog with two tails, bursting into our vardo with the news about Fredy Knie.

Ma glanced up from her sewing machine, looking anxious. 'I thought we were doing all right in the local taverns, Pa. Surely it's asking for bother. This is Berlin. Not some German village . . .'

But I knew that look on Pa's face. He'd been after something like this. '*Bother?* The Wintergarten's the most famous variety theatre in the world. And the *Knie Brothers*, no less! Come on, Ma. We ain't gonna turn this chance down.'

He flung himself into his chair and reached for his pipe, lighting it from his old tinder lighter with the wick hanging down. 'Don't look so troubled, Ma. You know the old saying. If you want to hide a stolen horse, hitch it to the front of your wagon.'

Ma snapped off a thread with her teeth. 'And I've never really understood what that means. It don't make no sense to me.'

'It means, if you want to hide something, you're best to hide it where people ain't likely to go ferreting. Look at it this way. We've been hiding in the open for three years already.'

Ma sighed and laid down the bolero she was working on. 'How come Fredy Knie wants us?'

'Well, I heard he was hiring from a roustabout in the tavern, so I went straight there before anyone else nobbled 'im. He's got problems, see. He's got a long run booked and not enough talent to fill the bill. The army's pinched most of his horses and that's the lion's part of the show, so he's got special permission from the German Ambassador to hire foreign acts from Europe.'

'What? From enemy countries?'

'That's about it. They're short handed and there's foreign talent kicking its heels. It's good money for us and it's safe. We'll just mingle with the foreigners. Fredy says the government's keeping the theatres open to stop folks complaining, 'specially now the war news ain't so good. Variety's the thing to keep people's minds off empty shop windows.'

Pa was chuffed as you like but Ma still wasn't sure. 'How will you get back every night? The weather's getting worse.'

Pa beamed. He'd got that one stitched too. 'There's a couple of apartments in Berlin we can have and big stables near the theatre, where Fredy's brother keeps his elephants.

You don't have to come, Ma. You can stay with Baba Sara and mind baby Franko for Florica. I'll need her in the troupe.'

Ma sighed, staring into the fire, but I could tell she was warming to the idea. 'Who'd have thought it?' she said slowly. 'Fredy Knie! My word, Pa. How do you always land on both feet?'

Pa chuckled. 'A dog that wanders finds the bone, ain't that so, girls?'

Me and Frieda were sitting by the stove. I was glad I had the firelight on me, so no one would see I was burning up. I felt like I'd swallowed a bag of butterflies. I'd been finding it harder to make excuses to get out since the weather turned bad and sometimes I thought I might die from wanting Max so much. *An apartment in Berlin!* I hugged myself. 'Fredy Knie,' I said, trying to sound casual. My mind was zipping ahead like a ladder in a pair of stockings. 'Did you say they were short of horses?'

Pa grinned. 'That's what they need most! He was that chuffed when I told him about you and White Lightning and the counting and all . . . and they want Pali and Tamas with Spitzi. Florica and Fonso and little Fifi's juggling. The Camlos. I told him straight out – *you'll not see better*!'

Ma sniffed, pursing her lips like she'd sucked on a gooseberry, but I could tell she was proud too. 'You're like Houdini, you are, Josef. You could argue your way out of a straitjacket!'

Running Water

COULD WE ALSO SUPPLY perch-pole dancing, springboard acrobatics and some high-wire dancers? Of course we could, said Pa, wondering where we'd find a perch pole in time. Ma raised an eyebrow. 'Never hide your talents,' laughed Pa. 'Modesty never set a purse jingling.'

Fredy Knie was delighted. They needed some sensational acts, especially as his brother Rolf was appearing at the Scala Variety on Lutherstrasse with their wire-walking elephant, Baby. So they were both up against it to fill their slots. Me and Frieda were hired, along with Pali, Tamas, and any number of our acts. And what's more, there was a stable for White Lightning, dressing rooms with lights all round the mirrors, and a place to stay, off a square called Hackescher Markt.

The apartment block was built round dark courtyards, one leading into another, with the year 1884 carved in stone over the archway. We'd never slept in brick before, although we never told that to the key lady on the desk. She was a shrivelled little woman, like a tiny black mouse, who kept her false teeth in a jar until she needed them for talking. She was nice but nosey, so Pa said we should mind our chatter.

The block was five floors high with an iron lift and metal gates next to the stairs. Me and Frieda kept going up and down in it till Frieda got her hair caught in the gates.

'What have the stairs done wrong?' Pa said. Lifts were for lazybones, he told us, whose legs had got weak from riding on trams.

Our two flats had iron balconies looking over a cobbled courtyard full of dry old plants, where street *chavvies* tried to make snowmen from the snow that fell from a square of grey sky. I felt sorry for them but Frieda said you'd maybe not miss lanes and hedgerows if you'd never known them. It was a lot warmer than our vardo. Our clothes dried out for the first time in weeks and our chilblains improved right away. We shared a toilet in the stairwell with a woman called Fräulein Frick. She had dyed black hair with a line of grey like a badger, and lots of men visiting. She kept moaning that there was never any hot water for a bath. We couldn't understand why she was so grouchy. When we'd first seen our kitchen we kept turning on the taps just to see the water coming out. And there were olive green tiles in the bathroom and a tub so deep you could sleep in it. 'The *gadje* have such *chikly* habits,' Pa said. So we piled it up with shoes.

We were all starry-eyed for Fredy Knie. He was only twenty-two and already the most famous horse trainer in Europe. Everything was romantic about Fredy. His grandpa had been a doctor's son and studying to become a doctor himself, and then one day he just upped and ran away with a travelling troupe and married a bareback rider. Fredy started in the ring at four years old and by the time he was twelve, he'd been to London with Bertram Mills himself. You might think Fredy's head would get stuck in the door, people bowing and scraping like that, but not a bit. He had a kind word for everyone. And for a few days, I swear Frieda's head was turned. Marko got that green look on his face I remembered from when I wore his *diklo*. But Fredy won Marko round and soon they were getting on like two bees in a jar. You see, Fredy was a real stickler about animals, like Marko. 'What you can't get out of a beast by human kindness ain't worth a candle,' Fredy used to say.

Everyone was friendly at the Wintergarten, even though the chatter backstage sounded like when God mixed up the languages. It didn't matter. Words don't figure much in circuses so long as you can walk the wire. There was a human pyramid from Russia – twenty-seven men with muscles like ferrets in a sack, conjurers with doves in cages that disappeared through false bottoms, contortionists who tied themselves in knots and a troupe of Chinese plate spinners in golden kimonos and scarlet slippers. But my favourite act was Fredy's own, where his beautiful stallion lay down on the stage in a nightcap, his head on a giant pillow. There was only one thing that took the shine off my kettle. Or one person, I should say . . .

Dario Gallo was a sword swallower from Seville. He was nice looking, a bit like Clark Gable from *Gone With the Wind*, but when he smiled it was like milk curdling. He set my teeth on edge. Lots of the other girls liked him and squabbled to talk to him backstage, but I knew he didn't give a fig for the others. I felt his eyes on my back all the time, like a shiver between my shoulder blades, and whenever he brushed against me, I felt like something had left a slimy trail.

It was 16 January – a Saturday – and the last rehearsal before we opened on Monday. I was sitting with Marko and Frieda in the auditorium, admiring the stage and watching an Italian firewalker sauntering through some flaming hoops. There wasn't a circus ring, just a huge long platform, curved at the front, with the thickest, heaviest curtains all ruched and fringed with gold tassels. When it came to Pa's turn there was no end to what he could do with the horses on a twenty-metre revolving stage: wheeling, dividing, threading. I could tell Fredy was impressed, particularly with Pa's act with the brown and whites, where Pa stood smoking a cheroot while the Shetlands arranged themselves like black and white keys on a piano.

My knees were jelly when it was my turn. I needn't have fretted. White Lightning's a professional and I was that proud of him, walking sideways, turning circles, then rising up on his hind legs, pawing the air as I held up numbers for him to add and take away. When I motioned him down with my whip, White Lightning bowed, going down on one knee, his foreleg extended so I could jump onto his back. Then in a jingle of harness bells, he carried me from the stage. I could hear the applause from the troupe wafting me backstage as I gave him his sugar cubes. Suddenly, there was Fredy Knie, hurrying up full of praise and shaking me by the hand. I'm sure he was like that with everyone but I didn't care. I felt like the star of the show.

Gypsy Trash

THE WIND WAS BITTER as I led White Lightning across the yard to the stables but I didn't feel cold. The Wintergarten was perfect. My act was perfect, and now the dress rehearsal was over, I was going to meet Max. His pa was holding a party at his house for some injured soldiers and Max was going to slip out and meet me in the lane. The Wintergarten doubled up as a picture palace and the manager had given us some free tickets for the film that evening – *Request Concert* with Isle Werner. Frieda and Marko were keen to go so it was a perfect excuse for me to get away. I had a bad headache, I told them. Would they mind if I saw them back at the apartment? They shook their heads. They only had eyes for each other.

It was peaceful in the stable. A wood fire burned in a huge brazier and the light from the oil lanterns pooled in a warm glow. *Typical Fredy*, I thought. *We might all freeze to death but there'd always be wood for the horses.* The stable was deserted. We'd run on late because of an air-raid siren that had turned out to be a false alarm, so Fredy had sent the grooms home. I spread White Lightning's blanket over his flanks and filled his nosebag from the trough, then breathed in deeply, enjoying my favourite smell of horse sweat, brass polish and old leather, and the comforting sounds of snorting and swishing tails. I reached up on tiptoe and traced my fingers down his white blaze and then I kissed his velvet muzzle until his nostrils quivered.

'Save all your passion for your horse, do you?'

I jumped out of my skin and White Lightning did too, his hind legs skittering in the stall. We hadn't heard Dario creeping up until he was right there, leaning casually against the wooden partition.

'I knew you were a hot little bitch, underneath that cool skin. I just wondered who you were saving yourself for.'

His eyes gleamed black in the darkness and there was a sour reek of beer on his breath as he stepped towards me, barring my exit. I tried to laugh, pretending it was just a joke, but my heart was thumping. Something in his face told me this wasn't a tease. I made a lunge past him, when suddenly he was on me, his hands on my bodice, tearing it down with a grunt. I tried to scream but his mouth came down on mine, our teeth crashing together as I tried to twist my lips away from his probing tongue.

'Don't mess with me, you little whore,' he snarled, trapping both my hands behind my back with one of his. Then he thrust his hips towards me hard. 'I know you want it. I've seen the way you look at me.' Then suddenly his hands were back on my bodice, pawing my breasts whilst his right knee pushed my legs apart, his mouth on mine. White Lightning whinnied. He knew something was wrong but he didn't know how to help. And then I had a sudden idea. I wrenched my head to the left, freeing my mouth to bite down as hard as I could on Dario's thumb. Then I pushed him with all my strength, screaming at the top of my lungs.

Dario stumbled back, crashing into a bucket of mash and sending it slopping. He was drunk, but not drunk enough. He scrambled up, his back against the partition, and stood glowering at me, head down like a bull. And then all of a sudden his face broke into a cruel leer. He held out his hand, blood snaking around the base of his thumb. 'D'you want to know a secret? Biting only makes me want you more. I love a wildcat . . . or should I say . . . a wild *gypsy*?'

The stable swung round and back again. I gasped, clutching the neck of my bodice, backing away from him as I pulled it up to cover my breasts. He was panting heavily, sweat beading his forehead. 'You can't fool me, *Antonia Escudero*, or whatever you like to call yourself. You're no more *Spanish* than Herr Hitler himself! Now, you lie down quietly, my beauty, and open your legs, or I go straight to Prinz Albrecht Strasse.' The street name meant nothing to me. He took a step forward, pinching me so hard under my chin that tears started in my eyes. 'I think Gestapo HQ might be interested in you. And you'll get worse than my cock between your legs if they get hold of you. And that's a promise.'

A rush of vomit rose in my throat and the shadows tilted as the stable rafters swung round to meet the floor.

'Is everything all right in here?' It was Fredy, picking his way across the straw, carrying a saddle, like an angel emerging through the lamplight. 'Who's there?'

'Er . . . it's Antonia. She must have fainted, Fredy,' I heard Dario say. 'I was just passing and I heard a cry, so I came to see what was going on. It's a good job I did. She might have got herself trampled . . .'

My head was throbbing. I gazed around, dazed, fingering a lump the size of a juggler's ball on my temple. 'I'll look after her, Fredy,' he said as if butter wouldn't melt. He began to help me up, and as he did he squeezed my hand, digging his nails into my palm. 'I'll see she gets home safely.'

I staggered to my feet, brushing strands of straw from my skirt. Dario grasped my arm, his fingers pressing so hard the blue marks would take days to yellow and fade. We made our way out through the foyer to the front of the theatre on the corner of Friedrichstrasse. His breath was hot on my ear. 'That was a lucky escape, *Zigeuner*, but don't think you've heard the end of this, *gypsy trash*!' And leaving me on the freezing corner in the snow, he swaggered off down the street, raising his hat in a cheery farewell.

I stood on the corner of Friedrichstrasse staring after Dario, numb with shock. A man brushed past me, chin buried in his coat, eyes on the pool of light cast by his shrouded torch. I leaped like a scalded rabbit, but he passed on by, hurrying into the foyer of the Wintergarten. I heard a train rumble over the huge iron railway arch and wheeze into Friedrichstrasse station, and the noise of slamming doors. I flicked a glance behind me, and then quickly turned right and began to stumble down Dorotheenstrasse, slipping and sliding along the glassy pavement, past block after block of grey buildings that seemed to lurch at me from the darkness, bristling with icicles sharp as daggers. At the end of the street the huge burnt-out bulk of the Reichstag loomed. I turned left and hurried on towards the Brandenburg Gate, draped in green netting and decorated with summer leaves like a mossy mountain.

The moon was high and almost full over the Tiergarten, a sad-faced clown peering between the snowy branches, gazing down on the snowdrifts piled against the bare black trunks. I shivered as I turned into the patchwork of shadows, feeling cold for the first time. In the shock of it all, I'd forgotten my coat.

Permanent Waves

ERIKA WAS THRILLED THAT Vati was holding a party for some wounded officers from the hospital. It was a welcome distraction to have something to plan for that didn't involve dragging sand buckets down to the cellar, and Erika and I had been busy rolling rugs and setting chairs against the walls, whilst Tante Ida made *Pflaumenkuchen* with some bottled plums and our pooled sugar rations. 'We'd have had hothouse chrysanthemums from Blumen-Schmidt's in the old days,' lamented my sister.

Tante Ida folded her lips. 'Really, Erika! You know that *all* flowers these days are reserved for funerals.'

Our maids, Mirka and Ludmilla, had made drop cakes with substitute eggs, substitute milk and saccharine from a folder of *sparrezepte* – economy recipes from the World War, and some nurses from the hospital had promised *ersatz* 'banana' sandwiches made with grated parsnips. Vati had surpassed himself with the drink. On our Christmas Day visit to the cellar to check the stirrup pump he'd brought up some bottles of his fine old Riesling and some Champagne he'd stockpiled after the fall of Paris. 'What's the point of saving it when the future's so uncertain?' he'd said. '*Carpe diem!* Seize the day!'

Gretchen thought he'd said *Karpfen* and got very excited that we'd somehow got hold of some fish, and Vati said, 'That's what comes of parading around waving flags and not going to school any more.'

By six o'clock I was ready to go downstairs. I knocked on Erika's door, gasping at the apparition that met me on the threshold. She giggled. 'This, my dear brother, is the new Wella Permanent!'

I was lost for words. I didn't know whether super-curly really suited her.

'Well, what's a girl to do these days? Tante Ida's surrendered our metal curlers for the war effort and pipe cleaners simply don't do the business.'

I sat down gingerly on her satin eiderdown, wondering how a butterfly could emerge from such a chaotic cocoon. There were clothes everywhere: silk petticoats, foamy nighties, stockings snaking from half-open drawers and a pungent smell of nail lacquer. 'If you wait while I put on my make-up, I'll tell you a funny story . . .'

She'd just had the permanent wave papers washed out of her hair at Fräulein Schneider's when the air-raid siren went off. The lady in the next chair started screaming, and who do you think it was? Frau Schneck, our snooping *Blockwart*, who'd just had the peroxide put on and was sitting with her hair in a plastic bag. And after all that the Führer had said against women using hair dye! Well, off they'd all scuttled across the road, trailing towels, to the safety of the U-Bahn – women in curlpapers, heads half-dyed or covered in foam. According to Erika, most ladies were more afraid of their hair going wrong than being caught in a raid, especially since we hadn't seen a bomb for fourteen months. There they'd all sat for half an hour, fretting until the All Clear sounded. And the entire time Frau Schneck pretended she hadn't recognized Erika. 'I'll have something to say next time Frau Schneck complains about my *nigger music*!' she giggled. 'Silly old goat!'

But then she grew more serious. Had I seen the new camouflage netting on the East-West Axis – a vast canopy of wire netting hung with strips of green gauze to make the road blend into the Tiergarten? And they'd painted the shiny golden angel on the Victory Column bronze so it wouldn't reflect the moonlight. What did it all mean?

Suddenly Frau Schneck's hair didn't seem so funny. My snakes had begun to move. I thought of Vati and the stirrup pump and the tin baths full of water in the cellar.

'Oh, come on, Max,' said Erika, straightening my tie. 'I didn't mean to spread gloom. Let's not spoil the evening.' So down we went together, but not before pinning another of our jokes on Gretchen's bedroom door.

Tante Ida was in the dining room arranging crockery and

glasses on our best damask tablecloths. 'New dress, Erika?'
she said with a disapproving glance at the new hairdo.

'Mmm,' said Erika, giving a twirl. 'From Khunen's.
Fräulein Spranger took it off the model in the window . . . in
return for the loan of your chinchilla. But don't worry. It'll
be back in the shop by tomorrow, and you can have your
coat back . . . more's the pity!'

She broke off as Gretchen stormed into the dining room
in traditional folk-costume. 'Who pinned this disgusting
notice on my bedroom door?'

Erika's face was all innocence. 'What notice might that
be?'

I decided this might be an appropriate moment to kneel
down on the parquet and start sorting records, concealed
behind the gramophone's brass horn.

Gretchen brandished the offending notice, quivering
with indignation. *BDM – BUBI DRUCK MICH!*

I'd enjoyed inscribing *SQUEEZE ME, BABY!* in large
gothic capitals four inches high. Safe in my hiding place, I
smirked in delight at my own wit.

'And that's only today's!' wailed Gretchen. 'There was
one yesterday too. *Bedarfsartikel Deutscher Männer.*'

Useful Things for German Men! How we'd laughed at that
one.

'And the day before it was *Brauch Deutscher Mädel.*'

That one was Erika's idea. *Make use of German girls!*

'It's got to be Max or Erika.'

Erika was frowning at Gretchen's waist, her head on one
side. She heaved a sigh. 'A circular skirt gathered onto a

waistband is a difficult shape for anyone to wear, Gretchen, dear,' she observed, winking in my direction. She held up her hands in mock surrender. 'I'm only trying to help . . .'

I crouched lower behind the brass horn, any feelings of guilt eclipsed by the joy of the moment. We'd had such fun devising saucy acronyms from the initial letters of the League of German Girls. We had another one up our sleeves for later. *Baldur Drück Mich! Take me, Baldur!* A reference to Baldur von Schirach, the ex-leader of the Hitler Youth. 'Gretchen asks for it,' we'd told ourselves over a shared *Himbeergeist*, a kind of fake vodka that nearly took the roof off our mouths. 'All that prating about having babies for the Reich . . .'

'Ah, there you are, Max,' said Gretchen, finally noticing me as I slipped Duke Ellington surreptitiously under a copy of Beethoven's Emperor Concerto.

'I'm sorting records for tonight,' I said airily. 'I'm removing the Mendelssohn and Mahler. And the Schönberg. We can't have any *Jewish* composers now, can we?'

Gretchen screwed our notice into a ball and flung it in my direction. 'This filth has got to stop. I don't care what you think! My den leader says I'm a credit to the BDM. I spent the whole afternoon learning how to put out incendiary bombs so the family won't burn to death.'

Gretchen stomped to the piano stool and started pulling out music, flinging it to the floor. I hugged myself with anticipated pleasure. Lili was coming round this evening after rehearsal. I could slip away easily without being missed, especially if the music went on long enough, and by the look of the pile at Gretchen's feet, she was planning a feast. I'd arranged to meet Lili in our usual place – the gate that led from our back garden into the lane behind. I could hardly wait.

Sweet Sue

SOME OF OUR GUESTS had spent months in hospital. I'd imagined the odd person on crutches, maybe a wheelchair or two, but the pile of sticks in the hall looked like kindling for a bonfire. 'Don't stare,' whispered my aunt, flashing a hideous grin at a man with his trouser leg pinned up over his stump. She was wearing my least favourite necklace – the chunk of amber with a real spider trapped inside.

Erika was looking pale, Mutti's borrowed pearls glowing warm against her white skin. She poured herself a second glass of Champagne and gulped it down in one. I knew what she was thinking. *If Georg ever does come back . . . might it be like this?* There were dark circles under her eyes. I felt sorry for her. I knew she'd imagined some dancing tonight. Maybe a bit of jazz if the parents retired to the drawing room but there wasn't much chance of a foxtrot with a soldier with only one leg.

This particular fellow was surprisingly jovial, given the circumstances. 'My right hand's done for too,' he declared, raising it in response to Erika's horrified stare. 'Three middle fingers froze off in Russia. But one can still hold a wine glass, ha ha! Just use your thumb and little finger . . . like so!'

Everyone was trying too hard to be cheery, as if by trying they'd convince themselves they really were. Erika swiftly refilled her glass. I could tell from the rising pitch of her giggle she'd already had too much, and people were still arriving. Some nurses had brought ten little sausages of dubious origin, each about the size of a grape, and some chalky red liquid they claimed was tomato soup but tasted like something you'd make in a chemistry lesson. Two young doctors brought a coloured paste called *Lachs Galantine* with a flavour like sawdust and half a bottle of an acid-tasting sauce. They propped an actual menu from Borchardt's, one of Berlin's finest restaurants, against the sauce bottle for a joke. Only Professor de Crinis, the director of the hospital, brought anything really edible, courtesy no doubt of his position in the SS: two jars of caviar, some real coffee, a tin of smoked herrings and a tube of Kolynos toothpaste for Mutti – a welcome change from our usual chalk and peppermint water, but not exactly something to soak up the alcohol. So it was hardly surprising that Vati's Champagne went straight to our heads. At first it loosened our tongues nicely. Everyone was grateful to Vati for the effort and Tante Ida basked in the compliments about her *Pflaumenkuchen*, but the faux jollity was short lived. As usual with too much alcohol and not enough food, there was trouble in store.

The man with the frostbitten fingers had been talking to Erika for half an hour and at first I thought all was well. I'd been making a special effort to top up glasses, especially his, as I felt sorry about his missing leg. But as I circled round once again I got the feeling things were not quite as jovial as they'd first seemed.

'The government does all it can to suppress the truth,' I heard him tell Erika loudly. 'Oh, some people out there in Russia remain loyal to the Führer but it's only a few fanatics . . .'

Mein Gott, I thought as I noticed the director's head swing sharply in the officer's direction.

'Do you know what I think?' he continued, raising his slurred voice even louder. 'The Third Reich is like a brightly painted carousel. Beautiful to start with, so on we all jump. Then it starts to go faster and faster until your head begins to whirl. You look desperately around for someone to stop it, and then at last you realize the ghastly truth. The man at the controls has gone insane!'

I watched with horror as the director approached in his black jacket, praying that Erika would keep her mouth shut. There was something deeply jarring about a doctor in an SS uniform, especially one approaching my tipsy sister.

'This is defeatist talk from an officer, Captain Hinkel!' said de Crinis, towering over the wounded soldier in his wheeled chair. 'You should be careful where you say that kind of thing . . .'

The director had an odd, heart-shaped face with a deep widow's peak and a strangely long nose. *A cold, hard face,* I remember thinking, *not like a doctor at all,* but then Vati said he was a psychiatrist. Maybe they were different from other doctors. Vati was at his elbow in a flash, refilling his glass. 'Come now, Professor. Surely wounded officers can be allowed a little moan when they've suffered so much for the Reich? Captain Hinkel is convalescing. He's been seriously ill. I'm sure a psychiatrist can understand the need to, er . . . more Champagne, Professor?'

I noticed with alarm that Erika was finding it hard to stand. *Why was Vati refilling her glass?* She slugged it down, almost in one, and then she gave de Crinis one of her most dazzling smiles.

'Who invited you?' she slurred. 'I mean really, *who* invited you?' She hiccupped twice. And then to my horror, my sister began to sing in English – a hit from the previous summer called *Sweet Sue*:

'*Every star above
Knows the one I love:
Sweet Sue, just you!*'

The blood rushed to my face. *Please, Erika, leave it there.* Some clever clogs had set the tune to German words. She'd sung the new version to me only yesterday. *Lieber Gott,* I thought as she lurched towards de Crinis, who was backing away, eyes wide with astonishment. And then to the tune of *Sweet Sue*, Erika began to sing:

> '*Lest das Mittagsblatt*
> *Lest das Tageblatt*
> *Alles Lüge, alles Dreck.*'

> *Read the midday papers*
> *Read the daily news*
> *All lies. All rubbish.*

And then she burst into hysterical tears. For once I was grateful to Tante Ida. She clapped her hands officiously, announcing the beginning of the entertainment, which was to start with Gretchen's song selection from *Wir Mädel Singen*. Vati seized de Crinis by the elbow and steered him hastily towards a chair, drawing up a table for his Champagne glass.

'My younger daughter . . .' I heard Vati say. 'The BDM songbook . . . lovely voice . . .'

I looked at my watch. Lili was due at the garden gate in ten minutes. This was pretty good timing. Nobody would notice if I slipped away. But first I needed to escort Erika to her bedroom before we all got carted off to Gestapo HQ.

The Hand
on My Shoulder

I'D NEVER SEEN the house on the other side of Max's garden wall. It's hard to remember, after you've seen something, what you imagined it would be like. Same as when I saw my first elephant. I'd pictured it for so long and it wasn't anything like I'd thought, but after I'd seen it I couldn't remember my picture any more. I think I imagined Max's house would be a bit like our apartment in Hackescher Markt, only a bit grander, with more rooms.

I knew it was wrong to open the garden gate. I'd always met Max in the lane at the back. He would slip out, shutting the gate quickly, before I had a chance to peep inside. Well, tonight I was going to see what he was hiding. I think it was the shock of what Dario had said to me in the stables.

Zigeuner! Gypsy trash! It had scared me at first but now I felt reckless. As if I knew our time was running out.

I suppose I'd pictured a sort of square garden, like the one we saw from our balcony. Well, Max's was like a fairy tale. Or that's how it looked to me. There was a little orchard at the bottom and a path snaking through it to a garden shed almost as big as our vardo, and then a flight of wide steps with big stone pots and beyond it the dark shape of the house, two floors tall, with grand, high windows reflecting a row of silver moons.

I couldn't believe my eyes. I thought of the tiny room I shared with Frieda in our wagon, the roof so close you could touch it, and the cracks in our windows stuffed with cardboard. I thought of our little apartment off Hackescher Markt, and how me and Frieda had run around flicking light switches on and off and trying out the taps. I suddenly felt very cold. Very cold and very small.

Music floated down the garden on a wave of laughter. Someone was singing badly in a thin, high voice. I dithered at the foot of the steps, and then crept closer, up past the urns and down a flagstone path towards the glittering windows. You'd have thought I'd be scared someone might see me, but I wasn't. I just had to see for myself.

Small chinks of light marked the outlines of the windows, except for a pane in the middle where a slice of light shone yellow on the snow. A curtain was moving inside the room, like someone was pulling it. 'A fifty-mark fine,' the false-teeth lady back at the apartment had told us, 'if you show a light in the blackout.' I held my breath as I crept up, then I crouched under the window, so low I could taste the snow on my tongue, and peeked inside.

I'd never seen so many glasses – crystal bowls on tall stems that glittered in the candlelight. There was a polished floor with blocks of wood in a zigzag design and bright, patterned rugs, silver candlesticks and a huge gleaming wireless with a front all woven with shimmering metal threads and golden knobs. And over in the corner, a big flat piano like the ones you see in films, with its lid propped up like a sailboat. Everyone was in uniform or long dresses and there was a man in that black uniform Pa said we should watch out for. What was one of them doing in Max's house?

For a minute I thought Max wasn't there and then he passed in front of the window, so close I could have touched him. He looked so handsome. Black suit, bow tie, shiny shoes, and his arm round a beautiful girl. She was tall and slim in a long green gown, her hair in crinkly waves like a film star. I swear my heart stopped beating. She was leaning against Max, her head on his shoulder. And as I stared, he bent towards her so his head was touching hers, and then he whispered in her ear, like she was the only person in the room he cared about. And then they passed through the door out of sight, the beautiful girl leaning on his arm so heavily he almost seemed to carry her away.

My heart was beating so loud now I thought they'd hear it in the room. Then suddenly my legs gave way and I sank to my knees in the snow, dropping my forehead on the icy windowsill as tears spilled between my fingers, burning my frozen cheeks. How could I have been so stupid? Why should someone like Max care about someone like me?

Slowly I stumbled away down the icy garden path. My thin circus boots had no grip and I skidded against one of the stone pots at the top of the stairs and bashed my shin. I was glad it hurt. Pain was good. It was something to take my mind away from the pain in my heart. Cold was good too. Maybe I could lie down in the snow and let it numb me till I fell asleep. I turned away from the fairy palace. There was a hollow space in my chest where my heart used to be. Of course our love was a fairy tale. A story from round the campfire that flares and crackles, but when you wake in the morning, you know it was only make-believe. Like Shon and Chakano – a tale, nothing more. My throat ached with tears. I closed my eyes and breathed in the cold night air. I used to tell Frieda after Rollo died that time would heal, but what did I know about broken hearts? Maybe it wouldn't always feel as bad as this . . . but just now . . .

I turned sharply at a footfall behind me. I didn't care any more if we were found out. I had nothing left to live for. I waited for the hand on my shoulder.

Cat's Cradle

'**Y**OUR SISTER!'

'Yes! Honestly, Lili. What do you take me for? Why were you spying on me, anyway? I was coming to meet you but my sister needed helping upstairs.'

I'd found Lili wandering in the orchard, a block of ice without even a coat. I was wearing Tante Ida's fur over my suit so I'd whipped it off and wrapped it round her shoulders and bundled her into our shed.

Herr Müller had certainly known how to make himself comfortable. There were wicker chairs with cushions, an electric lamp, a paraffin heater, a tin of biscuits with the Führer's face on the lid, half a packet of Trommler Golds. He'd even made little blackout curtains, rigged up on wires

– in case of bombs whilst tending his cuttings, I supposed. I stared around as Party circulars and tins overflowing with Party badges swam in and out of focus. I'd had too much Champagne myself.

Herr Müller's brown pillbox hat from his storm trooper days lay on top of a pile of plant catalogues, his brown jacket on a nail next to a picture of Hitler in red wax relief. I shifted the lawnmower to get to the biscuit tin, sending a huge pile of *Der Stürmer* magazines cascading to the floor. Three hideous hook-nosed faces adorned the top copy, peering down at a bloated baby with the caption: *Every Jewish infant grows up to be a Jew.*

Lili glared at me in silence and then she burst out again, her voice shaking with fury. 'There's one of those black uniforms in your house drinking wine . . . and this shed . . . packed full of Nazi stuff . . . even the biscuit tin! At least you're not in *your* horrible uniform tonight . . .'

I scowled back at her. I couldn't understand why she was so mad at me. 'The SS man is the director of the hospital,' I said defensively. 'This isn't fair. First you accuse me of having a girlfriend who turns out to be my *sister* and now you're suggesting . . . I've told you before. I'm in uniform because it's the law. It's not my choice.'

'That's stupid.'

'Well, that's just the way it is.'

'That's just the way it is,' she echoed. 'What do you want with me, Max? A dirty *Zigeuner*! You, with your fine house and dandy wine glasses! I could never fit into your life, and you know it. Why else do we meet in the lane at the back of your house?' She raised her arm aggressively upwards in a Nazi salute towards the Hitler portrait. '*Heil Hitler!*'

A bright wave of anger broke in my chest. I caught her hand in mine. 'Don't do that! It's not funny. Look, Lili! What have I done? Nothing's changed. So I happen to live in a big house. That's not my fault either.' I stepped towards her. Her hair smelled of hay and horses mingled with leather and her familiar rose perfume. 'And I can't help it if my father's boss happens to be in the SS. I never asked him to the party.'

She wrenched her hand away, her voice thick with contempt. 'There's a Romani saying: if you lie down with dogs you'll catch fleas.'

I took hold of her shoulders and shook her. She flinched and closed her eyes, turning her head away. I stepped back, ashamed of myself. 'It would be so much easier if . . .'

She stared at me with her seductive black eyes, angry and beautiful. 'So much easier if what . . . ? If you didn't want to kiss me, you mean? If you didn't want me so much?'

Then she leaned forward and brushed her lips hard against mine. Not a kiss. More of a challenge. And suddenly my arms were round her, pulling her close. I buried my head in the soft fur of my aunt's coat.

'Don't be angry, Lili. Don't.'

She leaned into me as I ran my hands through her thick, damp hair, kissing her throat, her neck and then lower, nudging aside the thin fabric of her blouse. She arched her back as I kissed the hollow between her breasts, my hands on her waist, her hips, her thighs. I shivered as she slid her cold fingers under my shirt. Still holding her against me, I dragged some cushions from the wicker chairs, making a bed on the floor, pulling her down with me and covering us both with the fur. And suddenly she was my Lili again, her silky-soft skin, her muscles hard as iron, her stomach smooth and flat under my hand.

'Don't be sad, Lili. There's no one in the world for me but you. Nothing will keep us apart . . .'

She smiled up at me, reluctant at first but then more warmly, just like that first time we made love, and just like the first time, her smile melted my heart.

'You're my Chakano,' I whispered.

She sighed in my arms. 'And you're my Knight of Wands.'

I think we must have slept. At least the wailing came from far away at first, growing louder and more persistent, a deep, keening lament. Lili was on her knees, eyes wide with terror in the light of the paraffin heater.

'Oh, Kali Sara! What's that?'

'Stay where you are!'

I opened the door just a crack, letting a knife blade of freezing air slide in. There it was again. The haunting wail of the air-raid siren – a menacing, angry howl.

'It's probably a false alarm, like this afternoon . . . my sister was at the hairdresser's having a permanent . . .'

Lili was at my side, gripping my hand. 'Hush . . . listen . . .'

I held my breath. There was no mistaking it. The distant thrum of aero engines . . . *throb, throb, throb* . . . growing louder and louder by the second, a dreadful rolling thunder getting nearer and nearer. I wrenched open the shed door and suddenly the whole sky was alight with searchlights, a cat's cradle of bright beams stabbing upwards like silver arrows into the sky. It was magnificent, thrilling and terrible . . . all at the same time. I peered at my watch. Eight o'clock exactly, and for once, not a cloud in the sky.

'The cellar, Lili. Let's go. We're not safe here . . .'

'The cellar?'

'It's the air-raid shelter for our street. Come on!'

'But –'

'Come on, Lili! This is real!' I was dragging her arm but she was standing firm, pulling back into the doorway.

'I'm staying here!'

'But you *can't* stay!'

'I can't go down there . . . not with *them*. I'm not going . . .'

Someone was shouting from the street. '*Lights out! Get that bloody light out! Turn off your gas! Leave doors and windows open!*'

Lieber Gott. The flak was already firing, like flashing birds up amongst the probing fingers of searchlights. I stared up at the house. I could hear the commotion inside: shouts, screams and sharp-rapped orders, the clatter of feet on the parquet and Siegfried barking. In some cool part of my mind I wondered how they'd get the amputees down to the cellar. They couldn't get wheelchairs down the steps, surely. I should be there to help. *Oh God!* I suddenly thought of Mutti. *What will she do when she finds I'm not there?*

The rumblings in the air were growing, rising in a thundering crescendo, then all of a sudden we saw them, a triangle of low-flying planes fast approaching, followed by another and then another, and then all hell broke loose. The earth trembled as if a thousand horsemen were drumming into Berlin. The huge anti-aircraft guns in the Tiergarten boomed into action as streams of heavy bomber formations swept over us heading west, their fighter escorts a mass of silver crosses caught in the searchlights. The roar of the guns so near our house was deafening, and then the aftershocks, like miniature earthquakes, one after another. *The best-defended city in the world!* That's what Göring had called Berlin. So how had the planes got through our famous double ring?

'Get back, Lili. It's too late,' I gasped, bundling her inside and slamming the door. I knew we might as well be in the garden for all the protection the shed would offer, but somehow it felt safer inside. There was a terrible crash and our only lamp went out.

Lili was trembling in strange little waves that came and went. 'Make it stop, Max. Make it stop!'

The whole shed lurched from side to side. We covered our heads at the sound of falling shrapnel, clattering down like deadly hailstones. The night was full of the scream of rockets, exploding shells, the shatter of glass. And somewhere in the distance I heard fire-engine bells. I hugged Lili close, my lips on her hair. 'They say if you can hear a bomb whistling down, it's not for you . . .'

For a long time after the last explosion there was silence, except for the sound of barking dogs and fire-engine bells.

And then the single constant tone of the All Clear and the blessed relief that brought tears flooding to our eyes. *It's finished. It's over and we're still alive.* I felt Lili relax against me, and then she struggled from my arms. After a second or two, I heard a match strike.

'What are you doing?'

The sulphur flared in her eyes. I could tell her hands were trembling as she struggled to connect flame with cigarette. She took a long, slow drag, inhaling deeply.

'I've never seen you smoke before . . .'

She laughed nervously. 'There's always a first time!'

Lili was badly shaken but she still had to go. She was frantic about her family and they'd be worried about her, and I was anxious about Mutti. I made her keep Tante Ida's coat and then kissed her goodbye at the gate, arranging to meet again after the show on Tuesday. We had tickets already, I told her, bombs willing. And I'd have eyes for nobody else, so she'd better give her best performance ever. I watched her disappear into the snowy shadows and then made my way back through the orchard, wondering how I'd explain where I'd been. Gretchen met me at the back door, her lips set in a thin hard line. I almost wept with relief to see her safe and sound. The feeling wasn't mutual.

'How could you be so *selfish*? Mutti is hysterical. Where've you been? And who on earth was that *girl*?'

I could hear people leaving by the front door. A flurry of goodbyes. The party, it seemed, was over. 'What girl?'

Gretchen's face looked ugly in the lamplight, her voice

heavy with contempt. 'Don't give me that rubbish, Max! We've just had an air raid with a house full of invalids and you were nowhere to be found. We could have done with your help but where were you?' She narrowed her eyes. 'What are you up to? Something you shouldn't be, I know that much. Something you don't want people to know about!' She turned on her heel and stalked into the house, pausing to look back over her shoulder. 'I saw you, Max. Don't think I didn't. I saw you at the garden gate.'

'But, Gretchen . . .'

She stopped again but this time she didn't look round. '*Gretchen, what?* If you wanted my friendship, Max, you could have had it. But you didn't. So don't start asking me to keep your secrets now.'

I made my peace with Mutti. I was smoking a cigarette in the garden, I told her, and I sheltered in the shed when the flak started firing. I tried to make up by helping clear away the glasses. As soon as I could, I slipped up to my room. I lay down on my bed but I couldn't relax. I was exhausted and confused and my head was aching from the Champagne. What had Gretchen said exactly? *Don't start asking me to keep your secrets now.* What had she actually seen? I sprang from my bed, darted across the room and wrenched open my desk. There was an empty space at the front where I'd left my diary that afternoon. I scrabbled towards the back of the drawer, then bent down and peered in.

My diary had gone.

Sunday Morning

THE SMELL OF REAL COFFEE wafted up the stairs from the kitchen as I came down for breakfast next morning. The director of the hospital was good for something at least. I'd had a sleepless night worrying about my diary, wondering what Gretchen was going to say and when she planned to say it. And on top of that I had a terrible hangover. I pushed open the kitchen door, waiting for all hell to break loose. Gretchen's place was empty.

My aunt smiled approvingly at the vacant seat. 'She's already left for the clubhouse to make straw slippers for the front. Typical Gretchen – up with the lark. That girl deserves a medal. I presume you're coming to Mass? Mutti might stay in bed . . .'

I breathed a sigh of relief. I would search Gretchen's room while she was away. Try to find my diary. Vati was reading the Sunday paper, the headlines two inches high:

AVRO LANCASTERS USED AGAINST BERLIN FOR THE FIRST TIME

A cowardly terror attack by the RAF against the German civilian population occurred last night. A bombers' moon made Berlin an easy target for the spineless air terrorists.

It had been a light raid, apparently, compared to cities further west. Two houses had been hit in Zähringerstrasse and a man killed by flak from our own guns. There was a photograph in the paper of the two buildings, furnished rooms exposed like dolls' houses, plaster hanging from the walls and a row of hooks with a dressing gown still dangling. A private life exposed.

'The siren was far too late,' complained my aunt. 'The planes were overhead before we could even think about getting to the cellar. I'll have to speak to Herr Müller.'

Vati sighed. 'I don't suppose Herr Müller holds the key to the siren control box.'

Erika still hadn't appeared downstairs although it would soon be time for Mass, but Rudi was ready, hair neatly combed, in his old loden coat and fox fur. 'Can Siegfried come down to the cellar next time there's an air raid? Can you get dog gas masks? Can you get parrot ones? I was worrying about Otto the whole time. I could hear him squawking . . .'

Tante Ida smoothed his head. 'Don't be silly, Rudi. Parrots aren't the same as dogs, but I'll certainly put Siegfried's spare basket down there so he'll feel more comfortable. Anyway, who says there'll be a next time?' She gave a nervous laugh. 'And even if there is, they'll have to do better than that if they're going to bring Berlin to its knees.'

Vati took off his reading glasses and folded the paper, laying it neatly next to his plate. 'You *really* think that's the best they can do, Ida? I think that was just a rehearsal. There'll be even more of the monsters next time. We can camouflage streets and lampposts, but we can't cover the River Spree for mile after mile. It will guide these new heavyweights right into the heart of –'

He broke off abruptly as Mutti walked in, white-faced, eyes red rimmed. I'd heard her weeping much of the night. He scraped back his chair and got up, putting his arm around her thin shoulders clad in shabby Sunday best. She smiled round weakly. 'I'm coming to Mass, after all.'

Vati squeezed her hand. 'Mutti and I have something to tell you. There isn't going to be a next time for some of you. Max and Erika are working, but Mutti is going to Bavaria with Gretchen and Rudi. I've been selfish. I should have sent them away weeks ago. Something tells me Berlin's got it coming, and the sooner we get them out of here the better.'

Rudi was jumping up and down with excitement. 'Can we take Siegfried?'

Vati smiled. 'As a special favour to you, my little Rudi,' he said, 'you can take that dreadful parrot too. Maybe Oma can teach him some Bavarian folksongs. I've certainly had enough of the *Horst Wessel* song to last a lifetime.'

I closed my eyes and sent up a silent prayer of thanks. *Vielen Dank, lieber Gott!* Gretchen was leaving Berlin!

Circus Knie

All trains out of Berlin were full until Thursday morning,
so I had three more days to worry about Gretchen.
I'd found my diary under her bed. Tante Ida had refused to
join Mutti in the exodus from Berlin, volunteering instead
for the new First Aid Squad operating from St Hedwig's.
'It's a shame about the delay,' she proclaimed, 'but at least
it means Rudolf won't miss the circus on Tuesday. Doktor
Goebbels is quite right to keep the theatres open – to show
everyone it's business as usual in the capital.'

'What if there's an air raid while we're there?' said Rudi.

'Then we'll use the Friedrichstrasse Underground, just
like anyone else who doesn't have a cellar of their own.'

Tuesday finally arrived – rainy but no more snow. I hadn't

seen Lili since the evening of the party. The troupe were busy getting ready for the opening night. We'd had another raid on Sunday but nothing on Monday. *What an odd life*, I thought. *Two nights of bombing, one night's reprieve, and we're off to the Wintergarten to see a circus.* 'They can't send those big bombers this far every night,' people reassured each other. 'We're just too far away.' Silence still from Gretchen, although she must have noticed I'd taken my diary back. If anything, she seemed to be avoiding me, her glance sliding away whenever I caught her eye. She's enjoying this, I thought – keeping me dangling on a thread. I felt like someone from the French Revolution, waiting for the guillotine to fall.

We hadn't been to the Wintergarten for some time and I noticed the peeling paint straight away. There was a shabby atmosphere inside the foyer too – frayed carpets and dusty plants. They'd done their best to cheer it up with circus posters. *Vollständig neues Programm!* screamed the huge colourful letters that snaked around a painting of a girl in scarlet ostrich feathers performing the splits on a high wire. *Completely new programme!* A clown with hinged hair that flicked up and down as he blew a horn was selling programmes outside the auditorium. Tante Ida purchased one to share, then, holding it above her head, ploughed through the sea of women, children and wounded soldiers to our seats in the stalls. I could hardly wait to look at the running order, so I took my chance as my aunt was fixing Rudi up with some opera glasses.

The Flying Meteors were first. That should be fun. I could enjoy the flying trapeze so long as it wasn't Lili up there. I might even watch through the opera glasses. *Chinese Plate Spinners* came next followed by *Dario Gallo – Schwertschlucker*. A *sword swallower*. How wonderful!

I scanned down the list, frowning as I reached the end of the first half. Two lines at the bottom had been scored through, but not so heavily you couldn't read the writing underneath: Florica and Fonso, *Spanish Flamenco* had been replaced by *Holländisch Klompendansen – Dutch clog dancers*. And *Die Brüder Orosco – die kleinen Leute von Córdoba* were replaced with Hungarian clowns from Budapest. My stomach clenched. *Die kleinen Leute? The little people?* Lili had told me there were dwarfs in their troupe, and weren't Florica and Fonso part of their troupe too?

My palms were sweating as I scanned the second half. A further three acts had been replaced by alternatives. Suddenly hundreds of bulbs began to dim and at a sign from the conductor, the orchestra launched into a jaunty German folk tune.

I squinted at the programme in the dying light. There was Lili's act: *Senorita Antonia and White Lightning – the Amazing Counting Horse* – scored through in black ink and replaced with *Polnische Volkstänzer – Polish folk dancers*. And then the lights went out.

I don't remember leaving the stalls, just the feeling of panic. Somehow I reached the stage door, hardly knowing how I'd found my way. I banged with my fists on the peeling paintwork. *Thump thump thump!* I stepped back and took a deep breath. *Calm down, Max. There must be some explanation*. And yet deep inside, my familiar snakes were writhing. I banged again, tears of frustration starting in my eyes. *Thump thump!*

A young man wearing the back end of a zebra costume opened the door with a flourish. 'Someone's in a hurry,' he said, taking a bow. '*Wunderzebra* at your service. Well, half of one, anyway, but the most important half.' He laughed and then frowned when I said why I'd come. Yes, he knew the Spanish troupe, he said. It was all very odd. I'd better come in.

'What's odd about it?' I demanded, almost shaking the zebra from his costume. The ringmaster was summoned.

'Fredy Knie,' he said, holding out his hand. 'What can I do for you?'

He was really too busy to speak to me but he snatched a moment when he realized why I'd come. Did I know anything about them? he asked. He seemed more puzzled than angry, although he'd had to do some last minute juggling for the show to go on. Five matinée acts hadn't turned up yesterday for the opening performance. He'd had to borrow some stunts from his brother at the Scala, but they were needed there this evening so acts were going to have to double up. He scratched his head. He just couldn't understand it. They were an excellent troupe. Very talented. And they'd left their horses behind too. Shetlands, and some beautiful Lipizzaners – abandoned in the stables! 'Something's not right,' he said, scribbling an address down on the edge of my programme.

10 Rosenthaler Strasse, off Hackescher Markt.

He snatched up his whip and hurried off. He hadn't time

to talk right now, he called over his shoulder, but if I found out anything about them, he'd be glad to hear it.

A strange little concierge fished her false teeth from a glass on the counter. 'Yes, this is ten Rosenthaler Strasse,' she said, munching her dentures into place, 'but they're not here now.'

A flicker of hope flared. 'When will they be back?'

She shook her head. 'They won't be back . . . ever. All gone.'

I stared at her. '*Where* have they gone? When was this?'

'Sunday night, a couple of hours after the All Clear. The Gestapo came and took them away. They weren't Jews, I don't think, but they still got took.' She shook her head. 'They were nice people . . . but you don't mess with the Gestapo when they come . . .'

'*The Gestapo!* Where did they take them?'

She held up her hands in a hopeless gesture. 'You think the Gestapo are telling me?'

'What number?' I shouted. 'What number apartment?'

'They're not there I tell you!'

I turned on my heel with a sob and began to run across the cobbles. I could hear her calling after me. 'Fourth staircase . . . use the stairs . . . the lift is broken . . . but you won't find them . . .'

The door of the apartment gaped open, hanging crookedly by one remaining hinge. I flicked the light switch illuminating the single bare bulb. Tattered chairs lay on their sides. Drawers had been pulled from a chest, vomiting their contents. I raced through the rooms. The bath was full of shoes and a tap was dripping, following the line of a dirty brown stain. My throat was aching, that horrible feeling when you're trying to hold back tears. I heard Lili's voice in my head. *It's like a palace. Lights come on from a switch on the wall and the water comes out of a tap*. I sank to my knees on the torn linoleum, resting my head on the bath. Great sobs rose up from my chest, tears splashing down my cheeks and dripping onto the pile of worn out shoes. 'Lili. Please, Lili. Don't leave me again.'

I turned at a wheezing breath. The little concierge was holding her side. 'A truck stopped outside and six men leaped out, leaving the engine running. I couldn't keep up. By the time I got here they'd burst open the locks. They had an axe and everything! The bell got stuck from too much pressing and I could hear it, ringing, ringing – long after they'd taken them away.' She gazed around the devastated room. 'All this mess. And no workmen left in Berlin . . . and no materials for even the smallest repairs.' She picked up a red leather strap from the floor and handed it to me. It was part of a horse bridle, decorated with silver bells. 'They were theatre people, I reckon. Foreign accent but very polite. Spanish, maybe. They definitely weren't Jews . . .'

The afternoon light was fading over Rosenthaler Strasse and it had started raining again. I pushed the circus bells into my pocket and pulled out the programme, as if staring at it might bring Lili running down the road, laughing and telling me it was all a mistake. I couldn't believe it. *The Gestapo!* What could I do against them? I could hardly march to Gestapo HQ and demand the release of my Romani girlfriend! Fear spread through me like blood through water. There were rumours about Gestapo interrogation techniques, and they didn't bear thinking about. I felt totally helpless. I knew nobody of any influence in the Nazi hierarchy, let alone the Secret Police. There was nothing I could do.

Huge pellets of rain fell from the grey sky, splattering on the cheap paper of the circus programme. The ink began to smudge, bright green running into the vivid red, mixing together and trickling down, like tears of dark blood.

My sister's face was pale.

'You've done a *terrible* thing, Gretchen! What right had you?' Tears sprang to her eyes. She put her arm up defensively, as if she thought I might hit her. 'Oh, don't play the victim with me, you little beast! Do you have any idea what you've done?'

Tears glittered in her eyes. 'I . . . I haven't done anything. I only read your diary!'

'*Only read my diary*, you little liar! You did more than that.' I took a step towards her. She flinched.

'I didn't! I didn't tell anyone. *You're* in the wrong, Max, not me, but I *didn't* tell on you.'

I glared at her, shaking my head. 'I don't believe you, Gretchen. It's just the kind of low down, interfering, priggish, self-important . . .' I stopped, breathless. I'd run out of adjectives. ' . . . *Gretchen* thing to do!' I turned on my heel. I was shaking with fury. 'You've not heard the end of this, but right now I'm leaving this room, because if I don't . . . I swear . . . I might . . . wring . . . your . . . bloody . . . neck!'

Echoes in the Wood

THERE WAS A HUGE BOMB CRATER in Tiergartenstrasse and beside it a grinning dead horse. I rode round it in a large loop and then off down Budapester Strasse towards the Ku'Damm, pumped up with newfound hope. It had come to me in the middle of my sleepless night. It was just possible the Gestapo had questioned the troupe and then let them go. So as soon as I'd finished my post round, I'd cycled to Rosenthaler Strasse to check they hadn't returned. No, they hadn't, the concierge told me, without even bothering with her teeth. 'It's three days,' she lisped, 'since they were took.'

I was undeterred. Lili used to say her pa could talk his way out of a pair of handcuffs, so why shouldn't he manage it this time? Entertainment was essential to keep up morale, so our Propaganda Minister said. It didn't make sense to arrest them. They were just circus people, working for the war effort. Her pa will have explained it. They'd now all be free as birds . . . Or would they? A memory of that horrible little book of Rudi's stirred in my mind – *Hitler and the Gypsies*. I shook my head, trying to dispel the image. No. It wasn't possible. Hadn't Lili told me their Spanish disguise fitted them like a glove? But then again, Gretchen had read my diary. Oh God! What had I written in it? If my stupidity . . . my carelessness had harmed Lili, I'd never forgive myself. But hadn't Lili told me often enough that they were safe in the circus? *Nobody cares who you are*, she'd said. But how could she have been so sure? And if Gretchen really had betrayed me, what had she told them? I pedalled furiously, taking the road out to the Grunewald, my hopes, once high, now back down in my boots. But on the other hand, I thought, sweat trickling between my shoulder blades, maybe Gretchen was telling the truth after all. The previous night I'd been sure she was lying, but hadn't she sworn she'd only *read* my diary? Nothing more. I swung wildly between despair and hope. Gretchen was an infuriating little prig, but she'd never been a liar. I pedalled faster still, my wilting hopes rekindled. I'd *definitely* find them all back there, I convinced myself. I felt sure of it. Somehow or other I'd get to see Lili. Just as long as they hadn't decided to up and leave Berlin . . .

I parked my bicycle in the usual place, under the holly tree at the side of the station, next to the freight yard where I'd seen the Jews, and pushing that uncomfortable image from my mind, I raced through the tunnel to the back of the station and plunged into the forest. The sound of rushing water told me I was close to their camp, near to the Hundekehle Lake. The temperature had risen and the snows were turning to slush, filling the river with meltwater. I kept stopping, stretching my ears for telltale sounds, listening for something different from the usual restless noises of the woods. Then I heard a strange sound. It was a high-pitched whine, almost like a baby's cry. I broke into a run, weaving through the trees, beating back the naked branches that bent and whipped, following the intermittent sound until the trees began to thin out into bushes. In a moment I'd catch a whiff of wood smoke and hear the sound of fiddle music, the clattering of cooking pots, the sharp cry of a hungry baby. Hope beat in my heart. Soon I'd emerge into a clearing and see their high-wheeled wagons sprawled out in a hollow . . . and then somehow or other I'd find Lili.

There was a strange smell, sweet and rotten, like overripe mangoes. About twenty dead dogs lay scattered around the clearing, legs askew, black tongues lolling. It seemed they'd been shot as they ran between the brightly coloured wagons that now lay smashed and splintered, their wheels upturned and pointing skywards. Everywhere iron pots and pans lay in disorder, broken musical instruments, flowered eiderdowns and mangled birdcages strewn on the ground between the ashes of burnt-out fires. I heard the cackle of a magpie deep in the wood, the harsh screech of a jay, and then the silence gathered in again, eerie, brooding, giving nothing away.

'Is there anybody here . . . here . . . here . . . ?'

The magpie's cackle answered my echo, and then as I stooped down to pick up the jagged scroll of a broken violin, I heard that desolate cry again.

Only one of the wagons was still upright. It was a deep azure blue, decorated all over with silver moons and astrological symbols. *Sara Escudero*, snaked the words on the side. *Fortunes read. Futures foretold. 20 pfennigs.* Its side was smashed in and the deep purple door hung askew on its hinges. There was an iron horseshoe above the door with the rusty nails still in, prongs pointing upwards like Lili said they should, to keep the good luck in. A pack of brightly painted cards lay scattered on the threshold, some face down, their purple and silver backs muddied with dirty boot prints, others face up, revealing their strange, luminous pictures, and tied to the bottom step was the source of the whimpering sound. A bundle of white fur lay on the cold ground in a puddle of congealed blood.

I prised the horseshoe from the doorframe with the blade of my dagger and dropped it in my saddlebag beside the broken violin scroll, collected up the tarot cards and slipped them into their muddy silk bag, then I took off my jacket and made a nest for the small white dog in the bottom of my bicycle basket. I rode home gently, careful not to jolt the basket, trying to avoid the bumps in the road, blinded as I was by tears.

Total War!

G RETCHEN HAD GONE to the country, and for the next two weeks I distracted myself with frenzied activity: making my post round, clearing rubble with the Hitler Youth, checking the Wintergarten stage door twice a day for any news of *The Spanish Troupe* as they called the missing acts. I'd grown quite friendly with the back end of the *Wunderzebra*, sharing the information I had with him, and hoping for some in return.

'Turns out they were gypsies, not Spaniards,' the *Wunderzebra* informed me one day. 'When I told Fredy Knie what you said about the Gestapo coming for them, he went straight over to Prinz Albrecht Strasse himself to find out what was going on. Camped outside Gestapo HQ till someone agreed to see him. Nearly got himself arrested as well. 'You should be careful who you employ in your circus in future,' they'd told him. 'Or else that special permit you've got from the German Ambassador won't last you five minutes!' But they wouldn't tell him what had happened to the troupe, and you don't argue with the Gestapo. It don't sound too good to me.'

When I wasn't bothering the *Wunderzebra*, I spent my time nursing the little dog back to health. As I'd cycled home from the ravaged campsite that day, I'd had a wager with myself. If I could save the dog, then Lili would be safe, as if by saving its life I could draw her back to me. The dog had lost a lot of blood but miraculously the bullet had passed right through from chest to shoulder, missing the vital organs. Shadow, as I called him, was a clever little thing, with thick white fur, brown eyes and a curly tail, and as he gained strength each day and followed me around, I convinced myself that soon I'd hear from Lili. But late at night I'd climb the attic stairs and stand on the shrapnel-covered rooftop and stare out over the darkly wooded Tiergarten. And then I'd feel that I was sliding towards an abyss. I still nurtured a dream that one day I'd pass the Wintergarten and see a freshly painted billboard: *Senorita Antonia and White Lightning – the Amazing Counting Horse.* But when the silence of days stretched into weeks, my hopes began to wither.

And then Stalingrad fell.

We were deeply shaken but not surprised. The radio announcers had been softening us up for days – '*General*

Paulus warns Hitler that the situation is hopeless. The Sixth Army is clinging to the ruins of Stalingrad' – little by little paving the way for the bombshell that fell on the afternoon of 3 February. The programme I was listening to that afternoon was interrupted abruptly for a special news announcement.

'After a crucifying struggle, the German Sixth Army has laid down its arms. Our beloved Führer has declared three days of national mourning. Heil Hitler.'

Three hundred and thirty thousand German soldiers killed at Stalingrad. And, for once, even Doktor Goebbels couldn't hide the seriousness of the defeat. The tide had turned. 'The God of War,' announced our Führer, 'has gone over to the other side.'

I don't know whether knowing or not knowing was worse for Erika. Every day she greedily scanned the papers, blighted with little black crosses, each one recording the death of a much-loved husband, brother, son. 'A few say fiancé,' said Erika, a catch in her voice, 'but we weren't even engaged.' I said she was jumping the gun. We should wait and see.

Erika received the news from Georg's grief-stricken mother. A shell had hit his tank at Lisichansk. Three days later the notice appeared in the *Deutsche Allgemeine Zeitung*. Georg had received the Iron Cross, an image of the posthumous medal appearing above the announcement:

Georg von Breuning
Killed in action during heavy fighting around Stalingrad
on 1 February, our beloved only son. He died as he had

lived, a brave Lieutenant and Company Commander and a faithful Catholic.

I don't think I'd ever known Georg's surname, although he'd spent enough time smooching to *In the Mood* on the gramophone at our house. How must it feel, I thought, for a mother to lose her only son? Two weeks later his mother brought Georg's last letter addressed to Erika. She'd found it in his jacket pocket when it was returned to her in a brown paper package stamped in red ink with the words, *Died for Greater Germany.*

Darling Erika,
If I ever get out of here, I'm going to ask you to marry me. One thing I've realized being in this hellhole is how precious ordinary life is. And if you say yes, we'll have Benny Goodman at the wedding, and to blazes with what our Führer thinks of American jazz!

'*Totaler Krieg!*' screamed Goebbels two weeks later to a packed audience in Berlin's Sportspalast. *Total War!* Hitler's Propaganda Chief was a magician, once again pulling a rabbit out of a hat. How could an ever more bitter struggle be presented as a triumph? And yet the people were all on their feet, roaring and waving their hands in the air.

'Do you want total war? For the salvation of Germany and civilization?'

'*Ja! Ja! Ja!*' they cried in hysterical frenzy.

Little Doktor Goebbels raised his arms in the air. '*Nun,*

Volk, steh auf, und Sturm bricht los!' he shrieked. *People, rise up and let the storm break loose!*

Two weeks later, 1 March 1943, the bombers came for us again, two hundred and fifty this time – the deadliest raid yet on Berlin, making the raid on the night of the party look like a children's firework display. The sky burned scarlet for three whole days, trees in the Tiergarten split as if by lightning, and a shell had fallen in the zebra compound of the zoo, killing all the poor creatures but one. Unter den Linden was hit. Friedrichstrasse, Wilhelmstrasse – all a sea of flames. And our own St Hedwig's Cathedral completely destroyed, its beautiful domed roof collapsing like a punctured balloon. And our beloved Frau Günther from the sweet shop was dead. She'd been working in the soup kitchen when the bomb hit. 'There's another angel in heaven,' said Vati, tears streaming down his face. 'I just hope God likes liquorice.'

Oh, and they bombed the Wintergarten Theatre too that night. I sent up a silent prayer of thanks that wherever my Lili was, at least she'd not been there. And nor had Fredy Knie. He'd escaped unscathed with all his animals. *Wunderzebra* included.

A Garden in Berlin
April 2013

THE CIRCUS BELLS gave one last silvery tinkle as Max placed them in the suitcase. There weren't many of his precious things left on the green table now. He picked up the violin scroll, cupping his left hand around the curled wood, then, extending his right arm at shoulder height, he raised his bow, making sweeping gestures across the phantom violin as the strange, forgotten music filled the garden. He paused, his right hand still hovering above the imagined strings and, smiling sadly, stared into the trees. There was a shadow where no shade should be.

'You never heard me play, did you, Lili?' he said. 'I was pretty good.'

'*So was I. You never heard me either. But I wasn't as good as Pa.*'

'We were going to play together, remember?'

'*One of the many things we never did . . .*'

The sun was past its height. Max shivered. He'd like to fetch his coat but the shadows were lengthening and there was no time to waste. He placed the broken scroll of the violin and the diary in the case beside the circus bells. Heaving a deep sigh, he picked up the last but one of his most precious things. A black triangle of coarse fabric the size of a fist lay on his palm, the letter Z roughly stamped in the centre. Gently he pressed the faded cloth to his lips. Then placing it on his lap he slowly unfolded a rectangle of cheap paper, smoothing it out on the garden table. Lili's face stared out at him from the portrait, a sky-blue kerchief wound around her dark hair, her eyes deep pools of pain.

There was a tremble in the leaves but no breeze. 'I tried to find you, Lili,' said Max. 'I thought Shadow would be my talisman. I thought if I nursed him back to health his strength would draw you back to me.' He smiled at the memory. 'Such a clever little dog! He could walk on his hind legs, you know.' Tears brimmed on the red rims of his lower eyelids. He pressed his hand to his heart, breathing deeply. 'Yes, he was a smart little fellow was Shadow. I loved him so much, but there are limits even to what love can do.'

PART THREE

RUMOURS OF DEATH

Marzahn Camp
Berlin – March 1943

MARZAHN CAMP WAS A FILTHY dump of shacks surrounded by barbed-wire fences on the edge of Berlin, squeezed in between a sewage dump and a cemetery. At first Pa thought there'd been a mistake, so he asked a guard to get a message to Fredy Knie. He was frantic about us not showing. The guard just spat in his face. And then Ma and Baba Sara turned up with the others from the Grunewald. Soldiers had gone to our forest camp and smashed our vardos, stolen our wagon horses and shot the dogs, just like in those stories Pa had heard when we were on the road. Baba Sara had almost got herself killed trying to save Pali's little dog that was tied to the steps of her vardo.

There'd been no mistake. Someone had betrayed us.

Blown our cover as the Spanish troupe, and it didn't take me long to figure out who that might have been. I blamed myself for what had happened. But what should I have done? Go with that Dario and let him do what he wanted with me? I knew I should have told Pa what had happened to me but I was ashamed, and anyway I hadn't really believed Dario meant what he'd said. But there was another reason I blamed myself too. And for that I hadn't an excuse. You see, I just hadn't been thinking straight, that was my problem. I'd been that obsessed with me and Max, with no room in my head for anybody else. So even when Dario threatened me, I hadn't taken his warning seriously . . . and now it was too late.

After we'd been in the camp a few weeks, a nice young woman visited us. We called her *Loli Tschai, the red-haired girl*, and we liked her at first. At least, she was nicer than the camp guards. *Loli Tschai* was a missionary, or that's what she told us. 'Call me Schwester Eva,' she said. She was a pretty lady, neatly dressed with lots of papers that she kept in a leather case, but she never talked about God or gave us Bibles. She just asked hundreds of questions and wrote the answers down and then she gave us sweets. She even gave Ma a calendar with pretty pictures of the countryside. Pa was like a dog with two tails. He loved talking about himself, so he prattled on for hours: where we came from, where we'd travelled, what circus acts we all did. Ma said he was blathering but Pa said it would help get us out of this place with only two holes in the ground for you-know-what!

One day *Loli Tschai* brought us some difficult puzzles.

Pa told us girls to do them double quick so she'd maybe give us jobs outside the camp. So we tried our best. I even did 364 x 50 really quick in my head. I can see Pa now, beaming from under the brim of his big felt hat. 'If you can find smarter girls I'll eat my shoes,' he said. 'I always sent 'em to school when I could.'

But Schwester Eva wasn't a bit pleased. You should have seen her face when she turned away. I could see the back of her neck, all red and angry. I felt sorry for Pa. He'd been that proud of us.

The last time we saw her, she brought a box of needles to take our blood and then she measured our heads with calipers. Then she held a chart with glass eyeballs against our faces and wrote the colour down. We found out later she was a kind of scientist. She was writing something for Hitler about how gypsies weren't as clever as Germans and shouldn't be allowed to breed. Then I knew why she'd been mad about the puzzles. Pa couldn't credit it. He said she was very wicked, pretending to be working for God when she was really working for Hitler.

I don't know what was worse – the stink of sewage, the terror of ghosts, or sharing two standpipes for water. And I couldn't sleep for worrying. What did Max think when we didn't show at the Wintergarten? He just wouldn't understand what had happened. He'd be frantic. I racked my brains about how I could send him a message. I was worried about White Lightning too. He'd be missing me. At least I could trust Fredy to look after him until they let us go. But Max had no one to turn to. He wouldn't know who to ask. I nagged the camp guards. When would they let us go?

A helpful Sinto told us it wouldn't be soon. He couldn't make head nor tail of it either. He'd lived in Berlin all his life. Worked for the civil service, and his wife was a teacher in a kindergarten in Potsdam – until last month when the Nazis arrested them. They were just ordinary German citizens, he said. 'Not like you lot.' He wasn't unfriendly. He just couldn't understand why they'd been lumped in with us travellers, although, looking round, it seemed there were more Sinti than us.

All the same, more vardos kept arriving and we met up with some old friends we hadn't kept company with for years. There was even a small travelling circus – Romanies from Turkey – with two curly-tailed monkeys that scampered round with a hat begging and a big brown bear with tattered fur that danced to a tambourine. 'Why are we here?' we all asked. 'What have we done wrong?' Nobody knew anything, except there'd been a gypsy camp here for years, ever since Berlin held the Olympic Games back in 1936 and they'd had a clean up of the city.

Then one morning in March Pa burst into our shack with news. I'd known there was something afoot because we'd seen soldiers arriving in trucks. 'I told you it would be all right, Ma. Everything's *kushti*!' he shouted. 'We're going!'

'Going where?'

Pa looked unsure. 'Where?' he called to an SS officer striding by.

The black uniform waved his Luger at Pa like he was a bothersome gnat. 'To work in the east. A new life. New homes. Quick! Quick! The trucks are waiting.'

Pa opened his arms wide then flung them round Baba Sara as she sat on a bucket, plucking a partridge she'd earned from reading palms for one of the guards. He was laughing for the first time in weeks. 'What did I tell you? It's been a terrible mistake. The police chief must have got my letter. It's like Ma always says. I can talk my way out of a room with six padlocks!'

Baba Sara swung the balding pink body over to her other knee with a slap. 'But *where* in the east? If it's a mistake, why don't they just let us go?' She clutched Pa's arm. 'It don't seem right to me, Josef.'

'Do as they say,' said Pa sternly, picking feathers off his sleeve. 'We're getting out and that's what matters. It can't be worse than here, so hurry up before they change their minds. One bag each, they said. And don't forget the fiddles. We'll need those to work when we get there.'

'Wherever *there* is,' muttered Ma.

Baba Sara heaved herself to her feet, looking pretty shaky. She'd had a bad winter and her chest rattled like peas in a jar. 'Lili! Frieda!' she croaked. 'Run round the family. Make sure everyone's got the message.' A violent fit of coughing rearranged the peas.

Pa squeezed her shoulder. 'We'll be all right now, Mother. The first thing we'll do when we get there is put that cough right.'

I could tell Baba Sara wasn't happy, but she wouldn't speak against Pa. Pa was all of a doodah, stuffing his poacher's pockets with his best things: his pipes, his tinderbox, his tin whistle. 'Tell them to hurry,' he called after Frieda, who was already running across the icy ground. I wasn't far behind, bootlaces trailing, weaving between groups of soldiers with those snarling wolf dogs. Everyone was running from their hovels like ants from a poked nest.

'Nano Florian,' I panted. 'Have you heard? We're leaving! Tell one of the girls to run to Florica's.' I raced across the camp, knocking on more doors, delivering the same message. 'We're leaving Marzahn! Free at last!' Had it really been only two months? It felt like years. But where were we going? My stomach double flipped. What if it was far away from here? And I still hadn't got a message to Max.

As I walked back across the icy scrub I could see more trucks arriving and SS jumping down with rifles. I took a deep breath and watched the air turn white. It was still very cold, though the calendar said it was March. As I pushed open our door I felt suddenly giddy. I steadied myself on the bin outside. I hadn't had breakfast. Maybe that was the problem.

Ma appeared from the back of the shack, her sewing machine in her arms. 'Pa said no sewing machine but I told him: *no sewing machine, then no fiddles!*'

I heard Pa laugh as he loomed at her shoulder, a kitbag on his back and two fiddles in their battered old cases. He frowned when he saw me. 'What's the matter, Lili? You look like you've seen a ghost.'

I suddenly felt so tired. As if I'd just climbed a mountain. 'I'm feeling a bit peaky, that's all. It must be all this rushing around.'

Frieda ran in behind me. 'What's the matter with Lili?'

'She's off-colour,' Pa said. 'I hope she's not coming down with something.' He clicked his tongue. 'Those filthy toilets . . . I wouldn't be surprised.'

I was trying to act normal, though all the time I was doing my best not to puke. 'Are you sure you're okay?' said Frieda. 'You look awful green.'

I was feeling worse by the second. 'It's probably my time of the month,' I said. 'Just my luck.'

There was a silence. Frieda was staring at the calendar that Schwester Eva had given Ma. I still remember the picture for March – bright blue gentians, poking up through the snow. Frieda flipped it back to the month before. Snowdrops – huge drifts of them under the bare trees. 'How d'you mean, Lili?' she said slowly.

I took a deep breath. I wished Frieda would shut up prattling. Spit was gathering in my mouth, like it does when you're going to be sick. I could feel Frieda's eyes boring into me.

'Well, it can't be that,' she said. 'It must be something you've eaten. We always bleed at the same time and I finished mine a week ago.'

The silence beat in my ears as Frieda's words sank through me like a pebble tossed in a pond, sending out ripples far wider than you'd reckon for a stone so small. The tin walls of the shack swam and suddenly I felt like a great hole had opened up and I was hurtling down it, as something I'd not even let myself think dawned in my brain. I'd felt so tired lately. I'd put it down to the troubled dreams I'd been having – about Max and being lost in huge houses where people find me in places I shouldn't be. I'd hardly slept for thinking of him and our stupid impossible dreams.

And now from far away I hear Max's voice in my head. 'Lili, we must be careful. You know –'

I'd put my finger to his lips. 'I'm a Romani, don't forget. I know my phases of the moon . . .'

And suddenly I knew. I could hear Frieda's voice far away as if she was under water, or maybe it was me who was drowning. 'Ma! Come quick. Lili's fainted!'

Devil Wagon

A RAILWAY STATION late at night, somewhere out north of Berlin, surrounded by warehouses and factories with the windows smashed in. 'Why so far out?' wondered Pa.

There was a huge Z chalked on the side of the wagon they stuffed us in – about eighty to a single wooden box. 'Hey, steady on,' shouted Pa. 'You can't cram any more in here!' But you don't argue with a soldier with a rifle. 'We can't be going far squashed like this,' said Pa, finding a corner for Baba Sara to sit and making a kind of bench for Pali and Tamas from a pile of bags. 'Jump up, you two. Little people could get crushed. You can hold the fiddles. Make sure they don't get trod on.'

Nano Florian made a stirrup with his hands for the dwarfs

to clamber up and then he lifted Florica's two *chavvies* to sit with them. Baba Sara was scared of the *devil wagon*, as she called the train. She'd never even sat on a bus.

At first there was chatter – people fretting about where we were going. Folks from the camp were just pleased to be going somewhere different, but some Sinti who'd only just been arrested were blabbing on about their apartments. Had they locked the door before they left? Who would feed the cat? Would the milk go sour on the doorstep? Then as day turned to night and then another day of hunger with the *chavvies* always crying, they forgot the small things and the fear started niggling in. It didn't seem right to be going so far. Why no food? Where were we really going?

'We're like cattle,' said Ma. 'They don't see the signposts either.'

Pa's face was grim. 'You'd treat cattle better than this!' he raged, one time when we'd stopped. 'Nobody told us we were going this far.' There were tiny slits where the air came in and Pa was shouting through. 'At least cattle get water.' Every time the train stopped he'd bang on the door. 'Water! Water for the *chavvies*. Open up! You can't do this.' Nobody came. The train blew its whistle. Its boiler hissed louder and it was off again, screeching through the night like a huge iron beast. Ma said it sounded like a cry for help.

For days we squatted in that animal wagon, so tired we could hardly stand, our skirts and trousers soaked with the foulness that soon began to spill over the rim of the tin buckets we'd been given for you-know-what. It swished round our feet, flowing from side to side like a river. By now we were thirsty like you can't imagine, our tongues like dry old meat.

'Hey, you,' shouted Pa to a soldier who appeared at a crack in the door. 'A drink for my mother. For God's sake, have a heart.' He thrust his hat through the tiny gap in the sliding door. 'Hey! Come back. Fill this for me!'

In all my life, I'd never felt so ill. The stink, the crush of bodies. Just one time, only one, a soldier took Pa's hat and filled it up, but by the time he'd squeezed it back through the gap the water had spilled everywhere, but people still lunged forward. One man started licking the brim. 'Spare a drop. Just a mouthful.' And the train set off again, the carriages lurching on with a groan of parched throats and dry tongues.

How much longer? I laid my head against the wooden slats and closed my eyes, beginning once again the pointless counting up of days. When was the last time I'd been with Max? Seven weeks? Eight? Was it really so long?

Baba Sara moaned in the dark. Someone was snoring. Would I ever sleep again?

I put my hand on my belly, as if by feeling I'd know for sure. And then I went over it all again, like a juggler, endlessly tossing the same old balls. It can't be true. It mustn't be true. It can't be true. Terror seized me by the throat and there it was again. That choking feeling of panic, like groping for the fly-bar and finding only air where the trapeze should be. I knew my moon rhythm like a loyal friend. So how come it had let me down?

The freight car shuddered. The whistle shrieked once

again in the dark and the full buckets spewed and splashed. How I needed some air! My belly clenched and suddenly I was retching. Once, twice, and then a third painful heave as my stomach lurched into my mouth. My eyes were stinging. My throat was burning. And then I retched again. *Oh, Kali Sara help me!* How had it come to this?

'Are you all right?' It was Pa, eyes wide with worry.

I wiped my mouth on my sleeve, hot tears spilling down my face. I didn't even try to blink them back. The shame of it. With child by a *gadjo*!

Pa reached for me in the gloom, pulling my head down onto his chest. 'Poor *chey*,' he soothed in my ear. 'Poor daughter. It can't be much longer, and then you can get some rest.'

I clung to him guiltily, soaking his shirt with my tears.

Roll Up!

A BAND STRUCK UP the first three notes. Two horns, a trumpet and a big trombone. A flute, an oboe, a clarinet. And then the strings played on their own, black notes scurrying, chasing each other's tails, and then those first three notes again. *Eins, zwei, drei,* rest. A joyful double four time. Pa knew it straight away as the door to the boxcar slid open. The overture to *die Fledermaus*. He'd heard it only once in Munich the year he married Ma, but you know Pa. He had tunes by heart, almost before he'd heard them. 'What did I tell you, Ma?' he said. 'It's all *kushti*. There's a band to welcome us.'

'*Raus! Raus, Zigeuner! Aussteigen!*' Out, gypsies! Get out! The doors were wrenched open. At first it was pure relief.

After days crammed together like crabs in a bucket the cold air was nectar as we tumbled out, blinking in the dazzling lights. We stood on tiptoe, desperate for a sip of air, so at first we didn't see the soldiers with rifles and dogs. Or the other carriages in front of ours with the word *JUDEN* chalked on.

And then we saw them crowded on the opposite side of the track – the Jews from the front carriages. There was a man in white jodhpurs and shiny black boots with a whip in his white-gloved hands, and a group of men in stripy suits and floppy matching hats, scurrying round with baby carriages and wheelbarrows, like nightmare clowns from some grotesque circus. They were picking up the Jews' belongings from the concrete ramp. Battered cases and knapsacks. A doll and a yellow teddybear. A jar of pickled gherkins. I stared in disbelief as the band played on.

'*Ja! Ja!*' yelled the jodhpur man. 'Leave your things there! You'll get them back later. *Schnell! Schnell!*'

We watched in horror as the Jews were herded, the stronger ones marched off with cries and screams as families were parted, men from women, old from young. We gazed after them, marching five abreast as they disappeared down a track that led from the ramp towards a gateway with a metal sign: *Arbeit Macht Frei. Work sets you free.* In the twilight just before dawn we could see beyond the gates to row upon row of barracks behind coiled barbed fences, and all along the outside, tall watchtowers on splayed giraffe legs, each with a soldier and machine gun, bright spotlights shining down into the camp below.

And then we noticed a sign that was hidden from view

before the crowd cleared. We found out later it was Polish: Oświęcim. And underneath that, there was a place name in German. The band crescendoed to the final strident chords of their piece and then fell silent. We all stared, open mouthed. *Roll up! Roll up! Welcome to Auschwitz!*

'Don't look so glum, *Zigeuner*. Get in!' The SS in a greatcoat pointed towards five trucks that had just drawn up at the ramp next to the railway siding. He waved his Luger in Pa's direction. 'Are you their leader?'

A stocky man elbowed Pa out of the way, like Pa wasn't our *Rom Baro*. 'He's not *my* leader. I'm not with them. I'm a respectable Sinto. A soldier of the Wehrmacht!' The man puffed his chest where he'd pinned an Iron Cross on a black and white ribbon. 'My wife and I are Berliners – same flat for forty years. I'm a decorated soldier and a Party member. I can show you my card. Now sort this mistake out, there's a good fellow.' He clicked his heels and stabbed the air. '*Heil Hitler!*'

The officer grinned like a slice of pumpkin. 'Don't worry, old soldier. Nothing bad will happen. You're off somewhere better than this. We've just stopped to unload the filthy Jews at the main camp, that's all. You're all going to the *Zigeunerlager*. The gypsy family camp a couple of miles away.' He jerked his thumb towards Pali and Tamas. 'Even them! They're lucky. Their sort would have gone to the left if they'd been Jews, I'll tell you that for nothing.'

The truck drivers revved their engines. There was a smell of diesel in the air. '*Schnell*, Oscar,' shouted one of the drivers. 'We haven't got time to stand chatting.'

'Up you get, then,' said the man called Oscar. 'Grab your bags and into the trucks. It's not far. Breakfast when you get there.'

The trucks reversed in a spray of mud and changed direction. Then at a sign from an SS, the leader of the orchestra raised his baton. The skinny players, sharp elbowed, hollow eyed, struck up a chord.

Pa shook his head in disbelief. 'Is everybody crazy? Wake me up. I must be dreaming!'

Zigeunerlager

O UR SPIRITS ROSE as the open trucks rattled along a bumpy road beside a railway line, mountains with snowy peaks on our left. A forest dotted with little white farms appeared, thin twists of breakfast smoke curling into the sky. We'd been so long cooped in the Marzahn camp it was good to be on the road. Pa smiled with relief, his arms around Ma and Baba Sara as we squatted on our bags. 'At least we're still together. Breakfast when we arrive, eh, Mother?'

Baba Sara was looking grey. She shot a fierce glance at Pa. 'I told you we should have brought my samovar.'

Pa squeezed her arm. 'We'll buy another one – soon as we get earning. And get you something for that cough. Lili still looks peaky. Don't fret, *chey*. A full belly makes everything feel better.'

My stomach heaved at the thought of food. I crossed my arms over my chest. My breasts felt different, fuller already, my nipples tender. I fixed my eyes on the distant mountains. Was there really another heart beating inside me, a tiny flicker of growing life? How alone I felt. I leaned my head against Frieda's shoulder and closed my eyes, willing myself not to be sick, though surely my belly must be empty.

I must have dozed. 'Lili! Look!'

I jerked awake. I was dreaming we were rolling along in the vardo. As the trucks juddered to a halt we saw a huge red brick tower with square black windows and a triangular tiled roof over a wide arch and metal gates, broad enough for a circus wagon to pass through. The lead driver jumped down from his truck in a spray of mud and ran over to one of the long, low buildings on either side. Then he came racing back, beckoning to the other drivers. *'Komm Kameraden! Das Frühstück!'*

'Breakfast for them,' muttered Pa, 'but not for us.'

By daylight we could see the ground was boggy, oily green water lying in pools in the rutted ground. The sky was dark, like someone had stretched a huge grey veil between earth and sun, trapping in the gloom. It was raining – that fine misty rain that seems wetter than proper raindrops. And suddenly we heard a band again. I couldn't see the players this time, but I could hear their chirpy tune. Then, like performers appearing from the wings, lines of ragged women came marching, dressed in awful shapeless dresses, striped like circus clowns with yellow stars on their chests.

They were marching in fives, guarded by women in grey with dogs, out through another arched entrance beside the main gate, some in wooden clogs but most on rag-bound feet, squelching through the mud. And as they came closer I saw they'd got no hair, only tufts of stubble sprouting from shaved heads. On they tramped, an endless column, marching to the music, out past a wooden sign nailed to the wall: *Frauenkonzentrationslager. Women's Concentration Camp. Auschwitz-Birkenau.*

Then all at once a great wail of fear rose up from our trucks – screams and curses, howls of betrayal. I stared at Pa. His face was quivering with rage. And what was worse, I could feel his fear for the first time. I found myself praying. *Please don't let Pa be afraid.* Pa's never afraid.

'They said this was a family camp,' whispered Ma. 'They said we'd be together.'

Pa's teeth were clenched, lips pressed white, like a scar. We watched in horror as the hollowed-eyed women marched past like puppets, heads down. Not one looked up. It was as if we were invisible. As if they couldn't even hear our screams.

Pa shook himself all over like a wet dog. And suddenly he was Pa again, spraying us with hope like drops of water. 'Ma's right. We've been cheated and no mistake. But I'll sort this out, you watch me. If they think they can trick us like this, they haven't met Pa Petalo!'

It had stopped raining by the time the guards had eaten breakfast, and at last the trucks were off again, bouncing along the furrowed ground around the edge of the camp beside a fence, coil upon coil of bristling wire stretched between concrete pillars three metres high. Every so often there was a sentry tower, like we'd seen in the other camp, and over it all the same sickly yellow lights on posts, glaring down like unblinking eyes. There were white signs fixed to the fences, black writing over a zigzag lightning flash of red:

VORSICHT!
Hochspannung. Lebensgefahr.

CAUTION!
High Voltage. Mortal Danger.

A sharp left turn and we were travelling up the side of the camp towards a small wood in the distance. Every so often there was a huge gate in the barbed wire and then a wide, deep ditch full of dirty water. We stared through the gates at row after row of wooden buildings, like stables for horses. We gazed in horror at the creeping grey skeletons of sickly looking men in shapeless zebra clothes, squelching ankle deep in slime. Gaunt faces. Legs like sticks. No one said a word, each of us wrapped in our own misery. And then the miracle happened.

The trucks slowed down outside a huge metal gate like the others – the same squat guardhouse, same armed guards. But there was no barbed wire. No grey, shrivelled faces or stripy uniforms. Some men in greatcoats trickled out of the guardhouse, yawning and rubbing their eyes.

The guard barked orders as we clambered down from the trucks. 'Stand together in family groups. Do as you're told and you'll stay together. *Schnell!* On the double.'

The family camp was waking up, and if the barracks had been vardos it might have been any other Romani camp – a splash of wild colour against an endless sea of grey mud. Women were wearing bright headscarves, exotic turbans and flowery-fringed shawls. The men in warm trousers and stout leather boots were playing knucklebones, smoking or strumming guitars. Men and women sat together on crates and buckets, chatting while *chavvies* played tag round their legs or football with a rag-stuffed jumper. Everything was life and bustle – or that's how it seemed at first.

A red-haired guard led us through the gate. 'I'm SS Wolf,' he told our group, beckoning with his clipboard. 'Your *Blockführer*.' Pali and Tamas had somehow worked their way into the middle of us, so they couldn't be seen above our heads. Pa was clutching his fiddles. 'Musicians, eh?' said SS Wolf. 'We like a bit of music in Block Six . . . and dancing.' He looked sideways at me and Frieda, his pink lips curling in a smile. 'You can dance, I expect?' He winked. 'All *Zigeuner* dance. Can you sing?'

'We're a travelling circus,' said Pa coldy. 'We can sing, dance, anything you like.'

I could tell Pa wasn't happy with an SS flirting with his girls, but there was something else. Pa was gazing into the distance towards a little wood of birch trees. There was no barbed wire, it was true, but dotted about under the trees were soldiers with machine guns pointing at us, and there was a group of long, low buildings with smoke blackened chimneys. In summer they'd be hidden by leaves, but not on that day. SS Wolf followed Pa's stare.

'What's over there?'

'Nothing to do with you,' barked Wolf. 'Showers and disinfection blocks for the filthy Jews . . . problems with lice. You'll get your own shower block soon, once we get the water running. That'll be your first job – to get us connected up to the water mains. This camp's not finished yet. Nobody's been here long.'

'Well, it's a bad place for a camp,' said Pa. 'Any Romani will tell you marshland's unhealthy. A swamp's a bad choice.'

The officer burst out laughing, like Pa had cracked the best joke ever. 'Ha ha ha! I'll tell the camp *Kommandant*.'

Pa frowned. He couldn't see what was funny.

'Or better still,' the man smirked, 'I'll get you an appointment. You can tell him yourself!'

The main street was a river of slippery mud that ran between two rows of barracks, all painted in the same grey-green paint with gleaming whitewashed roofs. The mud sucked my feet. 'A decent concrete road will take care of this,' said Wolf. 'That'll be your next job. And the toilet block's not ready yet either. But there'll be flowerbeds soon, an orphanage, a kindergarten, and there's a shop over there in Block Two if you've got any money – coffee, tobacco, razor blades. And the hospital's down the end there. There's plenty of work here, so you won't have to work outside the camp. You're on "special orders" from the camp *Kommandant*. You won't be treated like the Jews.'

I looked towards the next-door camp where even more of the grey-faced men were out and about, lining up outside the stable blocks in their ugly wooden shoes. A soldier with a clipboard was shouting out names, ticking them off on a list. 'Don't talk through the wire,' warned our block leader, 'or there'll be real trouble.'

Pa nodded slowly. 'So if we're not prisoners here,' he said, gazing back into the trees where the guards with machine guns hadn't moved a muscle, 'what exactly are we?'

'You're a nosy *Zigeuner* who asks too many questions, that's what,' said SS Wolf, suddenly less pally. 'You watch your tongue. Not everyone's as nice as me. Now you listen here. You're damned lucky you're in my block. And you're lucky you're over here and not there. You wear your own clothes, keep your own hair and you live with your family. So shut up and follow me. Step out of line and you're for the high jump. Do as you're told and your only enemy's the mud!'

That was the first time we were called lucky that day. It wasn't the last.

Florica fainted while she was getting her number. It was when they said little Franko's arm was too small and they were going to brand him on his bum.

'What's all this about?' shouted Fonso. 'You can't label us like cattle!'

An SS kicked him up the backside. 'You're lucky you've got a number, *Zigeuner*. Thousands never get that far . . . now move your arse out of here and take that screaming bitch with you.'

Queuing up to be tattooed with a sharp pen to become a number didn't feel much like luck. Before long, my left forearm was smarting like I'd slipped in a clump of nettles. Then off we marched back down the Lagerstrasse, the camp street, back to the clothes store to collect our triangles from a basket full of pieces of black cloth. *Winkels*, they called them. Black for *asoziale*, we were told. We had to sew them on ourselves next to another piece of cloth with our number. 'Don't look so glum,' said the Sinto prisoner handing them out. 'At least it's not the yellow star!'

We found out later that some prisoners helped the SS with their work. They were mostly ex-criminals brought in to do the dirty work. They called them *Kapos* or Trusties in the camp, and they worked for the Nazis in return for privileges. *Kapos* were never hungry. That's how the SS controlled the camp. They set the prisoners against each other, so no one trusted anybody. It took a while for us to work this out. We found out later most *Kapos* were beasts, but this one seemed pally enough, so Pa asked him what the officer meant about the numbers. The Sinto lowered his voice. 'It means they've still got some use for you. Why give you a number if they're going to send you up the chimney? Keep healthy. Keep working. That's my advice. What do you think those buildings are – over there in the trees? Bread ovens?' He winced as a whip flicked his knuckles.

'Keep your mouth shut!' the SS snapped.

There were some rules, it seemed, even for *Kapos*.

We found out about the triangles when we met our *Blokalteste*, the block supervisor. She was the prisoner in

charge of Block Six and a favourite with our block leader.
Luisa was a black-eyed Sintezza with an oval, brown face.
She wore a green triangle on her silver tunic next to a black
one. 'You're just asocial,' she said, pointing at the black
triangles we were clutching. She tapped her chest. 'I'm
asocial *and* a criminal. Beat that!'

Luisa kept order and doled out food. She shared a little
room with SS Wolf at the entrance to the block. They'd
made a private den for themselves draped with red blankets.
I sneaked a peep. There was a bed with a pink eiderdown,
a long silk bathrobe, a table and some flowers in a jar. We
wondered what she'd done to wear the green triangle. Pa
said it was enough for a Sintezza to go with a *gadjo*!

'That doesn't make her a criminal, Pa!' The words were
out of my mouth before I could stop them. I felt my face
burning up.

We soon learned we had to be careful of the green
triangles. They were mostly brutes, murderers and thugs,
but Luisa was all right for a green. She used to sing for the
sailors in Hamburg. One day a sea captain had his way with
her without paying, so she'd tied him up and stolen his gold
watch when he was asleep. Pa said she was a loose one, but
I thought the sailor had it coming.

'This is where you'll live,' Luisa said, showing us into the
long, dark tunnel of Block Six. She sidled up to me and gave
me a shove in the ribs. 'It's pretty bad in here,' she whispered,
'but a girl like you can make it better for yourself.' She
laughed and wiggled her hips. 'These SS! They'll give you
anything for a bit of what you've got. Sardines, Champagne,

and you can share it with your family.' I must have looked shocked. 'Don't give me that,' she giggled. 'You know what I'm talking about. These men have been here for months without a poke!'

'That's enough chatting, Luisa,' grinned SS Wolf, pinching her bum.

She patted my cheek in a friendly way. 'Suit yourself, love, but it's a hundred times better with an officer than without one. If you change your mind, just give me the nod.'

Ratten!

MOST PRISONERS SOON LOST COUNT of the days, but I had more reason than many to scratch each day on the wooden wall of our block that we shared with rats, lice and fleas. The buildings were stable blocks made for fifty or more horses. Well, there must have been three hundred of us crammed in there – and more arriving every day. The SS lumped us all together. *Zigeuner*, they called us, like we were all the same. But there were all sorts of gypsy tribes here. Lowari, Medvashi, Kelderari, Lalleri, Gelderari. Some were filthy dirty – never worked in their lives. And others were fancy types with book learning who'd done office jobs in the past, like the Sinti from Germany, the brick dwellers I've mentioned before. And then there were the ones we called *poshrats* – half bloods.

Some Sinti thought they were a cut above. This made Pa mad as a nest of hornets. There was a Sinto who'd owned a big factory in Munich, and lots of Sinti soldiers from the German army – still in the uniforms they had on when the Gestapo came for them. And there was a Sintezza who was a leader in the League of German Girls in Berlin.

'It's an insult to lump us with them,' they said. 'We're respectable Sinti. Roma beg and steal. They spoil our reputation.'

Pa squared for a fight.

'Leave it, Josef,' said Ma. 'We've troubles enough.'

My belly was growing in spite of camp food, though I pretended it was bloated from cabbage soup.

'You get better food than the Jews,' said SS Wolf.

Well, maybe Luisa did, but not us. *Kantinsuppe* was made every day in a great big kettle: red beetroot soup, cabbage soup, soup made out of old socks, so Pa used to say. It smelled foul but we fell on it like animals, fighting for the black bread that made our gums itch. On Sundays we got a thin slice of sausage but we didn't touch that. Pa said it was horsemeat and it's taboo for Romanies to eat horse. We couldn't understand why the rats were as fat as kittens, scurrying over us day and night, their long tails snaking in and out, swimming in the puddles or just staring at us from the rafters. 'What can they be eating?' said Ma.

We could smell Luisa's cooking in the room she shared with Wolf behind the curtain. Fancy stuff, she told me, pinched from the Jews. 'Best Slovakian salami.' She grinned.

'Greek olives. Hungarian gherkins. Dutch cheese.' I noticed she was wearing a new red skirt. She offered again to get me an SS. '*Du sollst auch leben,*' she said. 'Live a little. Why go hungry with tits like yours?'

Luisa was right about something. Our girls certainly got the SS goggling. They'd come at night in their jeeps, swaggering around with their pistols and their liquor, getting us to dance. And plenty went with them for food. They called us *niggers* in the day and then they'd come at night to lark around and go with our girls in the little rooms reserved for *Kapos*.

There were bunks down each side of the block, three tiers high. Pa called them shelves. Each shelf was home for a family – bare boards made of old doors or window shutters, with paper-thin mattresses. It was bad at the top and bad at the bottom. The place stank of bodies and everything that came out of them. At least at the top by the skylight you could take a sip of air but then you'd get drenched.

The bottom bunk was worst. The flimsy bunks collapsed sometimes, crushing the people – and that was mainly the old and sick. On the bottom you'd get splashed with everything that came down and that was bad in a place where everyone soon had the squits.

'Call this a family camp!' said Ma.

Luisa said there were icicles inside in February, but in spring it rained all the time, streaming through the rafters. We waded through stinking water. There was mud in our clothes, mud in our shoes, mud caked between our fingers. We tried to wash in puddles of mud.

There was a long brick chimney shaft down the middle dividing the block in two like a long table with a firebox at either end. There was no wood, so we ate, played cards and even slept on the stove. Our women gave birth on the stove while we tried to beat the rats away with sticks. Birthing in front of men was shameful for us, but so was eating from the same bowls we washed in, and being forced to you-know-what in rows of holes, men and women together. Sometimes a German midwife came from the women's camp across the big main road. She was a green triangle who'd done time in prison for getting rid of babies. She sneered when we complained. 'You *gypsies*! Where d'you think you are? A private sanatorium? You're lucky,' she said. 'At least in the *Zigeunerlager* you're allowed to keep your bairns. Jew babies are drowned in a bucket as soon as they're born.'

We huddled together on our bunks, trying to work out what was happening. People dropped hints all the time. Our family camp was up at the top end near the trees so we could see the chimneys better than most. We lived in their shadow and the birch trees couldn't hide the long columns of people walking towards the smoke stacks. Sometimes they'd herd us into the blocks for a *Lagersperre*, a *lock down*, and then we'd see the sky to the west, burning red through the thin ribbon of skylights and it smelled that bad you couldn't hardly breathe. It was sweet and sickly. Suffocating. Like musk.

A Polska Roma told Pa that two whole blocks of Sinti from Białystok were gassed before we arrived. To stop the typhus spreading through the camp, the doctors said.

'Pull the other one!' Pa said. He couldn't believe it. 'This place makes people sick in the head. They start dreaming things that ain't true.' But by this time even Pa had lost some of his swagger. Even Pa couldn't explain the smell and the ash that fell like filthy snow.

At night I fretted about the baby. I lay awake in my roost, listening to the scurrying rats, thinking of a way out. The first week we were there some men had tried to escape while out chopping wood for railway sleepers. The guards had brought them back riddled with bullets. They piled them up in the middle of the street with labels round their necks: *Because we tried to run*. It was bad but it set me thinking . . .

I could try to escape and forage until the baby was born, then leave it at a farmhouse. There was still no wire round our camp, just machine guns. I could run into the woods at night and if they shot me Pa would never know my shame. They'd cry for me and call me *poor Lili*, and they'd never know the terrible thing. But I didn't want to die. It's hard to believe but I wanted to live, even in the stinking rat hole of the camp.

My thoughts churned in my head. Maybe I'd tell Baba Sara my secret, make her swear not to tell. She could make me a brew to help me lose the baby. She knew all about herbs to make people get with child, so she might know how to make one bleed away. But I couldn't bother her with my problems. She was ailing really bad. She pretended she was mending but I knew she wasn't. At first she used to shake her fists at the guards and spit on the ground. But soon the fight went out of her. Her skin was like yellow paper and her lips were covered in sores. We'd all lost weight but she looked different from us. I thought she smelled of death.

One night I dreamed the baby bled away. Its life gushed out of me, dripping down like a red river onto Ma and Pa below, and then I woke up shaking. It's a sin to wish a life away, and the ghost of my dead child would come and get revenge.

And then I had an idea. I could pretend to Pa that one of the guards had forced me. That way it wouldn't be my fault. I suddenly felt calmer and at last I fell asleep, but in the morning the plan looked stupid. If any of the guards laid a finger on Pa's girls, he'd kill them with his bare hands. And then they'd shoot Pa. And where would we be without Pa?

Football

B Y APRIL WE'D GOT our own electric fence and sentry
towers and guards with guns. We heard some banging
in the night and next morning the fence was humming. Most
of the guards were cruel, but at least we weren't like the poor
souls we could see through the wire next door. Not at first,
anyway. We even had the chance to forage. One day after
Zählappell, that's *roll call*, when we'd line up in the freezing
rain, Pa was told to join a *Waldkommando* – a team of prisoners
chosen to chop wood in Birkenau Forest. 'We're adding a new
branch line to the railway,' the SS told us. 'We need strong
men to heave timber.' By this time Pa was our *Zählappell* clerk
and on kind of friendly terms with Wolf. So he asked if some of
the women could go with them to do some foraging. Wolf was

in a good mood that day, maybe because the rain had stopped. He said yes, so we ran and grabbed our bags from the block. Baba Sara was still asleep. Ma said maybe she should stay back with her but Pali told her to go. These days the dwarfs never left her side. Her skin was hot and clammy when I kissed her goodbye. 'Don't leave us yet,' I whispered.

Birkenau Forest stretched as far as the Sola River. It felt good to stretch our legs and hear the skylarks after so long cooped like chickens. At least I wasn't being sick any more – not like when I first came, retching in secret behind our block. Before long, we'd left the watchtowers behind. It was quiet round the chimneys that day but the week before, the sky had burned red for days. We weren't supposed to know what happened there.

'Don't talk rubbish,' said SS Wolf. 'Whoever heard of gassing people and burning them?'

So we tried not to think at all, or you'd end up losing your mind.

The guards had guns as we marched out that day and *they* carried the axes and saws until we got there. They weren't taking any chances after the break-out.

It was the rise of the leaf and the trees were jumping with nesting birds. In another life we'd be hefting our wagons out of the mud, changing our winter curtains and lighting the first open-air fires of the year. I watched Pa striding ahead with the other men, stretching his arms wide. I shut my eyes. If I tried really hard I could hear the rattle of wagon wheels, the jangling of chains and the soft plod of the horses' hooves. I thought of the circus. I thought of the Wintergarten. I thought of Max and the day we saw the rain bird. I thought of our baby and then my mind started churning again. And then I heard the river . . .

I'd considered drowning myself already. I'd heard drowning didn't hurt, though I wondered how people knew that. After all, you couldn't come back and tell people. I imagined the bubbles rising as I sank, my hair spreading out like a dark halo. They'd find my body in the river and everyone would be weeping . . . Suddenly I realized I was actually crying. Hot tears splashing onto my chest, staining my green blouse with dark patches like old moss. I took a deep breath. I mustn't let Ma see me snivelling.

Sunlight glistened on the dripping trees. Everything was soggy with rain, perfect for mushrooms and young snails. We found some black morels at the base of a rotten tree stump and a great clump of honeycomb mushrooms. Florica filled her bag while I collected snails and wild garlic. You could smell garlic long before you saw it and I followed my nose and sniffed out the broad, soft leaves. Ma found some wood sorrel and we crammed it into our mouths in great handfuls. It quenched our thirst but it stung our cracked tongues. The men were a long time sawing and we managed to fill our bags with nettle shoots for soup, dandelions for tea and heart-shaped birch leaves for salad. 'If we could do this more often our gums would stop bleeding,' said Ma. They bled every day and we'd got funny blue spots on our skin. 'And if only we had time to set a rook trap, we'd have more than a few snails tonight.' She wanted to gather birch sap. It was full of goodness but we didn't have anything to put it in, and anyway, the men had finished their chopping and it was time to go.

It broke my heart to leave the forest and march back to

the miserable camp. Our spirits drooped with every step, so think how we felt when we heard gunshots. Our hearts were pounding. The piece of spare ground between the *Zigeunerlager* and the chimneys was crawling with SS, and prisoners were flocking to the barbed wire. *Were they crazy?* Then we saw more prisoners on top of the blocks, standing about on the roofs. And then we heard more shots ringing out through the trees. Even our guards looked startled.

It turned out the SS had started a football match. Auschwitz main camp versus the *Zigeunerlager*. We couldn't hardly believe our eyes. We joined the crowd at the back. It was 2–1 to the gypsies, and the prisoners were charging up and down as if the ground outside our camp was any old village green on a spring day. The match was nearly over and the SS were cheering, each side shouting madly for their camps, shooting their pistols when their team scored. The gypsies won – a big surprise as the main camp team had four professional footballers from Poland. The players were slathered in mud but they didn't seem to mind that day. They were caught up in the thrill of the game. It turned out they'd switched the electricity off so the gypsies could cheer for their team at the fence. Later that day when they turned it on again the humming seemed louder than ever.

That was the first game but it wasn't the last. The main camp team came back for a return match and that time they beat us. And then suddenly the party was over. A new camp was built on the pitch. An infirmary for male prisoners. And then there was nowhere left to play any more, and even if there had been, the Polish players were dead.

Call Up!

Four months after Lili disappeared my call-up papers finally came. After the terrible loss of manpower at Stalingrad and setbacks in Africa, they'd reduced the conscription age to seventeen. New divisions were now urgently needed on all Germany's fronts and I'd been called at last to give my life for the Fatherland as a soldier of the German Reich.

My letter arrived at breakfast one morning in May, but not from Wehrmacht High Command summoning me to the *Luftwaffe* Flak Unit like my school friends, but to officer training in Beverloo, Belgium, for the newly created *SS-Panzer Grenadier Hitler Youth Division* – a unique tank division of the SS. Unique in that most of those enlisted were between sixteen and eighteen years old. The Baby-milk Division, the Allies called us. But we didn't hear that one until after the war.

'There must be some mistake,' said Vati. His face was white, if anything more shocked than mine. 'I thought you'd signed up for the Wehrmacht.'

I frowned at my papers. I had a vague memory of Hans Rust and Willi Bauer coming round a few months before on their way to pre-register at the Recruitment Office. 'Come on, Max. If you don't get your name down for the Wehrmacht you'll end up in the SS. And you know what their casualties are like!' I'd go later, I told them. I was too busy. Busy nursing Shadow back to health and haunting the stage door of the Wintergarten. Too busy standing on the roof of my house and staring out over the Tiergarten, licking my wounds and staring into the void.

Vati was horrified. He marched me round to Bendlerstrasse straight away. 'This can't be right!'

The recruiting officer scanned his lists. 'No pre-registration, I'm afraid.' He glared at me over his half-moon glasses. 'You've missed your chance, sonny.'

'But he's only seventeen . . .'

'SS divisions need replacements like any other,' he snapped. 'There aren't nearly enough volunteers. Where's the manpower to come from if not the Hitler Youth?' There was nothing he could do, he told Vati firmly. I'd left it way too late.

So instead of joining Hans and Willi as *Luftwaffe* telephonists at the Air Ministry, I was off to Belgium with the fighting wing of the SS – a fate that anyone with any sense had done their best to avoid. We'd prepared for war in Hitler Youth. We'd marched. We'd drilled. We'd played at being soldiers in the Grunewald. But the truth is, it had never seemed real to me. At seventeen you feel immortal. Does any seventeen year old really believe death might come for him? But my name was on the papers. My fate was sealed.

I dragged my bicycle up to the loft with a heavy heart and then began to pack my bags. Tante Ida gave me a cigarette case that had belonged to Onkel Manfred in the trenches with the words *Gott Mit Uns* – *God With Us* – etched on the front. 'One just like this saved a soldier's life in the trenches,' she said. 'Your uncle always kept this in his breast pocket . . . over his heart.'

Along with my kitbag I packed the small brown suitcase with the silk lining. In the bottom I placed a pack of hand-painted tarot cards, a rusty iron horseshoe, some bells from a stallion's harness and the broken scroll from a gypsy fiddle. Then I covered my precious things with a paisley scarf that still carried the scent of old roses, but only if you breathed in deeply and remembered very hard.

Mule! Mule!

I᷂T WAS MAY and we'd been in the camp two months. It felt much longer, and Pa was going crazy with nothing to do. The water had been connected and the camp road was finished. Luisa said he should be glad they weren't working us like the Jews, but work was what Pa wanted. He couldn't sleep all day or sit around playing cards like some. Already he knew everyone useful, from the SS women in charge of the kindergarten, to Erich the red triangle who ran the camp kitchen. Red was for politicals, and they were the best kind of *Kapo*s, said Pa. They'd got standards, not like the Greens. And it was from *Kapo* Felix, one of the Reds, that Pa heard about the Birkenau Camp Band.

Kapo Felix ran the 'sauna' – the delousing barrack down

the far end of the camp next to the infirmary. We went there once a month for *Lausenkontrolle*. We stripped naked in front of each other under the showers while our clothes got steamed in a wagon to kill the lice. Lice carried typhus, we were told, and the sauna was full of big notices: *Eine Laus, dein Tod! One louse, your death!* It must be a bad joke, we used to say. They fell out of our clothes like grains of sand. We were crawling with them, even our eyebrows, and the itching drove us crazy. I was always scared when we were naked that someone would notice my belly, but everyone was so cold nobody was looking, although Felix let us stand under the warm water longer than the other *Kapos*. He was kind.

He got chatting to Pa while we were fetching our clothes from the steamer. There'd often be fights after *Lausenkontrolle* and you'd be lucky if you got your own skirt back. 'Why not start a band if you're bored?' said Felix as Pa struggled back into some trousers that looked like his. 'I'm in the Birkenau Camp Orchestra myself.' He patted his belly. 'Players get better rations. You'd have to get permission, though.'

'Who do I ask?' said Pa.

'*Sturmbannführer* Schwarzhuber likes music. Ask him.'

Schwarzhuber was one of the deputy camp commanders who spent a lot of time in our camp. Felix lowered his voice. 'He's a drunken thug, though. You'd better pick your time to speak to him.'

Pa grinned. He was sure the trousers weren't the ones he came in, but they were a better fit than the old ones. 'Thanks for the tip, Felix,' he said. 'I will.'

Pa got on to it right away.

'A gypsy band! Why not?' replied Schwarzhuber. 'You've got your instruments.' He was a wiry little man from the Tyrol, a cruel man, so people said. Little eyes, mean lips, sharp nose, and much too fond of the liquor, but Pa got on with him all right. Pa knew how to butter his bread on both sides. Schwartzhuber seemed enthusiastic. 'Good idea!' he said. 'I've a taste for *Zigeunermusik*! There's a price for my permission, though,' he laughed. 'I want a concert for my wife's birthday on Sunday.'

I didn't like Schwartzhuber. Not one bit. I thought his face was like a wolf. But it gave Pa something to do and he looked happier than he'd done for weeks.

At last the day came. We'd been practising all kinds of things: acrobatics, violins, dancing. There'd be extra rations, we'd been told, if we gave a good show. But by the afternoon I was as jumpy as a flea. There were more SS than usual, standing around, whispering in groups. Something wasn't right. Then after roll call Ma sent me to the infirmary by the sauna – the *Krankenbau*, or Ka-Be, as we called it. Baba Sara had coughed so hard Ma thought she'd cracked a rib. There was never much there, except some sacks of white powder they called *Kaolin* that they handed out for everything. I went down anyway, just to please Ma. I'd got a hollow feeling in my stomach. Last night I'd heard Ma and Pa talking on the shelf below. Pa said Ma should warn me and Frieda about Baba Sara. 'She'll be joining Grandpa Guno soon,' he'd said.

I don't know why it was called the *infirmary*. It was really just a couple of stable blocks like ours. *Krankenbau*.

Eintritt Verboten – Entry Forbidden – it said on the door. If you wanted a doctor you had to hang around outside and hope one came out. The doctors were mostly Jewish prisoners from Poland and Czechoslovakia. They tried their hardest but there was too much illness. I hung around for an hour and nobody came out except a thin nurse carrying a cardboard sign with red writing. She pinned it on the door: *ACHTUNG! TYPHUS!*

'Can I speak to a doctor?' I asked.

She shook her head and scurried back inside.

'It's bad in there,' said *Kapo* Erich, passing me on the Lagerstrasse. He was a fat Sinto from Poland who worked in the kitchen. He had a thing about Frieda and she was tempted by his offers of food, but she knew what he wanted in return and Marko would kill him. Erich was carrying a bucket of shrivelled beets and my mouth was watering. He stopped to chat but he wouldn't put the bucket down in case he got mobbed. I told him I was waiting for a doctor. 'Haven't you heard?' he said. 'There's another typhus epidemic like in March. They're falling like skittles.'

Erich hurried off with his bucket and I passed the time of day with Katza, a mad old woman from Block Ten. Katza used to wander up and down the street all day in a wedding dress she'd got from a place we called *Kanada* – a big warehouse where the guards stored the stuff they'd pinched from the Jews. There were piles of fur coats in there, watches, cameras, children's toys. Her dress was held together with a nappy pin and she was carrying her usual bouquet of twigs. She wore a wide straw hat trimmed with pink roses. 'You'll all be bridesmaids,' she said, flashing me a toothless grin, 'when we get home.'

I'd nothing else to do so I wandered round the back of the sauna, hoping to bump into *Kapo* Felix for a chat when I noticed a rough wooden shed, like a kind of extension behind the Ka-Be. The door was padlocked but there was a window on the far side, high up. There was a swarm of black flies around the door. I stood on my tiptoes and peered in . . .

I was almost too stunned to be shocked. And then my guts heaved. There was a mountain of dead bodies about as tall as me – children, babies, grown-ups, all jumbled up, arms and legs skewwhiff. They were stark naked and covered in white powder. Rats were scurrying all over them and there were more flies inside. I backed away, slowly at first and then I turned and ran, back down the Lagerstrasse, my heart thumping like a drum. I burst into our block. By now I was screaming. *Mule! Mule! Corpses!*

Variety Show

THE SWALLOWS SWOOPED AND PLUNGED over the open space next to the kindergarten, their blue backs catching the light of the afternoon sun. They were hunting insects, and God knows there were enough of them in that swamp. The children had left early today so they could see the show. The roundabout and rocking horse were still. Everyone not sick or dying had turned out for the performance. Rows of wooden benches stretched out in front of the stage. They'd be for the SS, I reckoned. It would be a fancy audience that afternoon, so we'd been told. Not only *Lagerführer* Schwarzhuber and his wife, but the commander of the main camp, *Obersturmbannführer* Hoess was coming. 'He likes music too,' said Pa.

Schwarzhuber had told Pa what he wanted on the programme. 'It must be something different. We hear Schumann, Grieg and Mozart all the time from the main camp orchestra.' They had some of the best musicians in Europe, he told Pa. 'So we want proper *Zigeunermusik* from you lot. Understand?'

Pa understood a man with a pistol. He was off round the camp. There was plenty of talent. He knew at least three families who'd made their living as entertainers before coming to Birkenau, including the Turks we met in Marzahn – Ahmet and his family. 'Will your daughters dance?'

Ahmet looked doubtful. 'They like our girls too much, these SS,' he muttered, stroking his silver beard. But when Pa told him we'd get cigarettes and extra soup, Ahmet agreed. He waggled his finger at Pa. 'No bare bellies, though.'

Pa hired Franzi Daniel too. Franzi was a famous acrobat from Circus Busch. He came on the same transport as us, and Pa was proud to know him. We were short of props so Pa was chuffed when the dwarfs borrowed a wheelbarrow and ladder from the kitchen barracks for their act, and the Camlos and Nano Florian had been practising a human pyramid for days behind the block. Frieda was mad that I wouldn't perform with her. She'd found us some skin-tight leotards in *Kanada* but I couldn't do up the hooks down the sides. Well, I might as well have worn a sign on my head. Someone would have noticed my belly before my first cartwheel. I couldn't explain why and my sister was in a sulk.

Pa was happy with the music. '*Herr Schwindelig* will love

it,' he said. That was Pa's new name for Schwarzhuber. *Mr Dizzy*, because he was always wobbling about with drink. Pa had organized music from the Hungarian steppes, Anatolian dances, Spanish flamenco with Florica and Fonso. 'If they want *Zigeunermusik* – we'll give them the best!' said Pa. He'd learned a special tune for when Schwarzhuber's wife arrived. It was her favourite hit, apparently: *Die schönste Zeit im Leben – The Best Time of Life*. Pa didn't know it, so a guard took him in a jeep to the main camp so he could listen to the gramophone. 'I only need to hear it once,' said Pa.

When it was time for the show, Kommandant Hoess mounted the platform with two of his children, a girl about ten and a smaller boy, followed by Herr *Schwindelig*, leaning shakily on his wife's arm. She was very beautiful, in a well-fed blonde sort of way, with two little fair-haired *chavvies*, not a bit like their old man.

The performers stood in a semi-circle next to the block, waiting their turn as the Turkish band struck up the first piece. Ahmet, in a fresh white turban, played a pear-shaped *oud*. His father played a *tulum* with pipes and a goatskin bag, his brother on the goblet drum. *Dum, tek, pa. Dum, tek, pa.* We all swayed to the shifting notes and strange rolling rhythms. Pa was enjoying it. 'It's the quartertones that make the difference,' he said, 'like the cracks between the black and white keys. They've got more notes than Mozart, I reckon!'

It was a good show. After the band played there was a little whistling artist Pa had found in the kindergarten. Jerzy was a Romani from Poland. He could whistle songs from musicals, note perfect. And then came the acrobats, tumblers and the human pyramid. The SS *chavvies* whooped and clapped and then it was time for flamenco.

How thin Florica looked. Her dress hung loose and you could see the tendons on Fonso's neck, like ropes. They'd taken some chivvying to join in. 'This isn't the place for happy dances,' they said. 'The SS should give us better rations if they want Bulerías.'

Pali and Tamas were next on but they'd disappeared, so Pa brought on the belly dancing early. I watched the SS watching the girls and then their ma began to sing. '*When she danced, she was like a swaying branch . . .*'

Suddenly there was a drone of aircraft. We all looked up as the sound of engines throbbed closer. The music stopped. We all stared up into the sky as SS Hoess leaped to his feet. Maybe it's the enemy, we thought, come to bomb the camp. After all, there had been rumours.

'Play on! Play on!' shouted Hoess. 'Don't stop, you fools. They're filming! No extra rations if you stop playing!'

By now the planes were so low they were in danger of grazing the roofs of the barracks. *What were they filming us for?* And then, just as suddenly as they appeared, they wheeled about and flew away, disappearing over the horizon.

After the show was over, Schwartzhuber was as good as his word – or almost. As the SS wives hurried back to their cars, hustling their children away, we saw one of the *Kapos* from the kitchen wheeling a big urn of soup between the blocks. Ahmet frowned. 'I thought you said cigarettes, Josef,' he said. Pa shrugged, looking doubtful. 'Maybe later,' he said. 'Enjoy the soup.' Then suddenly we heard a piercing whistle.

'*Lagersperre! Lagersperre!*' *Lockdown!* 'Everyone to your barracks, immediately! *Schnell!*'

The SS were charging about with whips and pistols – the same ones who had been watching our show only half an hour before. They started herding everyone into the barracks and I heard the sound of engines and from the tail of my eye I saw SS Wolf running down the Lagerstrasse. 'Get inside!' he yelled. 'There's been a change of plan.'

Our block was cold and damp. Baba Sara was still sleeping, though how she could I don't know, with that rumpus going on around her. Pali and Tamas were with her. 'She's very bad,' they said. That's why they couldn't leave her and take part in the show. Tamas shook his head. 'She's been asking for Lili.'

I stared at Baba Sara on the bottom shelf. She was always so strong, was Baba Sara. She had cures for everything. But now she looked shrivelled, like a withered branch. There was a rattle in her throat.

'She's losing the fight,' said Ma.

As we all crowded round, she opened her eyes. The whites were sickly yellow. It didn't look like her.

It was quiet as a grave outside the block. The SS had enjoyed the show, so what was going on now? They'd locked the stable doors and it was dark inside. SS Wolf was with us. He was angry about something, we could tell. When people asked what was happening he shook his head. 'The left arm doesn't know what the right arm is doing in this place,' he growled. If he was mad, it wasn't with us. 'Go to your bunks,' he said. 'It's nothing to do with you. The show was good.' He threw up his hands. 'Just keep quiet.'

It was usually noisy as a hen house in the block but that night there was just a dull hum of mumblings, like wind in the stovepipe. We crouched on our shelves, stretching our ears. Fear crept like a wolf in the dark. And then we heard jeeps, rattling along the Lagerstrasse between the blocks. We held our breath as we heard them pass by, past block number four, number six, number eight. There was a sigh of relief as they drove on. I was holding Frieda's hand and she was holding Ma's. And then we heard shouts and wailing, terrible screams, curses and cries. Doors slamming. Engines revving. Shots fired.

They liquidated the Ka-Be that night – the night of the SS Variety Show. Gassed over a thousand patients, one of the doctors told Pa. Czech gypsies with the spotted typhus. We could smell the burning. And through the ribbon of skylights we could see the sky over our showground burning scarlet and black. Some people say these tales are all lies. Well, if I hadn't been there myself, maybe I might have said it was all dreamed up too. But it wasn't a dream. It was a nightmare.

I never planned to tell Pa that evening. About the baby, I mean. But somehow it just slipped out in the horror of it all. He stared at me for a long time in the darkness and then he bowed his head. I thought he was never going to speak and then, after a long time, he did. 'Oh, Lili. I'm sorry. The bastards!' His eyes glittered in the darkness. 'This hellish place, how dare they?' He grasped my hand so hard it hurt.

For a second I didn't understand and then the light suddenly dawned. I could have pretended one of the guards had forced himself on me. After all, I'd thought of it often enough. Tears were streaming down my face. I found I was sobbing – for everything. My broken heart, my shame. I couldn't keep the secret any more.

'Pa,' I whispered. 'I wasn't forced. I'm sorry.'

He gasped. He let go of my hand. I reached out and touched him but he flinched away, like I'd touched him with a branding iron.

Later that night we sat in stunned silence. Ma, Pa, me and Frieda.

'I didn't know Baba Sara was going tonight,' said Ma. 'Not tonight. All this rumpus going on, and she just slips away.'

The dwarfs were on the bottom shelf with my grandmother, rocking each other and sobbing.

Pa's voice was so low I could hardly hear him. 'She's better off dead.' I think that's what he said.

SS Wolf told Pa we had to take the body away. It might be infectious, he said, but Ma begged to let her stay – just for tonight. Pa went with SS Wolf to the room he shared with Luisa, taking Ma with him. Later, I heard them stumbling back to our bunk. I could smell their breath. I reckoned they'd shared a bottle of schnapps from the box SS Wolf kept under his bed.

I lay there in the dark, the weight of shame like a stone on my chest. I could hear Pali and Tamas, praying and singing softly to Baba Sara on the bottom shelf as if their songs could still bring her comfort.

And then I heard Pa's voice in my ear. 'There was a time when I'd have thrown you out of the tribe for this, Lili. But now . . . here . . . in this place . . . where people behave like animals . . .' He heaved a deep sigh in the darkness. I thought my heart was going to burst. *'Te aves yertime mander tai te yertil tut o Del,'* he whispered in Romani. *I forgive you and may God forgive you as I do*. He smoothed my hair like he did when I was a little girl and scared of the thunder.

I sent up a prayer of thanks to whatever God there might be. Because really I'd known all along that I wanted this baby. More than I'd ever wanted anything. Even in the camp, in the middle of all the misery. I put my head on Pa's chest. I could feel his body shaking.

Next day I told Frieda about Max, and all about his glamorous life that I could never have shared with him. I told her about the great house he lived in off Tiergartenstrasse and the windows that reflected the moon. I cried with relief that it wasn't a secret any more. Frieda cried too. We cried together for everything we'd both lost. We cried for Baba Sara. We cried for Rollo. We cried for what had happened to us all. I cried for Max.

Beverloo,
Belgium 1943

I DID WELL in my training for the 12th Panzer Division. The schoolboys I trained with were officially seventeen, although some were much younger, recruited from military training camps across Germany – fit and fired with enthusiasm, each carefully chosen for their intelligence and fearlessness. Or so we were told. Hitler had wanted a tank division of volunteers, and most had joined willingly, but some had been tricked into signing up. And some were plain conscripts like me, beset with misgivings that we didn't dare voice.

The volunteers were fanatical, many holding the Hitler Youth Achievement Medal for Outstanding Service and determined to live up to the honour. I gazed at the exuberant faces of my fellow trainees in the lecture rooms and wondered where I fitted in. At first I longed to be back in Berlin, manning telephones like my friends, instead of practising with live ammunition on the firing ranges. But after a few months in Belgium, my family home seemed like a distant memory, a black and white flicker, announcing the end of one film and the beginning of another. In some ways it was good for me. There was little time to think. It helped keep my mind off Lili.

Day in, day out, they brainwashed us with propaganda. When we weren't learning to drive tanks, we were lectured by men with the Death's Head insignia on their collars about the motives of our enemies: the Russians, the Americans, the Canadians, the British. The British were an outdated imperial force organized by freemasons, who wanted to turn back the clock a hundred years to the days when their word was law around the world. Whereas all Hitler wanted was justice and peace. Many British workers supported us, we were told. It was just their leadership who was against us. Of the Americans and Canadians we knew very little, except that international Jewish financiers paid for their armies, under instructions from Moscow. Our Führer had accomplished a wonderful thing, our tutors roared, their faces alight with passion – the unification of Europe under the German Reich – and now these foolish Allies, these agents of Jewish international finance, were seeking the destruction of the very order that Hitler had achieved with so much sacrifice.

They were harsh men who trained us on the tanks, and

who could blame them after what they'd been through? My tutor had no nose and was missing both little fingers – the fingers slightly less obvious at first than his lurching limp, due, he informed us, to the absence of a number of toes. He'd left those pieces of bone and cartilage behind in the snows of Russia. He used to be the most handsome lad in his platoon, he'd laughed grimly, until the frost had bitten off his nose.

He counted himself lucky, though. One tank crew froze to death in their vehicle one night at minus thirty when their fuel ran out. 'Like statues they were,' he said, 'when we winched them out. We lined them up on the snow like chunks of marble.'

It was hard not to be impressed by such men. We looked up to them. 'These men gave their lives for the Reich,' our tutors roared. 'Be worthy of their sacrifice. They died believing in you!'

Our training was intense – tank practice all day long with live shells to give us as accurate an idea of real battle as possible. If anyone showed weakness he was considered wet. A chicken and a coward. A disgrace to the whole platoon. 'Anyone who shows any sign of defeatism must disappear from our ranks,' yelled our training officer.

'I'd disappear with pleasure,' I unwisely told the volunteer who shared my bunk in the barracks. He reported me to our superiors and I had to crawl round the camp on my knees in the mud as punishment for showing reluctance for duty. I never confided in anyone again, although it was hard not to long for home, crouching in a trench while a captured T34 tank drove over the top of me. And yet gradually, month by interminable month, the propaganda seeped in. 'You're special,' we were constantly told. 'You're the best division in the army.'

And so we trained from dawn until dusk for almost a year, collapsing into our bunks at night, utterly exhausted. We were well fed and we slept soundly. And only occasionally did I dream of Lili.

We were in the Grunewald. It was morning and the sun was shining. She was running through the wet grass, her hands full of berries. I ran to meet her, but when I reached out I passed smoothly through her, like grey mist, my hands left clutching empty air.

I rose with the sun and pulled on my combat boots, washing my dream away with a bucket of cold water over my head. No more of that, I chided myself. There was nothing I could do to change what had happened. Lili would always be with me – her voice in my head, and sometimes at night in my dreams. But I had to start looking forward to a new life. There was training to be done. The Allies in the west. The Bolsheviks in the east. Who else would save Germany? Who else would save our mothers and sisters from enslavement under communism if *we* didn't? It was unpatriotic to long for home, and weak and feeble to wish for another life than this. We were the 12th SS Panzer Division, better equipped and better supplied than any other regiment. In spring we'd be sent to the front. East. West. We weren't quite sure. We'd go wherever we were needed. And we had to be ready. We had to do our duty.

Things You Learn
in the Camp

HUNGER HURTS. Like knives in your belly. People act bad when they're hungry but you can't point the finger unless you've been there. We pounced on rubbish bins, grubbed like pigs for rotten cabbage leaves. Fights blew up over half a black potato.

'Men are like fish,' said Pa one day. 'The big ones gobble up the little ones.' We mustn't be tiddlers, he told us, or we'd get eaten. He'd noticed we were growing lazy. 'Buck up, everybody,' he said. 'This won't do.' So we did as Pa said and we learned how to *organize*. That was camp lingo for how to get by.

There were jobs that could help you. *Good detachments*, we called them. So Pa got busy *organizing*. If you were in a band that was the best job of all. Better clothes, better food, and Pa got us all playing. We played for the SS when they came to the camp to get drunk with our girls. On those nights there was food for the whole troupe. Then there was *Kapo* Erich in the kitchen. He liked Frieda, so Pa got her a job in the storeroom. One day she pinched two potatoes and ran to our block with them stuffed in her armpits. Pa was mad at her. You could hang in the camp for less. But we cooked them all the same over a fire of wood splinters. There was only a tiny bite each but it tasted so good I ate it again in my dreams.

And then there was Ma and her sewing machine. Pa met a tailor one day – a Sinto from Prague. He'd got a racket going with the SS. They'd bring suits they'd pinched from *Kanada* for him to alter. Silk shirts, and dresses for their girlfriends. 'My Rosa's a wizard with the sewing machine,' said Pa.

Ma didn't like it at first. 'It's low,' she said. 'The SS thieve from the Jews and then we turn it into extra rations.'

Pa threw up his hands. 'Come on, Ma! Three soups to sew a blouse! Somebody else will do it if you won't. Anyway, everything we've got comes from *Kanada*: boots, combs, baby carriages. It's just a fact.'

Ma shrugged. 'You've got to take what's offered, I suppose.'

Pa looked suddenly weary. There was grey in his hair I'd not noticed before. He sighed. 'You know the old saying, Ma. It's hard to walk straight when the road is bent. We do what we can to get by.'

As for me, I made friends with a *Kapo* called Stefan. He was a red triangle from Krakow with pockmarked skin, sticky-out front teeth, and thick glasses that made his eyes look all goggly. I called him *Shushi* behind his back – that's Romani for *rabbit*. He used to hang round our block when he'd finished his work, waiting for me. Sometimes he'd send me letters, wrapped round a slice of bread or salami. Then one day he gave me a raincoat. It had a pointed collar and two rows of buttons and a belt with a buckle. He was kind and I liked him.

'Do you want to cook for me?' said *Shushi* one day, pressing two cigarettes into my hand. 'In my special room in my block?'

I stared at the cigarettes like they were bars of gold. I didn't want the cigarettes but I could swap them for soup.

'Only cook?' I said with a laugh.

'Only cook until . . .' he said, then tapped his belly and made a mound with his hand. By this time the baby was showing, even though I'd lost weight. 'And then after that . . .' He winked and made a rude sign.

I promised I'd *cook*, as he called it, after the baby was born, so he went round smiling and whistling all day. I never really meant to be his girl, but I'd fix that wheel when it was broken. He was funny and kind and that was enough for me. It might sound daft but I think I loved him a bit. Not passionate like with Max, but it's odd the people you make friends with when you're really down on your luck. Kindness counts for more than love sometimes. That's just one of the things I learned in the camp.

By July it was suffocating – the air hot and still over the

blocks. They'd made two new hospital barracks down the far end. There was more than just typhus by this time. There was typhoid and cholera. Scarlet fever too. Every time I went to the Ka-Be I learned about some new sickness.

'What do they expect?' moaned the doctors. 'What with the rats and the maggots in the drains?'

That was one job nobody wanted. The *Scheisskommando* – the work detail that emptied the latrines. We were dying like flies. We swabbed our bunks down with Lysol but the lice didn't seem to care. They put up extra notices in the sauna, warning about our itchy friends.

'It's a shame lice can't read!' is all one prisoner said, but a *Kapo* reported him, and he couldn't sit down for a week after the guards had finished with him. There was something else too. Something the doctors said they'd never seen before outside the gypsy camp. They called it *water canker*. It was mainly the *chavvies* that got it, and there were hundreds of them in the kindergarten by now. It was like rotting ulcers all over their lips and cheeks. It looked disgusting. One little mite had a hole in his cheek so big you could see right through to his teeth.

Then one day there was a rumour. A new SS doctor had arrived, all the way from Berlin. We heard about him from Milena, a Sintezza from our block. She used to be a secretary in a hospital, so she'd got herself a camp job keeping records in the Ka-Be. It was a good 'work detail' for her, especially as she'd got *chavvies* and no man to help out.

'The new doctor's very handsome,' said Milena with a twinkle, 'and polite too, not like an SS at all.' She was very beautiful and I reckoned she fancied her chances. 'He's setting up a laboratory in our camp,' she told us, 'to look into all the sickness. He's ordered extra rations for the chavvies already. He's going to make them better.'

I got to know Doktor Mengele pretty well later on, after my baby was born. Milena was right. He *was* handsome, like a film star.

That's another thing I learned in the camp. People who do terrible things don't always look like they're bad. Mainly, they look just like everyone else.

The Secret Name

THE GEESE WERE RETURNING to the marshes – small, ragged threads skirling over the swampy ground. On a clear day you could just about see Birkenau village, the spire of Oświęcim church and the mountains in the distance with snow on the tops. Sometimes I thought I could hear the church bell tolling and then I'd realize it was just me wishing.

The family camp was filling up. Every day new people arrived and we'd nag them with questions about the war. The news wasn't good for the Germans. Italy had surrendered and their leader had resigned. Sometimes there was a newspaper smuggled in. We'd fall on it like locusts, gorging on the bad news. More defeats on the eastern front. Hamburg destroyed in a firestorm. The guards said they'd let the gypsies go at the end of the war, so we prayed for Germany's enemies every day, facing in the direction of the church spire, even if we couldn't see it through the gunmetal clouds.

By October the winds were growing stronger. Leaves flew from the birch trees that hid the chimneys. The prisoners in stripes were building again, behind those bare trees not far from our block – more buildings with chimneys. Our camp was so close we could watch them. We could hear the banging all day and all night.

We used to talk about food all the time. It was mushroom time and we dreamed of chanterelles cooked in butter. We'd swap recipes for hedgerow jelly and pickled crab apples. If I'd been a hedgehog I'd have filled my belly with slugs and beetles and made a cosy womb of leaves under a hedge and waited for my time to come, but my breasts were flat and small, like empty sacks, even though Stefan had done his best to get me eggs and butter. By that time Ma was doing so much sewing for the SS that one day she managed to *organize* a lemon for me and I ate it, peel and all. I crammed it into my mouth, sucking every last juicy squirt.

A few days before my baby was born it started heaving. I could actually see a foot or a small fist, beating on my shiny mound of stretched skin. And then the day my pains started I woke early, terrified it had stopped moving. Ma said bairns often went quiet just before they were born. 'It's making the most of the warm,' she said 'Poor *chavvi*.'

Our women didn't give birth on the stovepipe any more. There was a special birthing room in a block next to the Ka-Be. It was just a small, square space, but there was a kind of washroom and four concrete holes in the ground. It wasn't much cleaner than our block and there was no fresh water. But at least it was private. So when my pains started Ma took me there.

Women never forget their birthing day. It's burned in their memory like a brand and a blessing. There's a storm outside, howling round the barracks. I can hear the rain drumming in between the waves of agony. I can feel it too, streaming through holes in the roof, and then my body's gripped again in a white-hot flame and I can't think of anything but that. I see volcanoes in my mind like the ones in picture books. My body's a volcano. Erupting. Spewing out life like boiling lava. Someone shoves some wood between my teeth. 'Bite down. Bite!' But I can't bite for screaming. I'm screaming all the time. Ma's at my head, whispering birthing spells in my ear. I can taste vomit in my mouth. I'm drowning in pain. 'Oh, *Kali Sara*. I want to die!'

The midwife is speaking, telling me not to do something but I can't hear her, I'm yelling so loud. I push down hard as pain rips my body in two. It feels like glass, splintering, ripping through my guts. 'Can't anybody hear me? I want to die!'

I'd seen so many newborns in the camp, yellow and sickly, with crumpled faces like sad, old monkeys. Yet my boy was big. His greedy little mouth clamped onto my nipple, sucking and swallowing as if he couldn't believe nothing was coming out. 'You'll never feed him,' said the midwife.

'There's not a chance.' But my boy was a fighter, and he sucked and sucked like a kitten and when my milk came in, he gobbled and slurped so he nearly choked. I saw Pa staring at my bairn out of the tail of his eye. His baby skin was paler than mine and his hair was a different colour. Linnet brown, I'd call it. Pa never asked and I never said.

One day I found a parcel from Stefan on my bunk and a note. He'd been moved to a new camp in Birkenau for Jews from a Polish ghetto. It was like ours, he said in the note, where they stayed together and kept their own clothes. It was close by, but camps never mixed, so he might as well have gone to the moon. There was a stuffed bear with black button eyes in the parcel and two nighties he'd got me from *Kanada*. Frieda tore one into rags for me, and Ma made nappies for the baby from the other. Like I said, he was a good man. I called the bear *Shushi*, so I'd never forget Stefan.

A few days later we gave my boy his Romani name – the one we'd all use in the family. Frieda cried when I told her the name but I knew that really she was pleased. There was no beer and brandy to celebrate the naming, so Pa just played his fiddle and after that we named my baby Rollo.

But that wasn't his only name. Every Romani has a secret name too. A name that our mothers whisper the moment they first hold us in their arms. It's meant to keep the demons and bad spirits in the dark. A Romani never tells his secret name, so no one knew what my Rollo's special name was. Only me.

Winter Snow

Snow in Auschwitz lasted until March and there were many deaths that winter. *There's ice on the rabbit's paws*, Baba Sarah used to tell the *chavvies* as the weather grew colder, but Auschwitz wind had teeth of glass. It gnawed our bones. We all had burning throats and coughs that racketed our ribs. Our teeth wobbled, our gums bled and our swollen legs were covered in boils. We weren't so crowded any more. After the summer typhus and the winter deaths there was much more room in the camp. Stars glittered in a frosty sky. Snow piled in deep drifts against the barbed wire and the guards in the watchtowers sang Christmas songs, calling out greetings in their sheepskin hats. On Christmas Eve the camp was full of singing and the roaring of drunken SS. We played for them till dawn.

Our shoes were full of snow and the piles of dead bodies were now part of our lives. We'd got used to seeing them stacked on the frozen ground, waiting for the carts that hauled them away. After the first few weeks, it hardly bothered us. It wasn't that we were heartless. It's just that you can only be shocked so many times and then your skin gets tough.

Our family survived the winter without loss, all except poor Florica and Fonso, who lost their little Fifi to pneumonia. I was lucky. Ma made me a fur nest for Rollo out of some offcuts from a fur coat she'd altered on her sewing machine for an SS. He'd pinched it from *Kanada* for his girlfriend who was half the size of the coat's real owner, and he'd let Ma keep the bits in payment. It kept Rollo snug that winter. I felt guilty, but there was only enough for a baby. After Fifi died, Florica just sat and sat, rocking little Franko in her arms. She wouldn't eat and she didn't care what happened any more. Some people got like that in the camp. We called them *Muselmänner* or Moslems. Don't ask me why. It was camp lingo for people who'd given up trying to survive.

'Come on, Florica,' said Fonso. 'Don't let them break us.'

'I'm already broken,' she said. 'There's nothing left to break.'

Then April arrived with gentle breezes, as sunny as the winter was cold. And with it rumours, spreading through the camp like typhus. Suddenly there was more work for our men. They were building a new railway spur with three tracks inside Birkenau, right into the middle of the camp.

By then we knew exactly why. So the trains could drive straight in, right up to that screen of trees at the end of the road that was meant to hide the chimneys. They were murdering Jews and burning their bodies. How could we go on kidding ourselves when our camp was so close to those trees? We gathered at the Ka-Be, gazing through the wire at the prisoners building the new ramp.

By May the railway line was complete. *When will it be our turn?* The fear never left us, however many times we were told it wasn't what they planned for us. 'They'll never let us go,' whispered Ma. 'They won't leave us alive after everything we've seen.'

'Don't talk like that, Ma,' said Pa. 'You'll turn into a Moslem.'

Then one day we heard news we couldn't hardly believe. They needed space for a big transport of Jews from Hungary, so some of us would be leaving to make room. We badgered the guards for details. 'How many will be going? How will they decide?' They want the able-bodied, we were told, to replace German workers sent to the front. 'Where will they go? To towns? To another camp?' Our trapped wings beat against the bars of our cage. *Anywhere* would be better than this. And when the SS came with clipboards and lists of names we all crowded round, trampling each other, desperate to hear if our names were on the paper. We tried to stand tall and stop limping.

'We're fit for work!' we cried. 'Take us! Take me!' Our new *Lagerführer*, SS Bonigut, was all right for an SS, and I could tell he felt bad he couldn't let everyone go. I heard him arguing with the guards, trying to push more people onto the trucks so they were spilling from the sides. 'I'm the *Lagerführer* here!' he yelled. 'It's up to me.'

The Petalos didn't expect to be chosen. That's the one thing Pa hadn't managed to organize. They needed useful skills, they told us, like knowing how to make bricks or fix boilers. 'They don't need acrobats for the war effort,' said Pa.

The lucky ones rushed to collect their things. Trucks came and they all piled in, pushing and shoving for fear there wouldn't be space. It was mainly Sinti on the lists – soldiers who'd been in the Wehrmacht. The SS barked like dogs, baring their teeth. 'Only the names on the list!'

Where were the lucky names going? Places we'd never heard of – *Flossenbürg, Buchenwald, Ravensbrück*. The SS might as well have said they were going to heaven for all we knew. We rolled the names around on our tongues. We smiled bravely and waved to the departing trucks. '*Latcho drom!*' we called out in Romani. *Good journey!* Maybe next time it will be us. Maybe next time.

How can I describe the madness that spring? It was Hitler's birthday – 20 April 1944. Otherwise we wouldn't have known the date. The camp was draped with those black and red flags and we had extra bread and potatoes. They'd built a mound of earth for a platform and Pa's band had to play – waltzes by Strauss and the German anthem: *Deutschland Deutschland über alles, über alles in der Welt*. And while we played we saw a long black snake of figures passing down the main street from the ramp, past our camp gates and into the trees and then suddenly it was, '*Lagersperre!*' The doors to our block were slammed shut and the sky behind the woods turned blood red . . . then black.

One day the air over the family camp thundered, and the wooden walls of the blocks rattled with the roar of engines. We rushed outside and stared up into the pale blue sky. The sun glinted on the white stars on the planes' wings. Suddenly air-raid sirens wailed through the camp, a sound we'd never heard before.

'American bombers!' people gasped, terror mingling with a strange feeling of joy. They were flying low over the chimneys, bellies shining in the sun. SS men raced for the woods. There must be shelters in there, we thought, but there was nothing for us. We stood right out in the open, staring up at the sky.

People were shouting from all the other camps, those stripy strangers from beyond the wires. 'Hooray! Hooray! Bomb the railway lines! Bomb the death camp!'

We were all terrified, of course, but we were happy too, even though we knew we might be killed. *Someone outside knows about us. Someone outside knows.* It must be hard to believe if you've never been in hell, but we were actually praying for bombs to fall.

They didn't. Just as suddenly as they appeared, the planes looped and turned. We watched, open-mouthed, as they disappeared over the horizon. We stared after them until the sky was empty and all we could hear was a distant throb.

There was a strange silence in the family camp. No one knew what to say. We crept back to our block and climbed onto our shelves, crouching together in the darkness. It wasn't like Pa to sound beaten, but he said he felt like a man stranded on a desert island, who'd just watched the ship that might have rescued him sailing away over the rim of the sea.

Caen and Calvados

FOR ALL OUR SWAGGER we'd been hugely relieved when, boarding our train from Beverloo in March 1944 it began to chug west towards France instead of east towards Russia. Our task was to reinforce the Hitler Youth Panzergrenadiers, a group of heavily armed infantry stationed in Normandy, just off the beaches north of the pivotal town of Caen. There were rumours flying of a possible invasion of France by the Allies, so we were needed to swell the coastal defences.

'Ha, ha, ha!' my youthful companions laughed, slapping each other's backs as the train clattered west. 'They think they can pinch France from the German Reich, do they? We'll show them who's boss. We'll throw those fish back into the sea!'

Most of us had never been to France before. The countryside was beautiful and our spirits were high as we disembarked the trains on a clear blue day. We assembled in a sunlit valley of the Odon River and then marched through a forest to a fortified farmhouse, requisitioned from a local dairy farmer. This was to be our living quarters, a few hundred metres across a lush meadow from where our Jagdpanzer IV tank destroyers stood camouflaged under the trees.

The farmhouse was huge and chaotic, with walls of honey-coloured stone and windows with pretty green shutters and a monumental Normandy fireplace. This was Calvados country and the farmer had kindly abandoned quite a supply of the fiery apple liquor in the cellar, and we all felt very grown up, sitting on the terrace in the evenings, drinking brandy and watching the nightjars catch moths.

My platoon was commanded by our *Feldwebel*, a Waffen SS veteran called Werner Merkel – a tough man in his thirties with a livid burn scar on his face. He'd been decorated in Russia with the Iron Cross, and we envied it immensely. Our platoon consisted of five sturdy Jagdpanzer IVs, each crewed by smooth-faced teenagers with a more experienced man as vehicle commander. In my case, this was a twenty-two-year-old *Unterfeldwebel* called Helmuth, who'd already seen active service. Helmuth was a jolly, confident fellow with sandy hair and a dusting of freckles like brown sugar. We admired him too, but more because of his 'friendship' with Marie-Claire, the farmer's buxom daughter, than for his wartime experience.

'Do you speak French, Helmuth?' asked Fritzi, our youngest comrade, a conscript like me, who seemed younger than his fifteen years. He planned to go to art college after the war, and spent his spare time sketching brindled cows in the meadows.

We all snorted with laughter as a deep blush flooded Fritzi's plump cheeks.

Helmuth tousled his hair in a brotherly way. 'Who said anything about talking?'

In addition to the commander, each Jagdpanzer had a gunner, loader and driver, and since the average age of my crew was sixteen, at the ripe old age of eighteen I'd been given the starring role of gunner, in charge of a magnificent 75mm gun. Young Fritzi was my loader, and our driver a boy called Peter from the school year below me. Our vehicle had a low profile, scarcely taller than me, easily concealed by leaves and branches. So with camouflage smocks pulled down over our field-grey uniforms and our MP40 machine guns, we felt confident that our equipment was superior to anything the Allies might have.

Our only mild anxiety was the curious lack of air cover. We'd seen plenty of Allied reconnaissance planes flying low, taking a good look at the terrain and escaping back over the water, but there'd been no sign at all of our *Luftwaffe*. 'Where could they be?' we wondered, with only vague disquiet.

'Not wasting precious fuel in reconnaissance,' laughed Helmuth. 'Don't worry. They'll be somewhere around.'

There was a quietly confident atmosphere during those spring days as we made ready our defences in the peaceful countryside around Caen. Our rations were basic but many of us traded with the locals who would happily swap milk, meat and bread for things they lacked and we had, such as petrol, cigarettes and bootlaces. We filled our stomachs with French ham and cider, and passed the time when we weren't training catching river trout and cooking them on our Panzer engines just for fun. A favourite treat was the local Camembert cheese made with the creamy milk from the farmer's cows, despite what Helmuth poetically called its odour of 'smelly gym socks'. As we licked the sticky residue from our fingers and cleaned our palates with Calvados, we thought of our fellow soldiers in Russia and felt guilty our life was so soft.

We found out later that even a place like Normandy can be turned into a living hell. When you've seen hundreds of men killed by shells in a meadow, so that you can't tell which body parts belong together, which head, which arms, which legs, then you try to blot out the memory for the rest of your life. Until, that is, you catch a whiff of a certain kind of cheese.

Dina

I WAS WALKING TO THE KINDERGARTEN in the baking sun to feed Rollo when I first met Dina. I was wearing my new *diklo* from the *Kleiderkammer*, the clothes store down in Block Three. It was a beautiful blue, shot through with silver thread. We'd all been trying to look extra smart so we'd be chosen for the transport out, but it hadn't worked for us yet. So I was scuffing down the street in my broken boots when I saw Dina walking towards me, waving.

'Can I paint your picture?' she said. 'Doktor Mengele says I can pick who I like.'

Dina was the most beautiful girl I'd ever seen. She had long red hair that curled to her shoulders, high cheekbones and wide-set eyes that creased up at the corners when she smiled. 'Come on,' she said, taking my arm. 'I noticed you yesterday at roll call. When Doktor Mengele said I could paint who I like I came looking for you. You get extra food if you sit for a portrait.'

I didn't understand. 'What does he want my picture for?' I said. It seemed a bit funny to me but I'd stopped being surprised by things in the camp.

'I'll tell you later,' said Dina. 'Just follow me.'

'I have to feed my baby first,' I said. 'I'll come after that.'

'Don't laugh at my clothes,' said Dina, leading me into a room in the sauna next to the Ka-Be. 'It's the only dress I have. It's made for a fat woman so I've hitched it up with string. My mother says I look like a Franciscan monk.' The dress was a shapeless sack but on Dina it looked amazing. I said I didn't know what a Franciscan monk looked like, but her laugh was so catching I joined in anyway. Dina was always laughing. I liked her straight away. 'And these boots!' she said, pointing her toe like she was a model. They were heavy and tied up with wire. 'Do you know what Doktor Mengele said when he saw them? *Can't you wear nicer boots than those?* I almost said to him, "Oh, I'll just pop to the high street and buy myself something more suitable," but you don't joke with an SS. So I just said, *These are all I've got!*'

Dina was a Jew, she told me, from another *Familienlager*, a *privileged* camp like ours. 'I didn't know there was another one,' I said. 'I thought everyone else wore stripes.' Oh, yes there is, she told me, or there used to be. Theresienstadt BIIb. They came here last September from a ghetto in

Czechoslovakia. Her camp in Birkenau was nearer the main entrance than ours, near the big arch where the trains came in. I didn't know, but then why should I? This camp was huge and we never went anywhere outside our own wire.

'I couldn't live here all the time like you do,' she said, 'so close to those chimneys.'

'You think I choose to live here?' It came out crossly but I didn't mean to be rude. It's just we were all frayed nerves at that time.

She made a funny shape with her mouth. 'Like I chose my boots, I suppose!' she said, and we started to laugh. She was always making funny faces, was Dina. 'We used to wear our own clothes in BIIb. We kept our hair and stayed in families like you. To start with we could even write postcards, except we had to pretend we were staying in a town called Neu-Berun, about five miles away . . .'

'To start with?'

Dina jerked her thumb in the air and made a noise like a firework going up. 'They're all dead,' she said. 'My father, brother, all my family. All except Mother and little Mischa here . . .'

The light wasn't good so I hadn't noticed the little boy at first, crouching over a bowl of water, washing paintbrushes.

'That's good, Mischa,' said Dina. 'Thank you.'

I stared at her. 'So how did you . . .?'

'Doktor Mengele saved me. He'd already chosen me to make the paintings when the *Kommandant* decided we were all going to the gas. He came to take me to the main camp on the afternoon they all went off. Of course I'd no idea where the others were going. The SS kept pretending they were going on a transport – to a work camp somewhere nicer – just to keep things peaceful. My mother wasn't well and I didn't want her travelling without me, so I told him straight: "I'm not going to the main camp without my mother and little Mischa here." The doctor said, "He's not family," but I told him he was my assistant, and that I couldn't work without him.

'That night trucks came and took the whole camp to the gas, all except the ones on the doctor's list: ten pairs of twins, my mother, Mischa and me. No one else survived. All dead. Babies, children . . . everybody gone.' Her voice cracked. 'They only realised what was happening at the end, but it was too late by then. They were all singing the *Hatikvah* as they went to the gas. And the Czech National Anthem.' Her eyes were deep pools of sadness. 'I usually cry buckets when I tell that story. So you see, Mischa,' she said to the boy, 'I'm getting better.'

I stared at her. 'How can you still laugh?'

Dina shrugged. 'Mother says despair is like a disease and living every day's the remedy. I hold on to that thought.'

Dina talked a lot as she got her paints out and positioned me on a chair like a model. I had the feeling it helped her. She was only twenty, just two years older than me. She'd been an art student in Prague with a scholarship to a college there. 'But how do you think they found out I could paint?' she giggled.

I shrugged. I guessed it was going to be funny.

Well, she only went and painted faces on other girls' bottoms with eyebrow pencil so they could *moon* at the SS behind their backs! She couldn't believe I didn't know what *mooning* meant. 'Maybe I'm just a naughty girl,' she said. Dina was one of the funniest people I'd ever met. Lucky for her their *Blockführer* had a sense of humour. And it got her the painting job.

To start with she just painted signs for the blocks with slogans like *Cleanliness is next to Godliness*. She laughed at how stupid that was. 'I got my own back, though. I painted tiny lice and fleas around the letters, so small nobody could see them – but *I* knew they were there and that was enough.' Then when they found she could paint properly she got work from the SS drawing their girlfriends from photographs in exchange for food and cigarettes. She even painted her camp kindergarten with Snow White and the Seven Dwarfs dancing together, ready for when the International Red Cross came to visit. 'I know it sounds like I've made it up,' she said, 'but everything's crazy here.'

'I'd believe anything,' I said, and I told her about the show we put on and the planes filming us.

Dina nodded. 'It's propaganda,' she said. 'To mislead the world into thinking this is a holiday camp.'

Anyway, one day an SS doctor called Lukas saw the Snow White painting in their kindergarten and brought Dina in a jeep to meet Doktor Mengele. 'He wanted an artist to illustrate his book about gypsies,' said Dina. '"Ten or twelve portraits," he said. Would I do the job? As if I had a choice! How I laughed when I told Mother. "I've been in a jeep to see Doktor Mengele . . . and I've come back alive!"'

I shook my head. I was starting to worry. There were rumours about this Doktor Mengele. How he experimented on twins and sick children, but no one knew if they were true.

I asked Dina about it.

She shrugged. 'Who knows if the stories are true? Many children die, but many children are sick. I often ask myself – what sort of a man would be a doctor in a place like this unless . . .' She lowered her voice. 'Look, Lili. If you want my advice, stop asking awkward questions. I do the paintings. You sit for them. Just understand what's good for you.'

I took a deep breath. 'So why do you want to paint *me*?' I could ask her that, at least.

Dina's face clouded. 'I don't *want* to paint you. It's an order. If the SS tell you to do something, you do it, unless you want to be . . .' She made that sound again like the whoosh of a firework. 'You know that as well as I do.' And then her face lit up. 'It's all right really. Better than hauling bags of rocks all day at the quarry. And if I have to paint to save my life, I might as well choose the prettiest girl I can find.'

Doktor Mengele couldn't get a decent photograph of the gypsies, he'd told Dina, for his book on genetic research. The colours weren't right at all. Too garish, apparently. He needed the exact skin tones for his work. 'He's a doctor of anthropology as well as medicine,' said Dina.

I didn't know what anthropology was. Or genetic research. I didn't tell Dina, though, else she'd think I was stupid.

'Can you paint as good as a photograph, with skin tones and eye colours just right?' he'd asked Dina, and she said she'd try. She'd done some men already and now she was painting women.

'The last one wasn't pretty like you,' Dina said. 'But there was something in her face that I liked.'

So there I was, sitting in a small room next to Doktor Mengele's office, like a real artist's model. The sauna was right next to the ramp, and through the flimsy wooden walls we heard the long, lonely whistle of the cattle trucks arriving. We held each other's eyes, listening, and then Dina shook her head. 'You can't save everyone. I saved Mother and little Mischa here. We just do what we can.' Then she smiled reassuringly. 'Don't worry. I've told you. Doktor Mengele's writing a book about gypsies. So he must mean to keep you safe . . . and me too, as long as I keep painting. So . . . if you can turn your head to the left, I'll make a start. A half profile would be nice.'

I turned my head. Dina's drawings covered the walls: paintings of heads, noses, ears, feet. There was a chart of eye colours, a picture of a heart. She must have seen me shudder. 'He puts them in a book,' she said quickly, 'and makes notes in the margins. It's important work, so that after the war he can become a professor at the university in Berlin.'

I sat as still as I could. I wasn't feeling very beautiful. I'd caught sight of my face in a mirror by the door. We didn't have mirrors in the block so I almost looked over my shoulder to see if there was someone behind me until I realised the hollow face was mine. The dark rings, the missing tooth. I told Dina I wasn't looking my best.

She got up, untied my *diklo* and arranged it in a different way so it surrounded my face. 'You're lovely,' she said. 'When I saw you yesterday, I knew I had to paint you.'

Dina took days to paint me and I got the feeling she was taking

longer than she needed, we had so much to say. She'd been in
love too, in the Theresienstadt ghetto, with a boy called Karl,
but she'd taken a lover in the camp – a *Kapo* called Willi. She
told me such funny things about him. He was nothing like her
Karl. Willi had terrible teeth when she first met him, and then
a prisoner in the camp who was a dentist patched them up for
him. He wasn't handsome but she'd grown to love him. He
got her food and made her laugh, and that was important to
Dina. She was incredible. One of the nicest people I'd ever
met. She told me she made a baby with Karl in the ghetto
but a lady got rid of it for her. I was shocked at first, but
I understood. After all, I'd thought about it myself, though
now the idea made my heart stand still. Rollo was my life
now. He was the one bright star in my dark night.

Dina knew I had a baby, though I didn't tell her about
Max. I only ever told Frieda and that was hard enough, but
I wanted to swap something for her secrets. So I told Dina
about Stefan and his bad skin and thick glasses that made
his eyes swim like fish and we held our sides laughing. She
knew I didn't mean it cruelly. Dina had learned the same
lesson in here as me: love comes with different hats on. She
still loved Karl, but Karl wasn't here, and Willi was a good
man. He helped her get by. I felt lucky Stefan had been sent
to another camp, because I don't think I could have gone
with him like Dina went with Willi. But I didn't blame her
either. We did things differently in the camp. We did what
we needed to survive.

Doktor Mengele

MY PAINTING TOOK TEN DAYS and I met the Doktor every day. He drove an open jeep or sometimes a motorbike. He was always dressed in a crisp white overall when he was working in his lab. It was hard to believe the things people said about him, though Pa said angel faces were often the worst. He was always whistling tunes from the opera and he loved *Zigeunermusik*, as he called it. Dina thought he looked half-gypsy himself with his dark hair and olive skin.

There were often children in the room next to where Dina painted. She said he was measuring heads and taking fingerprints, and there was a Polish assistant called Zosia, writing everything down: eye colour, skin colour, mouth shapes. 'The children seem to like him,' said Dina. 'He gives them sweets. They call him Onkel Pepi.'

Doktor Mengele played chess too, in the clerk's office with a Czech prisoner called Ivan who'd lost all his family to the gas. The doctor was good but Ivan was better. 'He has to be careful,' said Dina. 'Ivan could beat the doctor every time, so he has to make sure he lets him win.' Dina frowned. 'The day he gets to checkmate by accident . . .' That firework noise again. '*Whooosh!* Ivan plays chess for his life,' she said, 'like I paint for mine.'

Some days Doktor Mengele was silent with a faraway look in his eyes, and others he was whistling. One day he turned up in a jolly mood. He was carrying a bunch of photographs of Rolf, his baby. He was chattier than usual. He was writing a fairy story for his son, he told us. He sat down in a chair, dangling his legs over the side, all casual. 'Gypsies used to come to my hometown in Bavaria. I always enjoyed their music.' He fixed me with his brown gaze. 'I'm fond of gypsies, you know, the way you sing and dance. Oh, you'll never settle down like civilized people and you're a thieving bunch too. I said to Schwarzhuber, "You have to keep your hand on your pocket when you go into the gypsy camp!" But you certainly look on the bright side of life.'

I frowned. I hadn't thought life had a bright side lately.

'They told good stories too,' he said. He smiled suddenly, like he'd had an idea. 'You must know *Zigeuner* stories.'

'I . . . I know some . . .'

'Then tell me one.'

My mouth felt dry and my heart was thumping so hard it made my voice tremble. 'Well,' I said slowly, 'if you like

Zigeunermusik . . . I know one called *The Romani Fiddle* . . .'

He leaned back and closed his eyes. 'Go on, then,' he said. 'Tell me.'

I looked at Dina. I knew what she was thinking. *Some paint, some play chess, some tell stories . . .*

I took a deep breath. I couldn't believe this was really happening. But like I said, crazy things happened in the camp all the time.

Long ago, I began timidly, *there lived a poor girl called Lavuta. She was good and beautiful but no man would marry her, for she was a cripple with a leg all shrivelled from birth.*

I paused. I licked my lips like I always did when I was scared. My blood ran like ice, although my face was burning up.

'Go on,' snapped the doctor. 'I'll tell you when I've had enough . . .'

One day, as she sat weeping under a tree, a handsome forester appeared on a black stallion, dressed in a green hat with a fine big feather. At first Lavuta was frightened, for she hadn't heard the sound of hooves on the forest floor.

'Don't be afraid,' said the forester, 'for I have bread and honey cakes!' Then from his saddlebags he took a barrel of beer, half a roasted pig, a dish of herrings and a wheel of crumbly cheese – far more than could ever have fitted into the bags.

But Lavuta only clapped her hands and cried, 'You must be an angel. God bless you!'

'Eat! Drink!' said the woodsman, 'and afterwards I will take you to my castle. I have a healing well. If you drink the water your leg will be whole and I will make you my bride.' Then he kissed her, and Lavuta grew so warm in his embrace that she didn't notice his breath was as cold as the tomb.

The doctor grunted. 'So she was a fool then as well as a cripple.'

I licked my lips again. *It's me who's the fool*, I thought. I could have chosen so many tales. What made me choose this one? 'Sh-shall I stop now?'

He shook his head. 'Carry on. I like it.'

And when she had eaten, she climbed up behind him and they rode off together, and as they rode, she sang a joyful song.

'You will sing your song to me every night at my castle,' said the woodsman. 'It will warm my heart.'

The mountain path wound higher and as the sun began to set, Lavuta felt suddenly cold, so she wrapped her arms even tighter round her lover's back, but she drew no heat from him. 'Maybe he's cold too,' she told herself, 'with no spare warmth for me.'

I paused again. My throat was dry. Dina was listening, her lips parted, but I wondered if the doctor was dozing. After a second he opened his eyes. 'And then what happened?' he said sharply. 'Why do you keep stopping?'

At last they reached the castle, and the woodsman jumped down from his horse. Poor Lavuta was so tired she thought she must be dreaming when the wind whipped back the forester's cloak and she saw a pair of goat's feet poking out. But when the wind snatched off his hat, she knew it was no dream. Two horns sprouted from his black hair, and at last Lavuta knew that this was Beng, the devil.

'Where is the healing well?' she cried. 'Take me to it as you promised.'

At this Beng threw back his head and as he laughed his forked tongue quivered. 'What? So you can run from me? No! Now I have you here, I will never be lonely again.'

And that night, he made her his wife.

Outside the shadowy room I heard the shrill whistle of a train arriving. The harsh clanking of doors. I felt hot and cold all at once. I'd forgotten, when I started, just how the story went from here. I wished I'd never started but there was no going back. So I told the story of her broken heart and how she refused to sing her joyful song or eat Beng's food or wear fine clothes until at last he locked her in the highest tower with a scroll of parchment and a quill.

'You will write down the joyful song you sang when first

we met or you will be my prisoner here, even to the end of the world.'

And Lavuta bowed her head and wept. As weeks turned into months Lavuta's waist grew thin until she could put both hands around it so her fingers touched, and her hair grew scraggly long. And the more she grieved, the angrier Beng grew.

Every night at moonrise, the devil returned to her tower. 'Where is your joyful song?'

Now, unbeknown to Beng, four brown mice had pitied Lavuta in her loneliness, bringing her berries from the bushes every day. 'How can I ever repay your friendship?' she whispered as they ran about her shoulders and sat lovingly in her hair.

'You could sing your joyful song for us,' they said.

So Lavuta wrote down her song on the scroll and sang it for them, and as she sang they stroked her ragged hair. But still she would not sing for Beng.

I looked up. The doctor was staring at me in the fading light, a strange expression on his face. I glanced at Dina. Her face was tense. And yet I couldn't stop now. Doktor Mengele was waiting.

Then, one night, the four mice squeezed under her door in excitement. 'He has accidentally left the key on the other side,' they squeaked. 'We will nibble a hole so you can free yourself. But take us with you, dear Lavuta, or we will die of grief.'

So she gathered them up and placed two in each pocket. Then, snatching up her crutch and scroll, Lavuta fled into the forest, but as she fled, a raven rose up from the top of the tower and flew to the devil's chamber. When he heard how he'd been cheated, he gave a great roar of pain. Then, mounting his black stallion, he kicked its flanks with his spurs. And when he caught up with Lavuta, he raised his great club and struck her down and her life gushed out, drowning the mice in a river of blood.

There was a sharp knock on the door. I almost jumped out of my skin. It was the Polish assistant. 'Ivan is here to play chess,' she said.

Doktor Mengele looked surprised, as if he'd forgotten, although Ivan came every night at that time.

'Tell him to wait in my office,' said the doctor. 'Go on, *Zigeuner*,' he said, but his voice was less friendly now. 'You've chosen a miserable tale but I still want to hear how it ends.'

One day, after many years had passed, a Romani was walking in the forest, when all of a sudden he caught his foot on a gnarled old root. The root was the strangest shape he'd ever seen, like a woman's body, with coarse hair at the top and rounded shoulders and a waist. Four twigs stuck out from the body, one much thinner than the rest, and as he gazed upon the strange root, he thought he heard faint music. So he sat down on a log and, taking

*out his knife, began to carve the twisted root, and as he
hollowed and whittled, the sweet music grew louder.
Birds stopped flying to listen and the trees began to twist
and sway to the magical tune. Then out from the belly of
the root rolled four shrivelled stones and a twisted scroll
of parchment, hard and dry.*

*On and on the Romani carved, the music showing
his fingers where to shape, until the sun went down and
the moon rose and the song quivered gently to an end.
Then he gazed on what he'd made. It was the strangest
object he'd ever seen, with shoulders, a waist and hips
like a woman and four strings attached to four round
pegs and a long slender neck topped by a curly scroll.
For from Lavuta's body he'd carved the first fiddle.
And of the brown mice he'd carved four pegs to hold the
strings and on the top he'd placed the scroll that held
the joyful song. Then from Lavuta's crutch he made a
slender bow and strung it with her hair. And as he drew
the bow across the thinnest string he heard a voice from
the hollow belly.*

*'My name is Lavuta. Once I was silent, sad and
lonely. But a Romani has given me back my voice. Others
will learn to play me, but no one will ever play me like
the Roma, for above all other people on the earth, Lavuta
belongs to them.'*

It was almost dark. Doktor Mengele said nothing. He stared
into space, a frown on his face, his thumb resting in the
dimple on his chin. And then he scraped back his chair and

357

marched out, slamming the door behind him, so hard it quivered in its frame.

The next day he arrived at the sauna in a different mood. He stood at Dina's shoulder as she painted. His voice was sharp. He didn't like my picture. He didn't like the scarf over my ear. Had she forgotten this was a scientific portrait? He wanted to see the shape of my ear, not the colour of my kerchief. He pulled the fabric back and wound it behind my ear, not roughly, but like I was a specimen, like the ones Dina said he kept in jars in his laboratory. 'There. Like that,' he barked. 'Change it!'

That was the last time I saw Doktor Mengele, until . . .

Well, Baba Sara used to say, 'When you're a *chavvi* you have the face you were born with. And when you grow up you get the face you deserve.' Baba Sara was wrong about that. Doktor Mengele was handsome, with a face like an angel. But I think his heart was black – like Beng, the devil.

Waiting

WE WERE EXPECTING the Allies to invade Europe in
that summer of 1944, but the strain of not knowing
exactly where and when caused nerves to unravel, even
amongst the toughest volunteers. Even fifteen year olds
preferred cigarettes to sweets these days and when we
weren't out mapping the terrain, we'd gather in huddles
smoking nervously. Would they come by air or landing
boats? From the north or western coast of France? 'Probably
from Calais,' our commanders reassured us. 'After all, it's
the narrowest crossing-place. But it doesn't really matter.
The coast is bristling with heavy guns and we've mined the
dunes and cliffs right along the Atlantic Wall.'

On the rainy evening of 4 June we'd been disturbed

by the noise of Jagdbombers flying overhead – the Allied fighter-bombers we called *Jabos* for short. They'd flown over the beaches and inland this time, and we'd heard the noise of flak firing from south of our position. Nonetheless it was clear that something new was happening. We'd never heard so many planes at night before.

Unperturbed, Helmuth had brought the farmer's daughter, Marie-Claire, to the house again and whilst we ate bread and cheese and drank cider in the kitchen we tried to ignore the squeals of delight wafting down the rickety stairs. There was not a little envy amongst the rest of us gathered round the table, making do with a game of Skat.

'He's not even particularly handsome,' someone sighed. 'She can't have very good taste.'

'Maybe he has a *way with women*,' said young Fritzi, blushing scarlet. He was putting the finishing touches to a sketch of some striped kittens he'd found in one of the barns. He planned to send it to his mother in Munich.

I poked him in the ribs with a stick of stale bread. 'What do you know about women, Fritzi?' I teased.

He scowled at me, his flush deepening. 'About as much as you do, I expect!'

I glared back, stung by the implication. 'How do you know what I know?'

We'd had too much time on our hands lately, and all this hanging around was making us quarrelsome. In fact, I had a soft spot for Fritzi, really. He was a conscript like me, not a volunteer, and as a rule I got along with conscripts better.

'Oh, stop quarrelling you lot,' said Werner, our *Feldwebel*.

'You don't know when you're well off. You've got beds and food. Cigarettes. What more do you want?'

'It's all this waiting,' someone said. 'We just want something to happen.'

Werner smiled grimly. 'You'll feel better when it's started.'

We all nodded, reassured. We respected Werner. Naively, we believed him.

We sprang to our feet suddenly at the sound of another wave of bombers flying over, nearer this time. Tumbling over each other we grabbed our gas masks, preparing to scuttle down the cellar stairs.

'Stay where you are, lads!' Werner commanded. 'No need for the cellar. Our Jadgpanzers are well hidden. They'll look like hedgerows from above even with a full moon like tonight.' Sounds of explosions flared and died away. 'We're invisible as ticks on a dog here.'

We returned ashen-faced to our seats as dust drifted down from the rafters, glinting in the lamplight. The bombing couldn't be as far away as last night. It sounded closer – to me, at least. Reluctantly we went back to our game of Skat, our hands trembling as we dealt the cards onto the gritty table and Fritzi blew dirt from his drawing.

Werner Merkel pulled a dusty bottle towards him and lined up some breakfast cups. 'Any of you kids want brandy? This hanging about always jangles the old nerves. But you're going to fight those damn Tommies and you're going to win.' He fingered the lumpy scar on his face. 'We'll mine those meadows round the house tomorrow. Then the sooner they come the better, I say. We'll give those Allies a spanking they'll never forget!'

There was a burst of nervous laughter. Somebody clapped. Then someone fiddled with the dial on the farmer's wireless, trying to tune in to a German station. It crackled into life, easing the atmosphere as an orchestra struck up the opening chords of a song. I took a swig straight from the brandy bottle, shuddering as I felt the fiery liquid trickle down my throat. I began to relax, humming along to the familiar tune. What was it? Suddenly my voice faltered. *Oh no! Not that tune. Anything but that* . . .

Memories are like highwaymen. They catch you unawares. In a taste, a smell, in the dying notes of a verse. But my comrades had already taken up this favourite song of the German troops and were warbling along, happy to have a sing-song to take their minds off the sound of flak firing, cranking up the volume for the final words of the chorus:

'Mit dir, Lili Marlene . . .'
With you, Lili Marlene . . .

I scraped back my chair, stalked across the room and turned the dial. The wireless went off with a pop.

'Hey, wait a minute,' someone shouted. 'We were enjoying that!'

My feet echoed on the wooden treads as I stomped up the stairs and clattered open the wooden door of the room I shared with Fritzi. I scrabbled in my kitbag for the cigarette case; the one that had belonged to Onkel Manfred with the words *Gott Mit Uns* on the front. *God With Us*. He'd better be. I flipped a cigarette from the elastic, ignited a match with the nail of my thumb and took a drag, inhaling deeply as I pulled out my little suitcase from under the bed. Then, searching with my fingers in the darkness, I found the tarot cards inside. I didn't need a candle, since I knew the Knight of Wands would be on top. I pulled it from the deck and placed it in the cigarette case, and then remembering Tante Ida's story about the soldier saved from a sniper's bullet, I slipped it into the left breast of my jacket . . . over my heart. Flinging myself down on the bed, I stared up at the low wooden beams, watching the smoke coil upwards in the moonlight. Someone had switched the wireless back on downstairs and they were singing again.

I slept badly that night, thickheaded from drinking. The trees rustled in the wind, and as the shadows of their branches danced to and fro over the moonlit rafters, I fancied I saw a girl on a flying trapeze, swooping back and forth across the ceiling.

Next day, just before noon, Helmuth roared into the farmyard on his motorbike, scattering hens like skittles. The day was unusually wet and blustery. We'd been out ourselves that morning, laying mines in a meadow. Helmuth tipped back his helmet and peeled off his dripping goggles. 'Someone's seen paratroopers landing,' he panted. For once he was looking anxious. 'And we saw twin-engined aircraft with black and white stripes on their wings. I've never seen those before . . .'

Werner had come out into the farmyard at the sound of the bike. I remember that day so clearly, even the smell from the dung pit where the farmer kept stable waste for fertilizer. I remember the white gulls against the leaden sky tumbling inland from the shore.

'They sound like C47s,' Werner said grimly. 'The Tommies use them for personnel transport – paratroopers, that sort of thing. See any of our *Luftwaffe*, Helmuth?'

Helmuth shook his head. 'No, sir.'

Werner grunted. 'I can't understand it. Our warning level was two at the weekend but it's down to three today.' He scratched his scar. 'That doesn't seem right to me . . .'

It wasn't right. Not right at all. At dawn on the 6 June, as the sun rose over the grey Atlantic, a gigantic war fleet appeared on the horizon. The invasion of Normandy had begun.

Sardine Cans

WE FIRST SAW ACTION on 7 June, and to be honest our orders had come as a relief. There'd been confusion at first about the true scale of the landings. So we hadn't been ordered to the front until twelve hours after first reports of the invasion, but at last we'd received our briefing from German High Command. Believe it or not, we'd actually cheered, slapping each other on the back and toasting our comrades with what was left of the farmer's Calvados.

'You know what this means don't you, lads?' said Werner.

We all nodded.

We didn't.

Our 12th Panzer Division was one of the closest to the landing beaches and by mid-morning the following day we'd moved into a position north-west of Caen, with orders to crush the advancing Canadian infantry and tanks, and drive them back into the sea only a few kilometres away.

'Child's play,' said Werner. 'Those Churchills and Shermans are not a patch on our Panthers. Sardine cans, I call them!'

Our position consisted of a couple of platoons of tank destroyers, including my own Jagdpanzer IV, together with some artillery and a small group of Panther tanks that were joining us from nearby. We had a communication team of Hitler Youth in a *Kübelwagen*, a jeep-type vehicle with a machine gun mounted on the back, and Werner as platoon commander in a radio car. A dispatch rider on a BMW motorbike completed our force. I rather envied the biker, tearing around, looking important, although to be honest I was feeling pretty grown-up myself as gunner for my crew.

We'd advanced into an area of lush, wooded countryside and then out onto an undulating plain where the woods gave way to neat patchwork fields. This morning the sky was forget-me-not blue with clouds like wispy lambs' tails.

'You can put this in your sketchbook when we get back, Fritzi,' I said, 'so you won't forget your first taste of real action.'

Our reconnaissance unit had informed us that there were Canadian tanks about two kilometres ahead.

'Not long to wait now,' said Helmuth, punching me on the shoulder. 'Are you looking forward to painting your first kill-ring on the gun barrel?'

On Werner's instructions our five Jagdpanzer IVs fanned

out on the edge of the trees, three in the forward position and two in reserve, watching our flanks, and the crews all jumped out of the cramped interiors, racing round arranging camouflage foliage. Tanks move fast and there was no time to dawdle with the enemy so close. We arranged the branches and leaped swiftly back into our positions, Helmuth standing in the command hatch, his helmet sprouting twigs and leaves, with me on my circular gunner's seat. Peter settled down in the driving seat and Fritzi crouched to my left as loader, his small frame just perfect for handling shells in a cramped space. Our ambush was ready.

'All set, Fritzi?' I asked.

He'd seemed all right when we'd heard news of the enemy's approach, but now I could see he was shaking.

'Here, have some of this,' said Helmuth, offering round his hip flask. 'Take as much as you like. There's plenty more.'

We each took a hefty swig, coughing as the flask turned out to contain neat brandy. I grabbed the flask again and took another greedy gulp. Then Helmuth dug in his jacket and brought out some small pills from a brown tube with a buff label bearing the word *Pervitin* in black writing. I didn't know what they were.

'Break one in half and give half to Fritzi,' he said, sharing his own with Peter, who washed it down with another swig of brandy.

It's hard to explain how I felt, waiting for that first engagement. I'd read accounts of battles in France in the World War – of men breaking down and weeping, praying and crying for their mothers. It just didn't feel like that at all.

Our Jagdpanzer had a solid steel *Saukopf*, a curved pig's-head mantlet to repel armour-piercing shells, and I'd felt fairly invincible during training, snug in our little compartment with the hatch cover down. We'd performed so many exercises using live rounds I felt fairly confident I knew what to expect. Everything had an air of unreality, so I wasn't very scared at first, although the promised Panther tanks had not yet materialised as back-up, and Helmuth was cursing their drivers. He was smoking incessantly and that surprised me, as he'd never been much of a one for the cigarettes. Not until now, anyway – and that unsettled me a little. I took a deep breath to steady my nerves.

On the edge of the wood I saw some Hanomags full of Panzergrenadier boys, confident and smiling, and that reassured me – until, that is, I caught my first glimpse of the enemy. I had my eye to my optic sight when suddenly my heart gave a lurch. For a moment I thought it had forgotten how to beat and then it set up a strange percussion in my chest – a double thump that took my breath away. I stared at the horizon in horror. I thought I might choke.

They were Churchills, I was pretty sure of it. We'd seen a captured one on the training ground at Beverloo and I recognised that squat, domed profile with its 88mm gun. There were three of them, huge and green, moving rapidly from west to east across the plain in a fountain of dust, making swiftly for the cover of some trees. My stomach clenched as I put my eye to the sighting triangle and traversed the gun as I'd been taught, so the white mark rested on the first tank in line. I took another deep breath, but by now I was feeling light-headed. That special tablet Helmuth had doled out had made me alert and aggressive, smothering any last traces of fear. I put my hand to my left breast, feeling for the cigarette case with the Knight of Wands inside. I was a real knight now, I thought to myself, only my charger was a Jagdpanzer IV.

'Do I wait for orders, sir?' I asked Helmuth, 'or do I fire when I'm ready?'

'No – wait!' he said, squinting through his binoculars, his hand on my shoulder. He was listening to the radio, eyes narrowed, waiting for instructions from Werner. 'Let's see how many of the buggers there are first. We want to make the most of their vulnerable hull flanks before they spot our position. We can knock out the whole line of the beauties if we time it right.'

But my neighbouring Jagdpanzer had other ideas. Suddenly their gunner opened fire and I saw bright green armour-piercing tracer snaking through the air to score a hit on the front of the first tank. The Churchill lurched to the left, its track bursting from its metal plate in a shower of rivets and wheels. I couldn't help feeling annoyed with Helmuth. That first hit should have been mine.

'Fire!' shouted Helmuth suddenly. 'And keep firing!'

I fired my first round. I don't know whether it was my hit this time or my neighbour's. There was an almighty flash around the turret ring of the second Churchill, and Helmuth cheered as the enemy hatches flew up into the air, smoke billowing, the tank's turret spinning like a child's top. Another shell must have gone straight through the petrol tank. The rear end exploded in a sheet of flame, blowing out the rear plates, flinging the exhaust high into the air, oily smoke rolling upwards in thick black coils.

By now there were at least ten Churchills in the line, all of them exposed, their flanks towards our anti-tank guns as we sat like predators in the shadow of the trees. Our three most forward guns, including mine, were firing now, little Fritzi clearing the breech, shifting the long shells, then loading in a frenzy at my elbow as I traversed my gun to take fresh aim. My heart was racing, my ears ringing painfully with the shriek of rocket launchers, the thundering din of explosions. We could see the Churchills panicking now. We'd caught them entirely by surprise in the open and now they began to weave around, heading for cover in the woods, some reversing, colliding, spinning, spouting tongues of red and orange flames as our tracer rounds sped across the summer meadows, spent warheads tumbling head over heels across the fields.

'Shoot them up, Max!' yelled Helmuth. 'Knock 'em all out!'

Naively, we cheered again. We were hitting more and more of them now, and I watched in amazement as my tracer hit a Churchill on its centre flank. The turret burst from the hull, smashing to the earth and rolling away in a huge, fiery explosion. I saw some of the enemy crew flung clear, their bodies trailing fire and smoke. Others began to climb out, some with their clothing on fire, desperately beating at the flames while diving for cover, racing to get clear before their fuel tank went up.

In the lulls between firing I could hear cheers coming

from my comrades in the other Jagdpanzers. In the space of five minutes the first seven of the line of ten were totally wrecked or in flames, their caterpillar tracks sprawled out, and between the burning vehicles I saw many soldiers on the ground, wounded or dead, like bundles of bloodstained clothing.

These were the first casualties I'd ever seen. On the ranges we'd shot at empty tanks. Never with real people inside. Later, much later, these scenes would come to haunt me, but just now in the heat of battle we had no time to think of the carnage inside their hulls. We were fired up with adrenaline and amphetamines – just one thought on our minds: the sure and certain knowledge that it was them or us.

By now my gun barrel was red-hot. I just couldn't understand why the other Churchills weren't returning our fire. *They must have spotted us by now.* I placed my eye to my optic and traversed my gun again. Suddenly my hands were shaking, jumping with a will of their own. Three Churchills at the rear of the line had turned their front hulls to face our direction, and I watched with mounting horror as all three of them lowered their strange, fat guns. My bowels turned to water. For the first time in my life I was looking down the muzzle of a gun that would shoot to kill. And for the first time today the enemy tanks had our Jagdpanzers in their sights.

How to Make Omelettes

W^E DEFLECTED THE IMPACT of the enemy's first shell
from our mantlet but the force jerked my gun breech
violently upwards. I stumbled backwards so poor Fritzi got
the full impact in his face, breaking his jaw. He slumped
over the gun barrel, groaning as the whole vehicle rocked on
its suspension. 'I'm hit, I'm hit,' he screamed as he slumped
sideways, blood pouring from his mouth.

'Is there a round loaded?' shrieked Helmuth.

'I-I think so, sir,' I stammered, but as I tried to traverse
my gun there was a second almighty explosion as another
shell broke through our armour plate, the steel peeling back
like a can of vegetables. Shards of metal shot around inside
our compartment and with a jolt I realized that I too had

been hit. My seat was suddenly slick with blood, hot and sticky, pouring down my back. There was a numb sensation between my shoulder blades, as if someone were dragging me from behind. I tried to twist round to take a look but Helmuth aimed a kick at my head.

'Fire, you bloody fool!' he yelled. 'The bastards are shortening their range.'

I could hear the panic in his voice. The dials on my controls were darting madly. Desperately I tried to clear the gun breech and reload it myself before concluding with a curse that the bloody thing was jammed. *Any minute now and they'll hit us again.*

Then suddenly I heard another sound, unlike any I'd ever heard before – a low, screeching noise that set my teeth on edge. From the western fringe of the meadow I saw a vast curtain of fire creeping towards our position, a tornado of scarlet whirling upwards, ten metres into the air.

I heard Helmuth swear. 'What the hell?'

It was an awesome sight. I found out later it was a Crocodile. A Churchill tank fitted with a flamethrower in its hull that sprayed fuel mixed with rubber pellets – a deadly combination that stuck to anything it touched like burning jelly. Suddenly the entire plain was ablaze with yellow and orange flashes, bursting above the ground. And then through the din we heard the thrum of oncoming aircraft.

Please God let it be our Luftwaffe! I shielded my eyes but all I could see were dark shapes in the azure sky.

'*Jabos!*' somebody cried as I saw streams of bombs descending on the long-awaited Panther tanks, that had suddenly rolled into view.

'Get the hell out of here – NOW!' screamed Helmuth as the meadow erupted in a storm of red tracer from the enemy tanks.

In a grinding of gears I felt our vehicle shoot backwards, then Peter hit the accelerator. There were explosions all around us now, flinging up vast plumes of earth, and as our crippled Jagdpanzer lurched around a clump of trees I heard a screaming sound above my head as we were hit for a third time. I saw a huge spurt of blood erupting from Helmuth's leg, splattering Peter's hands as he gripped the wheel. Flames burst from the back of our destroyer.

'The engine's shot!' yelled Peter. 'The tank will ignite!'

As we juddered to a halt I sprang onto the roof, searching in vain for the fire extinguisher. Looking down through the gunner's hatch I could see oil on the floor mingling with the blood, an ugly thick mess of black and red. Already there was a strong stench of petrol. Suddenly everything seemed to happen in slow motion, so that afterwards I could recall every moment with perfect clarity. A fire had ignited in the hatch, oil from the engine feeding the flames. I remember the blistering heat and the flames so bright they left an imprint on the back of my eyes so that everything seemed edged with fire.

'Help me! For God's sake, help!' screamed Helmuth, grasping the hatch cover and trying to haul himself up. He scrabbled wildly with his hands on the roof panel, unable to lift himself out. 'My bloody leg's trapped!'

'Get Fritzi out,' I screamed at Peter, leaning over and

giving him a shove. 'Move yourself, for God's sake!'

I hauled Helmuth under his arms. I tugged and tugged but nothing happened. Helmuth was struggling in the flames, screaming and pleading with me as the fire down the hatch began to engulf him. Out of the corner of my eye I saw Peter. I stared in horror. He was slumped over the wheel with the back of his head missing. Killed outright.

It was all down to me now. I could see the agony in Helmuth's eyes, but he was firmly trapped. There were flashes of burning fuel spurting from the engine deck behind me. Any moment now and the whole thing would explode. Suddenly I knew what I had to do. Grabbing Fritzi under the arms I hauled him out and flung him wide of the vehicle with all the strength I could muster. Then, seizing the Luger from my belt, I leaped clear of the crippled destroyer.

I braced myself. I raised the barrel. I felt the click of the firing pin. I took careful aim and squeezed the trigger – two shots at my friend Helmuth, straight between the eyes. I jerked backwards with the gun's recoil. The terrible screaming stopped and Helmuth's body lay still at last, already engulfed by flames. For a moment I stood rooted to the spot, shaking, weeping, then, collecting my wits, I hauled Fritzi over my shoulder. Staggering under his weight, I began to stumble across the burning grass. Within seconds I heard a tremendous blast behind me as our Jagdpanzer burst into flames.

'Get in here,' screamed a voice. 'We're in retreat!' I hadn't seen the radio car approaching. Squinting through the smoke I recognized Werner next to the driver, filthy and covered in blood – sweat pouring down his face. He hauled Fritzi into the car and I dropped down into the back seat as the car rolled forward, earth and shrapnel exploding around us as we passed a shot-up Hanomag full of dead boys.

Werner sucked in his breath. 'Where's Helmuth?' he said.

It's strange, but I'd always imagined real combat in bad weather, in lashings of rain with the rumble of thunder rolling around the battlefield. I'd never thought that such destruction could be wreaked on a clear blue day. Or so many killed for the sake of a few metres of golden fields. We were all badly shaken and confused, those of us who had made it. Relief mingled with a certain guilt that others had perished whilst we lived to fight another day. We were filled with fury at the loss of our friends and the carnage these enemy tanks had brought to our peaceful European soil. I pulled my official booklet, *Facts About Europe*, from my pocket and flung it down on the grass. There was nothing it could tell me about anything I'd needed to know. Like how to shoot a dying friend between the eyes.

Werner sent Fritzi to a zone behind our line with other wounded boys in a cart drawn by farm horses. Then a doctor from a mobile hospital van prised out some shards of armour-plate from between my shoulders that had narrowly missed my spine. The medic gave me a morphine injection and a whole pill this time from one of those brown tubes like Helmuth had in his pocket. Later on I stood in the farmyard, smoking a cigarette with Werner, the Iron Cross at his throat glinting in the sun.

'Only a few pieces of shrapnel,' he said casually, glancing at my field dressing. 'This is nothing compared to what I saw in Russia. But you were brave today, I'll say that for you. You saved Fritzi's life.'

I took a long, shaky drag on my cigarette. Bravery had nothing to do with it. We'd rehearsed for war in the field, but a real battle? We just hadn't had a clue.

'Ready to fight again today,' Werner asked, 'now your scratches are sorted out?'

I had a feeling that 'No' wasn't an option. I stared at him through a drug-induced haze. 'Without Helmuth?' I asked.

He tousled my hair and touched the medal we'd all envied. 'You want one of these?'

I shrugged.

'You can't make an omelette without breaking eggs,' he said, flinging the butt end of his cigarette to the earth and grinding it under his boot. 'Life goes on, lad. Even without Helmuth. And by the way, someone had better break the news to Marie-Claire.'

Seven Dwarfs

THE AIR HUNG HOT and still over the barracks. Wild
rumours were doing the rounds. We'd heard news that
they were closing the *Zigeunerlager*. We were all leaving
to build a new camp where we could work and there'd be
better food and no chimneys. We were being transported.
Someone said Australia. Someone else America! Nobody
really knew. The camp was much less crowded since the
earlier transports had gone. Pa thought about five thousand
were left, though many were sick in the Ka-Be, so how they'd
manage on a long journey we didn't know. There were six
times that number to start with but so many had died. *Oh,
Kali Sara. America, maybe!*

I was jerked out of my daydream by a familiar voice. 'Lili!

I hoped I'd catch you.'

My spirits soared. I hadn't seen Dina for a week or so and there she was, walking towards me down the Lagerstrasse with her funny grin.

'Where did you think I'd be?' I said. 'At the *Solahütte*?'

It was one of our jokes. The *Solahütte* was the mountain retreat, where the SS went on leave from the camp. She'd heard of it from Doktor Mengele. 'I'm off to the *Solahütte* for a bit of sunbathing!' Dina used to say as she left our camp for her own enclosure, escorted by an SS on a bicycle.

Dina laughed. A jeep bounced past us down the camp street in a cloud of dust, bristling with guards. She pulled my sleeve. 'Come and sit down and I'll tell you why I'm here. But I can't be long.'

Apparently, that doctor, SS Lukas, had come to the women's camp again looking for Dina. He'd taken her to the SS barracks right down by the main entrance. Of course she was scared stiff but it was nothing bad. She thought she'd finished working for Doktor Mengele but he wanted her again for more drawings.

'More drawings of us?' I said.

Dina opened her eyes wide. 'You won't believe me when I tell you. If somebody told me, I'd think they were making it up.'

Then Dina told me about the seven dwarfs. She was right. Nobody would believe it. A troupe of seven Jewish dwarfs, two men and five women, had arrived on a transport from Romania. They were famous entertainers, so she said. Beautiful singers with miniature accordions, half-size cellos and tiny fiddles. And they'd brought their costumes with them. Glamorous dresses, silky evening gowns. Doktor Mengele was thrilled to bits, apparently. He'd even broken into song. She mimicked him, in a light tenor voice: '*Over the seven mountains come the seven dwarfs!*'

'Maybe he'll lose interest in the gypsies now,' she said. 'He told Doktor Lukas he'd found something to study for the next twenty years. Look, Lili, I must dash.' She jumped up and scooped me into her thin arms, hugging me hard. 'We might not see each other again if you're going on a transport. But don't forget what we said . . .'

I nodded. We'd talked of it before – about meeting up if we ever got out of the camp.

'Oh, I nearly forgot,' she said. And then she dug in her bag and pulled out a sheet of paper. It was the portrait of me in my sky-blue headscarf – only not quite. Dina had altered the painting to how it was before the doctor made her change it, so the scarf covered my ear like before.

She beamed at me. 'It's *almost* an exact copy. Only I like it better with your scarf this way. It makes you look like a Madonna.' There was a lump in my throat. Dina held me at arm's length and looked into my eyes. 'I loved painting you, Lili. I've never had a gypsy friend before, and now I've got you.'

I watched as she disappeared down the camp street, red hair shining in the sun, in her biker boots and her long black sack held up with string. I wanted to run after her and hug her again but something held me back. Somehow I knew I'd never see Dina again.

An Empty Train

PA BURST INTO THE BLOCK, crashing through the stable door. He'd been up and down the Lagerstrasse all morning trying to work out what was going on. And now we'd got something else to worry about. Pali and Tamas had disappeared. Someone told Pa they went with a man on a bicycle. Something about having their portraits painted. Pa was frantic. I suddenly remembered what Dina had told me about the seven dwarfs from Romania. I told Pa and he rushed off again.

I was going to the kindergarten to give Rollo a feed, though my milk had almost dried up. He'd been losing weight and I was scared. As I hurried down the Lagerstrasse I bumped into SS Bonigut with a clipboard. He was looking cross. Bonigut was nice for an SS. I asked him if he'd seen Pali and Tamas and he shook his head. I asked him if it was true that we were leaving and he said, 'There's a transport going out today. Everyone who can work will be on it.' I asked about the ones in the Ka-Be. He pressed his hand to his brow. 'That's not my department,' he said. His eyes slid away. 'I just do what I can. It's not my fault.'

'What do you mean?' You could usually ask Bonigut things, except that day he bit off my head.

'Shut up and mind your own business.' Then he looked at me and heaved a weary sigh. 'Listen,' he said, 'there's not room for everyone. The old, the sick – it's not my fault.'

I was trembling all over. 'What'll happen to them?'

He slammed the clipboard against his thigh. 'For God's sake, stop pestering. Just look after yourselves and make sure you get on that train. It's workers the Reich needs, not invalids. We're not the Red Cross, you know!'

I walked anxiously down the Lagerstrasse, startled by a sudden cloud of peewits that rose up from the marshy ground, flashing black and silver. Then suddenly I felt a fizz of excitement. Maybe we'd soon be free, like the peewits. And then I realized what had caused their sudden flight. I heard a long hiss of steam and a shrill whistle from near the kindergarten. A goods train was rattling up the track, belching steam as it drew up at the ramp beside the *Zigeunerlager*. I heard a cry from down by the Ka-Be. 'A empty train's arrived. An empty train!'

Oh, Kali Sara! Rollo! I raced to the kindergarten and snatched Rollo from his cot and then back up to the block to grab my things. There wasn't much. Just Rollo's bear with the button eyes and the picture Dina had just given me. I wrapped them in my raincoat, the one Stefan got me from *Kanada*, then I raced outside. 'There's a train,' I shouted. 'An empty train!'

Pa still hadn't found the twins. He was talking frantically to an SS with a dog. The SS shook his head and Pa ran off again down the street. And then I saw the SS we called Herr *Schwindelig*. He was arguing like crazy with Bonigut. 'No babies, I tell you,' cried *Schwindelig*, waving a sheaf of lists. 'You know the rules. No children under ten. That's my final word!'

Then a voice from a loudspeaker drowned out the row. 'There's no cause for alarm! This is an advance transport of able-bodied persons leaving for another camp. Line up in an orderly fashion. This is a relocation . . . relocation . . . another train tomorrow.'

Eager faces surged towards Herr *Schwindelig*, knees and elbows pushing to get near him. He was calling numbers and names. People no more than skin and bone pushed back their shoulders in a wretched attempt to walk tall. 'Take me! I'm fit and strong! I can work!'

'Damn it all,' shouted Bonigut above the racket. 'We can't take everybody!'

And then I heard our names called out. We were to line up by the fence next to an SS with another of those wolf dogs. I grabbed Frieda's hand and we started to run but Ma wouldn't budge.

'I'm not going nowhere without Pa!'

The freight train at the ramp snapped and clicked, heat shimmering around its engine. The first column of prisoners was lining up at the gate with their tiny bundles. A guard with a giant holdall was doling out salami and cigarettes to the ones whose names weren't on the lists. 'You'll join your families tomorrow. Make the most of the extra food.'

There was laughter, wailing, heartbreaking scenes of farewell. One old man ran at the electric fence, meaning to end it all, but for once it was switched off. He lay there sobbing, clutching the wire.

'Look here,' shouted a guard, waving a sausage. 'Better food already for those left behind!'

Suddenly I spotted Doktor Mengele. He was handing out sweets to two boys, cool as a pickled gherkin in his shiny black boots and brass buttons. I recognized the boys from the Ka-Be – his favourites who used to run errands for him. He waved them towards the gate like a kindly uncle. I wondered if I should ask about the dwarfs but I didn't dare risk it. I was too busy trying to hide Rollo.

And then at last I saw Pa. He was running back down the Lagerstrasse, in and out of every barracks, calling for Tamas and Pali. Ma ran to join him. I watched in silence as panic began to rise. We were all lined up by the wire now and the gates were swinging open.

'Ma! Pa!' screamed Frieda. 'Come *onnn*!'

They ran up panting. Pa couldn't hardly catch his breath.

'What about the Ka-Be?' I said.

'There's a guard on the Ka-Be,' said Pa, sweat pouring down his face.

'We can't go without them,' sobbed Ma. 'You all go on ahead. There's another train tomorrow . . .'

Pa shook his head slowly. And then I saw there was more than sweat pouring down Pa's cheeks. I could see defeat in every line of his face. 'When's that then, Rosa? When horses grow horns?'

I looked from Pa to Ma. He slid his arm gently round Ma's shoulders. She stared at him, tears brimming. 'If we don't go now, Ma, it's never. There'll be no more trains tomorrow.'

Allez! Hup!

DOGS WERE BARKING. Guards shouting. Whistles blowing. There was a wall of *Kapos* on one side, lining the rim of the ditch between our barbed-wire camp and the next. 'March! March!' they shouted. 'March!'

'Here, give me your bundle,' said Frieda. 'You've enough to carry with Rollo.' And suddenly we were moving forward in the direction of the gate, our bodies so thickly wedged we were carried forward without trying. Beyond the gate the train was waiting on the ramp, smoke pumping skywards from the engine into the shimmering air and behind it a long line of cattle trucks. Pa had squeezed himself into the line in front of us. He was gripping Ma's arm like he was scared she'd run back. I fixed my eyes on the gate as it slowly swung open. I couldn't believe it. Any second I'd be passing through for the first time in over a year. I closed my eyes and sent up a prayer to Kali Sara. *Please don't let Rollo cry.*

I was almost at the gate. My heart flipped a somersault. Out of the tail of my eye I saw Florica and Fonso slide through the gate, shielding Franko between them, merging into the press of people surging for the train. I didn't blame them. It was everyone for himself and I'd have done the same. I clutched Rollo to me so hard he started to cry.

'I said no babies!' yelled the guard. 'Understand? Prisoners fit for work only!'

There was a crush in front and a crush behind. I was jostled and pushed. 'Just one,' I begged, tears of terror springing to my eyes. *'Ich kann arbeiten!' I can still work with a baby*, I pleaded. 'Please!'

There was a moment of wild hope as he scratched his head, and then suddenly a *Kapo* was clutching my arms, dragging me from the line. My legs staggered. I fell to the ground, twisting to the side so I didn't squash Rollo. I felt the imprint of a boot in my belly but I still held Rollo tight in my arms, covering his head with my hands, as boots and clogs stamped over me, thundering towards the open gate. Several times I tried to rise and fell back, fighting my way to my knees only to be trampled again.

'Frieda! Frieda!' By then I was howling. There was a mad raging coming from my throat. My mouth was full of blood. I choked and spat, gasping for breath, clutching at people's clothes as they seethed past. 'Please! Help me, somebody! Pa! Pa!' And then I felt a wrenching as someone tried to tear my baby from my arms. 'No! No! Don't take my baby!'

'Lili! Let go of him. They'll trample him to death!' It was Frieda, reaching down, hands outstretched for Rollo. 'Give him to me. I'll send Pa back for you. Let go of Rollo!'

I was staring into Frieda's face as my fingers relaxed on the howling bundle. I had no choice. It was me or him. My eyes were blind with tears as I slowly let him go, my fingers uncurling, empty hands clawing the air. I rolled onto my belly covering my head with my hands as the tramping clogs clattered over my neck.

I heard Frieda screaming. 'Pa, Pa, Lili's fallen! *Paaaa!*'

And then I heard Pa's voice, shouting above the screech of the train's whistle. 'Somebody help my daughter! Don't close those gates! Somebody help us! Lili! Lili! *Liilii!*'

And then I felt boots kicking me aside. Rough hands around my wrists and ankles. And then I was hurtling through the air. There was a moment of floating, then falling, and then I was rolling. Down, down, over and over, and as I fell I saw dark earth rising. Rising up above my head.

When I first opened my eyes I couldn't see. There was a white agony in my head. In the distance, far away, I could hear shouting. *'Einsteigen! Einsteigen!' All aboard! All aboard!* The words echoed in my brain. They must still be loading the trains, I thought. I must be lying in one of the ditches that surrounded the camp. They were full of water in winter, but that day I could see the bare earth wall rising steeply above me.

Where is everyone? Where's my Rollo? I felt tears, hot

and wet on my cheeks. *Will anyone come back for me?* I was suddenly afraid, choking with terror. *How will they find me, lying down here in the dirt?* I tried to move my legs but they didn't want to move. I tried to cry out but my throat was bone dry and my mouth full of earth. I was thirsty – so thirsty I couldn't even speak. I tried to scream but no sound came.

I heard the camp gates clang shut and the harsh scrape of boxcar doors. Dogs were barking. People were screaming names. *Is anyone calling for me?* Something had happened to my legs. They didn't hurt but I couldn't feel them either. I heard the sound of weeping, sobbing, rising and falling, and then the desolate, lonely screech of a train's departing whistle.

It's getting darker now. I'm all alone. There's a stillness around me though I can still dimly hear sounds of camp life. The pain in my head is easier now but I'm growing cold, and with the cold a creeping numbness is spreading through my body. Is this how Lavuta felt, lying alone on the forest floor after Beng struck her down with his club? The story had a happy ending, though not for poor Lavuta . . .

And thinking of Lavuta, I'm warmed for a moment by the magical notes of Pa's fiddle, and on the strains float sounds of happier times – the shrill tinkle of circus bells, the gurgling of a samovar in a bow-topped vardo, the crack of a horsewhip. 'Roll up! Roll up! Welcome to Circus Petalo, the Greatest Show on Earth!' I can smell greasepaint, leather, sawdust and woodsmoke. I'm in the Red Barn. I can smell *hotchi-witchi* sizzling over a brushwood fire. I'm in Max's arms. He kisses my eyelids. I'm laughing up at him. *May kali i muri may gugli avela. The darker the berry, the sweeter the fruit.*

I'm colder than snow now. Colder than ice. My thoughts are slowing down, like a humming-top losing its spin. They come and go like wisps of smoke. I wish I was a little girl again, practising trapeze with Ma or sitting still as a statue while she binds white heather in my hair. I wish I was riding White Lightning with Pa and learning to fall without breaking my neck. I wish I'd told Frieda which songs to sing to Rollo. I wish I'd told her his secret name. I wish I could tell Max I still love him, even though it was never meant to be . . .

Darkness floods in like a freezing tide. I'm floating above myself now. I can see my broken body lying askew in the ditch, my head thrown back, my legs twisted in ways legs don't bend, my eyes closed against the glare of the dying sun. I'm so thin I can hardly believe it's me, lying there alone in the ditch. Higher and higher I float above the camp. The ramp is empty. The train has gone.

I'm high up in the big top now, balanced on the perch twenty metres above the ring, about to plunge down into the dark chasm of the swing. I'm holding the trapeze in both hands. I hear the roll of drums. The clash of cymbals. I know I mustn't look down. I'm too well trained for that. But I'm not afraid. There's no pain now. No pain any more. I wait for the shout to tell me it's safe to leap. *Allez! Hup!* I fling myself into the dark. *Here comes Lili Petalo. Queen of the flying trapeze.*

PART FOUR

TEARS OF A CLOWN

Re-education

B Y AUGUST WE'D LOST three thousand boy soldiers in battle and the fertile meadows of Normandy became fields of graves. Then in September we were surrounded near the Falaise Pocket, fighting to protect an escape channel for retreating troops, and I was taken prisoner – just twenty miles south of Caen.

We were sent to a prison compound near the coast and from there to another camp at Attichy in France run by Americans, along with thousands of other German schoolboys between twelve and nineteen, deliberately separated from our older comrades for purposes of *de-Nazification*. And it was there, in April 1945, that we heard that the war had ended. We could hardly believe that Germany had actually lost. Only gradually did we come to accept that Hitler was really dead and that Germany was now an occupied country.

Many boys couldn't believe at first that what Hitler had told us was lies. They knew of no other system than the one that had poisoned their minds and they stared at me sceptically when I said that my father had always hated Hitler. They didn't believe me. I was trying to curry favour with our teachers, they said. And I in my turn smarted under the stigma of association with the SS, since I'd been a conscript after all.

During our re-education programme we were incessantly questioned about why we'd joined Hitler Youth. Why had we submitted ourselves to such bullying? It was impossible to explain to anyone who'd not lived through that time – about the fear, the coercion, the indoctrination, but also the excitement, the renewed hope, the heady sense of belonging to something powerful and new. We needed substantial remedial lessons, so our captors told us, in free democracy. Of course there were still some boys who refused to see it our teachers' way, refusing to believe that we'd been fed such lies, and still professing their admiration for the Führer and National Socialism. It was painful for us all as we struggled to accept that we'd believed in something so wrong. But after a while few spoke openly of Hitler any more and many felt like fools, especially when we learned that our leader had not died at the head of his troops, but had taken the coward's way out . . . and shot himself.

It was a confusing time. I was much troubled by events in Normandy. I found it hard to sleep. Scenes of the battlefield haunted my dreams – the sound of shells, the screams of the dying, the stench of blood. I felt I had witnessed the most appalling sights any man could see. Slaughter like that twists every nerve. It leaves an enduring image on the mind.

We were not mistreated. We were permitted to send letters although we received none in reply and we were allowed to attend lessons in school subjects we'd been forced to give up under the Nazi regime. Nonetheless, I yearned to see my family again. I longed to speak with my father about my bewilderment and anguish. Then in September 1945 we were released. I wended my way back home along with other soldiers like myself, in tattered tunics, travelling by any means available – on foot, in horse-drawn carts and, only occasionally, with a lift from a passing truck.

At last I arrived in the devastated streets of Berlin.

I could hardly believe my eyes. There was nothing left of Alexanderplatz. Parizer Platz was in ruins, the famous Adlon Hotel entirely gutted, the guardrooms at the Brandenburg Gate just a pile of stones. Tanks were scattered on broken pavements like stranded corpses and over it all hung a sickly stench of rottenness and death. Gone were the swastika flags and propaganda posters. Just notices everywhere: *Beware of mines and falling masonry*. Disorientated, I could barely find my way home. Most familiar landmarks and street signs had disappeared beneath the debris, but I found it at last, our house miraculously still standing in our shattered street. The destruction all around should have prepared me for what awaited me at home. But somehow it hadn't.

It was Tante Ida who broke the news that my father was

dead. He'd been killed at the Charité in the last week of the war by a Russian grenade lobbed in through a window whilst operating on an injured child, as fighting raged in the hospital grounds outside. It was a swift end, Tante Ida told me, tears spilling down her wrinkled cheeks, for the doctors and patient alike. And thus ended the life of my beloved Vati, devoted paediatrician and opponent of Hitler to the end.

My mother never recovered. Always a frail spirit, she took her own life a couple of years after the war. Living without Vati was simply too unbearable. So the Second World War, as it came to be known, finished for her what the First War had started. Just one poor life amongst the millions, ravaged by conflict.

Rubble Women

TANTE IDA STEPPED INTO the void left by Vati's death like the invincible spirit she was, organizing our rations that had begun to trickle through again, courtesy of the occupying forces, making trips to outlying farms to trade crystal and porcelain for food or exchanging her jewels on the black market in Alexanderplatz. She'd return, worn out, covered in grime and soot but triumphant, with a piece of unidentifiable meat. 'Don't ask,' she'd say, as Erika made as if to vomit. 'At least we're not like some poor souls, living in cellars without water and electricity.' Erika had the grace to look shamefaced. She was working as a cleaner in a house occupied by some American officers. One soldier had asked her out to a jazz club, she told me, but she'd refused – 'for the moment!'

Tante Ida never mentioned the name Hitler again, passing by with pursed lips when we happened upon sarcastic slogans daubed in blood-red paint on crumbling walls: *HITLER MASS MURDERER! FÜHRER WE THANK YOU!*

It was a strange phenomenon, how everybody claimed they'd always been against Hitler. I remember Erika saying that she couldn't understand how he'd ever become Chancellor, since nobody seemed to have voted for him. 'Thank heavens we'll never have to say *Hiel Hitler* again,' exclaimed Frau Schneck, our ex-*Blockwart*, scuttling down the street of roofless buildings with her empty string bag. Herr Müller, our old gardener, had not been partial either, as it turned out. He just appeared one day in his familiar gardening overalls and began digging over the vegetable patch, as if he'd never left us. I must have seemed surprised.

'Neue Besen kehren gut, aber der Alte kennt die Ecken,' he mumbled, reddening slightly. *New brooms clean well, but the old one knows the corners.*

At least Rudi seemed pleased. He'd missed his friend, Herr Müller. I came upon my brother one day in autumn 1945, helping Herr Müller clear out his garden shed. There was still no school for Rudi and Gretchen due to teacher shortage, and Rudi had grown bored of collecting up steel helmets to be melted down and turned back into saucepans. Herr Müller had a fine blaze going in the orchard, and as I stood watching the flames, I pretended not to notice the piles of Nazi Party circulars he was hastily tossing onto the bonfire along with the red wax portrait of Hitler. We watched as the wax dissolved, Hitler's face first distorting into a hideous grimace before melting into nothing. *'Das dreckigen Hund! Das schmutzige Schwein!'* snarled Herr Müller, stroking his moustache, which was already sprouting into something much more like the handlebars Rudi used to pull. *That dirty dog! That filthy pig!*

Only once did I venture as far as Friedrichstrasse to take a look at the wreck of the Wintergarten. Splintered mirrors. Shattered tiles. A tangle of electric cables. It was hard to tell the back from the front, let alone where the stage door would have been. I stared unfocused at the rubble mountain as tears welled, shutting my eyes as memories surged in.

Wunderzebra at your service . . . at your service . . . at your service.

No. We have no idea at all where they've gone . . .

Christmas came and went – a curious affair with little to celebrate, and no cake either with flour at 150 marks a pound, and then the New Year arrived, also without celebration. Everyone looked pinch-featured and broken. There was so much we had to tangle with in those months.

Struggling to survive in the ravaged city, we were also trying to cope with the full enormity of the atrocities we soon learned had been committed in the death camps. There was hardly anyone who'd not seen the compulsory film by now – *Die Todesmühlen, The Mills of Death*, with its horrifying footage of skeletal corpses and emaciated survivors in striped suits, and the pathetic piles of personal belongings: the clothes, the shoes, the toys, the wedding rings. Some people claimed they'd never heard about the camps. Others still didn't believe they were real. For myself, I was haunted by those miserable people I'd seen at Grunewald station on the day I met Lili in the Red Barn. I was only a schoolboy, but was I also guilty of looking the other way? There was so much soul-searching. Such disillusionment. I though of Vati constantly in those days and how bravely he'd refused to join the Nazi Party, and how he'd died as he'd lived, saving human life. How I missed my father. How I longed to talk to him.

Spring is always welcome, even in a city full of unexploded bombs, and this one brought fresh optimism, at least to doughty spirits like Tante Ida. 'It's miraculous how nature takes over so fast,' said my aunt heartily one day, as we walked Shadow across the Tiergarten, over ground pitted with bomb craters. She was as fond of the little dog now as I was, especially since Siegfried had died. 'Just look how the shattered trees still struggle into leaf – a promise of hope amidst all this destruction.'

I'd been saying that I couldn't imagine how the indescribable mess would ever be cleared up, despite the bands of *Trümmerfrauen*, the rubble women, ordered to clear the streets by the occupying forces.

'And yet, just smell that blossom!' said my invincible aunt. *'Alles neu macht der Mai.' May makes all things new*. 'And look!' she said, pointing to a poster pasted onto the side of a burnt-out tank. 'The Berlin Philharmonic is performing Haydn's Four Seasons in the Titania Palast cinema.'

Visitors

Iт was a Sunday morning the following year. One of those freezing March days where sharp drizzle falls from a leaden sky – a day calculated to depress anyone, even if they weren't shivering in a house with panes of glass still missing. Vati's study overlooked the front garden and I was sitting at his desk, a tiny fire in the grate, trying to complete my chemistry homework. I'd claimed Vati's study as mine since my return from France and I spent much of my time in there surrounded by his precious medical texts. Somehow it made me feel closer to him, and besides, I liked to keep busy. Studying helped keep my demons at bay.

By this time I'd enrolled in a school with a few buildings left standing on the other side of the Tiergarten. I was in the de-Nazification category that had received a 'youth amnesty' from the Allied authorities, and I was busy making up for lost time, along with a number of other ex-soldiers who were preparing for entry into the university. The rest of my family had gone to Mass in a small, recently reopened Catholic church – but since I felt little inclination to bother God these days, I'd made the excuse of a cold coming on.

Our front garden was full of new rubble. The house next door, just a burnt-out frontage for the last two years, had collapsed onto our path a few nights before, a chimney pot somehow finding its way into the middle of our drawing room. For the last few days we'd been using the back door so I was surprised to see a woman in a dusty red skirt, picking her way through the remains of next door, a small boy in her arms.

My heart double thumped. A sudden piercing memory. A bubbling surge of joy. I raced into the hallway, wrenching open the door before even a knock was heard. *'Lili!'*

I couldn't hide my disappointment but I didn't need to. The stranger was too nervous to notice my confusion. With hindsight I understand how much courage she'd had to muster to come here. She was clutching a map and I was impressed that she'd found her way since maps were still pretty useless, main roads still obliterated by mountains of rubble. I saw at once that the girl wasn't really like Lili at all. She had a rounder, softer face, wide eyes and dark, curly hair, strangely streaked with silver for one so young. I remembered Lili saying that Frieda was more like her ma and that she was more like her pa, with her long, straight nose and hair like a horse's mane. Instinctively I knew who she was, and besides, the child that stared up at me, his thumb in his mouth and his eyes like dark berries was Lili to the life, although his skin was paler and his hair not so dark. I stared and stared as tears welled in my eyes and constricted my throat. Then I heard Lili's voice in my head. *The darker the berry, the sweeter the fruit.*

Second sight. That's what Lili would have called it in her inimitable way. A sixth sense. Words were superfluous. I knew why Frieda had come.

Had I known in my heart that Lili was dead – like a fairy-tale character with a premonition at the point of their lover's death? I'm sure Shon or Chakano would have known, and yet I must have been in France at the time with my regiment, in the middle of another kind of death. Another kind of hate. And anyway, real life isn't like fairy tales. I'd nurtured a dream that one day I'd see Lili again. And now at last I knew how it felt. The death of all hope.

I led Frieda into the study and closed the door. No. She wouldn't sit down. She seemed ill at ease, constantly plucking her skirt, eyes darting around the room, but the child broke the tension between us.

His name was Rollo, she told me. Lili had chosen it. He was three and a half, she said. He was agile as a mountain goat, climbing onto the coal box and then balancing along the fender on his tiny, nimble feet, tumbling off and getting up again without a whimper. Then from fender to chair in one leap, he climbed onto the arm, reached out for the edge of my desk and swung himself up.

'He plays like this all day long,' she said, in a deep brown voice, with the familiar Romani burr. 'When he's five he'll start on the bar. He's a natural. Just like me and Lili.'

She relaxed when she spoke of Rollo and we stood in silence for a while, the child an unspoken link between us. And then all of a sudden Frieda began to speak rapidly, her black eyes only occasionally meeting mine, smiling apologetically when a cough convulsed her chest. She'd had it since the camp, she said, and couldn't shake it off.

Frieda talked and talked. And I listened, my heart overflowing. I listened and said nothing. When she had finished the room was deathly quiet. Words were inadequate. There were no words to say.

After seventeen months in Auschwitz, the Petalos were taken to another camp called Ravensbrück, and yes, Frieda was sure that Lili was dead. She'd saved Rollo in the crush for the train but they hadn't been able to save Lili. Not even Pa. Swept on by the press of bodies they'd been crammed into trains like animals, the SS with dogs and whips barring any chance of return. She'd slipped past the guards with Rollo while Pa had gone back to help Lili, but the gates to the camp had already closed. He'd watched through the wire as they flung her body into a ditch like a dog. Then the doors to the cattle trucks slammed shut. They'd all got on that final transport, the remnants of Circus Petalo. All except Lili and the two dwarfs. 'We all wept and wept,' said Frieda, 'all through that night. We wept and howled until no more tears would come.'

A few weeks later they found out what had happened

that night, after the transport had left. Two women called Elisabeth and Hillie, Sinti who'd worked in the Birkenau camp office, arrived in Ravensbrück on a transport from the Auschwitz main camp. On the very same night Frieda's train had left, the old, the sick and the children, the ones unsuitable for work, were taken in trucks and murdered in the gas chambers behind a grove of birch trees. All three thousand of those left behind in the family camp. After their salami and cigarettes. After they'd waved goodbye to the train through a fence of barbed wire. 'Until tomorrow,' they'd cried. 'Until tomorrow!' And the sky over the camp was filled with the scent of burning flesh.

I needed air, so I went in search of some coal, leaving Frieda and Rollo alone in the study. When I returned, it was as if a door between us that had been briefly open was shut again. I knelt by the grate, trying to coax the fire into a blaze, and whilst I had my back to her Frieda began to speak again. The dark clouds were clearing, the sun struggling in through the study windows' grimy panes. And as she talked and the little boy played, the shadow of Vati's desk crept across the Persian rug and began to climb the wall.

The family had been split up for the first time at Ravensbrück, the men imprisoned in the men's camp and the women on the other side of a wall, and it was there that Ma Petalo died in the winter of 1944. She died slowly, said Frieda. From exhaustion and cold and tuberculosis of the lungs, but mostly from grieving for Lili. Pa could have consoled her, said Frieda, but Pa was in the men's camp, working in a building supplies yard, after being sterilized along with the other men. The Petalos were detained there for five months, until one day some wagons arrived and they were taken to Sachsenhausen, another camp north of Berlin. Then one night in mid-April there was a hurried evacuation, as reports of the advancing Red Army came through. Thousands of prisoners were force-marched northeast with no food, some without shoes – twenty miles a day. All stragglers shot.

Then one morning they woke to find the guards had disappeared. They'd fled into the surrounding woods, taking their guns and wolf dogs with them. The prisoners hid amongst the trees and bushes. They didn't know what to think, and then some soldiers came and said, 'You're free. The war is over!'

Portrait of Lili

I MET FRIEDA AND ROLLO every day for almost a week. She never came to the house again, but as we walked in the Tiergarten amidst the scorched and blasted trees, she told me their plans for the future. They'd met up with a Romani circus from Brandenburg who'd been hiding there during the war and were now on the road again. The circus had a variety of acts but no animals, they'd told Pa, so if Pa Petalo could find some livestock they'd be welcome to join. And that had set Pa thinking.

There was a story doing the rounds about the butchers of Berlin. The war had left lots of stray horses wandering wild. Military horses. Farm horses. Pa had heard that the butchers were rounding them up and selling them for meat, so he had the idea of buying some up for their circus. The ones in the poorest way were going cheapest and it was amazing the horseflesh you could purchase in return for a few nights' entertainment.

I knew on the last day I saw Frieda that she'd come to say goodbye. She'd been restless the day before, talking about the rising of the leaf. Pa Petalo had bought a dozen horses that week and now spring had come the new circus were heading north towards Schwerin. Pa had heard a story about two dwarfs from a roustabout he'd met in a tavern – clowns who rode ponies bareback. The man didn't know details but he thought they might be twins. Frieda had urged Pa not to raise his hopes too high. He wasn't as strong in his head as he used to be, not since Ma died.

For a week I'd walked and talked with Frieda. Not just about the death camp, although that was always on her mind, but I learned much I'd not known about Lili and their lives together. She seemed to need to talk and I liked to hear, and as she talked I watched my tiny son chase rabbits and squirrels in the Tiergarten. We never spoke about his future. It went unsaid that Rollo would stay with the circus.

'We have a saying in the tribe,' she'd said on that last morning we ever met. 'With one behind, you can't sit on two horses.'

I told her I'd heard that one before.

'It means you can only live one life,' she said.

I said I knew. '*Gadjo* with *Gadjo*. Rom with Rom,' I said. 'Lili told me that one too.'

Frieda shook her head. 'Lili always went her own way.'

She smiled sadly at me. 'I promised Lili when we were in the camp that if ever she didn't make it I'd raise Rollo like my own. He's everything to me and Pa, now Lili and Ma have gone.'

I nodded. Of course she was right. I'd applied to study medicine at the university. What would I do with a child in bombed-out Berlin? My eyes followed Rollo as he trotted on his stocky legs, climbing tree stumps, falling off and clambering back again.

'Rollo's going to be a star,' said Frieda, her voice breaking, somewhere between a smile and a sob. 'Remember my words. One day you'll see his name in lights.'

I nodded, swallowing down my tears. I knew the time had come. Then Frieda held out a small package, wrapped in a piece of newspaper. 'These were in Lili's bundle I was carrying for her . . . that day . . . the last time I ever saw her. Only don't open it now. Wait till I'm gone.'

My heart was breaking. I watched Frieda as she gathered Rollo into her arms and swung him up onto her shoulders. He squealed with delight and I stood on tiptoe to kiss his forehead. And then I kissed Frieda's.

I stared after her as she picked her way across the ruins of the Tiergarten. Before she passed out of view she turned and waved to me, this brave girl so like and so unlike my Lili. And I waved back at her and my little son on her shoulders. It would be many years before I saw Rollo again.

I opened the package with trembling hands. There was a black triangle of rough fabric stamped with a Z, a plaited twist of hair – part brown, part black. And a portrait of Lili.

She was wearing a sky-blue headscarf shot through with silvery threads. Her face was thinner than I remembered and there were hollows under her eyes where the darker skin used to glow with a purple-brown sheen. My whole body was shaking. I turned the portrait over, reading the words in pencil on the back: *To my dear friend Lili, with love from your Dina. Auschwitz, 1944.*

And all at once I knew what the poets meant when they said that a heart could break. I felt mine, caving down inside my chest in ugly, jagged fragments, and then the searing pain of the splinters, sharp as death and cold as ice.

Confidences

IT WAS MANY YEARS AFTER the war that I told Erika about Lili. By 1960 I was making my way as a cardiothoracic surgeon, having finally followed Vati into the medical profession. Somehow a musical career no longer appealed to me after the war. I couldn't bear to hear the violin, let alone touch it. But at least I could try in my own small way to make the world a better place and follow where my father had led.

Erika was well over her own broken heart and happily married to a successful Berlin lawyer with two teenage girls and a pleasant apartment in Charlottenburg. We were having dinner together one night while her husband was away on business – and I'd had too many glasses of wine.

'I've given up on any of my siblings having children,' pouted Erika, blowing smoke through her pastel-pink lips. *Heart of Pink*, she informed me, had long replaced *Scarlet Velvet* as the choice for the fashionable woman. 'I mean, why have none of you married, for heaven's sake? I've abandoned all hope of cousins for my girls.'

'I thought you'd given up on me long ago,' I said, referring to the countless failed dates she'd arranged in the past with hopeful single friends.

'Well, I can't rely on Gretchen. What man in his right mind would want a ferocious nursing sister with her sights set on the matron's office? And Rudi with his architecture training – it'll be years before he settles down.'

I'd opened another bottle of her husband's fine old Riesling and suddenly I was telling Erika my story. I'd never told anyone before.

'What a dark horse you've been, Max, all these years!' She was astonished, incredulous, fascinated – everything except judgemental. So typical of Erika, and I loved her for it. But she'd asked too many questions. By the time I said my goodbyes that evening I was regretting the confidence, and wishing I hadn't opened that second bottle of wine.

The evening had unsettled me, and that night I dreamed of Lili again – one of the recurring dreams I used to have in the early days, but hadn't had for years. Lili is with me in my bed in our house in Berlin, curled small against me, my body curved around her. She's holding our child in her arms. And then in my dream I get up and look out of my bedroom window. The moon is full and there's a mesh of stars against the blue-black sky over the Tiergarten. Then, gradually, as my eyes adjust to the moonlight, rank on rank of stable barracks swim into focus and beyond them rolls of barbed-wire fences. And there in the distance stands a grove of birch trees, screening the chimneys beyond.

Suddenly I feel Lili's arms, snaking round my waist. Warm breath on the back of my neck. I turn from the window with a cry of relief but my arms pass through empty air. The room is empty. My bed is empty. And then I scream.

There's a phenomenon well known to psychologists, where a word, a name or a person who has recently come to your notice suddenly seems to appear with improbable frequency. Some would call it mere coincidence, and yet it still struck me as curious that only a few days after my dinner with Erika, one sunny morning in August 1960, I received a mystery letter. The hand was round and childish, the envelope cheap, so that I could almost see through it to the colourful contents inside. My hand was trembling as I picked it up from the doormat. There was no note. Just a circus ticket with a PO Box number on the back.

CIRCUS PETALO
THE GREATEST SHOW ON EARTH
Starring: Rollo Petalo – Trapeze Artist Extraordinaire –
and his Death-defying Triple Salto Mortale
Saturday 13 August
Tiergarten 7.30
Admit One

413

Triple Salto Mortale

A LEAPER STANDS on a narrow perch, a dizzying twenty metres above the sawdust ring. He's a slightly built young man but powerful too, his muscles in their fleshings rippling as a spotlight plays upon his white-spangled figure and gilds his mid-brown hair with gold. His skin is dark olive, but not as dark as his catcher's, who already hangs by his hocks from the catch bar, his feet in the cradle.

The leaper's hands are white with chalk, his body taut, his pulse steady. He won't look down, however much he longs to see. He's too well trained for that. There'll be time enough to turn cartwheels in the ring, to skip and smile and take his bow. But before the final curtain falls, there's a yawning gulf to cross, between a narrow perch high up in the dome and the sawdust ring below.

The magnificent ringmaster in the scarlet coat has nearly done his work. The audience is mellow now, like putty in his hands. He's given them liberty horses and tumblers, jugglers and fire-eaters, contortionists, high-wire artists and custard-pie clowns. The trapeze artists have thrilled the crowd with spectacular twisting doubles, pirouettes and passing leaps. The crowd has shrieked with surprise, wept with laughter, gasped in wonder at the magic of it all, but still they stamp their feet and howl for more. And who can blame them? Danger is as much part of the circus as magic and laughter – and the show's not finished yet.

The ringmaster's lips are scarlet and full beneath his impressive waxed moustache. 'And now . . . laaadies and gentlemeennn. Children of all ages! The moment you've all been waiting for. A stunt so dangerous it has killed more people than all other circus acts combined – the triple aerial somersault! At twenty metres in the air, at more than sixty miles an hour, the boy who makes a speciality of extracting teeth from the jaws of death will attempt the Triple Salto Mortale. The Deadly Leap!'

A frisson of delicious apprehension crackles through the audience as the low dramatic rumble of the bass drum begins, bubbling, rolling, mounting by degrees, rising in a crescendo to a clash of cymbals. In his ringside seat, Max Hartmann is biting his lip so hard it starts to bleed. There's a tang of metal on his tongue as the ringmaster's voice fades in and out.

'. . . *the most DEATH-DEFYING . . . PERILOUS . . .*

DARING DISPLAY of timing and precision ever attempted before in this big top . . . Laadies and gentlemeeen . . . the only living artist able to perform this stunt . . . THE EXTRAORDINARY . . . THE DAZZLING . . . THE SPECTACULAR . . . THE INCOMPARABLE . . . ROLLO PETALO!'

Max closes his eyes for a moment, his knuckles white on the edge of his seat. He can't bear to watch. And yet he can't bear to look away. The ringmaster solemnly raises his hand. There's a flurry of nervous coughing. A child cries out and is shushed by its mother.

'Quiet, ladies and gentlemen, if you please.'

The leaper looks towards his catcher. He's straining his ears for the signal that his partner is ready. *'Allez!'*

He takes a deep, slow breath, stretches his neck from side to side, flexes his fingers, then slowly places his hands on the fly bar, calculating time and distance with his eyes. Then Rollo Petalo leaps into the void, plummeting down, down, down the dark chasm of the swing.

In scarcely a heartbeat he's hurtling back up, up into the pinnacle of the dome. At the peak of the swing he kicks out, a trick to gain some extra height. The crowd gasps. He's vertical on the fly bar now, his feet pointing up towards the dome, and then down he swoops again, gaining momentum as he flies across the ring. His body is a jackknife, hurtling up once more into the dome. Another kick out, and down he glides in yet another impossible arc. There's a collective sigh from the mouths in the upturned faces twenty metres below as he soars to the pinnacle once again. *Will it be this time? Will it be now?*

'*Hup!*' Rollo's cry echoes around the canvas walls. The first somersault takes him higher still, momentum defying the laws of gravity. He flips a perfect second, spinning forward into the third, a ball of light and shadow. Then his arms shoot out, reaching for his catcher, flying into his grip of steel. The audience is on its feet as both flyer and catcher continue to swing, caught in the force of the impact, their bodies horizontal above the ring. The air is full of whistles and shouts and thunderous applause. Only Max Hartmann's palms are bleeding, half moons of scarlet where his nails have pierced the flesh.

Back down in the ring, the leaper joins his catcher, as two diminutive clowns in enormous shoes waddle into the ring and fall over their feet before presenting the triumphant pair with bouquets of flowers. The audience roars with delighted laughter at this exquisite combination of grace with absurdity that is the special charm of the circus. Then joining their free hands together, the leaper, with his catcher, take a deep, low bow, slow and strangely humble. For they know that a fraction of a second makes the difference between life and death, triumph or disaster, and complacency plays no part in the circus. Then Rollo Petalo, like the great showman he's now become, flings both his arms high in the air with a joyful whoop of triumph.

Tears brim in Max's eyes, welling over, spilling down his cheeks. And yet there's joy in his heart too. In the ring the tiny clowns are leading the procession of acrobats in the grande finale, flapping along at the front in their oversized shoes and kissing their hands to the applause.

Max finds that he's smiling at them through his tears, as memories crowd in from cobwebbed corners of his mind, of another August day, in 1939, here in the Tiergarten, as Europe teetered on the brink of war. His brother Rudi is skipping along beside him, holding tight to his hand.

'Why is that clown's face sad and the other one happy?' Rudi asked his big brother.

Max thinks he knows the answer now. Clowns hold up a mirror to our lives. There's no joy without grief, laughter without tears, triumph without tragedy. After all, we can't really claim kin with the high-wire artists, the stars of the flying trapeze. Their skill and daring is beyond our wildest dreams. But clowns, now, there's another matter. We can learn from the clowns, if we have courage enough. To take knocks and still not be defeated. To be trampled on yet still rise up to take the final bow.

A Garden in Berlin
April 2013

AN EVENING BREEZE lifted the hairs on Max's wrists as he pushed the close-written pages of his manuscript into a buff-coloured envelope and addressed it in a crooked, old man's hand. *Herr Rollo Petalo*, it read, followed by the number of the PO Box where he'd sent a cheque every year since he'd known where to reach his son. Then picking up the portrait, Max smoothed it out on the table one last time, tracing the beautiful line of Lili's jaw with his finger – then he laid it in the suitcase next to the faded black triangle. Finally, he lifted the paisley scarf to his face, buried his nose in its silken folds and breathed in deeply. Then, with a sigh, he spread it tenderly over his precious memories and very softly closed the lid.

'*So it was you who took my* diklo! *You've been caught with rabbits in your sack. I always wondered if it was you . . .*'

Max turned quickly. The leaves shifted and rustled in the orchard's fading light.

'You never asked,' he said. 'I'd have given it back . . . although I was glad I'd kept it . . . after I lost you.' He pressed the stiff clasps of the small suitcase home with a rusty click. 'It's where it belongs now, anyway,' he said firmly. 'At the beginning and the end of our story.'

Max smiled sadly to himself. A lifetime of mending other people's hearts and yet he'd never been able to properly heal his own. He remembered giving a speech at the retirement dinner they'd held in his honour at the Charité, after a lifetime of medical service. He'd made a joke as he was winding up, that in all his years of practice he'd put dozens of dodgy hearts back together again. He'd fixed the 'plumbing' as he used to call it, so those vital organs could pump the blood for a few more years. But he'd never managed to find a cure for a heart broken by love. He'd smiled around the room of well-wishers and said that he'd leave that unfinished piece of research in the capable hands of Professor Seligmann, the new director of the cardiac unit. Everyone laughed, and Max had laughed too – although his eyes were dim with tears.

Max shivered and put his hand to his chest, pressing down hard just to the left of centre. He took a deep breath, grimacing slightly. 'I know one thing, though,' he said out loud. 'This old ticker's almost done. There's not much Doktor Seligmann can do for me any more, whatever Gretchen believes.' He rolled his cramped neck and shoulders to the right and left, and then, painfully slowly, Max eased himself to his feet, groping for his stick. He grasped the shiny brown handle of his box of memories, and hobbled stiffly across the grass to the hole he'd asked the gardener to dig in the sandy Berlin soil.

Gretchen turned the key in the lock, then pressed her weight against the stiff front door of the old house near the Tiergarten, making a mental note to oil the hinges first thing in the morning. She was too tired to do it right away. Bridge was exhausting if you took it seriously, and Gretchen did. She'd always put her all into anything she turned her hand to: the League of German Maidens, matron at the Charité, secretary of the district Bridge club in her retirement, and self-appointed nurse to Max, since Rudi was dead and Erika, poor soul, in a nursing home. Gretchen stood, legs apart, in her stout brogue shoes, hurriedly unpinning her hat in the speckled mirror of the coat stand in the hall as the clock struck seven. Max would be starving. She should never have stayed for that final round of Bridge. 'I'm home, Max,' she called. 'Maaax! I'm home!'

She crossed the black and white tiled floor, bathed in scarlet and amber light as the last rays of the setting sun shone through the stained-glass panels of the door, an arrow of concern between her thick grey eyebrows.

There were no lights, but then Max often sat too long in the gloom; a legacy of wartime frugality, Gretchen always thought. Of those long dark days without electricity after the war.

'Maax!'

She noticed with irritation that the kitchen door was open to the garden. No wonder the house felt so chilly. Surely he couldn't be outside at this time. A worm of worry shifted in her stomach as she hurried down the stone steps from the back door, shooing away the neighbour's cat with an impatient *pshaw!* She must have a word with Frau Mann about Flocki – always leaving dead birds on the lawn. Or maybe it was Herr Strachan's Sammi. All cats looked grey in the dark. She squinted shortsightedly across the stone-flagged terrace and down towards the orchard, her stomach suddenly dropping away. 'Maax!' Gretchen began to run.

Max's body was still warm when Gretchen found him, slumped sideways by the granite stone, so carefully erected just a few days before. And there was dirt in his fingernails, as if he'd been digging. Burying something, maybe, under the freshly packed turf.

Afterwards, when she told Erika about it, Gretchen felt rather foolish. She'd never been a romantic. Plain Gretchen, that was her. Sensible and down to earth. So it did her good to talk to someone with more romance in her soul.

'I suddenly felt a strange shiver, as if I wasn't alone,' she told Erika as she pushed her wheelchair down the path of the nursing-home garden. 'I felt the hair prick up on the back of my neck. Then, above the sighing of the breeze, I heard a deep gurgle of laughter and the gentle sound of a soft voice in reply. I turned and stared into the fading light and for a moment, just for a moment, I swear I saw two figures in the orchard. They were holding hands, facing each other and gazing into each other's eyes. The wind rustled the leaves, the trees shivered, and then they were gone.' Gretchen sniffed, wiping her eyes with her handkerchief. 'It's silly, I know. Psychology can account for every kind of illusion. I'm a nurse so I should know about that sort of thing. And yet, it's odd . . . but it seemed rather real at the time.'

The Inspiration for
A Berlin Love Song

When I was a child growing up in Yorkshire our next-door neighbours, the Adlers, were German Jewish refugees who had fled to England during the war. Mr Adler had been imprisoned for a while in a concentration camp. He was a dentist – a proud, kindly, professional man with his own business. He didn't talk about his wartime experiences very much, but when he did, he used to shake and cry. This had a profound effect on me as a child; seeing an adult who I respected reduced to tears by memories of his past.

In 2011, on one of my many visits to Berlin, I happened upon an exhibition in the Deutsches Historisches Museum entitled *Hitler and the Germans: Nation and Crime*. It was a courageous exhibition – the first time since the war that a major museum had explored the relationship between Hitler and the German Nation, addressing the question of how Hitler had managed so successfully to seduce an entire country. It was fascinating. I was astonished by the boxes of Christmas baubles depicting Hitler's face, the jewelled swastika for the top of the Christmas tree, the beer mats and the playing cards, all decorated with Nazi symbols. Nearby there were the striped uniforms worn by prisoners in the concentration camps and street signs bearing the words *Juden verboten*.

In one small corner I found a few showcases dedicated to the wartime persecution of the Romani people. I discovered that in addition to six million Jews, up to half a million Romanies from Europe had been exterminated by the Nazis and I wondered why relatively little had been written about this. On my return to London I went to the permanent Holocaust exhibition in the Imperial War Museum. There I found another a small corner dedicated to the Romani story, but again, not very much. I set about discovering all I could about the persecution of the Roma.

It was not long afterwards, in October 2012, that I read about the long-awaited memorial to the Roma and Sinti that had just been opened by Angela Merkel, the German chancellor, in the Tiergarten park in Berlin, and her moving tribute to the victims. 'Every single fate in this genocide,' she said, 'fills me with sorrow and shame.' I felt I had to visit the memorial. Situated in the shadow of the Reichstag, it consists of a circular pool of water, at the centre of which there is a triangular stone, a reference to the badges that were worn by concentration camp prisoners. In bronze letters around the edge is the poem 'Auschwitz' by the Romani poet Santino Spinelli that appears at the front of this book. As I stood reading these poignant words, I finally resolved to write a story about the Romani Holocaust.

This novel is a work of fiction, but many of the characters in it are inspired by real people I have known or read about in diaries and first-hand accounts during my research. Max's father for example, the anti-Nazi paediatrician Julius Hartmann, is based on a German pastor who was a close friend of my father; the Jewish painter of portraits in Auschwitz was inspired by Dina Gottliebova, a Czech artist who really was forced to work for Dr Mengele, painting portraits in the Gypsy Family Camp. So although my novel is a product of my imagination, I believe everything I have written could have happened.

If you would like to read more about the persecution of the Roma and my inspiration for this book, please visit my website sarahmatthias.co.uk